Beneath
the
Cornflowers

Beneath the Cornflowers

Book Four

J. L. Robison

For information, contact J.L. Robison at joanlrobison@yahoo.com or https://linktr.ee/j.l.robison

First edition
ISBN 979-8-9907451-1-7

Beneath
the
Cornflowers

Book Four

J. L. Robison

For information, contact J.L. Robison at joanlrobison@yahoo.com or https://linktr.ee/j.l.robison

First edition
ISBN 979-8-9907451-1-7

Edelweiss Saga

SOMEDAY WHEN THE PAGES OF MY LIFE END, I KNOW THAT YOU WILL BE ONE OF ITS MOST BEAUTIFUL CHAPTERS.

—Unknown

I would like to dedicate this book to my family who (mostly) stayed patient while I spent countless hours writing it, and to my sister, Jane, who is one of my biggest fans. Thank you!

Chapter One
ॐ

August 18th, 1942

E va stared out over the horizon, watching the evening sun glitter off the blue sea and the soldiers who scattered along the shoreline. The German population of Dieppe and its surrounding areas had doubled in the last few weeks. A German garrison had moved into the area along with a large number of planes and a Luftwaffe fighter force. Nothing appeared to be amiss in the city, but the Germans obviously knew something she didn't.

She decided to hike to the top of the hill today as she often did and watch the troop movements on the beach. They were no longer allowing civilians on it, so this was as close as she could get.

She rested her hands over her growing stomach as the hot August breeze blew her hair and whipped her dress around her legs. Eva thought she was about ten weeks pregnant, but she was already starting to show. She was almost the same size as Ingrid had been at fourteen weeks, and she wondered why. She attributed part of it to the fact that Ingrid was heavier for her height than she was. Ingrid was two inches shorter than her, but they weighed the same. Although now that she was pregnant, she had been losing weight, not gaining it. The rations were limited, and she only got around a thousand to fifteen hundred calories a day, which was less than the daily average for a person who wasn't pregnant. She was always trying to find extra calories for herself and her growing baby. Ingrid often wanted to give her some of her food, but Eva wouldn't hear of it. But when Dr. Möller took her out to eat or offered her some of his food, she no longer told him no.

Aside from worrying about food, she would soon have to conceal her pregnancy or lose her job at the hospital, and then she wouldn't have money or food. She considered lying about the father's identity once she was too far along to hide the pregnancy. It would be better if people thought the father was French. To be pregnant with the child of someone who was considered the enemy, a man from the other side, would be detrimental. If a woman who was a collaborator became pregnant with the enemy's baby, they would never know what might happen to them. Except she did. It could cost her her life, or at the very least, it would earn her a beating or the public display of shaving her head that was common after the war ended. At best, the woman might have a genuine relationship with the man, and if she is lucky, he will marry her, and they will make a life together after the war in the man's home country. This, of course, would not be easy because the woman would no doubt be met with suspicion and hostility from the Germans as a foreigner. The alternative was to be left holding the baby and ostracized by their own community for

❧

2

having a child of the enemy. Either way, to fall pregnant as a collaborator was to ensure nine months of misery, uncertainty, and worry, followed by a life of conjecture and exclusion.

She sighed and looked down at the bump beneath her white dress. Wilhelm Bauer would be more than capable of providing for her and the baby, but that wouldn't happen because she was not going to tell him.

She turned to walk back down the hill, but four soldiers were coming up towards her. Her heart rate ticked up a notch, and she tried not to look in their direction as she walked past them. They said hi, and she turned their way and gave a forced smile that she knew they thought was genuine. They kept looking back at her, and it made her nervous.

Once she was in the apartment, she called for Ingrid. "Ingrid, are you home?"

Ingrid came out of the kitchen. "Hi. How was your day?"

"Ummm… kind of terrible, actually. I ate stale bread on and off, took three naps, and threw up. Oh, and I cried a lot."

"I'm sorry that I had to work today. I would have been here for you if I wasn't. Working must be terrible for you."

"It is."

"That's normal, though. It will get better. I was going to make something for dinner. Maybe that will help."

"Oh, what are you making?"

"We have a few extra potatoes and some carrots. I thought I would boil them."

"Sounds good. Even though my stomach is upset, I'm actually hungry."

"You're always hungry."

"I know. If only it wasn't so hard to keep it down."

Ingrid gave her a sympathetic look. "I remember the feeling, but I wasn't as sick as you."

"I'm hoping it will be gone by the second trimester. I'm only a couple of weeks away."

"When are you going to tell Dr. Möller?"

"When I can no longer hide it. He has noticed my loss of weight." To change the subject from her unfortunate condition, she decided to ask Ingrid about the increase in troops. "Have you noticed all the extra troops in the area?"

"It is hard to miss. What do you think is happening?"

"I don't know. Maybe the British are planning something." Eva wished that she knew the reason for the influx of troops.

"I'm sure you hope they are?" Ingrid wasn't trying to be hostile. She said it, wanting to give Eva something to hope for.

"I'm not sure how it would help me if they did." Eva knew the Allies didn't take France back from the Germans until D-day in 1944.

"What if they invade and take Dieppe?"

"Then that would be good. But I doubt that will happen. Most likely, they would attack, many of them would die, and the Allies would be no closer to winning the war."

Ingrid gave a nervous laugh. "Maybe it's nothing, and they just needed to move the troops somewhere."

"With the war in the east? No, they need all the troops there they can get. Something is going on."

"Let's hope it's nothing bad then," Ingrid said. "We should go to the market. They might have fresh fish this time, and we can have more than just potatoes and carrots."

4

"Sure, let's go." Eva stood to leave when three quick knocks echoed from the front door, and she halted, the hair on the back of her neck standing on end. Ingrid glanced at her, then went to the door. When she opened it, an officer was standing outside in the hall. He looked to be a little older than Wilhelm, with dark brown hair and blue eyes. Eva could not make out his rank, but she knew he must be a high-ranking officer. He also had the death head on his cap, but she did not see the SS runes on his collar.

"I am here to see Eva Abrams." He looked between the two of them.

She took a deep breath to calm her nerves. "I am Eva Abrams."

He gave her a smile that did not reach his eyes. "Nice to meet you." He looked to Ingrid. May we have a few minutes alone?"

She looked back at Eva but didn't move. "Of course," Eva told him. "Ingrid, would you wait out front, and I will meet you shortly?"

"Sure." Ingrid looked at the man, then walked out of the apartment and down the hall.

He came in and closed the door, then Eva nodded towards the kitchen, and he followed. "Word has gotten back to me that you said some pretty nasty things to SS Obersturmbannführer Bauer, but I don't think you know what you have done," he said as he walked behind her.

She looked up into his bright blue eyes. Who was this man, and how did he know what had happened in private between her and Wilhelm? "Oh, I think I do. It was no less than he deserved. I know what he did."

5

He sat in one of the kitchen chairs and held his hand out to the other one. "Please, sit down." Eva went to the other chair, lowering herself into it. "I am SS Oberführer Wulfekuhle. What you think you know, you don't."

"What does that mean?" Eva sat straight in her chair and did not break eye contact with him. She was not going to let this man have the upper hand.

"You say you know what he did, but every story has two sides. I'm going to tell you the other side, but I need you to listen and never repeat it."

Eva was leery of this strange man. "Alright."

"You should be in a camp right now. Wilhelm had information blacked out in your file a long time ago. It had been suspected that you were somehow involved in the resistance in Berlin, but to what extent, I don't know. One of our spies had infiltrated the resistance, and when they gave us the members' names, Wilhelm wanted to personally interview each of them. When your name was mentioned, he didn't add it to the list with the others, but our spy didn't know that. She was unaware that he knew you. Then we had our first arrest, and Wilhelm was there during the interrogation, but he wasn't alone with him. When the other man helping with the interrogation left for a few minutes, Wilhelm told the prisoner not to give your name, that if he did, he would go after his family, but if he didn't, they would be left alone. You were, of course, brought in for suspicions, but he had you released as soon as he found out. Because they did not have the same information on you as the others, he could do that. And that was because of his efforts to keep it that way. Once the man gave up the other names, Wilhelm had him shot before he could speak yours. They were going to shoot him, anyway. Then, a roundup was planned, and he knew he had to get you out of Berlin, so he approved your pass to the Russian front. Though it is dangerous there, it was far more dangerous for you to stay in Berlin at that time. Once you were gone, he went after the others, but a few escaped, who he believed were now in France working with the resistance. The resistance here is larger, more organized, and far more dangerous than the one in Berlin. That is why he used you to get to them. The sooner he caught them, the safer every German in France would be, and you. And in a way, it made the people of France safer as well because if he caught the resistance, there would be no more reprisals as a consequence of their attacks. Of course, he did not catch all of them in France; it is an ongoing thing, but he cleared most of them out of Dieppe."

His words penetrated deep. Had she been stupid in Paris for shutting Wilhelm out? "You said I was supposed to be in a camp already. What did you mean by that?"

"Even though you could not be directly linked to the resistance, they still deemed you a threat, so once again, a warrant was put out for your arrest."

Eva had no idea. After that last time she was arrested, she assumed it was over because no one ever came after her again. Wilhelm had said nothing to her about the other warrant. Of course, he didn't. He wanted to keep it from her.

"So why am I not in there now?"

"Wilhelm and I have been friends for a very long time, and he has helped me in the past with some things, so I owe him. He put in your file that you had been arrested and sent to Camp Royallieu-Compiégne because there were already French resistance fighters there, but, of course, you were not actually in the camp. About a week ago, Berlin contacted him and said that several high-ranking officers, including his superior, were coming to France to inspect the camps. I forged paperwork to say that an American woman had died recently in the Royallieu-Compiégne Camp. If he hadn't lied and asked me to do the same, he would have been relieved of his duties and most likely shot for what he has done for you. And they would have hunted you like the others in the resistance, and he would not be there as your buffer to stop them. I want you to know that it is very uncharacteristic of Wilhelm to do something like this. I don't want to sound mean because he is my friend, but he is ruthless in his pursuits. I have never seen him not get those he is after, and I have only witnessed rare instances of his mercy."

"So, he decided to take pity on me then."

He shook his head. "No," he said, slow and deliberate. "The only reason you are alive and sitting here now is that he fell in love with you. It is the one thing that has kept you alive. I believe if you hadn't secured the love of that man, you would have been dead a long time ago, and he probably would have even watched them do it and not flinched. It wouldn't be his first time attending an execution or performing it himself. I know you had seen the other side of him before he loved you, but that is the only side most people ever get to see."

Eva was speechless. She honestly didn't know what to say. How could she have been so wrong about him? "I had no idea," she said in a low, weak voice, trying to keep the emotions out.

"I know."

"Why didn't he tell me?"

"I don't think he wanted you to know. It was better that you knew as little as possible."

"He let me yell at him and say all those mean things?"

"Because he knew that he hurt you and that you needed to vent. He already felt bad about what he had to do, and then you found out. I can't say that it will ever be the same between the two of you again."

Eva felt a sinking feeling. "Is there a way I can fix it?"

"I don't know, maybe just give him time."

"So, he risked his life for me, and I made him feel bad about it?"

He looked down at his hands resting on the table and was quiet. "Wilhelm is a strong man. He will get over it. But he should know that you are aware of the facts now. And he should hear it from you." He lifted his down-turned eyes and looked around the kitchen. "I believe you were getting ready to leave. I will go. But I thought you should know that he isn't the man you think he is."

Eva walked him to the door. "Thank you for telling me, but I need to think about what to do with this information. I don't think he would see me now, anyway."

He held his hand out for her to shake. "Time," he told her when she took it.

She watched him leave, then got her purse and met Ingrid outside. They walked towards the center of town, where a market was held once a week in the summer. The street shops would sell fresh foods and goods that were made locally in Dieppe and fish the local fisherman would catch. Any fisherman had to get permission to have a boat and required a special license to operate it. That way, the Germans knew who was on it, what time they

9

would be out, and when they would return. They also had to have an escort with them, a soldier from the German army.

"Who was that man?" Ingrid asked as they walked.

"A friend of Wilhelm's."

"What did he want?"

Eva decided to tell Ingrid everything he had told her. There was no reason to keep it from her.

"Then you must try and make it up to him. If he truly loves you and risked everything for you, the best thing you could do is give yourself to him. After all, weren't you the only thing he truly wanted?"

"I don't know what to believe anymore. He probably never wants to see me again after Paris. That train has left the station, I think. But even though I hate him, I still love him. When you have known someone for as long as I've known him, and the two of you have so many shared experiences, quitting them is like losing a part of yourself. I may have run away from him, but I can't run away from how I feel. It's odd that you can know something isn't good for you but still want it so badly."

Ingrid didn't say anything but linked her arm through Eva's as they walked down the cobblestone street and pushed through the crowds of people. The smell of the food made her mouth water. She closed her eyes and took in a deep breath.

Once in the market, they bought a loaf of bread, some local honey, and some Camembert cheese, then headed to the end of the street where the seafood market was. They sold some of it raw, but you could also buy it cooked. They found a tent with various kinds of seafood, wooden boxes full of shrimp on one table, lobsters on another, scallops, and an entire row of mackerel on a side table. The little grey fish were lined neatly side by side. Ingrid leaned over the table to speak to the man and tell him how much mackerel they wanted.

While Ingrid ordered, Eva looked up and down the street at all the tents and people that crowded the street. Most of them were French people, but there were still a lot of Germans amongst them. She turned back to the table they were in front of but snapped her head back to the street. Standing three tents down was Wilhelm. He was looking at her, his face set to a callus mask of indifference. He had that same look on his face the day she saw him in her room in La Chapelle. His emotional barrier was now back up. She had probably undone all the progress she had made with him over the years in that single moment in Paris. He made no move to acknowledge her, not even a simple smile. He just turned away and walked in the opposite direction. She knew she had hurt him badly, but he also had hurt her. This gesture was symbolic. He was turning his back on her literally and figuratively. Wilhelm was rejecting her and withdrawing him love and affection. Just then, she realized that if he was back in Dieppe at the same time they were increasing the troops, that meant something was about to happen. What if this was finally it, a means for her to go home?

Chapter Two

August 19th, 1942

Eva jolted awake when the sound of large ship guns firing rumbled in the distance. She hopped out of bed and ran to the window, pulling back the curtain. The sun was still rising, and the buildings blocked her view of the beach. She ran to the wardrobe closet to get a dress. She had to see what was happening. She didn't care if she hadn't eaten breakfast. This could be her ticket out of France and away from the Germans. Her door opened suddenly, and Ingrid ran in.

"Eva, do you know what is happening?"

"No, but I plan to find out."

"You shouldn't go out there."

"I won't get hurt. I will only get close enough to see what is going on."

Ingrid hesitated for only a second. "I'll come with you."

Eva didn't object. Ingrid had as much right to go as she did. Eva changed, brushed her hair but didn't put it up, went to the bathroom, and then put on her shoes. Ingrid was waiting for her by the front door. They left the apartment and headed towards the beach, and Eva led them up the hill she always walked. They got close to the edge and stood in the high grass to watch. What she saw was absolute chaos.

Large guns were shooting from the hilltops down onto the beach, and what looked like cannons to her lined the shore, shooting out into the water.

The ground was shaking beneath her, with one explosion after another. It was continuous and loud, and the water would spray up from each blast. Planes were flying overhead, dropping bombs on the boats still coming in, but some had made it to shore.

Men were running, trying to make it up the beach to the city, but the Germans were unrolling barbed wire to prevent anyone from getting through. Men from the boats were falling like flies, littering the ground, some floating in the water. Tanks and trucks were coming ashore but were getting bogged down in the deep gravel. Eva would flinch every time someone was shot, but she gasped and clasped her hand over her mouth when a shell from a heavy artillery gun directly hit one of the boats, causing it to explode before her eyes. All the men on that boat were dead now. She couldn't look anymore, so she turned away and sat on the grass. These were people on her side, and they were getting blown apart. She didn't know if they were British, American, Canadian, or Australian, but it didn't matter. They were all her people. They all fought for the same cause. She put her fingers in her ears to block out the sound of the gunfire and explosions.

13

Ingrid sat next to her. "We should go home.

Eva shook her head. "No, when this is over, they will need us. I can't just sit in the apartment and wait."

They won't let us on the beach, but I suppose they'll need us at the hospital. Do you know where they're from, the soldiers?"

"I don't. They are most likely British."

She chanced a glance back at the beach, and it was so much worse than before. The water was a crimson color, and she knew she could never look at that beach the same way again.

"Maybe we should head to the hospital. We can wait there. Wounded will probably start coming in soon.

Once they were down the hill and in town, she realized some of the Allied troops must have made it off the beach and into the city. They had just turned onto a street when she watched a potato masher, which was a German grenade, fly through a building window and explode. Glass, debris, chunks of concrete, and plaster blew outward from the front of the building. Eva and Ingrid both screamed and ducked down, feeling some of the tiny pebbles of cement and glass rain down on them. Eva was squatting down with her hands over her head. Her ears were ringing, but she could still hear shouting in the background. She couldn't tell who it was. Eva looked over at Ingrid, covered in plaster dust, and shook her.

"We have to get off the streets."

Ingrid nodded her head, and Eva pulled her up by the arm; then, they turned around and ran. They had to get farther away from the beach because the part of the city closest to it was where any fighting would be. They ran over a few streets, then turned east again to try to get to the hospital. Gunfire echoed all around them, but they kept running, knowing they would get out of it faster that way.

There was a gunshot, then a ping sound, and Eva felt a burning sensation in her left thigh. The pain was growing intense with every movement of her leg. She stopped and looked down at her side. Her light blue dress was turning a dark brown color in the spot covering her left outer thigh. She pulled it up and looked at her leg. There was a hole in her thigh, and blood was trickling out.

Ingrid stepped off the sidewalk and came to her side to look at it. "Oh, my God. You have been shot." Her mouth was open, and her face was etched with horror. She took the scarf Eva had around her head and tied it to her leg, pulling it tight.

"A bullet must have ricocheted. It is not a direct hit," Eva told her.

"You are lucky. If it wasn't, it could have shattered your femur." Ingrid put her arm around Eva and helped her walk.

The pain was intense now, and she could hardly use her left leg. They were further from the fighting now, but the hospital was still blocks away. No one was out on the streets, and Eva didn't blame them. When they reached the hospital, Ingrid helped her into a chair in the lobby.

"I'm going to get Dr. Möller."

Eva didn't protest but instead nodded. She was feeling a little queasy and lightheaded. She looked at her leg; blood had already soaked through the scarf. She looked up when she heard voices coming toward her. Dr. Möller was walking fast down the hall in her direction, with Ingrid trailing behind. He came to her side and knelt down, taking hold of her leg.

15

"Let me see." He removed the scarf, and again, blood slowly ran down her leg. "It's only about three centimeters in," he said. She didn't know how deep that was, but when she looked at the hole, she thought the bullet was only in maybe an inch.

"We should get her on a bed so we can take her to the operating room," Ingrid said as she watched Dr. Möller inspect Eva's leg.

"There aren't any here," he told her. "In preparation for the incoming patients, they have moved them to the loading dock. I'll just carry her." He put an arm around her upper back and one under her knees, then lifted her from the chair. He carried her up the stairs to the first operating room and set her on the operating table. "Ingrid, I'll need you to assist me. But first, get another nurse to come and administer the anesthetics."

Eva grabbed onto Ingrid's arm, stopping her from leaving. "Ingrid, I don't know if it's safe."

"It's perfectly safe, Eva," Dr. Möller assured her.

She looked at Ingrid, who understood her meaning. Eva turned away from Ingrid and stared up at Dr. Möller. "I don't know if it's safe for someone who is pregnant."

Dr. Möller blinked a few times, then locked his gaze on her, looking at her differently this time. His eyes going right to her stomach. "How did I miss that?" he said to himself. "I see it now, the bump."

"I'm not sure what pain medication would be safe for the baby. The bullet isn't too deep, so I want you to take it out without giving me anything."

"Are you certain about this?"

16

"I didn't save this baby just to kill it later." He wrinkled his brows. "I'll explain later," she told him.

"Alright. After we get this bullet out of you, I can give you a barbital pill. It will help you sleep and shouldn't hurt the baby. You won't be taking it long term, just a day or two."

"I have heard of it. It's a sleeping pill, right?"

"Yes, it is used for that. Lay back on the table so we can get started."

She did, and he and Ingrid scrubbed in, then went to work on her leg. She gripped the side of the table to control the pain. Taking the bullet out was straightforward and didn't take long, but sowing it closed took much longer and seemed far more painful. She clenched her jaw closed every time he would put the needle through her skin. When he was done, Ingrid cleaned it with alcohol and wrapped it in white gauze. Dr. Möller carried her to a hospital room with a single bed. He laid her down, then left to get her the sleeping pill.

"Well, he knows now, but who knows how he will handle it," Ingrid said.

"He will definitely have questions later."

Just then, he returned with the pill and a glass of water. He held it out to her. "Take it."

With her thumb and index finger, she picked up the yellow pill from his hand, and he gave her the glass of water. She swallowed the medicine with some water, and he took the cup and set it on the side table. "I'm sorry I won't be assisting today. I sure picked a bad day to get shot."

He smiled. "We'll be fine without you. I'll visit you after the storm I know is coming is over."

"I would like that."

"And then you will explain to me how you got shot because you shouldn't have been anywhere near that beach. And when you are done explaining that, you can tell me who the father is, although I think I know. And then you will tell me why you put yourself in that position in the first place."

She felt like she did every time she got into trouble as a child, and her father chastised her. "I will explain it all to you."

He turned his head when the sound of commotion echoed from downstairs. "I think the wounded are arriving. I'll check on you later." He patted her arm and disappeared out of the room. Ingrid lingered for a second, then left too.

Eva tried hard to stay awake. She wanted to know who won and who lost and listened to the noises coming from the main floor, but it was getting harder to keep her eyes open. The medicine was in her system now, and she couldn't fight it. Her eyelids were growing heavy, and when she closed them, she fell into a deep sleep.

She was dreaming that she was traveling south on Interstate fifteen towards Provo. She was on her way to visit her parents, driving in her marine blue Geo Metro. It was a hot sunny day, and she had the windows rolled down, her arm resting on the door. She was happy, unconcerned with the troubles of life. It was a typical day, and there was the excitement of going home to see her family so they could go camping over the weekend. All her stress was gone as the hot, dry air caressed her face, whipping her hair all around.

Unexpectedly, her body jerked, and her eyelids flew open. Everything was dark, and she looked around, slowly realizing where she was, remembering what had happened. The ache in her leg registered with her, and she reached down, feeling the bandage. She was unusually hot, so she threw the blanket off and sat up. She did not know what happened with the raid, but it was dark now, and it must be over because she no longer heard shelling or gunfire.

She put her legs over the side of the bed and slowly lowered herself onto her right foot, trying to keep her weight off her left leg. Her stomach was nauseous and cramped from not eating all day. She limped across the floor to the door and felt that it was closed as she rubbed her hand along the frame. Someone must have shut it while she was sleeping. She opened it and peeked into the hall, and it was empty. She wondered what time it was because it was dark outside now. She limped down the hall, hanging onto the wall as she went. She had to know what happened, who won, and who might be at the hospital. The largest area with beds was on the main floor, and she looked at the stairs dauntingly. She held onto the banister and very slowly took one step at a time, wincing whenever she would put too much of her weight on her left leg. She got to the bottom and turned right, again hanging onto the wall. She went into the main patient area and saw that all the beds were filled.

She limped to the first one and looked down at the man lying on it. He was not in a German uniform but wore a brown one with a maple leaf patch on the shoulder. She took in a breath. He was Canadian. She scanned the room, but there were no doctors or nurses around. She looked back at the man to see what his wounds were and saw that his arm was wrapped in gauze, but that was all

19

she could see. She lowered herself onto his bed and tapped his leg. He jerked and opened his eyes, staring up at her, fear in them.

"Shhh... I will not hurt you. I'm American," she whispered to him in English. It was so foreign to her, speaking her own language again.

His fear was replaced with confusion. "American. What are you doing here?"

"I have been trapped here since 1939. I'm a nurse at the hospital, although I'm a patient right now. A bullet during the fighting ricocheted and went into my leg. Can you tell me what happened?"

"It was a raid to see if a full-scale invasion was possible and to gather intelligence, but it went downhill before we even reached the beach. The entire operation was a fiasco. Things immediately went wrong for the landing force on the eastern shore. They encountered a small German convoy, and the firefight between them alerted the Germans on the beach. The whole thing only lasted around six hours. I think some of us made it out, so maybe they were able to get some information they needed."

"I'm sorry it was a failure. I think the Germans knew you were coming. They had increased the number of troops in the area a couple of weeks ago, and I saw the head of the Gestapo for France here yesterday. So they must have had a tip that you guys were coming. They will send all of you to POW camps, but I don't know where. They have them all across Europe."

"And I am sorry you are stuck here. It must be hell living amongst the enemy."

She looked around the dark hospital room. "It has been at times. Are all of you Canadian?"

"Most of us, but there are British and American too."

Her eyes lit up. "Americans?"

"Yes, a small group of rangers. Maybe fifty."

"Are any of them here in the hospital?"

"I think some were captured and some wounded. I don't know if any are here, though."

"I can look. The Germans will probably move you guys to a camp in a few days. What is your name?"

"Sam. What is yours?"

"Eva. What part of Canada are you from, Sam?"

"Manitoba. A small town called Brandon. It's west of Winnipeg.

"I'm from Utah, near Salt Lake City."

"I've heard of it."

"I'm going to search the other patients. I wish you luck. And don't give up. We will win this war."

"I hope so."

"We will." She slowly pushed herself to her feet and made her way around the room, looking at the other patients' uniforms. They were all Canadian except for two who were British, but there were no Americans that she could see. The man she had been talking to could not understand the feeling of being amongst him and the other patients. Finally, being with people from the same continent who spoke your language, sounded like you, and whose country was allied with your own was of immense comfort.

She walked back towards the door and let out a little yelp when she ran into Dr. Möller.

"Eva, what are you doing?" His face was grave, and his voice disapproving. You aren't supposed to be here."

"I was just talking to them?"

"I understand your desire to speak with these men. But if you were caught here by anyone other than me, there would be serious consequences. And you should not be out of bed on that leg, either. Come on, let's get you back upstairs." He put his arm around her to help her walk.

"What time is it?"

"Ten."

"Can I go home tomorrow?"

"No, you need to stay for a few days." He helped her up the stairs, into her bed, and then sat on the edge. "How did you find yourself on the streets near the beach during the fighting?"

"I went to see what was happening. I knew the Allies must be attacking, and that was the closest thing to hope I've had since being here."

"It was reckless, but I understand." He met her gaze. "And what about this?" he asked, pointing to her stomach.

"That, too, was something reckless. A mistake."

"A mistake that alters your life forever."

"Everything that has happened to me since I've been here has altered my life forever."

"Not like this will. Does this person know that they are going to be a father?"

"SS Obersturmbannführer Bauer, and no, he doesn't know. And I will not tell him."

"Can I ask why?"

"For all the reasons you warned me about. He was not who I thought he was."

22

"No, I'm sure he's not. But now I don't see how you can be free of him."

"If I don't tell him, it's like I'm not even pregnant."

"That's not how it works. And you don't think he will find out?"

"How could he?"

"Well, one, he is here in Dieppe. But I'm sure he keeps tabs on you. Trust me, he will find out."

Eva looked down at her stomach. "I know."

"And he was at the hospital tonight. He doesn't know you are a patient here, though."

She met his gaze. "And he won't."

"He doesn't need to find out you're here to learn of your condition. Soon, you won't be able to hide it from anyone, and if he sees you, he will know."

"So what am I supposed to do?"

"As much as I don't like the man, it might be better if you tell him."

"No, I can't do that. Not after what he did."

"What did he do to you?"

"The resistance he hung in the street, he used me to get to them. And he is the reason Gerhardt was sent to the Russian front, and when I was in Paris, he was getting ready to round up the Jews and send them to the East. I'm also starting to think that he had Dr. Lavigne killed. He was supplying medicine to the resistance, and he had just given me some right before he fell to his death. But I think he was pushed and didn't jump."

"I wouldn't be surprised if SS Obersturmbannführer Bauer had him killed, and I shouldn't be surprised that you were involved with the resistance, but I am. Have you no sense? You got involved with the resistance, which was stupid in itself, but then, after you were tangled up with them, you got in bed with someone in the Gestapo. And he knows you were with the resistance?"

"Yes."

He let out a breath. "Then you have a hold over him, one I didn't realize you had."

"I don't believe me."

"Eva, there is no way you would still be alive, much less walking free if he didn't. I know he is capable of unspeakable things, but use what you have with him to your advantage. I normally wouldn't tell you to do this, but now you are carrying his child. You can't expect to work through your whole pregnancy, and who will support you and the baby once it is born?"

"You want me to turn to someone like him purely for self-preservation?"

"Yes, for the survival of you and your baby."

"I can support the baby and me. I don't need him."

"No, Eva, you can't. Not the way they have the system set up. You will not be allowed to work as a nurse once they discover you are with child."

"Then I can work as a maid or something. I won't go back to him." Part of her felt bad for saying that after learning all he did for her, but she was also trying to protect her own feelings because she didn't think he would take her back. So it was easier to reject him than be on the receiving end of it.

24

He stood. "I will let you get some rest. Think about what I said because I don't see any other way."

August 21st, 1942

After two days in the hospital, Dr. Möller told Eva she could go home, provided she rested. He told her not to move around too much, to get lots of sleep for her leg and the baby, and to make sure she ate enough food and drank plenty of water.

She hated feeling trapped in the house, but she couldn't argue with his reasons this time. She had thought a lot about what Dr. Möller told her, but she didn't know if she could ever forgive Wilhelm for what he did. She couldn't deny that she was still in love with him, but sometimes love wasn't enough. But he had done all those things for her. Kept her out of a camp. That in itself deserved her gratitude.

She didn't want to think about him right now, so she laid on the couch and tried to get some rest. Ingrid was good about taking care of her. Covering her up, bringing her food, and sitting with her. She felt she didn't deserve Ingrid.

She had finally fallen asleep while Ingrid cleaned the kitchen. But when a knock came from the door, she jerked awake and lifted her head. Ingrid walked past her, out of the kitchen, and went to answer it. When she opened the door, a man spoke.

"Is Eva Abrams at home?"

Eva watched the back of Ingrid at the door but could not see the man on the other side because she was blocking her view. "Who wants to know?" Ingrid asked him.

"I'm sorry. I cannot share that information with you. Is she home?"

"Yes."

"I need to speak with her. May I come in?"

Ingrid looked uncertain. "Yes, but she isn't well."

He didn't respond but brushed past Ingrid and walked into the living room. He looked down at Eva lying on the couch. She pulled herself into a sitting position, noticing he was in an SS uniform. Her mouth was dry, and her heart raced. This could not be good.

"Are you Eva Abrams?"

"I am."

"I have orders to bring you to Paris. Back a bag and come with me, please?"

She was terrified now. This had to be Wilhelm's doing. "Am I being arrested?"

"No."

"Then why am I being brought to Paris against my will?"

"I'm sorry, ma'am. I can only tell you that I am here to get you."

Ingrid stood behind the man, looking helpless and scared. "I will pack a bag. Can my friend come?"

"No, only you."

She slowly got off the couch, and Ingrid helped her to her room. After Ingrid shut the door, she whispered to Eva. "What do you think is happening?"

"I don't know. But I do know who's behind it. That man's uniform has the SS runes, just like Wilhelm's. He is probably Gestapo too."

"Do you think you are in danger?"

"He said I'm not being arrested, and if I was, there would probably be more than one man here to get me. But I cannot think of what he wants with me."

"Maybe he wants you back."

Eva frowned. "I don't think so. Not after what I told him in Paris."

"What did you tell him?"

"That I hope he goes to hell where he belongs."

"Oh, you should not have told him that."

"It's too late to take it back now. But I would retract my words if I could. I ruined what we had, but so did he."

"What are you going to do about your belly?" She pointed to Eva's stomach.

"Hide it from him."

"Hide your pregnancy? You are already popping."

"I'm not popping. I just ate a lot of food an hour ago."

"Eva, you look pregnant. You are very skinny with a big stomach. It's going to be hard to lie about your condition. You don't look like you are in the latter half of the second trimester, but it's obvious you are pregnant."

"I will just have to hide it better then. Wrap it or something."

"But you said that is bad, dangerous for the baby."

"I know what I said, but what else am I going to do, Ingrid?"

She shook her head. "I don't know."

They looked at each other, resigned to what had to be done. Eva pulled the flat sheet from her bed and cut a strip the length of it, then held her dress up as Ingrid wrapped it tightly around her stomach while she sucked it in. It was more uncomfortable than she thought it would be, verging on painful.

When they finished, Ingrid helped Eva stuff clothes into her bag, which was enough for a week because they didn't know how long she would be there. Then Ingrid carried her bag to the living room and sat it on the couch.

"How long will I be gone?" she asked the man standing in her living room.

"I don't know. They did not give me that information."

Of course, you weren't. "I am ready," she said to him.

He picked her bag up from the couch and waited. She embraced Ingrid in a tight hug. "I'm scared," she whispered in Ingrid's ear.

Ingrid's eyes moistened. "I'll tell Dr. Möller why you aren't here." She rubbed Eva's arms. "You'll be fine. He won't hurt you." She nodded her head, wanting Eva to agree with her.

Eva blinked back tears. "No, he won't... he won't."

She rode in the backseat, and the man who picked her up drove. There was no one else in the car with them. She wouldn't be stuck in the car with this strange man for long because it was only a three-hour drive from Dieppe to Paris. It was just after eleven, so they would arrive around two. Wilhelm had a reason for bringing her to Paris, but all the scenarios in her head worried her.

She watched out the window for a while but decided she had to see what this man knew. She leaned forward closer to the front seat. "Did SS Obersturmbannführer Bauer send you?"

He looked at her in her review mirror. "He did."

"And you don't know what he wants with me?"

"No, ma'am."

"Where will I stay while I'm there?"

"I don't know that either. He will tell you, I'm sure, when we arrive."

"So, where are you taking me once we are in Paris?" He again looked at her in the review mirror. "Is it 84 Avenue Foch?"

"I have instructions to take you to a very specific place, but I am not to tell you where."

She tried to curb the growing trepidation she was feeling. There was no way this was some secret date, but not knowing what was happening made her crazy.

They drove into Paris but didn't stop in the city's center, and like he said, they did not go to 84 Avenue Foch. She watched which roads he turned down, realizing they were heading south, and felt ill at ease. She looked from window to window, trying to see if anything specific caught her eye. But there was nothing out of the ordinary.

Finally, something did catch her attention. There was a tall stone wall, and above it rose two tannish grey buildings set side by side. They had red roofs and rows of windows that ran the span of each building. Whatever this place was, it was massive. As they got closer, she had a better view of it. It reminded her of an old fortress or an old prison. She tensed. *Oh God, a prison.* She froze in the backseat as the structure just beyond them seared into her eyes. They were fixed on it, and terror, like a hot iron spear, moved through her. The panic rose, and she looked around, desperate for an escape. "Stop the car!" she shouted at him."

"I cannot do that." He pulled up to the gate, rolled down the driver's winder, and spoke with the guard. After a few seconds, the guard opened the gate, and the car pulled through, parking in front of the main entrance. She opened the back door and leaped from the car, breaking into a run.

"Stop her," he yelled.

Two prison guards took off after her, chasing her to the gate. It didn't take long for them to catch up, one grabbing onto her arm and pulling her to a stop. They all but dragged her back to the car but didn't release her arms.

"I see we are going to have to escort you inside with guards." He nodded to the door. "Take her in."

The two men pulled her to the door and the man she came with opened it. They all went inside, and then he closed it behind him, locking it.

"They are going to let go of you now. If you run, they will be forced to take physical action. Do you understand?"

She nodded, too afraid to speak, and he gestured for her to follow the two men as he walked behind her. They led her to a cell and slid back a piece of metal that covered the small square window in the door. One of the men motioned for her to come closer and look inside.

Reluctantly, she walked up to the door and peered through the glass. It was a tiny room with a tabletop screwed onto the wall and a metal chair next to it, and on the back wall was a small window that looked over the enclosed courtyard. The room was plain, made of white plaster. On the other wall, from the table, was a single cot; on it was a man curled into a ball, facing the table. His hair was messy and matted, his face and hands were dirty, and his clothes were stained with blood. She looked back at the three men for a fraction of a second, confused as to why she was brought here. Then she turned back to the window and studied the man harder. He looked half dead, and both of his hands were wrapped in dirty gauze that was hard and crusty with dry blood. There was something familiar about him, but she couldn't quite figure out what or why. She tapped on the door, hoping he would turn his head slightly so she could see his face better. Just barely, he moved his head and looked at the door. She peered into his empty brown eyes and almost despaired. She pressed her face closer to the window and knew she hadn't mistaken him. It was Jon lying on the cot in the tiny cell, near death. The color drained from her face, and she took in a single explosive breath, on the verge of hysterics. She didn't know what to do and stood there indecisively.

She pounded on the door with both hands. "Jon," she cried, her voice fracturing. She turned to the men, not knowing what to say or do. "Can I see him?" her voice quivered.

The one man nodded to the other, and he went to the door and took a key from his belt, unlocking it. The door made an eerie screech as he pulled it open, echoing in the large building. She barely waited for it to open when she ran in and dropped to her knees on the floor beside the cot. She reached up carefully and touched the side of his face, misery threatening to break loose from her throat. Her eyes locked with his, and horror filled her every fiber. Tears spilled on her face and fell onto the cement floor. He tried to rise, but she held him down.

"No, stay still." She looked over his broken body, only realizing now that he was missing fingers on both hands. A fresh wave of tears filled her eyes and the sadness, anger, and sorrow she felt made her want to enact violence on the men who did this to him and the men standing on the other side of the door now.

"I came... to bring... you home." His voice was dry and hoarse, barely above a whisper. He had to pause between words as his breathing was labored.

"Shhh, I knew you would come for me, that you wouldn't go back without me. I never lost hope." She continued to rub his hair and the side of his face. A tear ran down the side of his nose, and it broke her in half to see him cry. "Jon, I am so sorry. You should have never come. I'm fine. I was not worth the risk."

"They got me just off the shore of Dieppe. I didn't know there would be so many troops on that beach."

"There was a raid. The Canadians and British came, but it was not a success."

Another tear escaped his eye and ran down onto the pillow. "I'm so sorry, Eva. But I told them."

Her eyes grew wide. "Told them what?"

"That I knew you. That you were the reason I came here. The Germans think I'm a spy, and now they think you are one too. They will kill me soon now that I've talked."

She blinked away the tears and leaned in close to him. "Don't worry about that. It wouldn't be the first time they thought I was a spy. Sleep. I'm going to get you out of here, no matter what it takes." And she meant it too.

She continued to try to comfort Jon, easing his pain by being affectionate and letting him know she was there for him. She couldn't even process that he was here, finally. Much less that he was in prison. There was no way on God's green earth that she would let them kill Jon. No one else was going to die because of her, and Jon was her only way back to the future. She stared at the plaster wall, and her resolve solidified. She had to win Wilhelm over, regardless of what that meant. She had to save Jon, and she suspected she didn't have much time.

Jon was asleep now. Her being there seemed to comfort him, she thought. Eva stood and walked to the door, knocking on the metel. The guard opened it, and she stepped out into the hall.

"I want to see SS Obersturmbannführer Bauer." The guard who opened the door looked at the man who had brought her there.

"My orders are to bring you back to Dieppe in the morning. SS Obersturmbannführer Bauer is too —"

"I don't want to hear that he is too busy to see me. I know where he lives and will sleep on his doorstep if I have to."

The man drew in a deep, long breath before speaking. "Give me a minute." He disappeared out of sight, then after several long minutes, he returned. "I have permission to bring you by his office, but I cannot guarantee that he will see you."

She gave one last sorrowful look at Jon, then turned back to the man. "Let's go."

She was feeling braver than she ever had before, now that it was Jon's life in danger. There was an echo of anguish trying to swim to the surface, but she found the strength to stamp it down. She had to be strong and brave for Jon, but she wasn't convinced she could. They got in the same car, and he took her to 84 Avenue Foch.

They turned down the wide street, and it was hard to believe such horrors that were only specters of hell in her time happened here. The city was infamously the stuff dreams were made of if you didn't know what was really happening beneath the surface.

She looked at the posh 19th-century mansions that lined the street and rows of sky-high chestnut trees. It was one of the wealthiest streets in Paris, yet it was the most notorious street in Paris. It had grown even more overcast, and there was an uncomfortable chill in the air now. Eva watched the military vehicles and uniformed men ornament the city from the car window, mirroring the somber mood of the day. The weather seemed fitting for where she was going.

When they reached the military headquarters, she got out of the car and looked around. Her stomach tightened as her boots contacted the damp ground, apprehension sparking at the thought of facing Wilhelm again.

They approached the building's entrance, a large white door before them. The SS man with her announced who she was to the grim-faced young soldier posted at the door. The man gave her a stern once-over before he nodded and disappeared inside. Everything about his demeanor unsettled her, everything about this place disturbed her, but she tried to ignore it. She had only been inside the building once when she barged in to talk to Wilhelm, only to be stopped in the lobby and told to leave. She was surprised there wasn't a guard at the door that day.

The soldier reappeared and motioned with his hand for them to follow. She and the other man walked behind the soldier as he beckoned them forward down a long beige corridor with light wooden floors to a door at the very end. The soldier opened the door for her, and she stepped inside, then he shut it behind her.

To face Wilhelm, Eva closed her fists and considered the viciously bad terms she and he parted on and how she was going to deal with that.

She noticed the SS man didn't enter with her. She was unprepared for what a frigid shock it was to see Wilhelm again. Her nerves rose to extreme heights. Wilhelm was seated at a large desk on the other side of the room, and other soldiers were standing around it, waiting. None of the soldiers she could see had the SS runes on their collars like Wilhelm. She noticed he was the only one in the room with them and wondered why that was.

Wilhelm was signing papers on his desk and took his time as he did it. He occasionally spoke to the other soldiers in the room, handing one of them a form after he signed it. When he was finished, the men saluted, then left to carry out the orders Wilhelm must have given them. As usual, he emanated power, the obedient actions of every soldier in the room demonstrating it.

It was hot and muggy in his office, but there was still the onset of a chill that was not caused by the temperature. The windows were open, and the gentle breeze rustled the thin white curtains. Wilhelm continued to work with some papers on his desk, and if he noticed her presence, he gave no indication. She searched his face but had no perception of his mood. His face was straight, closed off from showing any emotions. If only she had the same level of control over her own feelings, but she felt like they were always written on her face for everyone to see.

She stood still in the same spot she had been the whole time. Her heart was pounding as she drew on her courage, the little she had. As she stood in this large, warm office, she felt oddly disconnected from her surroundings. She had never been here in his Paris office before, and it was all strange and uncomfortable to her but, at the same time, familiar. It was ironic that she was again asking for his help, needing his favor, back in the pampered, opulent arms of the Nazis. And unlike Jon and any other American, British, or French, she was sheltered in her connection to Wilhelm Bauer. But he was dangerous and could sniff out her true feelings and intentions if she wasn't careful.

Wilhelm was a formidable presence, and his ambiance of power combined with his acute intellect was unnerving. Her recklessness had led her down a path that might benefit her in the end, but her treatment of him the last time they met could have been a deadly mistake. She had caused him heartache, and for that, he could easily bury her alive. It didn't matter if he was good or bad for her. She was having a hard time giving him up. What had she allowed herself to become? But maybe more important than that was what had she allowed herself to do? She put herself right in the path of this soulless person, and by doing so, he brought her into his world, which there was no coming back from. She wasn't sure she was capable of leaving anymore because she had fallen in love with the devil who had pulled her down into his hell.

Her emotions were turbulent inside as she continued to stand by the door, waiting for some sign that she could approach. Her leg was throbbing, and she had to keep most of her weight on her right leg, which was fatiguing it. And her stomach hurt from the material that was tightly wrapped around her abdomen.

There was a knock on the door, then three other men entered, walking right past her to Wilhelm's desk. They didn't acknowledge her and had a disregarding attitude towards her, like Wilhelm, ignoring her completely. She clenched her hands together, trying to be patient. The memories slammed into her of the times he had her arrested. And then Jon, beaten within inches of his life, missing fingers on both hands and imprisoned by soldiers just like the ones here now. He would never be able to do things normally again. Inside swelled a hatred of the German military, and she worried it would surface when she finally got to speak to Wilhelm.

Her gaze moved from person to person, lighting on every officer's hat and the picture of Hitler hanging on the wall behind Wilhelm's desk. It made her sick to her stomach, and while she was searching the room, her eyes fell on a gun lying on the desk, Wilhelm's gun, the one usually kept on his side. The idea of taking it and shooting everyone in the room ran through her mind, but she pushed it away quickly. Thoughts like that would not help her free Jon.

The room gradually emptied until there was only a single soldier and Wilhelm. She stared at him, and the young man's eyes met hers, his piercing gaze setting her even more on edge. He was tall, his expression serious, his angular features Aryan and he had Wilhelm's same voracious energy. Also, like Wilhelm, his military uniform's collar was edged with the two SS runic insignias of the Schutzstaffel.

Wilhelm signed a few more papers and handed them off to the young man. "You may go, Lieutenant Bonnet," Wilhelm said without looking at the man as he slid a stack of papers in front of him.

Lieutenant Bonnet saluted Wilhelm before he gave another quick, harsh look in her direction, then strode towards the door, being careful to not look at her again as he passed, putting on his officer's hat as he walked out of the room, leaving Wilhelm and her alone.

37

She tried to force herself to smile and appear calm, but the weight of her anger made it difficult. Although the familiar desire to be close to him filled her, at this knowledge, she could only stand there, fists clinched as a hatred for Wilhelm that was so intense it hurt slowly replaced that feeling. But she couldn't let it get the better of her. She needed him, and if she blew it, Jon would die.

Wilhelm moved the papers to the side, leaned back in his chair, and finally leveled his hazel eyes on her with an icy stare. "What can I do for you, Eva?"

You hurt Jon. You killed Gerhardt, you heartless bastard, she internally seethed.

She tried to relax her body and control her voice when she spoke. "I need you to release the American man you have in prison. I am willing to do anything for that to happen. Anything," she stressed, forcing the words out, trying to disguise her anger. The anger that she had been brought so low as to gravel at Wilhelm's feet chipped away at her.

He narrowed his eyes, and made a sound of contempt, then turned his attention once more to the papers on his desk. He took his time, not looking back up at her, but she saw his lips turn up in a mocking grin.

"Did I arrest your American lover?" Wilhelm retorted.

Rage pulsed through her, and she clenched her teeth tight, trying to control her emotions. "He is not my lover. We worked together at the Friends Service Council." That wasn't exactly the truth, but close enough.

Wilhelm laid the papers in his hand on the desk in front of him and leaned back in his chair again, impassive, then his eyes met hers in fervent, and his expression darkened. A flash of anger passed over his features, and his eyes flared with a violent gleam as he glared at her.

"You think I'm going to release him?" he said, his tone hard and uncaring.

"I need him alive. If he dies, I might never make it home," she said, chastising herself quickly after for her choice of words. She had to fight the urge to be hateful towards him and tried her best to seem friendly so that she might convince him. She struggled for composure and tried again. "Tell me what you want of me, and I will do it?" The words come out slow and forced.

"Commander Bauer, I'm sorry to interrupt." She turned to find another SS officer standing in the doorway, his intense gaze briefly darting to her, then back to Wilhelm. "We are ready."

"Tell them to load up," Wilhelm ordered, not looking at her, his expression one of indignation as the anger in his eyes was once again hidden. "Miss Abrams and I are finished, anyway."

She felt queasy and lightheaded, and her panic spiked. She had to get Jon out. "But, Wilhelm—"

"Show her out," he interrupted, ordering the man to escort her, but Wilhelm never once looked up.

"Wilhelm…" she choked out, on the verge of tears. Her thoughts swirled, and her mind and emotions were in chaos. The man approached and took her arm. He was gentle but insistent.

Filled with anger and an all-consuming fear for Jon's life, she flinched when the man touched her and pulled away. Wilhelm calmly turned his attention back to the papers on his desk, and the man retook her arm. As they walked away from the desk, she cast one last glance at Wilhelm before leaving the room. The man held

39

her arm as they left the office and guided her to the front door. She stepped out of the building, her whole body feeling numb. Her eyes met the SS Captain who escorted her out, and he eyed her with conjecture. She pulled her arm away again and started walking down the street, not caring where she was going or where she would stay.

Chapter Three

"Miss Abrams," the man called after her, but she ignored him and kept walking. She swiped at the tears in her eyes with the back of her hands. She wanted to give up, and to not be here anymore, and have her old life back.

It was now twilight, and the air was finally starting to cool. Eva crossed her arms over her chest and grappled with escalating panic. She didn't know what she was going to do now. A piece of her hair fell out of the hairpin, and she reached up with trembling hands and tried to re-secure it. *How can I save Jon if Wilhelm won't help me? Because if I do nothing, he will undoubtedly die.*

She walked the streets of Paris, not knowing where to go or what to do. Suddenly, she realized that she had left her bag in the car back at the Gestapo headquarters. She didn't even have her things, and she had never felt so alone in her life. She sat down on the sidewalk to get off her aching feet and sore leg and leaned against the building wall. She focused on her breathing to try and calm her frayed nerves. She still had her purse and some cash with her, and she knew that soon she would need to find a cheap hotel for the night.

"Miss Abrams?"

She was startled by a male voice close to her. She hadn't seen anyone approach. She looked up into the face of the harsh featured soldier who escorted her out of Wilhelm's office and wondered how he found her? He was peering down at her, his eyebrows pulled together. There was sincere concern in his expression.

"SS Obersturmbannführer Bauer has instructed me to take you to the hotel."

She stared at him in confusion, struggling to understand what this meant, but her stress and sleep-deprived mind couldn't process it.

"But he told me to leave. He will not change his mind about my request. Why does he care where I go now?"

He held out his large hand to her. "All I know is I have been instructed to take you to the hotel tonight, and tomorrow, you'll be traveling to Obersturmbannführer Bauer's home in Berlin. Your things are still in the car."

There was a moment of excitement at the mention of her things, but it was brief. Why was Wilhelm taking her to Berlin, and what did this mean for Jon? She sat there looking at him, confused by this news. Finally, she raised her hand, and he pulled her to her feet.

"Will Obersturmbannführer Bauer be coming to Berlin as well?"

"Yes," he replied. There was an enigmatic tone to his voice, and they stood staring at one another for a protracted moment.

There was something he wasn't telling her, but now was not the time to try and pry it from him.

"He still has some things that require his attention here in Paris, but he will meet you in Berlin when he is finished. I understand that will be soon."

"Will I be traveling alone, then?" she pressed.

There was the same cagy look on his face as before. "No, Miss Abrams. I will be accompanying you, along with two other soldiers, in a separate car."

Why did this feel strangely like captivity? "Alright. You lead the way back to the car, and I will follow." In truth, she didn't remember how to get back. She had blindly turned down street after street and didn't even know what part of Paris she was in. She tried to steady her nerves and walked beside him back to the car.

All night, she wondered if she would wake to find Wilhelm in her room, but he never came. He had put her up in the hotel she stayed at with Ingrid, the Hotel Lutetia. Now she was back at the Gestapo headquarters, and the SS officer who brought her from Dieppe was waiting by the car. Apparently, her meeting with Wilhelm wasn't going to take long.

Like the day before, she stood in his office, waiting for him to speak to her. He combed through papers on his desk, signed a few, then laid them to the side. Finally, he stood from his chair and went to the window, crossing his arms, watching her from across the room, his expression jaded.

She couldn't live without her family, and if Jon perished in this time, she would never see them again. She tried to imagine a family of only one and realized with sadness that most of Wilhelm's life had been that way. Only having his mother to truly care about him.

She leveled her gaze on him. "If you need someone to punish, then punish me. Put me in that cell, not him. If that is what it takes to free him, I am willing to sacrifice my life for his."

Wilhelm was silent for a moment, his gaze fixed on her. "I could." His eyes met hers. "But then I would mourn you for the rest of my life. And I don't give a damn about him."

Tears stung her eyes as she held Wilhelm's ardent gaze. She was touched by his words for her, but her heart fell to the pit of her stomach at the thought of Jon and how she had failed him.

He broke their gaze and looked back out the window. "I released him from prison. He is now in a hospital in Paris." His eyes gave a brief flare, and she could see the conflicted emotions in them. "When he is better, I will decide where to send him. You overestimate my power and my reach. I cannot simply let him walk free, but I will try to put him somewhere he will survive."

She let out a long, shuttering breath, astonished and grateful, more than he could ever know. She didn't try to hold back the tears. "Thank you for saving his life."

He smiled with polite deference. "I didn't do it for him."

"I know."

He looked at the tears that glistened on her cheeks. "Eva, you have to toughen up. This war is a brutal thing. Too much gets to you." Wilhelm's voice was unsympathetic. "You cower when faced with any hard choice."

Annoyance cut through the gratitude and relief she was feeling. "I am not like you. Fear is a reasonable response to me. It is for most people, Wilhelm."

"No, it isn't," he countered. "It is not a reasonable response. It is an irrational response. When you react to a situation in fear, you think with your emotions, not common sense, not your head."

"So, if you had been in my shoes and the resistance was trying to kill you, you wouldn't be afraid?" She hated that she couldn't keep the trimmer from her voice.

"They did try to kill me, remember? And no, I don't fear them even a little." Wilhelm eyed her coldly, then looked back out the window. "I see them like I see all enemies, as something to pick apart so I can find the best way to dominate them. You can learn, but it will take time and a lot of effort." He turned from the window and set his relentless gaze back on her.

It was ruthless how he looked at things, but she realized with perfect clarity that she needed to learn to think like him. She wanted to believe that she could be more like him; she wanted to be strong enough to face this, and Wilhelm's faith in her fortified the little courage she had. He had never coddled her, even though so many times she had hated him for it, but he was right.

"How did you teach yourself to be so confident?" she asked, frustrated tears blurring her eyes.

"Control and knowing when to not care," Wilhelm said. "One thing I learned about what it takes to be strong is recognizing and acknowledging any weaknesses in yourself and then making adjustments to counter them. It's a skill that you can learn. The reasons you cower are because you care too much, you lack control, and you don't believe in yourself. You need to overcome this weakness, or your enemies will take advantage of it, and they will win."

There was an unspoken tension in the room, and she had to clear it. "Tell me what you want in return for releasing Jon? Whatever it is, I'm ready," she forced out. She wasn't exactly ready for anything, and she had her limits. She just wasn't sure what they were yet, but she would know if she heard them.

Wilhelm laughed, the sound harsh and critical. "Really, Eva? You would be mine in every way? Should we get married tomorrow and consummate it that very night, so you will officially be my wife?" He looked at her cynically as if he already knew the answer.

Her fear notched up to panic. "Being friends isn't enough?" Her question was weighted, and she knew it. If marriage was his price, would she really accept? She was already carrying his baby, so would marrying him be any worse? And soon, she would be limited in her access to an income. She looked into Wilhelm's rapture, sharp gaze, a rush of heat igniting between them, sending a shiver through her, their draw impossible to fully suppress.

Wilhelm walked to his desk, shaking his head as if at war with himself. They were silent for a long moment, and when he brought his gaze back to hers, his brow was furrowed with a bitterness she had not seen in him before, a profound hurt. Her anger and resistance to him crumbled. He could have any woman in Berlin, but he didn't want to be with them. He chose her, an outsider, an enemy of his country, someone who despised him for the longest time.

"If that is what you want of me, then I will do it. I will be yours in every way."

46

Surprise spread across his face, and he stared at her, searching, then looked at his watch. "The car is waiting for you outside. We can talk more about this when I arrive in Berlin."

"Won't your mom wonder why I'm there?"

"No, I told her you were coming to visit."

He called in the officer who brought her there, and he escorted Eva out. She left Wilhelm's office, feeling everything around her was spinning. The SS officer opened the back door for her, and she slid in. Once the car was on the road, she laid down in the back seat and fell quickly asleep.

Someone was gently shaking her by the shoulder. "Miss Abrams, we are here."

She sat up and looked around, momentarily confused. It was dark outside, and she could barely make out the man's face. "Here where?"

"SS Obersturmbannführer Bauer's apartment."

The memory of earlier came rushing back. "Right."

She slid to the edge, and he helped her out of the car. He carried her bag up the stairs to the top floor, then sat it outside the door.

He tapped the bill of his cap. "Have a good night, ma'am." He turned on his heels and left.

She looked at the door, still feeling the throes of sleep. She knocked twice and waited. This was a familiar place to her; she had been here so many times, but not for a long time.

The door opened, and Wilhelm's mom gave her a warm smile. "Eva, come in."

Eva picked up her bag, walked past her into the apartment, and Marie closed the door. "How are you, Marie?"

"I have been well. How have you been?"

"I'm fine. I hurt my leg, but I'm better now."

"Oh, how did you hurt your leg?"

Eva felt embarrassed at how she got hurt. "I got shot."

Marie's eyes widened, a look of horror spreading across her face. "What? How did you get shot?"

"It's a long story. Really just a case of wrong place, wrong time."

"Here, come and sit down," Marie insisted. Eva followed her to the couch, and Wilhelm's mom took her bag, disappeared for a few seconds, and then returned. "You will sleep in Wilhelm's room tonight." She sat on the couch beside Eva.

Eva gave a constrained smile. "Thanks."

"So, Wilhelm tells me you will be staying with us while you are in Berlin?"

"Yes, that's right."

"How long will you be here?"

Eva took in a breath to say something but then paused. She didn't know how long she would be in Berlin because she didn't even know precisely why she was there. It was time she learned more about Wilhelm and told his mother the truth.

"Marie, what exactly has Wilhelm told you about me?"

She tilted her head to the side and observed Eva with a look of perplexity. "Just that you are visiting."

"No, I don't mean only now. I mean, about me in general."

"He doesn't tell me much about anything, really. But I've guessed that you two are friends, even though I think he tries to hide it from me."

Eva cleared her throat. "Friends, huh? I'm not sure about that."

"You are. Wilhelm has never brought another girl to the apartment. He doesn't even bring his guy friends here. You must be very special to him, or he wouldn't have let you see where he lives. And now he has let you come back again."

"Well, I'm not sure we are friends, but I think I need to be honest with you about what we really are. We are lovers."

Marie looked at a picture hanging on the wall as a way to focus her thoughts. "I had wondered. But now you have confirmed what I had already suspected."

"That's not all. If I tell you something else, would you promise to not say anything to him?" She looked back at Eva, her eyes full of questions, but she didn't say anything. "You have to promise, or I won't tell you."

Marie nodded her head. "I promise."

Eva tried to find the courage to say the words. "I'm... pregnant, and Wilhelm is the father." She choked up as she said the words.

Marie covered her mouth with both hands as her eyes teared. She shook her head several times, then moved her hands and took Eva's in her warm ones. "I never thought those were words I would ever hear. You asked me not to tell. Is that because he doesn't know?"

"Yes. He has told me several times that he doesn't want children."

She moved one of her hands from Eva's and gently wiped at the corner of her eye with her index finger. "He does. Part of it is this war and how much he works, but that is not the main reason."

Eva mentally tried to prepare for what she was going to say. "Then what is the real reason?"

"Do you want some water?"

Eva thought she was stalling. "I am a little thirsty."

Marie got off the couch, went to the kitchen, and filled two glasses with water. Eva wondered what could be so hard to say that it made her apprehensive to talk about. Marie returned to the living room, handed Eva one of the cups of water, then sat back on the couch and drank from her own glass. Eva took a few sips, then sat the cup on the coffee table.

Marie looked at Eva's face, and something was burning in her eyes, sadness, Eva thought. She took one of Eva's hands again and held it with both of hers in her lap. "Let me tell you about Wilhelm in all the facets that are my son. When I look at him, I see something different than what you do. I sometimes still see that twenty-three-year-old young man who took care of his mother and sick sister. I see a person who is devoted to his country and those he loves. His heart is strong, but it can still break. If he loves you, he will go to the ends of the earth for you. I don't know if he has, but if he ever hurt you in some way, I know it wasn't intentional. Most people don't know this about him, but if you look beneath the surface, you will see it. He wasn't always the way he is now. He used to not be so closed off to everyone. Let me tell you why he is this way."

She paused and took another drink of her water, and Eva watched her, tense as her mind ran wild with thoughts of what she might say. Eva took a sip of her water and then waited for Marie to continue.

Marie sat her cup back on the table, looked at her hands, and spoke at last. "You see, I grew up in an orphanage. My parents weren't married, so my grandparents made my mom give me up. I spent my entire childhood in that orphanage. When I was sixteen, I thought I was in love with an older man. He was the director of the orphanage, and he was nice to me for a while, at least. He flirted with me and snuck me things that no one else got. He made me feel special. I didn't realize at the time that he didn't really love me. We found ways to be together, and eventually, I became pregnant. When I found out, I told him, hoping he would take me from that place and that we would start a family together. But that is not what happened. He denied being the father and said that I had been sleeping with the boys in the orphanage and the baby was one of theirs, which wasn't true. He said it to keep himself out of trouble. When I gave birth, he tried to have my baby taken from me, so I escaped the orphanage with my child. By that time, I was seventeen and went to work for a family as a nanny to their children. They let me keep my baby with me in the nursery. I had given my baby my last name on the birth certificate, and I left the line with the father's name and information blank. When I finally got married, I gave him my new husband's last name and had it put on the birth certificate that he was the father. If I had given him his real father's last name, it would have been Steinbach. You see, Wilhelm's father is a Jew, so he is half-Jew. No one knows that except him and me, and now you."

Tears escaped Eva's eyes as she looked at his mother in astonishment. That was the farthest thing from what she thought

Marie was going to say, and it kicked up a whole host of conflicting, powerful emotions. "Is that why he hates Jews?"

"It is, and why he doesn't want children. His children would be a quarter Jew."

"But you aren't Jew?"

"No. I don't have any Jewish blood in me. It is good that I put his stepfather's name on his birth certificate. It protects him from his own party. Your last name is Abrams. Are you Jewish?"

"No, I don't think so. Will Wilhelm be mad then when he finds out I'm pregnant?"

"I think he will struggle for a while to come to terms with it. But he will in no way be upset with you." She searched Eva's face. "My son is dear to me, so when you told me you were pregnant, I was relieved. I never thought I would meet a woman who deserved him. Before he met you, he was lost and alone. I am happy he has finally found someone who can save him from his loneliness. But I think it's more than that. You are still in his life after all this time and carry his child. You have given him love, and life without that is grim. He has had his flings with women, and plenty here chase after him, but there has never been anything there on his part. Those women would turn him over in a heartbeat if any of them knew he was half-Jew. I told you because you have given me a reason to trust you, and I know the blood that runs through his veins is not a problem for you."

Eva drew in a breath and squeezed Marie's hand. "No, of course not. I don't care who his father is, and I would never turn him in for being a Jew. But I don't think it's love."

Marie's face grew strained. "You don't love him?"

"I do, more than anything. But sometimes I wonder about him. He is nice to me at times, and…" she flushed, "obviously is attracted to me, but I don't quite know what to call what he feels for me."

"Has he ever told you he loves you?"

"Yes, he has, more than once."

"Then he loves you." Her tone was certain, and there was no doubt in her words.

"Can I tell him that I know who his father is?"

"When you feel the time is right, but I would plan it carefully." She finally smiled. "I don't care that you are not German. I'm just relieved he has someone. He is expected to marry a pure Arian German woman, someone who fits a mold, as opposed to someone who you were destined to be with, but it makes no difference to me. What my son did shows the difference between making decisions with your head versus your heart. He hasn't had it easy from when he was born to now. His stepfather was mean to him, I think because he wasn't his own son. So, as a boy, he used to get into fights as a way to relieve the anger he felt towards his stepfather. I think that is why he started boxing. He needed an outlet for all his anger and the disappointment he felt towards the world. But everything he has done has been for his sister and me. He is strong, loyal, and a hard worker. I do know that when Wilhelm did not have a stable job, he would not have done what he did to father a child. And he would not marry someone if he didn't think he could support them. He has suffered a great deal and is familiar with solitude, lack of love, and abuse. However, his biggest weaknesses are that he is guarded, abrasive, and cold towards others. So, I think you truly surprised him, taking him off guard when you were kind to him. I suspect he is uncomfortable when people are nice to him."

He might be a monster, but he loved her in the only way he knew how. He gave her everything he had, and she understood that now.

"His sister, she doesn't have the same father?"

"No. His stepfather was her father. She was not part Jew, and Wilhelm wanted me to keep it from her that he was, so I did. She never learned the truth." Marie looked at the small grandfather clock. "It is very late. We should get some sleep."

Eva realized she was exhausted and knew Marie must also be tired. "I am sorry I kept you up so late."

"I don't mind. You have given me something tonight that, just yesterday, I would have never dared hope for. Do you know how far along you are?"

"Around eleven weeks."

Her eyes lit up. "Oh my, almost done with the first trimester. Let me see you." She stood and motioned for Eva to stand, too.

Eva had been wearing loose-fitting dresses to hide her growing stomach, but she probably wouldn't need to for much longer. Eva still had the material from the sheet tied around her stomach. She stood and lifted her dress, untying the material and unwrapping it from her stomach, and then she dropped the skirt of her dress back around her legs.

Marie watched as Eva did this. "So that is how you have kept it hidden?"

"Yes."

Marie observed her, then took her by the shoulder, turned her to the side, and pulled at the back of her dress to make it tighter around her stomach. "I can see it. If you wore dresses that fit you properly and didn't keep your stomach wrapped, he would have noticed already."

"I have been trying to hide it," she admitted.

"I understand. Let's get some rest. You need it. I wouldn't put that back on while you sleep. I can't imagine it's good for the baby or you." She looked at Eva closer. "And you are skin and bones, don't you eat?"

"I eat what I can afford it."

"Well, that's going to change. I won't allow the mother of my grandchild to waste away before my eyes." She ushered Eva down the hall to Wilhelm's room. "I'll make a nice breakfast in the morning." Then she went to her own room and closed the door.

Eva changed and crawled into bed, thinking what an unexpected night it had been.

Chapter Four

va jolted awake, momentarily disoriented, as she looked around the room. Her mind soon caught up as she took in the surroundings, Wilhelm's stuff, his bed, and his room.

She glanced at the things on the wall and on his dresser, and last night rushed back. He is half Jew, the reason for his hatred towards them and his mom's sad upbringing in an orphanage.

She sat up, feeling Wilhelm's absence keenly, and the desire for him to be there now roused her emotions. She looked to the window and at the predawn sky through the partially open curtains. Then, the sound of Wilhelm's deep voice flooded in.

She moved the blanket off, got out of bed, and went to the door. She opened it a crack and looked through the opening to see Wilhelm sitting at the kitchen table with his mother. She opened the door all the way and stepped into the hall, making her way towards them, her leg stiff from the bullet wound.

She took in Wilhelm's unbelted jacket as he leaned over the table, deep in conversation with his mother, but sensing her presence, he looked up and met her eyes. His dark hair was messy from showering, and she noticed his distractingly muscular frame, and an intensity passed between them; then he looked away back to his mother. She felt the sharp sting of his guarded behavior as she turned and went to the bathroom.

She was reeling by the knowledge of who Wilhelm really was, of how strongly he felt for her, and saddened to know why he was always closing himself off. She and Wilhelm would have to set their complicated emotions aside, though, if this was going to work.

While in the bathroom, she checked in the mirror to ensure that her nightgown hid her stomach. It was baggy enough that you couldn't really make out her shape, and she was satisfied. She returned to the kitchen and sat with Wilhelm and his mom at the table.

"Let me get you something to eat," Marie said, getting up to dip some food from a pan on the stove.

"My mother is leaving for a few days to visit a friend. That will give us some time alone." Wilhelm stared her down, his lip lifting with the trace of an emotion that didn't reach his eyes.

Both frustration and anger flared in her in response to his demeanor, but she thought she understood a little now why he acted the way he did. *Calm down, Eva,* she told herself. *You need him, and Jon needs him.* She gave him a nod, and his mom sat a plate of fried eggs with a side of potatoes in front of her. Eva picked up the fork but kept her eyes on Wilhelm.

"Well, I have eaten, so I'm going to pack a bag," Marie said. She squeezed Eva's arm, then walked out of the kitchen.

Eva watched her leave, feeling unexpectedly nervous about being alone with Wilhelm. She couldn't make out his mood but knew she would find out as soon as his mother was gone. He watched her eat, but she looked away and kept her eyes cast down. She finished her food and washed her plate, putting it on the rack to dry.

"Is it all right if I take a shower?"

He didn't turn his head but lifted only his eyes to her. His expression was severe. He gave one nod, and she hurried out of the kitchen. She got some clean clothes from her bag, then went to the bathroom, making sure she locked the door behind her. She showered quickly, put on her dress, and made sure not to pull the belt too tight, then combed through her wet hair. She went back to the bedroom, put her dirty clothes in her bag, and walked down the hall.

Wilhelm and his mother were standing by the front door, apparently saying their goodbyes.

Marie noticed Eva loitering by the couch. "Come here." She held her arms out to her. Eva closed the distance between them, and Marie pulled her into an embrace. "It will be all right," she whispered in her ear. Eva moved her head back a few inches and looked at her.

Marie patted her on the cheek, then let go and picked up her bag. She leaned in and kissed Wilhelm, then glanced at Eva before he opened the door for her, and she stepped into the hall. Eva sat on the couch to wait for his mom to leave.

"Bye, Mother."

"Goodbye, Wilhelm."

When he closed the door, Eva bolted to her feet, anxiety and fear coursing through her. He turned slowly to her, both caught up in a chaotic blaze of emotions. She could feel her heart pounding in her head, and Wilhelm's obvious frustration set off a spiraling anticipation deep inside. *I must do this for Jon, no matter what is coming my way*, she told herself.

The heated stare continued between them as she threaded her fingers together in front of her, and then her eyes wandered towards the door as she could no longer hold his intense gaze. She inhaled and exhaled, struggling to keep her emotions at bay.

Wilhelm eyed her hands, his brow tightening, and in one decided movement, he closed the distance between them, pulled her in, and brought his mouth to hers.

She gasped against him as his passion blazed through her staggeringly hot and fierce. He threaded his fingers through her hair, clenching tight, keeping her mouth pressed firmly against his. She gripped the sleeve of his jacket as he kissed her deeply. Wave after wave of blistering hot passion burned away her fear, but she could sense something else was stirring in him.

Then he pulled back, his hazel eyes boring into hers. Her breathing was uneven, and her skin was feverishly hot. She held his stare, his eyes set intensely on her, and then he took her hand and led her down the hall to his bedroom.

He pushed her face down on the bed, bending her over, and pulled up her dress. He took hold of her underwear, ripping the fabric and pulling it away from her body, tossing it somewhere in the room. The air and adrenaline caused goosebumps to form on the bare flesh that was now exposed. He kicked her legs wide apart, stepped between them, undid his pants, then drove his organ deep into her and violently took her over the bed.

Eva moaned at the roughness and the swiftness of the thrust. She felt the pressure as she was driven harder and clenched her fingers around the comforter, pushing against the pain.

He leaned over, took some of her hair in his hand, and pulled her head back towards him. "You will never defy me again. Do not make the mistake of thinking I have forgotten a single thing you have done. I may love you, but I don't trust you," he hissed in her ear. "I know you went to see the Canadians in the hospital. Did you think I wouldn't have someone watch you after the Allied countries landed on French soil?"

She wasn't wearing any shoes, and her feet were bare against the rug in his room. She tried to focus on the soft weave beneath the soles of her feet and on nothing else, but she was failing. Her mind kept going back to the pain between her legs. She held tightly to the comforter as Wilhelm gave a final thrust and let out a deep guttural growl, his weight pressing into her as he let his pleasure course through him. His body was hot and pulsing, and she could feel the fast beats of his heart on her back.

When he was through, he released her hair, and she laid still, thinking he was done with her. After a few seconds, she started to straighten, and he grabbed hold of her waist, turned her around, and pulled her to him. She stared into the threatening gleam in his eyes, a warning in them, his body giving off heat from the exertion, and then she felt his seed run out of her and down the inside of her thigh.

"Is what I said understood?" he hissed menacingly. She nodded. She could see something dark growing on his face. "Let me ask you. Do you know why I had you followed all that time in Dieppe?"

Because you are a bastard, the words screamed inside her mind. "So you could catch the resistance," she told him.

"Because I had to lie and deceive you. It was the only way to keep you out of prison. So that I could put on your record that you were working with the Gestapo to help catch them. Only you didn't know that you were. What I did, I did for you. Not for me or anyone else. I would have captured them without you. Maybe not as soon, but I would have had them all in the end, anyway. I used your betrayal against me to my advantage and to yours."

She was surprised at his words, but more by the fact he was admitting it to her than by the notion that there were conspiratorial motives surrounding her and him.

"It was the only thing I could do to protect you from my men and yourself. Think hard about what would have happened if I had not lied for you. I may be a monster, but I am one who cares about you enough to not want to watch you be shot or hung from a rope in the town square. I am a better alternative than either of those choices. And one last thing. You and that American, there is more than you or he is saying. No one would be stupid enough to risk their life and come to the French shore for just anybody. Either he is in love with you, which I'm not sure that's it, or there is something else at play. Something I am missing. But I have you, and I now have him, and I will learn what it is." She opened her mouth to speak, but he put his middle and index finger against her lips. "There is nothing you can say that will break the chain that's been forged between us." He pushed her back onto the bed and wrapped his hands around her wrist, holding her arms out to the side. His grip was as gentle as it was threatening. "I know that to you, I appear severe and unkind, but when it comes to you, it is to keep you safe. To other people, it is because I don't like them. But Eva, you have to meet me halfway once in a while."

She swallowed hard, aware of the muscles tensing in his arms and hands. Her mouth had gone dry, and she frantically searched for words. "Halfway? What does that look like?"

"You not always fighting me. And for once, doing what I say, and not always being so goddamned hardheaded."

"OK." Her voice was hoarse.

He moved back a fraction and gently caressed her cheek with his hot palm. "Good girl." He lifted himself off her and fixed his pants. "You should go clean yourself up. We have dinner reservations tonight."

"With whom?"

"With other officers and their wives."

"And you think I should go to this? I'm not your wife. I'm not even officially your girlfriend."

"And we are going to change that, starting with this dinner tonight."

"And I'm going as your girlfriend?"

"Yes. There is no reason to hide it. I will get some disapproving stares from some of the others, but I don't care."

"Is it formal?"

"No, just wear the nicest dress you brought."

She went to the bathroom and took another shower, washing off what he did and trying to make sense of everything that happened. She remembered the saying from Oscar Wilde. 'Everything in the world is about sex except sex. Sex is about power.' She understood that was exactly what had just happened between her and Wilhelm. What he did to her was not like any of the other times. This time, it was to show her that he was the one in charge. She wanted to have some control, but that would never happen with him.

She put a hand on the tile wall to steady herself and tried not to vomit. Her stomach churned from the food she ate and the events that took place shortly after. Eventually, she was going to have to tell him she was pregnant. The next time he made love to her or fucked her, whichever one, he would notice her growing waistline. But she didn't want to tell him right now. She was angry and hurt. She felt like she had to constantly remind herself that this was who Wilhelm was. And what about Jon? She would have to find a way to speak to him again. He was only God knows where, and that could only mean that now both of them were stuck in this time until the end of the war. And that was not for another three years. And getting back to their time was not guaranteed even then.

Wilhelm had left her alone for a while because he had a meeting, and she slept on the couch while she waited. But right after he returned, they left.

She kept looking over at him across the seat, trying to gauge his mood. But no matter what it was, she was going to have to ask questions. "If we are dating, what does that mean? Do I stay in Dieppe, move to Paris, come to Berlin...?"

He looked at her, his face hard. "Naturally, you will move to Paris."

"Alright. I guess I can work at the hospital there." She had to tell him about the pregnancy, unsure what would happen when they returned to his apartment. She met his gaze and held it.

"Wilhelm, I have to tell you something." She noticed the tension in his face now and thought he must be preparing for bad news again. This wasn't exactly bad, but it would be a shock. His brows creased with an unspoken question as he focused on her.

She took in a shaky breath, dropped her eyes to her lap, and spoke, not wanting to look at him when she said it. "I'm carrying your child."

His eyes widened, and he smacked the back of the seat in front of him. "Pull over and get out," he instructed the driver. His voice was firm and imposing. The driver pulled off on the side of the street. He turned off the engine, got out, and shut the door, leaving her and Wilhelm alone. Wilhelm turned and looked at her slowly and deliberately.

She froze, waiting for him to do something, anything. She couldn't tell what he was thinking. Was he going to hug her, slap her, kiss her, yell at her? What?

"How long…" he cleared his throat, "how long have you been pregnant?"

"A little over eleven weeks."

"And how long have you known?" His words were strained.

"When I was about five weeks."

"And you only decided to tell me now?"

"Yes. I wasn't originally going to tell you at all."

His eyes darkened, and his face took on a look of intense hurt. "And you didn't think until now that I had a right to know?"

"No, not after I found out what you did."

"What I did? You tried to kill me, and I forgave you for that. Look at all the other things I have done for you. I have lied for you, defended you, almost killed someone for you at the risk of my career, and you weren't even going to tell me you are pregnant with my child?"

"I wanted to, but you told me you didn't want kids."

"I wasn't planning on having any, but things change when you find out you are going to be a father, and it's no longer just a passing thought."

"I guess I figured you would want me to get rid of it if you knew." He looked at her as if she had just pulled a gun on him. To her utter surprise, his eyes glossed with tears, ripping at her heartstrings. She had never seen him cry. Somewhere inside, she thought he was incapable of it.

"Why would I want you to get rid of it?"

She was now lost for words. There was such furious passion in his voice that she flinched. "I will tell you when we get back to the apartment, not here."

"As soon as we get back."

"I promise." She knew now that he never would have forgiven her if she had aborted the baby, and he found out. Just knowing that she went to get an abortion would send him into a rage. "So, you aren't mad?"

His demeanor was softer now. "Of course, I'm not mad. But this changes everything. I never asked you to marry me because I didn't want to trap you here, but I see now this is where you need to be."

His words scared her more than she could express. Not because she didn't want to be with him, but because she didn't want to be trapped in 1940 Germany. "And what of my family?" She tried to keep the panic from her voice.

"I didn't want you to resent me for keeping you from them, but now there is no other option. You can see them, of course, but this is where you will live."

"Why?"

"Because your future husband is from here, works here, and therefore can provide for you and our baby here."

What did she say to this? She couldn't tell him no, that she was going to go back to America without him. Oh, and with his baby, who he would probably never see if she did. There was no way in hell he would allow her to do that. "Is this what you want, a wife and child?"

"It was a want I put in the back of my mind as something that was unlikely to ever happen. There were many reasons I had planned for it not to. But the two things I wanted but didn't think would happen have. And you ask me if I want you and the baby you are carrying or if I am upset about it." He looked at her, disbelief evident on his face. "You and that child are exactly what I want."

What he said touched her on a deeper level than anything ever had. He told her the truth, which could not have been easy for him. He tore down his walls to do it, and she appreciated every word. He made her cry, and she realized how much she loved him. But there were so many questions now. Did she stay the rest of her life in this time? Did she return to her time with a child and have her family ask questions, hard questions that she could never fully answer? How could she possibly know what the right choice was? She was glad she didn't have to decide today or in the next few weeks or months.

"I am relieved that you are not upset. And I will marry you on two conditions."

He narrowed his eyes at her. "Depends on the conditions."

"That you let me see Jon again and work for as long as I can before the baby is born."

He didn't immediately answer but thought about her condition. "I will consider letting you visit Jon. But the answer is no to the second one."

"Why? What am I going to do for the next six months?"

"What pregnant women do. Stay home and rest."

"That is not all they do, and I am capable of working."

"The answer is no, Eva."

She had to pick her battles, and this was not a hill worth dying on right now. He said he would consider the main thing she wanted. He was going to try and let her see Jon.

Wilhelm told the driver to get back in, and they rode the rest of the way to the restaurant in silence. She understood he was trying to process this new information, so she didn't talk and let him think.

The restaurant was a typical, upscale German establishment packed full of officers. They were led to a table with half a dozen officers, all accompanied by women.

Wilhelm pulled a chair out for her next to a tall, slim woman with hair so blond it was almost translucent. Then he took the chair beside her.

Their food came quickly after they ordered, and Wilhelm fell into a conversation with the officer next to him. She didn't think he was trying to ignore her, but it must be hard for him not to talk to her about it, so the easiest way to distract himself was by talking with someone else.

"How do you like your food?" The woman leaned over so she could speak above the noise at the table.

"It is good."

"I never liked fish much myself, but Sebastian does." She gestured with her head to the man Wilhelm was talking to.

Eva gave her a questioning look. "Is he your husband?"

"You wouldn't think so with how much he is gone."

Eva gave a side glance at Wilhelm. "I imagine that comes with the job."

"It does. I know Wilhelm isn't married, but how long have you been together? We have never seen him with a woman until now, and he has never talked about anyone before."

"He likes to keep things to himself. He is a very private person. I have known him since thirty-nine. But we have only been together since the beginning of the year."

"So you know he will be gone all the time, and you are alright with that?"

"I guess I'll have to be." She noticed Wilhelm occasionally glance in her direction, but he didn't talk to her. It was apparent he didn't want to be here but was being a dutiful German and mingling with his fellow officers.

When they got back to his apartment, the details of how to move forward had to be hammered out.

"Do you live here in Berlin?"

"I used to, but I now live in Dieppe, France."

"Oh, the same country as him. That is smart. Doesn't he live in Paris, though?"

68

"He does."

"Isn't that hard, trying to find time to be together?"

"It is, but I'm actually moving to Paris soon."

"That will be nice."

Eva took a bite of her food. "Uh-huh."

"I'm sorry to cut dinner short, but there are things that await my immediate attention," Wilhelm said to the men at the table.

Eva stood when he did and turned to the woman. "It was nice meeting you."

"You too. Look me up next time you are in Berlin. Petra Huber."

"I will." Wilhelm held his arm out to Eva, and she looped hers through his.

They got into the car, and Wilhelm told his orderly to drive fast, and of course, he obeyed, getting them back to the apartment in record time. Once they were inside, Wilhelm took off his cap, shrugged off his jacket, and pulled off his boots, then sat on the couch and patted the spot next to him. She lowered herself down and waited for him to speak first.

"I think it's better if we get married before you start to show."

She looked at her stomach. "I'm already showing." She got up from the couch and smoothed her hands over her stomach, pulling the dress tighter around it as she held the back.

He stared at her in astonishment, noticing the small round bump under her dress for the first time. He stood and came to stand in front of her. Slowly, Wilhelm moved his hand towards her as if at first he was debating whether or not he should, then he placed his large palm over her stomach with his fingers splayed. He

69

looked at his hand on her like it wasn't real and brought his eyes to meet hers.

"This is still hard to believe."

"Try being me. I'm reminded of it every day. It's hard to ignore." A smile broke across his face as he looked down at her, and she could see complete happiness. "Wilhelm, I know why you didn't want to have children, your mother told me."

The joy she saw on his face disappeared, replaced by resentful anger. He dropped his hand to his side and sat back down on the couch. "Did she?"

Eva sat next to him. "It's alright. You know I don't care about that."

"But I do." His face was etched with a bitterness that surprised her. There was intense pain in his eyes. "They are not my people. I am not one of the lost, forgotten members of that race. Nobody has ever wanted them, not then and not now. Even their own God has abandoned them. And now, when they tried to take our land and our humanity, there is no one to save them." She could see that his hatred ran deep.

"You are part Jew but you're anti-Semitic and say such awful things about them, your people." She hesitated with the last two words. "You think lesser of yourself because you are part Jew. Just because someone is imperfect doesn't make them any less deserving of love. The things that have happened in your life have made you think that, especially the men in it. If you believe you don't deserve love, then just look at me. I am the proof. That idea you have is false. And I want to preface by saying that I do not believe you are lesser than anyone else because of your heritage."

70

"Do you think this is unique to me? You are so naïve, Eva. Show me one person who hasn't made some anti-Semitic remark or thought it, and I will leave Germany, forsaking it. And I told you, they are not my people."

She scooted closer to him, took his hand, and held it tight in hers. "I don't feel about the Jews as you do, but no matter my opinion of them, someone's race or nationality does not define who they are as a person. If it did, I would not be with you or pregnant with your child. Not because you are half-Jew but because you are German. Right now, we are natural enemies, but I have looked past that. We are going to have a baby, so nothing matters but you and me. Not who your parents are or mine."

"Don't worry. I have no intention of shirking on my responsibility."

"I never thought you would. You are the most responsible, hard-working person I have ever met. And no matter how much I fight against it, I must admit that I'm glad you are the father. I think sometimes you understand me better than anyone else. And so, raising a baby with you isn't the worst thing in the world," she confessed. "And often, you even seem to know me better than I know myself. I fight against it, but you can see it clearly, what I want but tell myself I don't, or what I need but am too afraid to do."

His lips turned up with a slight trace of amusement, breaking his stern expression. "That is because I do know and understand you better than anyone else. Eva, we are perfect for each other. I know you better than I have ever known anyone, and now you know more about me than anyone else, and you understand me on a level not even my mother could." His grin turned into a smile.

"And when I look in your eyes, I can read your emotions like an open book. You should really work on that." She glared at him, her mouth opening slightly. "Like now, you are angry with me."

She nodded. "You are right. I am annoyed with you." There was a prickling from a flush heating her neck and face as the affection for Wilhelm warmed her heart. "It's also that we have been thrown together. We both need something from one another."

There was a rakish glint in his eyes. "You are right. We do need each other. We are both, in a way, rebels. We are from very different backgrounds and upbringings but have found ourselves on the same path, finally meeting on common ground."

"I guess we have. But it is a one-way path. There is no turning back for us." In her heart, she could feel the emotions stirring.

Something deep and raw flashed in Wilhelm's gaze, the silence between them growing heavy as it became emotionally charged. "I know," he admitted.

She loved Gerhardt, and she might never completely get over him, but her heart was now Wilhelm's. And she understood from her love for him that a heart can repair.

"It has been a long day, and I'm ready for bed." She took his hand and led him to the bedroom. She removed her dress, only leaving on her slip, washed her face and brushed her teeth, then slid under the blankets.

"Would you hold me?" she asked yearning to fill up the last empty space in her heart with him. She wanted to keep hold of him there forever, to drive away the fear.

Wilhelm gave her an intense look. "Eva, I'll hold you all night if you want me to."

The ache to be close to him intensified. He climbed into bed beside her and held her tight against him. She drifted off as a sense of relief lifted from her shoulders. She was glad he knew she was pregnant and that she knew about his past.

Chapter Five
❧

September 3rd, 1942

E va sat quietly during the drive to Berlin from France, as did Wilhelm. Both caught up in silent anticipation of the wedding that would take place tomorrow. The light from the oncoming cars' headlights passed over Wilhelm's sculpted face, the two of them seated on the far ends of the backseat of his military vehicle.

Wilhelm looked out the window as if lost in thoughts of his own, his brow deeply furrowed as the car made its way through the vast farm fields that lay between Paris and Berlin. There was a weightiness to Wilhelm's demeanor that overpowered his usual calm arrogance. Every so often, he looked over, his jaw set tight, and when he looked at her, his face was etched with an expression that suggested he was considering her like she was a particularly vexing puzzle to him. Then he looked away again as she studied him in the same probing manner.

She watched for a bit as the car's headlights fell across the black road, then turned to her window and peered out, letting her gaze wander across the fields that seemed endless. The partial light of the moon shone down on them in a faint blue hue, and she could make some of the fields out as corn and others as wheat. She turned back to Wilhelm and saw that he was watching her with a fixed focus so intense it unsettled her. She dropped her gaze and looked at her growing stomach, wondering how she would hide it beneath a wedding dress. She was almost thirteen weeks, and other people noticed it now too.

This was the first time she and Wilhelm had seen each other since they had left Berlin on August 24th. They had gone their separate ways, him back to Paris and her to Dieppe. She had to pack her things so they could be retrieved later, inform the hospital she was quitting, and tell Dr. Möller and Ingrid what was happening. She broke the news to them that she was going to marry Wilhelm and move to Paris. Ingrid had cried and asked if she could move there too, and Eva told her she would ask. Klaus's response was as she had expected. He hugged her like a father, offered some advice, told her he would walk her down the aisle, and fought to hold back most of what he was really feeling. Then he told her he would probably return to Germany, where he was needed the most.

She side glanced at Wilhelm, wanting to know what he was thinking. She loved him but worried she was straddling the line between the civilian he was protecting and his military prisoner. When they stopped to get gas, she took the opportunity to use the bathroom. She was back in the car before Wilhelm and sat still on the brown leather seat, clenching and unclenching her shaking hands in an effort to calm herself. She flinched as the door abruptly opened, and Wilhelm slid in and then closed it, leveling his gaze on her. Her breath grew shallow as she stared into his intense eyes.

"Alright, we need to talk." There was an edge of challenge in his voice as if he thought she would object.

"Alright." Her voice was tight. "We are going to Berlin, right?"

Wilhelm tilted his head and took in her demeanor, fixing her with a look that said, 'Why, should we be going somewhere else?' "Yes," he assured her.

She swallowed, still finding it hard to believe that she was marrying Wilhelm Bauer. The man she met at Madame Blanc's and who was in her bedroom waiting for her all those years ago. A man she had hated and despised with every fiber of her being.

He leaned back in the seat, his stare on her cold and severe, one hand absently fingering the handle of his holstered gun. "Why is the thought of being with me so upsetting to you?"

She stared at him, her mind falling into panic, and her lips parted in surprise. Wilhelm, in every way, seemed to be her friend, ally, and protector, but he was also firmly seated in the German military and unshakable in his beliefs about their ideology. She did not want to be an accomplice or attached to the German army with questionable motives and morals. Eva wanted to stay separate from them and remain loyal only to her country.

Not wanting to answer, she looked away and scratched her stomach through her dress. "I'm just exhausted, that's all." Her heart was racing, and she was desperate to divert his attention and ease his suspicions. She chanced a glance up to see if she elicited his sympathy, but he seemed unmoved, his eyes narrowed on her. She fidgeted, dropped her hands, and clutched at the edge of the seat.

"You are marrying a woman you arrested in the past and had, or I guess still have, suspicions about. Won't they find this union odd?"

Wilhelm considered this, his brow tightening in thought. "Some will, I'm sure. But no one will challenge me on my decision."

He looked at her hands, and she self-consciously folded them into her lap. "It would have been easier for you if you married a German, Wilhelm," she reminded him, but he wasn't listening. He was watching her, lost in thought.

Wilhelm's eyes hardened. "Give me your hand?" he insisted, holding out his own.

"Why?" She moved her hands to her sides, partly tucking them under her legs. Wilhelm kept his hand extended, insistent. She eyed his hand but knew if she refused, it would make him angry. Reluctantly, she moved her left hand from her side and held it out to him.

"No, your other hand."

Filled with a profound sense that she was rapidly sinking under quicksand she couldn't escape from, she held out her other hand. Wilhelm took it in his and pulled something from his pocket. It was a ring, silver with a single diamond in the middle. He slid it on the finger of her right hand, then looked at it on her, inspecting the ring.

"Well, at least non-Germans won't know I'm married because it will be on my right hand."

He glanced up at her and pursed his lips as if making fun of the hand Germans wore wedding rings on, and the comment of disguising her marriage to him was of poor taste, then went back to eying her hand, the wheels of his mind visibly turning.

"I understand. Really, I do." His hand slid around her wrist, his thumb tracing her palm. Tiny sparks trailed in the wake of his touch, setting her further on edge. "I understand your reasons more now than I did in the past. I understand a lot more."

She pulled her hand free, not knowing what to say to his words. "Do you?"

His brow furrowed, and he looked at her, searching. "Are you and Jon here as spies? Did you come together as partners?"

"What?" she let out in a low squeak. "You think Jon is a spy? And you think we came together?"

"You tell me, Eva."

"You know me. Do you think I have what it takes to be a spy?"

"You do lack certain qualities needed for spying. Wilhelm settled back in his seat. "I would be willing to wager there is far more going on with you and Jon than you are telling me." His gaze was formidable as he stared at her, unflinching. "I still want to know why he risked so much to come for you."

"I don't know. There is nothing more to it than a friend trying to save another friend." The lie stuck at the base of her throat.

Wilhelm's mouth turned up into a smile, and he tilted his head, resting his hand on his thigh. "It's not. I know it, and you know it. You're going to have to do better than those hollow lies." He shot her a sly grin.

She bit her lip, not knowing what to say but understanding if she said nothing, it would look like an omission. For a long and awkward moment, Wilhelm studied her, then seemed to have worked out what eluded him. He clenched his hand into a fist and leaned forward, his hazel eyes searing into hers. "I think I have figured some of it out. I think while you were working with the resistance in Berlin, they found out somehow that you were involved with a German and thought you betrayed them. Then they decided to kill you because they couldn't decide if you could be trusted." He paused, watching for her reaction, then continued when she didn't say anything. "Jon knows something about this. I know you kept correspondence with him, and he knows more about the war than I think I give him credit for. But you," he pointed at her, "are tied to all of it." He seemed to take her silence as a confirmation that he was right and leaned against the door, looking at her, feeling satisfied. "In any case, I have him now, and whatever his plan was, I thwarted it."

She turned to the window, her thoughts waging war against each other. How could she possibly tell him the truth that she and Jon traveled from the future? But not telling Wilhelm the truth might be just as dangerous. It was so strange. How could it be that part of her wanted to cling to him, but another part of her wanted to run and hide? She wondered if she would ever get over that feeling. She turned back to Wilhelm.

"And you won't torture him more than you already have to try and learn whatever you think he is hiding?"

Wilhelm shook his head. "No, I have no need to. I am in possession of both halves of the equation. He is locked up, and you soon will be mine." He set his gaze on her again. "What did they send you here to find?"

"They who?"

79

"Whoever sent you."

How did she dance around the truth? She wanted him to keep believing his version of events so she would assure him of them. "I came to help Jews escape, and he was to come get me in case there was trouble. It obviously took him this long to figure out where I was." That was kind of the truth.

"No." He shook his head. "Charity is not the only reason you came here." He stared at her, deep in thought, his expression taking on a harder edge. "Why did you come here, Eva? I don't mean the story you told me about wanting to help people who were displaced. I mean the real reason. Why did you leave your home?"

What could she tell him that was the truth but wouldn't get her into more trouble? "I was running away."

"Why?"

"My life wasn't what I thought it would be. I had these ideas as a kid, you know, about plans and the future. But it was different. Even the things I had counted on were different. I guess I was disappointed. And then, of course, there were the things I hadn't planned on, the things life throws at you. But nothing could have prepared me for the things that have happened to me here. Is that how your life was too? Or did you always want to be a soldier?"

"No, I didn't really have a choice. My country needed me, and I obeyed the call."

"Didn't you ever want to do something else with your life? Free to choose your own path?"

"I thought you would have learned by now that freedom is an illusion. We all, in the end, do what we are told."

80

His words seemed to have some hidden meaning that she didn't understand. "I have learned that."

"Any other reason you came?" The inflection in his voice told her that he still didn't think she was telling him everything.

"And to observe the war, that is it." She chewed at the inside of her cheek, not wanting to talk about this anymore.

The silence hung in the air, and his complacent attitude disappeared. She turned in the seat towards him, her gaze flicking over the iron cross first class pinned just below the pocket on the left side of his jacket and the other one where the collar of his shirt came together.

"I think we both hide things from one another. I'm not saying that to be mean or because it's how I think things should be, but because that is how it is and will stay, I suspect."

He leaned close to her. "No, Eva," he said succinctly. "I'm not hiding things that matter from you. There are military things I can't tell you, but they don't concern you and would be of no interest to you. But when it comes to everything else, my wall is gone." She stared at him, questioning if he was telling the truth, and his eyes said that he was. "Your turn," he challenged. "Tell me what you are hiding."

Her throat went tight. There was no way to tell him. She had to keep lying. "I am not hiding anything. I have poured my soul out to you, and there is nothing left."

"Nothing left? I think you have more to give than you know."

"I don't understand what you mean."

"I'll show you. Kiss me," he told her, his voice raw with desire.

Her eyes widened in confusion, and the feelings inside changed egregiously. Wilhelm's tone sounded like a challenge, a demand, and she could feel the warm sting of a flush on her cheeks and neck. She looked to the driver, then back to him. "But—"

"Don't look at my uniform or worry about him. In this car, I am not Gestapo, I am not German, I am just Wilhelm." She hesitated, not moving, and his eyes narrowed. He slid on the seat, closing the space between them, his leg resting against hers. "Eva," he said, gentler now, his hazel eyes caring and inviting. "Show me?"

She reached up and touched the side of his face with her trembling hand. As soon as her fingers made contact with the skin of his cheek, it was like electricity went through her. She could feel Wilhelm's reaction to her touch. He tensed his body and closed his eyes. Inside, a nervous feeling settled in the pit of her stomach. Overwhelmed by the sensation, she moved to pull her hand away, but he caught her wrist, held her palm to his skin, and opened his eyes, looking into hers.

"Your hand is trembling," he said, his voice husky. "And clammy." He brought it to his lips and kissed her palm and then the tip of each of her fingers.

Her emotions spiked, and the air in the car felt thick and heavy. It was impossible to fight her intense draw to him, to hide the fact that inside, she craved him, the savage pull burning through her fear of tomorrow. The raw emotions between them were all she was feeling now.

"I know why your hand shakes." Wilhelm's words were rough, with an obvious desire for her.

They stared at each other, and she clenched her jaw to keep control. Right now, she hated him and wanted him in equal measure. He leaned in, his lips coming down hard on hers. She gasped against his mouth, her emotions burning hot, escalating into a force that rocked her to the core.

Wilhelm drew back a fraction. "Give me your other hand," he said raggedly as he grabbed both sides of the skirt of her dress and pulled her closer, her knees now between his legs as he had one on the floor and the other bent on the seat. He took her other hand and put it on his neck. Her heart was pounding hard and fast in her chest, her breathing was ragged, and on some level, she knew they shouldn't be doing this in the car with his driver in the front seat. They were crossing the line of appropriate behavior, but the pull between them made it hard for her to care.

Wilhelm kissed her deeply, his lips moving against hers, and her mouth opened in response. Her body felt like it was on fire, and she wondered if he could feel the heat, too. He grabbed hold of her with unrestrained force as his hands caressed every part of her he could reach, his touch impossible to resist as it permeated through her. Wilhelm pulled her body hard against his own, and she gasped against his kiss as everything around them blurred. She breathed hard, and her hands found their way into his open jacket, sliding around his sides to his back, and every muscle of his body tightened, a deep groan escaping his lips. Nothing mattered to her at this moment but their passion.

But soon, some level of her senses returned, and she needed air and her heart to slow. She pulled her lips from his and her hands out of his jacket, the inferno between them fading enough for them both to suddenly realize that the car had stopped. They turned as the car door was being opened by his orderly, who was regarding them both with a forced neutral expression.

Wilhelm straightened his jacket and acted as if nothing was happening in the back seat. Then, he exited the car and she slid out too, her heart still thudding hard against her chest. To her surprise, another German car was waiting in front of his apartment building. Two men leaning against the side walked towards them once she and Wilhelm were out of the car.

One of the men came to stand opposite Wilhelm, then leaned in closer to him and, in a muffled voice, explained that they arrested a group of resistance on their way out of Paris and that they were carrying information about his command and his schedules.

"We have to assume that more of them know this information," the man continued.

Wilhelm put his hand on the man's arm to stop him from talking. "I'm sure they do." He glanced at Eva, then back to the man. Wilhelm's face morphed into an impassive mask.

The man looked at her, then turned his gaze on Wilhelm. "I will accompany you to the Reich Security Main Office. We have more to discuss with you."

Wilhelm nodded to him, then turned to Eva. "I have to work for a while." His expression and tone were oddly formal. He pulled her to him in an embrace and leaned his head down to hers, giving her a kiss. As his lips made contact with her cheek, his hand clenched around her arm, tight as a vice. He leaned in closer, putting his lips to her ear, and whispered into it. "Tell no one what you just overheard."

She nodded, and the man waited for Wilhelm to follow. He released her arm as he gave her an intense look. He seemed hesitant to leave, and it made her nervous. Masking his feelings, Wilhelm gave her a final offhanded nod, and then he got into the car with the other men.

She picked her bags off the ground and headed up the stairs to Wilhelm's apartment. She knocked on the door and moved from one foot to the other as she waited. Her thoughts were warring inside her head when the sound of a door opening broke her thoughts.

"Eva, come in." She bent to pick up her bags, but Marie stopped her. "Here, let me help you with those." She took the two largest bags and left the others for Eva. They took them to Wilhelm's room and set them on the floor in the corner. Marie gave Eva a warm embrace, put her hands on Eva's shoulders, and held her at arm's length.

"You look tired and a little worried. The time leading up to a wedding is always more stressful than the wedding itself. It will all get easier after tomorrow."

Eva gave her a smile. "I hope so."

"Why don't you lay down and get some rest, and I will make some food."

Eva peered at the bed, and it looked inviting. "I think I will. Are you sure you don't need help?"

"No, I'm fine." She turned and left Eva alone in the room.

Eva moved the blankets back and laid down, pulling them over her. She closed her eyes, and her mind went to what had happened between her and Wilhelm in the car. Her heart sped up just thinking about it. It was the first time they had been intimate in any way after he took her over this bed and since she told him she was pregnant. She couldn't help but wonder how he would be on their wedding night. Her mind then turned to the men who were waiting outside his apartment. They worried her; she didn't know what they wanted with Wilhelm. And from what she heard, would the resistance try to kill him again? That, too, had her worried. She tried to ignore the thoughts and the fear settling deep in her stomach and closed her eyes, finally falling asleep.

Heavy footsteps thudding in the sitting room woke her, and she bolted into a sitting position. She threw the blankets off, hopped out of bed, and quietly tiptoed to the door, putting her ear to it. Relief rushed through her at the sound of Wilhelm's level voice. She closed her eyes and pressed her forehead to the cool wood. Thank God he was here and OK.

Slowly, she turned the doorknob, hoping they didn't hear the creak of the hinges, and opened the door a thin crack and peered out. Wilhelm was standing by the fireplace in the living room. There was a clink of crystal on crystal as he poured himself a drink from the flask he kept on the table beside the couch. He held the glass in his hand and casually rested one elbow on the fireplace's white granite mantel, his side to her as he sipped his drink and looked at his mom, who was sitting on the edge of the couch, legs crossed.

"Wilhelm, I have to ask. You know that she will want to return to her country someday. Is that something you can let her do?" Her words were clipped.

Wilhelm shot her a sly smile. "Yes, because I know she will come back."

"You are in love with her completely, and I know she loves you, but do not underestimate how important someone's family is to them. Where she is from and her way of life there is foreign to you but comforting to her. She might be able to give up her country for you, but she won't give up it and her family. She won't surrender both."

"It's funny you used love when you mentioned Eva because she has never actually said that word to me. And her family, we are her family now. And she and I will soon have a family of our own."

"She isn't losing a family, Wilhelm. She is gaining one, as will you. But to give them up entirely, I know she won't do that. I never would, and I can't imagine she would either."

"I'm not asking her to. As you said, we will be joining two families. Tomorrow, we will get married, and eventually, she will have this baby, which will be the first of many, I am sure, and we will make it work. This isn't the first time people from different backgrounds and cultures have married and split their time between two countries."

The blood rushed from her head as she listened to him and felt dizzy. He obviously expected her to live in Germany, which she already knew, but she never even thought about having another baby after this one. Was he really planning on having more kids with her? Did he want to?

"Her family won't even be going to her wedding," his mom continued.

"If it was feasible for them to come, I would have had Eva invite them."

Surprised to hear them discussing her family, she moved a fraction away from the door, the full implications of the wedding rushing over her. Feeling shaken, she peered back out at them, wanting to hear more.

His mom let out a heavy sigh. "Well, as much as I like Eva and want grandchildren, which I am at least getting one, I think this is more complicated than you realize. I understand she didn't like you initially, but you kept her here, and now you are marrying her. And I know she would not be carrying your child if you had not prevented her from leaving and had allowed her to go home."

Wilhelm sipped his brandy and looked down at his mother, his hazel eyes glinting. "See, there are some advantages to my general lack of morality and empathy."

Eva covered her mouth and breathed deeply. She knew he was not being completely honest with his mother and keeping a lot from her. So, she had to try not to be angry at him for what he was saying.

His mom narrowed her eyes at him. "I know you did not get her pregnant just to placate me. And don't pretend you are with her on a whim."

"Of course not. I'm with Eva because I love her, and I only recently found out she was pregnant." He looked down at the drink in his hand. "Is she sleeping?"

His mom looked to his room, and Eva pulled back, not wanting them to know she had been listening to their conversation. "Yes. She laid down to rest a while ago. I had thought about waking her after I made dinner but decided she needed the sleep."

"I'm sure she does. It will be a stressful day tomorrow." He set his cup on the mantel. "I'm going to check on her, then I might go to bed as well."

"I know you two have already slept together, but don't wake her. Leave that until tomorrow on your wedding night. You have thrown off tradition enough."

"I'll let her sleep," he promised unconvincingly as he started for his bedroom.

Eva quickly closed the door and moved lightly on her feet back to the bed as fast as she could. She laid down, covered herself up, and closed her eyes. Her heart was hammering in her chest, and she tried to slow her breathing so he would believe she was asleep.

The door opened, then clicked shut. The bed dipped with his weight as he sat beside her, placed his hand on her hair, and leaned in, kissing her on the temple. She opened her eyes and rolled partly on her back to look up at him.

He lifted a brow at her. "Hi."

"Hi." Her thoughts turned in her head as she stared at him. "I want to be able to trust you. You told me you wouldn't hurt Jon anymore and that you would let me see my family."

He took in a deep breath, his gaze steady on hers. "Eva," he calmly but firmly said. "I wouldn't lie to you about that. Just like I hope you wouldn't lie to me. Although I know you struggle to believe it." His lips quirked into a jaded half-smile. "Believe me, I had lied to you before, and look where that got me."

She pulled herself into a sitting position. "Jon is how I can see my parents again, so I need to see him. Is that something that can be arranged?"

89

His expression turned tense and strained, and all traces of hummer were gone. "Maybe. I cannot make any promises."

"Where is he?"

"He is no longer in that prison like I told you."

Her expression turned grim. "He isn't in a concentration camp, is he?"

He narrowed his eyes at her. "No. This is something we will discuss after the wedding." He looked around the room, then settled his gaze back on her. "Something else. Tomorrow, I need you to appear as the in-love, dutiful bride. There will be a lot of the high command there, and they already have questions about my choice of bride and wonder why I'm marrying an American. Some know that I once thought you were a spy."

"Do you think they suspect me of being one, too?" Wilhelm's split-second hesitation caused a spark of fear in her.

"No," he finally said. "If any of them did, they would have brought you into custody by now. They trust my judgment, but I suspect some of them think you are a traitor. Many of these men are good at sniffing out insurrection, and Eva, you exude it."

"Well, it doesn't come as easy for me as it does you with your unquestioning obedience and abiding loyalty."

"You are right. They don't question my loyalty, just my morality and choice of a wife."

"And your total disregard of others' opinions or their view on conventionality," she noted.

Wilhelm made a bitter sound. "There is my complete lack of it."

She searched his face, and for a brief moment, she felt an understanding between them. "Will marrying me make them less trusting of you?"

"No, not as long as you appear firmly under my control."

She snorted out a breath. "I'm sure that would do it," she sniped, anger rising in her at the thought. "But it will not be that way, Wilhelm. Regardless of what they might think, I am not giving up who I am when I marry you. And I'm not something to purchase like an object. You'll never own me, even after the wedding."

Wilhelm's look blazed with intensity. "I don't know about you, but I consider us to be friends," he said unequivocally. "I want a wife, not a servant, not a prostitute, but a companion."

She believed him and knew they had fallen into an unexpected but genuine love for one another.

Wilhelm's lips turn up into a grin. "Play the submissive wife for tomorrow, and then you don't have to act. Of course, I expect you to do some of what I tell you, but you are not my slave."

She had to remind herself that she was in the 1940s, in Germany, not twenty-first-century America. Women were expected to be obedient to their husbands, but not the other way around.

"At least you aren't one of those men who think it's OK to beat their wives."

"Who says I'm not?" Her eyes grew wide, and he chuckled at the sight of her, but there was a tinge of bitterness in his laugh. "Of course, I wouldn't. Because that always works so well. I was beaten regularly by my stepfather when I was a child. All it accomplished was making me angry and defiant."

She inwardly wept for him, and a look of understanding passed between them. Outraged on his behalf, she tried to give him a smile and rubbed the back of his hand.

"I don't know what you are talking about. You are the perfect example of docile submission." He grinned, a mischievous glint in his eyes, and she couldn't help but feel an attraction to him, a pull towards his intimidating demeanor. "There was a time when I seriously had toyed with the idea of marrying you. I wanted to know what it would feel like to be with you, to be yours. I want you to know that, and it wasn't just for your position, your access to things I didn't have, or your power."

A hint of ardor flashed in Wilhelm's eyes as his emotions momentarily escaped his control. "Eva..." he said, his tone heavy with intensity. "I wanted to marry you after that day you first came to my apartment."

Remorse for what she did to him and the ardent love she felt for him now swelled inside her at his confession. She tried hard not to cry and stared into those warm hazel eyes of his.

Wilhelm reached up and caressed her cheek, then rubbed her hair back from her face. His touch was light and gentle, his expression slightly pained. He was attempting to comfort her, and it made her feel worse about herself.

She wiped at the tears brimming in her eyes as she took in the level of emotion in his. She was saddened by the loss of Gerhardt, but in time, her heart would heal, and Wilhelm is here now, always ready to help her, sometimes at the risk of his own life, and he is willing to bind himself to her in every way, unlike Gerhardt who chose someone else.

"I still love Gerhardt, but if I'm going to be bound to you, I have to give myself to you completely."

Wilhelm's eyes tightened. The pain in them edged with understanding. He stayed quiet, but there was an emotional shift in the air. "I want to tie myself to you," he said impassioned. "But I know my heart has been sealed to you for a long time now."

Eva laughed despite the tension between them. "I just realized I never picked out a dress, shoes, or a veil for tomorrow."

"Mother has already arranged things. You go for a fitting early in the morning."

"I'm glad she thought about it before now." Eva didn't know why, but for some reason, she remembered the attack in the garden and, for the first time, wondered what became of the man Wilhelm beat. "Whatever happened to the man who attacked me?"

The side of Wilhelm's mouth curled up, a hard glint forming in his eyes. "Jurgen isn't going to be attacking anyone else for a long time," he said, a wicked look etched on his face. "I won't be killing anyone right now, but he is on my list. And when he wakes up to find out we are married...."

She watched as he was caught up in that thought. *Oh, he liked the idea of that, sticking it to Jurgen while he was laid up in a hospital.*

"I hope it lures him to me." He smiled bigger, and the chilling look in his eyes raised the hairs on the back of her neck and arms. He had the face of a killer just before an attack. "He and I had left matters unfinished before we were interrupted. I hate leaving loose ends."

He squeezed her hand as he spoke of Jurgen, and she understood the full extent of the power that coursed beneath his skin and how dangerous he was if unbridled. He was intimidating, and a nervousness rose at the thought of being intimate with him again as the memory of how he was when they were together flooded back. Bedding him was like getting caught up in a force of overwhelming fury trapped inside a powerful body to go with it. And it scared her that she liked it. Sometimes, she wished she had someone to talk to about these feelings. Ingrid was the only person she would even consider speaking with on this topic. Most of the time, she was utterly unprepared for the things she did with Wilhelm and him in general. She had never discussed sex with anyone, really, not even Gerhardt. The night they slept together it had not been planned or discussed prior. And in her family, you just didn't speak of such things, and she never had a sister to confide in. Gerhardt took it slowly and did things more at her pace. That could also be because when she slept with him, he knew she was a virgin. But Wilhelm could be unpredictable and aggressive.

He stood and looked down at her. "Sleep here tonight. I'm going to sleep on the couch."

"Why? You don't need to. Stay here with me."

He shook his head. "I told my mother I wouldn't touch you before the wedding, but if I'm in the same bed with you, I'm not sure I can hold to that. I don't trust myself."

She didn't know what to say to this. She could see there was something in his eyes, an emotion he was struggling to keep under control.

"Try to get some sleep," he said, averting his gaze from hers. "We both need to be well rested for tomorrow."

She swallowed and eyed him, wishing she knew what emotions he was hiding. She stared at him standing in front of her and couldn't imagine her life without him now, and that was, in a way, an unsettling thought. Not having him around would feel like a part of her was missing. They had come so far, her and him. Looking back, she could not have fathomed what they would become to one another.

She looked at the empty side of the bed, then back up to him, and this felt like another rejection, even though she knew it wasn't, but she hoped this would be the last time she had to feel this way. After tomorrow, she would be his, but he would also be hers.

"Goodnight then."

Wilhelm shot her a cryptic look, turned, and walked out of the bedroom, closing the door behind him.

Chapter Six

September 4th, 1942

Eva stared at the image in the long, gold-framed mirror as Ingrid stroked her hair with the heavy, silver brush. Ingrid pulled it through rhythmically, then rubbed her hand over the top after each stroke. It was just the two of them, alone in the room brides used at the back of the church. The windows were open, letting in the fresh scent of the fall air and the birds that chirped from bushes outside.

The early afternoon light reflected in the mirror, casting scattered rainbow colors throughout the room. Black storm clouds were collecting in the distance, but right now, it was a beautiful day. Outside was unusually calm, not even a breeze to move the leaves of the trees.

Wilhelm had not arrived at the church yet. It was just her, his mom, and Ingrid. It felt strange being there without him, and she wished he was in the room as Ingrid helped her get ready, watching her as she did.

She drew in a shaky breath and looked at Ingrid's reflection in the mirror. She gave Eva an encouraging smile, and Eva returned it with the best smile she could force. She rubbed her hands down the bodice of her dress, feeling the material under her palms. She didn't know how much the dress cost, but it must have been a lot. It looked like it was made of real silk, covered in yards and yards of shimmery white lace and a lace ribbon that hung down the back. It had taken Ingrid a while to pull the stays in the back. Eva told her to pull it tight enough to hide her stomach. The train of the dress was bunched on the floor behind her chair, and the veil was hanging from a hook on the wall, waiting to be put on. Once attached to her head, it would drag behind the train of the dress. She had tried the dress on that morning with Wilhelm's mom, who had them alter it in the middle to make it fit a little looser to accommodate her stomach but tight enough to hide it. Although, if someone paid close enough attention, they might be able to tell she was pregnant, so she would try to hold her arms at her sides to hide it the best she could.

"Can I come in?" came a woman's voice from the doorway.

Ingrid's fingers halted their motion on Eva's hair. They both turned towards the door, and surprise rammed through Eva as she looked at the woman from the party in Berlin, standing there with her gaze fixating on her. Ingrid's hands fell to her sides as Eva's chest tightened, and for a moment, she couldn't breathe.

"I wanted to have a word alone with the bride before the wedding, if you don't mind," she said, looking right at Ingrid.

Ingrid turned to Eva, who gave her a nod, letting her know that it was alright. "I'll wait just outside," she told Eva and laid the brush on the dressing table. Ingrid walked past Klara and closed the door.

Klara came and stood behind Eva, picked up the brush, and started brushing through her hair.

"I haven't seen you since the party," she said with forced pleasantry. "I didn't know Jurgen would ever try something like that. I hope you believe me. I had not expected him to actually hurt you. I just wanted you to leave Wilhelm alone."

"You left me with a man that is a rapist. There is no way you didn't know that when you called him over," Eva returned, barely able to resist the urge to grab the brush from her hand and hit her in the face with it.

Klara stopped brushing and looked at Eva in the mirror, a wry smile reflecting back at her. "I could not figure out why he would marry you, but I now see the reason." Her head was cocked to one side as she focused on Eva's stomach. "He is marrying you because he got you pregnant. And you know what the worst part of this is? He doesn't even love you. You have trapped him, and there is no other way out for him now. I love him, but I will have to stand in the pew today and watch him marry someone else. Do you understand how painful it is to know that another woman will get him, to have his child, and I never will? He should be with me and not you. I thought you never stood a chance with him." Her face tightened into a painful grimace. "And you're one of the worst choices of all. You aren't even German?" Her voice broke on the last word.

She raised the brush and resumed brushing the back of Eva's hair again, and Eva tensed. "You and Wilhelm mingled your blood, and then you will take the child back to your country."

"Yes, I do know how that feels," Eva told her, thinking of Gerhardt and the pain it caused her, knowing it is his ex-fiancée who will be with him. "And I told Wilhelm I will live here, but if I ever move back home, I would imagine he would come with me."

Klara's eyes widened a fraction as if she was seeing into her soul. "That is what you want, isn't it, for him to betray his country and move to America with you?"

"It is not. Did you come here to try and ruin this special day for me?"

"No. I came here to speak with you and try to make you understand the implications of your actions. You are taking something from someone else."

"I didn't know he was yours."

"He would be if you had never come here."

"I know you think he doesn't love me, but he often tells me that he does. Last night, he said he had wanted to marry me for a long time. I don't know that he would be with you even if I wasn't here. I am not marrying him to make you sad or to prove that I have won some competition I didn't even know I was in. I am marrying him because I love him. If I didn't, I wouldn't be here today, even though I'm carrying his child."

Klara dropped her hand with the brush to her side and pursed her lips at Eva in the mirror. "So you love him?"

"Yes."

"And I would even go so far as to say you adore him. Am I right?"

"I... yes, I guess you could say that."

"And would you say he is a monster?"

Eva's eyes shot up to hers. "What?"

"Admit it. He is a monster. We both know it."

"I don't know it, and I don't know what you're talking about."

Klara laughed cynically. "Yes, you do. I want to hear you say it. Don't worry, I won't tell him."

Eva's pulse rushed in her ears, and a sense of fear streamed through her. "He has his daemons."

"You have called him a monster before. He told me you did."

Eva narrowed her eyes at Klara. "Why would he tell you that?"

"Because we are friends. Now say it." Her words were forceful.

"Yes, he can be. Is that what you wanted to hear?"

"Close enough. I wanted you to acknowledge that this man we both love and adore is a monster. And yes, he has his daemons and is reckoning with his past. But the real question is, how does somebody who has been closed off for that long open up to love? He is emotionally complicated and has always had nuanced relationships when it came to women." She saw the look on Eva's face. "I understand. It's hard to reconcile with that brutal reality. The truth is, in my own way, I, too, am a monster. I won't admit that to many people, but it's relevant to tell you now. He and I have something in common, which is why only someone like me could ever understand him. For him to truly open up to a person, he would have to know they could meet him on equal ground."

She started on Eva's hair again, weaving braids that she pinned with jeweled clips. "This is when someone is supposed to tell the bride what to expect on the wedding night." She looked down at Eva's stomach and arched a brow. "But I think we can dismiss with that. No one has to impart the secrets of the bedchamber to you, do they? You already know what to expect from a man's attention." Her gaze was fixed on Eva in the mirror. "But tonight will be different than the others because it is your wedding night. I hope whatever he does shocks you and he is as rough with you as possible. Although he doesn't want to harm this one, does he?" She poked Eva in the stomach with her index finger, and Eva flinched away. "Not all men are the same in bed, nor do they all have the same desires, wants, or needs. The way each man makes love can be very different. I'm sure you know this by now. He isn't like the man you had before him, and I hope you realize what you are getting yourself into."

Eva could only stare at her in the mirror, tears brimming in her eyes as Klara stared back, satisfaction written on her face as she continued to pin her hair.

Klara looked at the bouquet of mixed flowers lying on the table beside the jar of face powder. "I noticed when I came in that the wedding flowers you chose were orchids and so many of them. White, pink, red, and purple, but the ones I especially admired were the black ones. Do you know the meaning of that flower?" she asked as she deftly continued to braid pieces of Eva's hair.

"No, I don't. I've always just thought they were pretty."

"They are pretty and quite fitting for a wedding. But they couldn't be more perfect for a wedding to Wilhelm Bauer. They have several meanings and myths associated with them. The black orchid, with its dark color and mysterious beauty, signifies great power and absolute authority and commands submission." She paused, giving Eva a significant look in the mirror. "Did you know that the word orchid means testicles?"

"No." Eva knew there was some deeper meaning to everything she was saying about the flower. It all underlined some message she was conveying to her.

"Orchids derive their name from the Greek word for testicles because of features seen on the plant's tuber. This is why they are used to symbolize manliness. They represent sexual desires and are symbols of virility and fertility. But they have some interesting stories too. The first story is from an ancient Greek myth. Legend says that the goddess Aphrodite, Venus to the Romans, was out hunting with the handsome mortal Adonis when a powerful storm forced them to seek shelter together in a cave, where they made love while waiting out the storm. When the storm was over, the lovers ran off, Venus losing one slipper. A mortal human came across the shoe and reached down to pick it up when suddenly it transformed into a flower with a slipper-shaped petal of gold. But I personally like the second story better, the Roman myth. A character named Orchis was the son of a satyr and a nymph. While partying one evening during a feast to honor Bacchus, Orchis, having drunk too much wine, tried to force himself on a priestess. The normally happy Bacchus was not pleased with this behavior. So, he had Orchis ripped to shreds by wild beasts, and the pieces of his body were thrown far and wide. But, wherever those pieces landed, an orchid flower would grow."

"Why are you telling me these stories and the meanings of a flower?"

"Because they are here at your joining with Wilhelm, but they represent a darker side to human sexual desires. And because it represents authority and submission. Authority Wilhelm will exert over you, and submission he will expect from you. And the stories both represent love and desire that is unattainable, and therefore tragic."

"I think you don't know him as well as you think you do. And what I have with him is not unattainable or tragic." Eva struggled to believe her own words.

Klara stared at Eva for a long moment, her face hard. "I will get your friend to come back in and finish with your hair." She turned her head towards the door. "You can come back in now," she called loudly.

Immediately, the door opened, and Ingrid strode in. Klara handed her the pins she was holding, then gazed at Eva, a victorious expression on her face. Then she turned and sailed out of the room, shutting the door loudly behind her.

Angry, chaotic feelings lashed through Eva, and she wanted to find Wilhelm and have him wrap her in his loving arms, but she couldn't. He was no doubt preparing for the wedding too and attending to the guests as they arrived. Eva let out a long, shuttering breath and looked at Ingrid. She turned her gaze down, realizing her hands were trembling in her lap.

"Can I get you something, anything?" Ingrid asked.

"A glass of water. My mouth is oddly dry."

"I'll get you some water." She lay the pins on the dressing table and disappeared out of the room. Ingrid wasn't gone long before returning with a cup of water. She handed it to Eva and waited for her to tell her what to do.

Their eyes meet in the mirror. "She told me things I can't get out of my mind. I don't want them to be true, but I think they are. And, of course, she tells me today of all days."

Ingrid's voice was calm and controlled when she spoke. "She only said those things to upset you, and she has, but you can't let it. Do not allow her to be the person you are thinking of today. Today is about you and Wilhelm and no one else.

Eva set her cup down and looked at the ring on her finger, the knot of stress in her stomach tightening. "Do you think I'm making a mistake?"

Ingrid shook her head, honesty in her expression. "No, I don't."

The sound of car doors slamming and voices echoing outside filtered in through the open windows. Ingrid quickly looked to the windows, then at Eva. We better finish you up. I think people are arriving."

Ingrid finished putting up her hair, then Eva stood, and Ingrid moved the chair from behind her. She pulled the train of the dress out around her, then went to get the veil.

Eva stared at her complexion in the mirror, the thick mascara, dusted face with rouge on her cheeks, and red lips. She almost didn't recognize herself.

Ingrid came to stand beside her with the veil and placed it gently on her head. "You're lovely. An absolutely beautiful bride," Ingrid said, seeming momentarily transfixed.

A small clock on the wall ticked. Eva peered at it, and there wasn't much time left before she and Wilhelm were to be married. She took one last look at herself in the full-length mirror, the shimmering white dress, and how strange she felt in it. A multitude of emotions spiraled up inside her. She was sad that her mom couldn't be here to help her get ready for her wedding and that her dad wouldn't be the one walking her down the aisle like she always thought he would. Her brother taking a hundred photos, and all her friends, there for her big day. Jenny would be helping her get ready as the maid of honor usually did. Oh Jenny, how she missed her! None of this is how she thought it would be. Almost everyone important to her was absent on such a momentous day.

A knock came from the door, and Klaus' voice sounded muffled from the other side. "Everyone has arrived. They are waiting in the chapel. I am here to get you."

Ingrid went to the door and opened it. "Come in. We are almost finished."

Klaus walked in dressed in his full military regalia. It was pressed, and his boots were a glossy black. He looked at Eva, and his face took on an expression of intense affection.

"Eva, you are a vision."

Her eyes watered. "Thank you. I'm sure I look better than I feel. I might throw up from the nerves or pass out while walking down the aisle."

He came to stand beside her. "You'll be fine. I'll have your arm the whole time."

Ingrid inspected her, making sure everything was in place. "You are ready, Eva. It's time to go," she told her.

Eva gave a nervous nod, and Klaus held his arm out to her. She looped hers through his and held it tight.

Ingrid opened the door and followed them into the hall. Klaus guided Eva towards the chapel, and they paused at the threshold.

She looked up into his fatherly face, his round spectacles pushed far up on his nose. He smiled at her and squeezed her hand in an attempt to comfort her.

Ingrid opened the door, and Eva pulled in a sharp breath at what lay in front of her. The pews on both sides were filled with officers in uniforms, and they all turned to look at her when the door opened. Her pulse spiked as Klaus took a step with her into the chapel, the heels of her shoes clicking on the marble floor as they made their way down the aisle. She held his arm tight and willed herself to move forward.

There were steps leading up to the altar, covered in red carpet, and standing at the top was the priest. The building was massive, with a domed ceiling, but it was deadly quiet other than her and Klaus' shoes on the floor.

They reached the red carpet, and she froze, looking up at the priest waiting at the altar for her. She had the urge to pull up the hem of her dress and run for the door, but that was no longer an option. The intensity of the moment and a wave of trepidation filled her. It was all so surreal. Her surroundings, the people, the smells in the church, and the realization of what was about to happen ignited a deep-seated fear.

Klaus could sense her hesitation and started walking up the steps with her in tow as Wilhelm came towards the altar, her only now noticing him. Her heart thumped slowly and hard in her chest at the sight of him. He was striking, and she couldn't take her eyes off his tall form.

Wilhelm's gaze met hers, and he did a double take. His eyes glided over her with a flash of intensity, and with her locked on his, she forgot how nervous she was. She was taken aback to see

Wilhelm in something other than his uniform. Like her, he was dressed in formal wear, his tux perfectly tailored, and it complimented his muscular physique. She had fully expected to see him in his uniform, but deep down, she knew why he didn't wear it. He knew it would make her feel more comfortable if he didn't, so he wore a tux for her.

This man is my protector, my friend, and I love him. A fierce yearning for Wilhelm gripped her as Klaus placed her beside him. Keeping her gaze firmly on Wilhelm, she closed the final distance between them, noticing the intensity in his expression. Wilhelm took her hand, and his fingers gripped tightly around it.

The people simultaneously sat down on the wooden pews, making a loud plopping sound that echoed through the building.

She took one quick glance around her. It was as if every high-ranking military officer and their significant other were invited to Wilhelm Bauer's wedding. Wilhelm's mother was seated next to Ingrid and Klaus in the first row. And at the sight of them, she faltered a little, struggling to maintain her courage.

The priest had them face one another, then did a quick blessing, making the sign of the cross. Wilhelm held his hands out to her, his gaze fixed on her as she placed her hands in his. He wrapped his fingers firmly around hers, and she knew it was to comfort her and let her know she was not alone. The priest wrapped a purple cord around their hands, then placed his pudgy red hands atop theirs. Eva drew in a breath and held it, waiting for him to start speaking. She glanced at the priest, and his pale blue eyes met hers, but Wilhelm's hand clamped tighter around hers, and he pulled her closer to him, breaking her gaze with the priest.

He didn't want her to feel nervous, and the best way to achieve that was to keep her eyes focused on him.

The priest finally spoke. "We are gathered here today in the sight of God and these witnesses to join together Wilhelm Bauer and Eva Sofie Abrams in holy matrimony, which is an honorable estate instituted by God since the first man and the first woman walked on the earth. Therefore, it is not to be entered into unadvisedly or lightly but reverently and soberly. Into this holy estate, these two persons present come now to be joined. Therefore, if anyone can show just cause why they may not be lawfully joined together, let them speak now or forever hold their peace."

She squeezed his hands tighter and closed her eyes, half expecting someone to say something, not having the courage to look into the pews. But no one spoke, and she opened her eyes and met his warm hazel ones. He held her gaze, an ardent look in them.

After the priest's brief pause to see if anyone had any objections, he continued. "I will now read from the Apostle Paul, the first letter to the Corinthians, Chapter 13, verses 4 through 7: Love is patient, love is kind. It does not envy, it does not boast, it is not proud. It is not rude, it is not self-seeking, it is not easily angered, and it keeps no record of wrongs. Love does not delight in evil but rejoices with the truth. It always protects, always trusts, always hopes, always perseveres. Father, as they pledge themselves to each other, help them and bless them that their love may be pure and their vows may be true. Through Jesus Christ our · Lord, Amen." The people in the pew all repeated the Amen. "Wilhelm Bauer and Eva Sofie Abrams, you have come together this day so that the Lord may seal and strengthen your love in the presence of his minister, his word, and this community of family and friends. And so, in the presence of this gathering, I ask you to state your intentions. Have you both come here freely and without reservation to give yourselves to each other in marriage? If so, answer by saying 'I have.'"

"I have," Wilhelm said.

She took in a shaky breath. "I have." She couldn't keep the tremble from her voice. She didn't know how Wilhelm sounded so calm and confident when he spoke.

"Wilhelm Bauer, do you take Eva Sofia Abrams to be your lawfully wedded wife from this day forward? To have and to hold, in good times and bad, for richer or for poorer, in sickness and in health? Will you love, honor, and cherish her for as long as you both shall live?"

"I do."

"Eva Sofia Abrams, do you take Wilhelm Bauer to be your lawfully wedded husband from this day forward? To have and to hold, in good times and bad, for richer or for poorer, in sickness and in health? Will you love, honor, cherish, and obey him for as long as you both shall live?"

She took note of the fact he only added the obedience part to her vows. "I do."

"Wilhelm, please take the ring you have selected for Eva. As you place it on her finger, repeat after me. With this ring, I thee wed."

Wilhelm took her hand in his, his fingers warm against her clammy, cold ones. "With this ring, I thee wed." He slid it on the finger of her right hand. It was just a silver band that matched the diamond engagement ring she was already wearing.

"May Jesus Christ Our Lord, and Savior, always be at the center of the new lives you are now building together. That you may know the ways of true love and kindness. May the Lord bless you both all the days of your lives and fill you with his joy. Amen." Again, the people in the pews repeated the Amen. "Those whom God has joined together, let no man put asunder. In so much as Wilhelm and Eva have consented together in holy wedlock and have witnessed the same before God and this company, having given and pledged their faith, each to the other, and having declared the same by the giving and receiving of a ring, I pronounce that you are husband and wife. I ask you now to seal the promises you have made with each other this day with a kiss."

Most of the time, Eva was lost in thought and could hardly pay attention to the words the priest had been saying. Her gaze jerked to Wilhelm, her breathing erratic, her eyes brimming with fresh tears. Wilhelm narrowed his eyes at her as he took her in with a long, searching look. She blinked fast, trying to blink away the tears. She felt the sudden need to get away from all the Germans in uniforms, away from the church and the prying eyes.

"Eva," Wilhelm whispered, his gaze locked on hers as he prompted her to remember they were being watched by an entire church full of people. She glanced back up at him, a heightened awareness flooding into her. His hands reached out and took hers in his again, his thumbs stroking circles on her palms as he so often did when attempting to comfort her. "Eva," Wilhelm said again, his voice cutting through nauseating emotions that were overpowering her. "We are supposed to kiss."

Chapter Seven

September 4th, 1942

They walked into the reception area of the Hotel Adlon, a luxurious establishment on the main boulevard in the central Mitte district of Berlin, directly opposite the Brandenburg Gate. It was a large room surrounded by high arched windows on all four walls. Three-quarters of the room was filled with tables covered in white cloths, but the last quarter of the room was left clear for dancing. The last time she had been here was when Oberst Heinrich Schmitt invited her to a ball here.

Wilhelm held firm to her hand, and she clung tightly to him as they stepped into the crowded room. Her chest tightened when they crossed the threshold onto the carpeted floor. Wilhelm met her nervous gaze with a look that told her he would be with her every step. She forced a smile, and they made their way through the room, down the aisle that was left in between the tables. She followed Wilhelm to the empty part of the floor so they could dance the traditional bride and groom dance.

To the side of the room was an orchestra, waiting for Wilhelm's cue as he got them into position. He placed his left hand on her lower back and took her left hand in his right. People usually did it opposite of how they were, but he was left-handed and would use that hand to lead. He started the first turn, and the music came to life, echoing loudly through the room as the orchestra played a waltz. He guided her farther onto the dance floor, then pulled her closer and held her tighter with his arm.

Other people gathered around them on the floor, twirling to the waltz. Eva looked around at all the soldiers in the room, their eyes on her and Wilhelm as people murmured, the women obviously appreciating the dancing. Wilhelm seemed on the surface as unphased as he always did, but she could tell he was a little less confident than usual.

All the eyes of high-ranking officers staring at her, watching her every move, had her feeling uneasy. Instead of a wolf in sheep's clothing, she felt like she was a sheep in wolf's clothing, trying to hide amongst the pack. But any wrong move, and they would sniff her out. Her breath was increasing with every turn as the faces at the tables passed her by, and she leaned in to whisper in Wilhelm's ear. He immediately responded by pulling her closer.

"All the attention on us is making me feel light-headed."

He gave her a look of concern. "I won't let you fall. We have to finish this dance, then you can sit down," he whispered, tightening his arm around her.

The song's crescendo rose, and Wilhelm continued to glide them over the dance floor. She was happy to be close to him, but

113

the yearning to be alone and to discuss what was next for them pressed on her.

As the song came to an end, he lifted her hand high above her and turned her around once, then pulled her to him. Her stomach and chest bumped into his from the force. The people in the room clapped, and then a new song started as some couples on the floor returned to their tables while others came to take their place.

Her heart thudded hard against her ribs as her chest rose and fell, and his searing eyes dropped from hers to her low dress, then back. He took her hand in his and guided her off the floor and towards a long receiving table at the end of the room. Gathered around the table were mostly people she didn't recognize, probably Wilhelm's friends. His mother was placed in the chair next to his, and Klaus and Ingrid were seated next to her chair. But sitting only one table away from the bride and groom table was Klara, who stood like the others when she and Wilhelm approached.

Eva and Wilhelm made their way to a few of the tables, greeting the people at them before they sat. Eva's nerves spiked when she got to Klara's table. Her hands were shaking, and there was a tingling feeling in her fingers.

Klara leaned in and kissed Eva on both cheeks. "May you... continue to be blessed in this union." She put emphasis on the word 'continue.' She pulled back and gave her a look of censure. "Misses Eva Bauer," she said, drawing out each word.

Eva involuntarily flinched as she heard her new name spoken out loud for the first time. She was no longer Eva Abrams. She was now and would forever be Eva Bauer. It was so final, so permanent, that it punched through her well-fortified defenses to stab her with a pang of grief for Gerhardt, but she quickly pushed it back. *Eva Schulz,* she bleakly considers for a second, hearing the name inside her own head, but knowing those two words spoken together would never be said aloud.

They came around the table and sat in their chairs, and she looked at Wilhelm seated beside her, now as her husband. She appreciated Wilhelm for all he had done for her and the friendship he offered. Her gaze swept over his frame as he stood to greet another officer. Wilhelm's posture was casual but dominant as they briefly embraced over the table. Then, he took her hand again once he was seated. As the people came and went from their table, the man who stopped Wilhelm from killing Jurgen in the garden came to stand in front of them.

Wilhelm rose from his chair when he stopped in front of the table. "Someone finally managed to subdue you. Well, I suppose it's about time," he said to Wilhelm in a boisterous voice. "Congratulations to you both. Maybe you will spend enough time with her to have children. The Führer expects men like you to help add to the German population."

Wilhelm gave a wry smile. "I have no doubt that I will help add to those numbers," he countered, a reticent glint in his stare. They gave one another a solute, and then Wilhelm sat back down, pulling her hand into his lap.

They watched as the food was brought out. Waiters in white uniforms milled around the room while they placed finely decorated gold-plated china with lobster and steamed vegetables in front of people. She could smell it, and her stomach gave a rumble. She hadn't realized how hungry she was with everything that was going on.

People began to eat their food, and she was happy the attention was finally off her and Wilhelm. The sound of silverware clinking the china echoed through the room, and she looked to Wilhelm. He didn't speak to her but started a conversation with his mom about some of the people in the room, but his hand continued to hold hers in his lap.

When the dinner was over, it was time for the guests to form a line and begin streaming by, offering up the customary congratulations. A group of high-ranking officers paused before them. Eva looked at them, and it all seemed so surreal. Here she was, a girl who had an average life in the twenty-first century living in upstate Utah, now sitting in a room with a large percentage of the German command, and none of them had a clue about where she really came from.

"Congratulations to you, SS Obersturmbannführer Bauer," a gray-haired officer zealously offered his adulation, giving a quick solute. He had the SS runes on the collar of his shirt like Wilhelm, but there was something unsettling in his demeanor. As she watched this man, she leaned further away in her chair.

The officer's eyes flicked from Wilhelm to her, a look of impropriety on his face. "Your new wife seems a bit jumpy."

"She should be," the younger officer behind him said, smirking playfully as he looked at her. "She knows what's coming after the reception."

The material of her dress was bunched as she sat, and her right hand was covering her stomach. She realized now that most of the people here didn't know she was pregnant. She had tried to conceal it but only now knew it was working.

They all looked to Wilhelm now, him being the only one they included in their teasing. Her cheeks turned pink as they burned hot, and she felt resentment towards these men but kept her focus on the table. She didn't want to look at their faces or have them see her embarrassment. She would let them have their private joke at her expense. They spoke as if she wasn't even there, and it wasn't right how so many men in the 1940s, especially Germans, treated women. Like the way they were now, treating her as if she was a new pet Wilhelm had just got simply because she was female.

The younger man made an offhanded joke about noises she would make while in the bedroom. Wilhelm let go of her hand and eyed them. "I think you should stop talking now," he said in a calm, pleasant tone, but there was an unmistakable edge to his voice that put an abrupt stop to the men's laughing.

"I wish the best for you two," the officer said, his attitude now completely formal. The other officer behind him echoed the same good wishes, and then they both turned and left.

Wilhelm took her hand again in his and rubbed his fingers softly on the underside of her wrist, his thumb making circular motions over her pulse. He gave her a decided look, then rose from his chair and pulled on her hand.

"Come with me, Eva."

She stood and followed him through the room as they made their way down the aisle and out through the door. He led her down the long hall of the hotel to the other end and pulled her into another reception room, letting the door close behind them. It was smaller than the one they were using and was empty and dark, with only the city lights coming in through the windows and a small amount of light from under the door. The smell of stale cigarette smoke lingered in the room, but it barely registered with her as she struggled with the tide of her emotions.

He pulled her to him, wrapping his arms around her as he held her body tight against his. She suspected he took her out of the room so she could calm her nerves a bit, but wanted the people in the room to think they had snuck away to make out.

She brushed her lips against his ear and whispered in it. "Thank you for taking me away from there. And thank you for stopping that man from saying anything else."

"He was dangerously close to being knocked on his ass, but I figured words would be better suited at a wedding."

She still had her lips to his ear. "I don't think I would have minded, strangely enough," she said in a soft whisper. He rubbed her back rhythmically, sending a shiver through her as she looked up into his hazel eyes. "I'm scared because I don't know what comes next, and I'm nervous about going back into that room. I guess a lot of things are making me uncomfortable tonight."

He leaned in close to her ear, the sweet scent of her perfume filling his nostrils. "Well," he said, his voice a slow, gentle thrum as he walked her backward against the wall. "After, we will go to our room, and as I am unlacing your dress, I will be doing this." He brought his lips to hers, and there was a hot intensity in the way he kissed her.

She reached up, gripped the back of his unbuttoned tuxedo jacket, and ran her other hand through his hair, messing up his neatly combed side part. He bucked hard against her, pushing her firmly to the wall, her soft curves pressing against the hard lines of his body. His breath hitched as she gripped his hair more fiercely. He tightened his hold on her as one hand slid down her back to rest on her butt. She breathed heavily against his mouth as he kissed her passionately, her ribs straining against the dress as she tried to take in more air. She clung to him, getting caught up in his wild ferocity. He slid his fingers down the side of her neck and then to her cleavage that was exposed, tracing his hot fingertips over the top of the soft skin.

"And after I'm done, I want to see those flushed cheeks in the morning." She liked it when he took control, even though she didn't want to feel like he owned her.

Wilhelm's fire escaped his tight hold a number of times this evening, but his desire would be heated to a scald by the time they were done in this room. If he didn't stop, they wouldn't be going back into the reception room, and she wasn't sure she could get back into her wedding dress. It was pulled as tight around her stomach as was comfortable and safe, but to do it again like that could be challenging.

To her relief and disappointment, he pulled back a fraction. His breathing was heavy, and there was a fire in his eyes. He looked at her, searching.

"Is that better? I could see your anxiety and that you were straining to hold it together. I didn't want you to lose your self-control in front of everyone, and my ability to keep you calm is limited in there. That is why I brought you out here."

"I was close to losing it. But I am better now," she said as her breathing slowed.

He gave her a heated smile. "Good. Now you do know what will happen after the ceremony."

Her heart rate spiked again, but the knowledge that they had to return to the ceremony cut through her desire. "I look forward to it."

He moved away from her, rubbed his hand over his hair to fix what she messed up, straightened his jacket, and then held his hand out to her.

"Are you ready?"

She pushed away from the wall and put her hand on her stomach, taking a few deep breaths.

"I am."

She took his hand and could still feel the hunger and attraction to him coursing through her. They walked with their fingers laced together to the reception room, and he looked down at her, affection warming his gaze.

"Hopefully, there won't be any more comments like before," she said.

"I doubt there will be."

"It's unfair the way some men treat women. And this morning, I had someone tell me they hoped you would be rough on the wedding night."

He stopped walking and looked at her, raising a brow. "That certainly is not the evening I've envisioned."

"I know you didn't, but it still makes me angry. They said they wanted you to shock me with what you did."

His lips lifted into a smile. "Oh, I hope I do. But I'm sure it won't shock you for long. You catch on quick."

She gave him a frustrated look. "That is not what they meant."

He gave her a look of equal intensity. "I know that's not what they meant. And it's good that it makes you mad," he said, losing the smile. "Hold onto that anger because it's much more useful than fear."

She looked at him, surprised but also not surprised at his comment. That was who he was, and he was now her ruthless soldier husband.

Wicked mischief lit in his eyes. "When I'm done doing things that will shock you," he said, clearly finding the idea humorous. "I need to teach you not to let things get to you. You are vulnerable the way you are now. I know you have not had the need in the past to wear emotional armor, but you are too dependent on me."

She hated the thought of hardening her heart for any reason, but she knew, to a certain degree, he was right. And she was thankful that once again he was trying to look after her. She gave him an appreciative look, remembering just how much he was sacrificing for her. He was throwing his lot in with her, and that meant with anyone she was associated with. If he was caught, he would suffer a terrible fate at the hands of his own people. He was ready to help her at the cost of his own life but wasn't willing to risk it for anyone else other than his mother and his country. It struck her that she didn't mind so much being Eva Bauer as she faced down the rest of this war.

Chapter Eight

September 5th, 1942

E va looked at the building the car stopped in front of, but it was not his apartment. She turned to Wilhelm. "Where are we?"

He gave a sly smile. "Home."

She narrowed her eyes and turned back to the car window. "This isn't your apartment."

The building was a two-story tan stone structure on a row with other luxury apartments in the traditional French architecture.

"It is our new home."

Her mouth opened, and she eyed him in confusion. "I can't afford to live on the arrondissement. Do you know how expensive the apartments are here?"

"Of course I do. And this is where all the high-ranking officers stationed in Paris live."

"But you didn't live here before."

"No, I didn't need to. A small apartment suited me just fine when I was single, and I am often gone from Paris, so it stayed empty a lot of the time anyway. But now I find myself needing a larger place as well as a nicer one, and it will no longer sit vacant." He focused on her. "I will be away a lot, Eva. At least I can leave you and the baby in comfort while I'm gone."

This was something she hadn't really considered. She remembered that he was gone all the time before they were married, but it wasn't something that was at the forefront of her thoughts. Too many other things had been going on for her to consider all the other things that came along with marrying Wilhelm. She knew already that she wasn't going to like him being gone all the time, but she wasn't going to be able to change that fact.

"I would have been just as happy in the old apartment."

"It was too small for three people. Besides, you deserve to live in something nicer."

Did he think she would be happy with him only if he gave her material things? She didn't care about any of that. All she wanted was him. If she could trade the fancy apartment for more of his time, she would in a heartbeat. She knew this marriage wasn't going to be easy, but she was only now starting to realize how hard it might actually be.

"Can I go with you when you leave? I don't want to be alone all the time."

"Sometimes, maybe. It just depends on where I go and for what reason. Let's go inside, and you can pick out what room will be ours."

Wilhelm opened his door, and his orderly opened hers. She stepped out, and Wilhelm came around the car and held out his hand. She didn't hesitate but put her hand in his and let him lead her to the front door.

"I chose the apartment on the ground floor because of your condition. I know it will be easier for you, especially later in the pregnancy."

She smiled at his consideration. The security guard at the door opened it for them, letting them into the building. "You will go back to work tomorrow then?" she asked as they stepped through the front door.

"Unfortunately, yes. I would spend all the time in the world with you if I had it, but the war won't allow us more time." His warm hazel eyes bore into her, and she saw in them the regret at how it had to be.

She picked the largest of the four bedrooms to be theirs and the one closest to it for the baby's room. It dawned on her when she chose the room that soon they would have to buy a crib and all the other things babies required. But she didn't know what all those things were. There was a lot she would have to learn, and she didn't have her mom here to ask or help, which kicked up a whole host of powerful conflicting emotions. The best she had was Wilhelm's mom, but she didn't think she would mind. There was no furniture in the apartment yet, and their voices echoed off the empty walls.

"So, where are we going to sleep tonight?" she asked, turning around in the empty bedroom to look at him.

He was watching her, both of his hands tucked into his pants pockets. "Everything from my old apartment should be moved over tomorrow, but if you are feeling adventurous, we could sleep here tonight on the floor. We could get the blankets and pillows from the other apartment."

She gave him an amorous smile. "I think I'm feeling adventurous."

He cracked a smile. "Let's go get it then."

They slept with layered blankets on the floor in front of the fireplace. Wilhelm had a small fire burning, so they didn't get cold as the temperature dropped. It was late at night, but she struggled to stay asleep. He appeared to be sleeping, and she pressed against him, holding on tight. They were wrapped in the covers, but he was her blanket. His arm was around her, and she had her head on his chest and hand resting on his stomach, with a leg draped over him. She would have gotten closer if it were possible. She enjoyed the rise and fall of his chest and the slow rhythmic beating of his heart. For some reason, it was soothing to her.

Tomorrow, he would return to work, and she would go to Dieppe to collect the last of her things. She would only be gone two nights but was worried he would be somewhere for work when she got back. She didn't want the loneliness to start so soon. She had also mentioned to him that Ingrid might move to Paris. And made sure to say how happy it would make her if she had a friend in the city. He didn't seem to mind but told her Ingrid couldn't be at the apartment all the time. She understood why. When he wasn't working, he wanted to be the one she spent her time with. And as a newly married couple, that made sense to her.

She lifted her head and removed her leg and hand from him. Then, as softly as she could, she moved his arm from her. She

125

scooted out from under the blankets and tiptoed to the bathroom. When she finished, she didn't feel like going back to bed just yet. She crossed her arms over her chest and walked from room to room in the apartment. It was so big, and she had no idea what she would do with all that space. She went to the un-curtained windows and looked out at the dark city. She loved Paris but never imagined she would ever be living here. One good thing was that Paris never got bombed. The memories of the bombing raids in Berlin sometimes gave her nightmares. Everything going through her mind was slowly whittling away at her nerves.

She turned and went back to the bedroom and stood in the doorway, watching his sleeping body on the floor. She walked across the wood floor, the gentle patter of her feet the only sound in the apartment. She looked at the relaxed expression on his face. While sleeping, he seemed younger without the worries he carried while awake creasing into his forehead, and he didn't wear the guarded mask of detachment. She thought he had a handsome face with his defined jaw, high cheekbones, and strong browbones. His thick, curly brown hair was messy, and his head was turned slightly to the side.

She pulled her fingers into fists, trying to keep herself from touching him. She wanted to but didn't want to wake him. They had not been intimate on their wedding night. She was so exhausted from the day's events and felt sick from the stress of it all that they just went to bed on the pallet he made them. She knew that was not how he wanted to spend the evening, but he was understanding and didn't get upset with her. Any disappointment he felt, he kept firmly inside.

She took another piece of wood and put it in the fire. It crackled and popped, the flames growing larger as they wrapped around the log. She looked back to Wilhelm, pondering her future. Was she being reckless when she fell for him? He was her life now, even if that was not what she had initially wanted. It was a lot to bare, and in a way, it still upset her that she was now so tied to this time, but life wasn't fair. Although it has taught her that you can still find happiness and contentment in the unexpected. She had tied herself to this man she once wanted dead. It just goes to show how life can surprise you. The person she thought would be the death of her turned out to be her savior, offering her a glimpse of what she thought heaven must be like.

She lowered herself onto her knees beside the bed and sat on her feet. She tenderly brushed a piece of hair from his forehead. He turned his head slightly but didn't wake up. She smiled and watched the firelight reflect on his face. Why did she love this man so much? And how could she go home without him? That was something she had to work out. She wanted to see her family again, but she didn't think she could leave him now. Just the thought was painful and caused a tightness in her chest.

She ached to touch him, but she needed to let him sleep. He would be gone early in the morning for work.

She continued to sit beside him, watching the fire burn for more than an hour before finally crawling back under the blanket and scooting next to him. In his sleep, he draped an arm over her stomach, and she placed a hand on his arm. She closed her eyes and drifted to sleep in the early morning hour.

She woke to find Wilhelm gone from the blankets. Stiff from sleeping on the floor, she sat up and stretched, then threw off the covers and stood, the floor cool on her bare feet. She hugged her chest to ward off the chill in the air and walked into the dining room, the large family room, and finally, the kitchen. He wasn't in any of the rooms, and she stared at the empty kitchen, the gray light of dawn coming in through the window, and outside, a hazy mist hung in the air, making the city appear dreamlike. The defined edges of the buildings were hard to see. Something on the counter caught her eye, and she walked over to it. A plate with fresh fruit, cheese, and an assortment of pastries was sitting on the counter. Beside it was a coffee pot, a cup, and a note. She unfolded the paper and read it.

Eva,

There is no food in the house, so I brought you this. There is coffee in the pot that you will have to heat on the stove. You didn't wake up when I gave you a kiss, so I let you sleep. Please be careful going to Dieppe. I wish I could go with you. I will see you in two days.

-Wilhelm

She smiled and laid the paper back on the counter. She put the pot on the stove and lit it, then stood by the counter and ate the food while she waited for the coffee to get hot. When steam rose from the pot, she took it off the burner, poured herself a cup, and carried it to the bedroom where her suitcase was. She got some clean clothes and her toiletries, then went to the bathroom and took a quick shower. She put her hair up while she drank her coffee, packed her stuff, got her purse, and left for the tram. She rode it to the train station where she would wait for the twelve o'clock train to Dieppe.

Soldiers were coming and going on the trains, as well as French people. She watched them as she tried to stay awake. She was more tired than usual from not being able to sleep, had heartburn from the food she ate, and a sharp pain in her forehead and between her eyes from the onslaught of a headache. She had always heard that it got better around twelve weeks, which she guessed she was, but she couldn't be certain since they didn't have ultrasounds in the forties. But her symptoms didn't seem to be going anywhere. Her nausea, headaches, bloating, and sore breasts were all still there, and now she had heartburn to add to the other symptoms.

She needed to get her mind off how she felt, and her thoughts went to Jon. She didn't know where he was or how he was. Wilhelm had not told her anymore about him. All he had said was that Jon was no longer in the prison where she visited him and that he wasn't in a concentration camp. So then, where was he? She would ask to see him when she returned from Dieppe. Just because she was trapped here didn't mean Jon had to be. With her, it wasn't just physically being trapped. She was trapped here by her heart, but Jon wasn't. Her future wasn't certain anymore, but Jon's seemed to be much clearer.

The train pulled into the station and she stood, picked up her bag, and walked along the tracks. Once the people on the train unloaded, she stepped on, found a private box, and slid the door shut. With both hands, she hoisted her suitcase on the top rack and sat on the red satin cushion. She laid down on the seat and covered up with her jacket, tucking her hands under her head. She fell asleep quickly before the train even left the station.

Eva could hear people talking and sat up, realizing the train had stopped. She scooted on the bench and put her head close to the window. She recognized the station; they were in Dieppe. The trip seemed like it only lasted a few minutes. She put on her jacket and got her suitcase down. She remembered that she was going to have to carry it all the way to the apartment. If Wilhelm was here, he would carry it for her, and that thought brought a smile to her face.

She stepped off the train onto the platform and left the station. She still had her key to the apartment, so she would go there. Eva walked the familiar streets, remembering all the things that had happened here. Some were good, and some were bad, but they all connected her to the city forever, the way her experiences in La Chapelle, Paris, and Berlin did to those cities.

Unlocking the door, she entered the apartment and took her bag to her old room. She sat on the bed and looked around, feeling nostalgic. She rubbed her hand over the comforter, her emotions turbulent. She sighed, knowing the reason for some of the feelings she was having. It was because she was pregnant. Her life was chaotic enough; she didn't need to add to it. This certainly wasn't the most convenient time to be pregnant, the same way war was a bad time to be in love. For a long time, it was a love she dared not speak of, not even to herself. She worried about what people would think, the hate that no doubt would be directed at her for her choices. But what scared her the most was the fear of allowing herself to fall for someone like him.

She ate a little bit of food from the fridge and then cleaned the apartment while she waited for Ingrid to get home. She had called the day before to make sure Ingrid would be home today. She was sweeping the floor when Ingrid came through the front door.

"Eva," she quilled. She hadn't even removed her nurse's cap when she ran to embrace her. "I have missed you. It is lonely here without you now. While you were getting married, I watched from the pew and thought, who will be there to dry my eyes when I cry now that you are gone? You have Wilhelm, but I only have you."

Ingrid had left the morning after the wedding and had only been home a day and a night alone, but she was already lonely. Eva cupped her hand over her cheek.

"Maybe right now, but you are so young. And when this war is over, your life will be very different." She thought about what would happen to the German women when the Russians invaded. "Ingrid, you have to promise me something. If it looks like Germany will lose the war, would you stay in France and not return to Germany?"

She pulled her brows together. "Why?"

"Because if Germany loses the war, I don't think I have to tell you what will happen to the German women. Especially if the Russians get to Germany first. Just promise me?"

"I promise." Her face had worry etched in it. "Has Wilhelm told you something?"

"No, but we both know Germany could lose this war. And if that happens, Germany is where everyone will be fighting to get to, and it will be surrounded by all sides. Wilhelm said he is fine

with you coming to Paris, only that you have to give us our space."
She flushed, knowing Ingrid would understand why.

Even though there was still worry in her eyes, she smiled. "I
will let them know at the hospital. I will leave as soon as I can. Do
you think you can find me a place to stay before I get there?"

"I will look and try to find something cheap that's nice." Eva
looked at her watch. "I thought we could have dinner with Klaus
tonight."

"He is at work. We can go over and see him. Have you heard
he is leaving in a week to go back to Germany?"

Eva shook her head. "No. I guess it's not surprising that he is
leaving."

Eva was astonished when Klaus took her and Ingrid to the
same restaurant where they met Wilhelm. Where they played the
piano together and then went to the cottage and made love for the
first time. It made her uncomfortable to be here and also made her
miss him. There were butterflies in her stomach and an intense
want to be near him. This worried her because the more she loved
him, the farther away she felt from her family and time.

"How has the pregnancy been? Have you had any problems?"

The sound of Klaus' voice pulled her out of her mental
monolog. "It has been OK. Some days are better than others. I
have all the normal symptoms. I was hoping to skip a few, but so
far, I seem to have them all."

He looked at the bump beneath her dress. "How many weeks
are you now?"

"I think twelve."

"You carry it in the front, so you show it earlier."

She put her hands on her stomach. "I've noticed."

"Was he happy when you told him?"

"Yes, in a way. It was a shock to him. Honestly, I think he is happier about it than I am."

"You aren't happy about it?"

"Yes and no. It's hard to explain." She wanted to change the topic from her. "So Ingrid tells me you are leaving in a week."

"I am. I'm sure you know that I only came here for you?"

She gave him a warm smile. "I do. And I can't thank you enough for being there for me in so many ways."

"I am happy we met, Eva. But it saddens me that you've had it so rough since you've been here. And I need to be honest about something. You are playing a dangerous game. You are pregnant with Obersturmbannführer Bauer's baby, which has bound you to him. I understand that. And you need him to help financially and in other ways, but I wish it wasn't necessary. I would normally say it was cruel to keep a child from its father, but in your case, it would be better for you and the baby to leave and find someone else who can help you. I know I told you in the hospital that you should tell him, but I regret saying that now. I hadn't thought about what the consequences would be if you did." He looked at her stomach and shook his head. "That poor child. Its father is a killer, a cruel man, and if Germany fails to win the war, its mother will be seen as a traitor."

He was making her sad. Not on purpose, but his words stung like being poked with a thousand needles. "So you believe I should have gotten rid of the baby?"

His eyes grew wide. "No, I don't think that at all. I'm just pointing out the gravity of your situation. Everything that has happened to you, including that baby, I blame him for."

"It took both of us to make it."

"Yes, but he should have never done to you what it takes to make a baby."

"I'm not a child. I knew what I was doing with him. And it was my choice to do it. He didn't force me."

"Maybe not physically, but he knew anything that had to do with him was bad for you, and he did it anyway. I'm sorry, Eva. But I will always hate him for it. You have been deceived into thinking there is good in him somewhere inside, but you have made the mistake of underestimating him. He is well educated and intelligent. He may be charming, even seem human, but don't forget that he is a man driven by his Nazi ideologies."

"I'm sorry too." Her eyes filled with tears. She loved two men, but one would always hate the other. Why did life have to be so cruel? She had seen what lay underneath Wilhelm's hard exterior and knew that, at his core, he was not all bad.

"I know you wonder how two people who seem so different can be together. I often wondered that myself, but I know why. Love. It goes completely against all reason, and love doesn't make sense. I'm beginning to think it never did. We tell ourselves we don't love someone because our brains don't want us to, but our hearts never listen to our brains. His love might be my damnation, but I will love him to my grave."

His blue eyes penetrated hers. "I know you love him, which is why you will never leave him. Even if someone told you all the reasons why you should. And he might love you. It might be achingly strong, but it doesn't matter. It won't change a thing in the end. Some sins can't be washed away, even if you try."

"Please don't think poorly of me for my choice?"

He took her hand in his. "I don't think ill of you, Eva. My only hope is that by the end of this war, you will no longer be his concern."

She flinched at his words. "What are you saying?"

"Only that I hope someday you will be free of him."

"Maybe I don't want to be free of him."

"Then you're a fool."

Ingrid cleared her throat. "Shall we order?"

Eva had almost forgotten she was there. She was thankful for her interruption. She didn't want to fight with Klaus, and she didn't want to be angry with him. But his words scared her and hurt deeply. She thought about how it would feel to live without Wilhelm, and it was almost more than she could bare. She was nowhere near ready for him not to be in her life, and she didn't think she ever would be. She had to put the thought of him dying out of her mind or even going back to her time without him. She realized that she had just confirmed to herself that, at her core, she loved him more than life itself.

"Yes, Ingrid, let's order."

They ate in relative silence, but Klaus continued to glance at her, and Ingrid looked between them. While eating, she decided she would return to Paris a day early. She wanted to see Wilhelm and didn't want to wait an extra day. Klaus' words only made her want to be with him more and miss him with an intensity she was unfamiliar with. She thought it was because Klaus had put the thought of him dying in her head.

When they returned to the apartment, Klaus walked them to the door and paused next to Eva. "Ingrid, can we have a minute?"

"Sure." She went inside and closed the door.

Eva waited for him to speak first, and when his words came, they were soft and kind. "I am sorry if I upset you tonight. But I felt I had to be honest. I am not your father, but I imagine he too would have the same opinion of your union with Obersturmbannführer Bauer. He would want to protect you from him, so he would warn you about his character, as I have done. Nothing I have said was meant to hurt you in any way. I love you like I would my own daughter, and I feel like I would be failing you if I at least didn't try. I can't make your decisions for you, but I can at least help you make the right ones."

She didn't say anything but took two steps forward and wrapped her arms tight around his large torso. He wrapped his arms around her, too, and pressed his cheek to the top of her head. She cried into his army jacket and wished she could change so many things about her life and the world she lived in. After several minutes, she pulled away and looked up at him through the blur of her tears.

"I'm glad you care enough to be honest with me. I'm not mad at you for what you said. I'm mad that it's true, but I can never leave him. I hope you can understand that at least a little."

He looked through the round lens of his glasses at her. "I do understand." He put his hands on her cheeks and brought his lips to her forehead, planting a kiss, then let go of her. "Please take care of yourself, Eva."

"I will. Wilhelm wouldn't hurt me."

He looked conflicted. "I trust you, and if you tell me he won't hurt you, then I believe you."

She blinked away the tears. "Klaus, would you be the one who delivers the baby?"

This seemed to take him by surprise. "When it is close to your time, you let me know, and I will try to come to Paris and stay until you give birth."

"Thank you," she said in a whisper.

"I'll let you get to bed." He put on his cap and gave her a nod, and when he walked past, she thought he looked like he was on the verge of tears. She had never seen him cry, and his tears meant more to her than he would ever know.

Chapter Nine

September 7th, 1942

Eva had left that morning after saying bye to Ingrid. She hadn't told Wilhelm that she was heading back a day early because she wanted to surprise him. She didn't know when he would be home, so she was unsure how exactly she was going to do that.

When she was back in Paris, she went straight to the apartment. She asked the guard at the door not to tell Wilhelm that she was home, that it was a surprise. He told her he wouldn't say anything, so she gave him a warm smile and thanked him. Once inside, she hid her suitcase in an empty room and waited by the window, watching for him to return. She hoped it wouldn't be late, but it probably would.

She left the window long enough to see if there was any food in the fridge. There was the leftover fruit from the morning she left, some cheese and meat, and a half loaf of bread on the counter. She put some on a plate and went back to the window to keep watch. She checked her watch, and it was fourteen minutes till ten. She looked down at the dark street, hoping to see the headlights of a car.

She took her plate to the kitchen and washed it, putting it away so he wouldn't see a dirtied dish in the sink. When she returned to the window, the faint light of a car's headlights at the far end of the street was drawing closer. She watched the car until it finally stopped on the street in front of the apartment. When Wilhelm got out of the car, she ran to the empty bedroom and hid in the closet. She felt giddy, like it was the first date. Her palms were sweaty, and her heartrate was elevated. She still didn't know how she was going to surprise him.

Heavy footsteps creaked on the wooden floor as Wilhelm passed in front of the bedroom doorway. She listened to the sounds he made in the other room. He took off his boots and dropped them on the floor, walked across the room several times, then went to the kitchen. After a while, he came back down the hall. The footsteps stopped, then, a few minutes later, the shower turned on. She smiled to herself because she knew exactly how she was going to surprise him.

After the shower had been on for several minutes, Eva came out of the closet and tiptoed down the hall to the bathroom. The door was open, and she leaned around the doorframe and peered in. The shower curtain was pulled closed, and the steam had fogged up the mirror. She unbuttoned her dress and slid it off her shoulders, then pulled her slip over her head and dropped it to the floor in the hall with her dress. She slid her underwear down her legs and stepped out of them, then undid the clasp to her bra, letting it fall.

Again, she walked on the balls of her feet into the bathroom. She stopped when she reached the shower and paused. Slowly, she lifted her hand and, pulled one side of the curtain away from the wall an inch, and peeked through. His hands were braced on the shower wall while steaming water cascaded over him. The water streamed down his muscular back and the defined glutes of his butt, then his powerful legs. He moved his hands from the wall and rubbed them over his hair to push the soap out, and his powerful arms flexed, the veins in his hands and forearms bulging, and his skin glistening under the water as the muscles rippled through his back. Her breath hitched as she watched the strong form of his body.

While he still had his back to her, she pulled the curtain open a little farther and stepped onto the beige-tiled floor of the shower. She brought her right hand up, placing it on his back to trace her fingertips along his shoulder blade, but before she had time to do anything, he rounded on her. She had not expected him to suddenly turn and attack her. His hand was tight around her throat, and she looked up at him with wide, terrified eyes as she struggled for air. Wilhelm breathed a sound of disbelief, and his face changed from a look of fury to perplexed confusion. He suddenly dropped his hand to his side and took a step back, his eyes burning into hers. She brought her hand to her throat and coughed. The whole thing lasted no more than a few seconds, but as he gripped her throat, squeezing the breath from her, time seemed to stop.

He stepped forward, only inches from her now, and took her chin in his hand, lifting her head as he moved her hand from her throat. His sudden movement as he reached for her made her flinch, and her first impulse was to back away, but she held still.

He inspected her neck and brushed over her skin with his fingers, checking to see what damage he had done. He let go of her and then backed away again; his gaze on her was fierce. She could see the question in his eyes.

In a rough voice, she spoke. "I came home early to surprise you."

He put his thumb and middle finger on his temples and his other hand on his hip as he looked to the floor. "Eva...you should not have snuck up on me like that." There was frustration in his voice. "I could have seriously hurt you."

She reached up and touched the tender spot where he had squeezed. "I'm sorry. I didn't think about how you might react."

He watched her rubbing her neck, and anger flashed in his eyes. She didn't think it was anger at her so much as it was anger at himself. She moved her hand from her throat and stepped forward, closing the distance he put between them.

"Let's just forget it happened."

He narrowed his eyes at her. "How can I forget it happened? Eva, I put purple spots on your neck with my fingers. You will be lucky if they have disappeared by morning."

"You weren't trying to hurt me. You are a better man than any I have ever known. Once I got through your layers, I saw you, the real you, and I knew you wouldn't harm me."

"If only that were true."

This certainly isn't how she thought this was going to go. She assumed they would be making out by this point. But she was going to try and salvage the evening. She stepped even closer and put her hand on his chest, rubbing her palm over his pec muscles and down to his stomach. He didn't move to touch her, but he didn't stop her from touching him. She slid her hand even lower, and that is when he finally took her by the wrist, holding her tightly. She looked at his hand on her, then up to his face. He was giving her a heated, significant look. They stared at each other for a long moment as the tension flared between them.

Finally, Wilhelm drew her in, pressing her against him, his lips grazing her ear. "Are you sure?" His gaze on her was molten now.

"I'm sure," she said as her desire rose, and she was surprised at how much she wanted him. "You can have me any way you want."

"Any way I want?" he whispered, his deep voice thrumming through her.

"Yes, anywhere, anytime." Her words came out in a breath.

He pulled her under the water with him and brought his mouth to hers. She relished in the heat of his desire, the way he wanted her, and how he always made her feel alive.

"Fuck," he growled.

Before she had a chance to register what was happening, he got down on his knees and hooked her right leg over his shoulder. He put his head between her legs and took her into his mouth. Assaulting her fast and hard with his tongue and teeth, claiming her.

"Ohhh," she breathed.

He sucked her clit into his mouth and then released it, rubbing his tongue over the sensitive skin again and again.

She screwed her eyes shut. "Oh my God," she choked out.

He took her into his mouth again like he was starved. She fisted the hair on top of his head, arching her back as he nibbled, sucked, and licked.

"Damn, you are nice," he whispered against her skin. She watched him as he licked the length of her, starring up into her eyes. Then, he slid his tongue inside of her, and she groaned loudly.

"Oh, Wilhelm, don't stop." There was an ache building deep inside, and the feeling between her legs grew until it reached a pinnacle.

He put two fingers against her and glanced up. She nodded frantically, telling him she wanted him to, then he slid the two fingers inside her as he continued to circle her clit with his tongue.

"Yes, she moaned," feeling the orgasm build as it gathered deep in her belly. Her muscles started to prickle and feel sluggish as her breaths came faster and faster. She groaned, tightening every muscle in her body as the orgasm erupted inside. "Oh shit," she cried in English as her body tensed, then exploded from the inside, and she rode it out, grinding herself against his tongue. "Ahhh, Wilhelm!" Her clit throbbed, and she felt slick between her legs. She heaved, trying to catch her breath as the bursts of pleasure inside and between her legs pulsed and spread, then slowly dissipated. Her body shook with aftershocks, and Wilhelm's mouth slowed, licking her soft and gentle now. He kissed her clit, and then drug his bottom lip between his teeth.

He stood, then brushed his lips across her jawbone up to her ear. "Come with me," he said in a serious tone.

She knew what he was offering. He wanted her to go to the bedroom with him so he could have her again, but it was more

143

than that. She could hear the longing in his voice, how everything in him pulled towards her. And she wanted him with a profound depth, and not just physically. She wanted to permeate what he was and claim it for her own because he was everything she desperately wanted and needed.

He turned off the water, took her hand, and pulled her out of the shower, then reached for the towel, lifting it from the hook. He dried her body and then his own.

She thought how this felt like something new, like the last missing pieces of her broken heart were being put back into place, becoming his fully.

He led her to the bedroom, and she saw the queen bed from his other apartment, its headboard pushed against the far wall of the large room. He took her to it, then stopped just at the edge.

She let her gaze roam freely over the hard plains on his body as he stood naked in front of her. Fire rose in the pit of her stomach in a slow burn. His gaze fixed on her, and they both stilled as their eyes met. She took him in, the familiar lines of his face, his hazel eyes, his messy brown hair that hung in wet clumps around his face. Heat bloomed on her cheeks as she remembered the wild thrill of the last few times they were together. Not when he took her over the bed, but as they were in the meadow, or when he made love to her in her hotel room, and just a while ago in the shower. She remembered the feeling of his unrestrained power she now wielded because he was all hers, unconditionally. He had given himself to her fully and repeatedly.

She lifted her head to him, finding his eyes blazing as he stared at her, and she was intimidated and excited by the wild desire that was riding with it. She wanted him with everything in her.

He put his hands on her hips and pressed her hard against him, then wrapped his arms around her, almost in a protective manner. There was an intense emotion in the way he was holding her, in the way his desire filled her. Suddenly, it all rushed over her, how she had held herself back from him, unable to move past her grief over everything that was lost to her, possibly forever. Jon, Gerhardt, her family, her time, and her country. So many things she was giving up for him. Letting go of the last of her heart's hesitation, she pulled back slightly, stood on the tips of her toes, and kissed him in a shuttering rush of intense passion, and he inhaled sharply, his gaze growing fervid. She pulled away but kept her hands on the sides of his face.

"I'm sorry," she told him. Her voice filled with the affection and desire she had for him. "I'm sorry it's taken me so long to feel the same devotion for you that you do for me."

"It doesn't matter now," he said with tenderness. He backed her up until her legs hit the bed, then lowered her down onto it. He moved on top of her, laced his fingers through her hair, pulling gently as he brought his face to hers, and kissed her long and deep.

"Give me your passion. I want every part of you, Eva," Wilhelm whispered. "Give it all to me. I have your body, but I want all of you, heart and soul."

"It's yours; take it."

After her words, he didn't hold back. He touched and kissed her with a feverishly hot and frantic hunger. She thought he would crawl inside her if he could, which mirrored her own feelings. She couldn't get close enough. She craved for him to fill her completely. She wanted him to consume her and was ready to give in to the pull she was drowning in. She rubbed her hands up his muscular arms, over his sides, and through his hair. Then he pushed inside her, and she put her head back, opening her mouth as she drew in a long breath. She lifted her arms above her head, gripping the blanket tightly in her fingers. He placed a hand on her hip and leaned down, kissing her throat, and she moved a hand to the side of his neck. She lifted her leg and brought it over his head, rolling slightly to her side without him moving, and he continued doing her from behind as he leaned over her. She turned her head towards him, and he came in close, kissing her. The look in his eyes was intense and unrestrained, blazing with his passion for her, and he had her emotions in a tangle. He then thrust, and she screamed, her thoughts blurring. He was lighting up her body, and she was caught in a haze of desire. He let out a groan as he pushed in hard, then stayed that way for a few seconds. Finally, he leaned in and kissed her softly on the shoulder, and lifted himself off her. He moved to the head of the bed and leaned against the headboard, placing a pillow behind him.

She rolled to her other side and watched him, her breath still coming hard. He watched her, too, a haze still in his eyes. Her body was reeling from the elation he just gave her, and she wanted him to do it to her again. She couldn't keep her hands off him, and she couldn't stop thinking about having sex with him, and wondered if part of it was that her hormones were riding high because of her pregnancy. But she knew most of it was simply her draw to him and the fact that he turned her on.

Eva placed her hands on her stomach as her heart fluttered, and she almost couldn't believe that she and Wilhelm had created a life together, which made her feel even more connected to him. It made being intimate with him even more intense, and she was enjoying the ride, figuratively and literally.

She turned, laying her head at the foot of the bad as she stretched her legs out beside him. He watched her, scanning every inch of her body, then reached over and took one of her feet, pulling it onto his lap. He pressed his thumbs into the arch of her foot and rubbed. Her eyes closed as his rough, strong fingers pressed deftly into her skin. He was putting her to sleep, but she didn't want to, so she opened her eyes and watched him. His gaze was fixed on her leg, so she looked down to see what he was staring at. The scar from the bullet wound was visible on her outer left thigh.

He lifted his eyes to her, his expression stern. "How did you get that?"

Now she knew he hadn't noticed the bandage on her leg when he took her over the bed. He had been too caught up in the moment. "In Dieppe."

"You got that how while in Dieppe?"

"The day of the raid."

"Yes, and the fighting was mostly on the beach and on a few streets close to the beach."

"I was at the cliff watching. A bullet ricocheted and hit me in the leg as I was walking home."

His eyes were steely as he looked at her. "I think sometimes you need to be locked up to protect you from yourself."

"No. I felt I needed to see what was happening."

"So you could watch men get slaughtered on the beach?"

"No. So I would know if they were successful."

His face hardened at this, but he only took her other foot and started massaging it instead of responding. "The other officers' wives get together every Thursday for tea or coffee. You should join them."

"For what reason?"

"For something to do. It will give you a reason to leave the apartment, and maybe you can make friends here."

"Working at the hospital would also give me something to do."

He narrowed his eyes but didn't dignify it with an answer. She knew his feelings about her working now that she was pregnant. "I gave them your name and our address; one of them will be phoning tomorrow."

"I suppose it wouldn't hurt." She watched his hands work her foot and ran her eyes over him. The scars from his wounds were evident on his skin. She felt a pang of guilt and sadness that she was partly responsible for marring his body. Then she remembered Jon's missing fingers and closed her eyes, hiding the pain in them. She wondered if now would be a good time to ask about seeing him. "Wilhelm?"

He was rubbing up her calf now and looked from her leg to her face. "Yes."

"You told me to ask you after the wedding about seeing Jon." His hands stopped, and he eyed her cautiously. "I wanted to know if I could see him?" His hands remained still as he watched her, and she could see him considering her question. He didn't immediately answer but held onto her leg as he thought.

"I will arrange for you to see him in my office," he finally said.

148

She could feel the relief settling over her and smiled at him. "Thank you."

"I will try to bring him to Paris next week, but I don't know what day, so don't ask me. When he is brought here, I will tell you."

She knew this was the best she could expect. "I won't ask."

She pulled her leg from his hands and got on her knees, moving across the bed, and then straddled him. The frustrated look on his face that had settled there while they were discussing Jon disappeared and was replaced with a brazenly wanton look. She took both of his hands and placed one on each of her full breasts.

"So, I'm going to go shower, and if you come with me, you can have me in there too, again."

He leaned forward, bringing his face to hers. "Is that so?"

She felt a twinge of embarrassment at her forwardness. "I mean, I can shower alone if you don't want to."

He wrapped his arm around her waist and turned, sliding his legs over the side of the bed, and then stood. As she had her legs wrapped around him, he walked them both to the bathroom.

Chapter Ten

September 10th, 1942

Eva didn't need a jacket while she walked as the early September days were still warm, even though the near-autumn chill was fighting to dominate the warmth from the sunlight. She had told Wilhelm she would meet with the other officers' wives on Thursday. One of the women called the day after he told her and invited her to join them for lunch. Eva wrote down the restaurant they were meeting at and what time so she wouldn't forget. It was on the arrondissement across from the Arc de Triomphe, the same street she and Wilhelm lived on.

As Eva made her way to the restaurant, she found she was enjoying the exercise. Wilhelm worked all the time and would leave early in the morning and typically return late at night, so she was alone most of the day and night. But she was often too tired to go out and no longer had a job that forced her to.

She stopped across the street from the restaurant and stared at it. A large white sign across the top of the building read in bold, black lettering, Soldatenkaffee Madeleine. Two large windows made up most of the front of the building, and in between was a door. She hurried across the street, pulled the heavy door open, and stepped inside, looking around at the many tables. It was crowded, mostly with off-duty soldiers, but in the middle was a table with four immaculately dressed women. They all wore elegant dresses, heels, expensive furs, and excessive jewelry that glittered in the light coming through the windows. One of them had a hat pinned to the side of her neatly placed curls.

Eva looked down at her casual dress and plain, flat brown leather shoes that laced up the front. It was very basic and not at all sophisticated.

One of the women saw her, then waved for her to join them. She obviously had the right place. Eva weaved through the crowd and stopped at the edge of the table. They were all the ideal German wives, with their blond hair, blue eyes, and fair skin. She didn't look anything like them with her neutral under-toned skin, dark brown hair, and hazel eyes. The women all had fixed smiles on their faces as they stared up at her.

"Eva Bauer, right?" The woman's red lipstick made her teeth appear extra white.

"Yes."

The woman who spoke stood and pulled the empty chair out for her. "Sit here. I'm Lorelei Vogel," she said as Eva lowered herself into the chair. "And this is Anna Meier," she pointed to the woman to her right. "Petra Weber," she pointed to the woman across from her. "And Amelia Schröder," she said, nodding to the woman Eva was sitting next to.

Eva put her purse on the floor at her feet and looked around the table at the women. "So, do you guys meet here every Thursday?"

"We meet every Thursday, but not always at the same place," Lorelei answered.

"OK." The women were all staring at her with curious amusement on their faces. She felt like a tiny animal they were all gathered around, observing.

"My husband said that your husband told him you are American," the one named Emelia said.

She had a kind sort of face, almost innocent in a way. "Yes, that's right."

Lorelei looked down at her stomach. "And I see you are expecting. You must be thrilled?"

She subconsciously placed her hand over her stomach. "It will be different."

The women at the table chuckled. "Different for sure," Petra said. "I'm sure your husband is excited."

Eva thought about his reaction when she told him and how his eyes teared up when she thought he would want her to get rid of it. "He is. Do any of you have children?"

Anna spoke for them. "Oh yes, we all do, except Petra."

"How old are your children?" Eva looked at the women, and Lorelei was by far the oldest of the four. Eva guessed she was in her early to mid-fifties. The other three looked to be in their late twenties to early thirties.

"I had two," Lorelei said, staring into her coffee.

Eva noticed the change in her demeanor. "Had?"

The silence at the table was palpable. Lorelei turned the cup back and forth on the saucer. "Two sons, but both of them are dead now."

Eva felt terrible for this woman and the loss she must be enduring. "I am so sorry." Eva couldn't think of anything else to say. How could any word be enough to equal the pain of her loss? But saying nothing would be worse.

"My oldest son was a pilot and was shot down last year over the English Channel. And my younger son was killed last month at Stalingrad in Russia.

Eva knew exactly how brutal and bloody that battle was. She didn't know what else to say or how exactly she should act. A sincere sorry wouldn't even come close to matching her suffering. "When I was a nurse, I was stationed on the Russian front, and the men, more like the boys that would come in, was heartbreaking."

"I didn't know you were a nurse."

"Yes, I have been a nurse since 1940."

"That is a noble profession for a woman. But you aren't working as a nurse now?"

"No, not for several weeks now." She looked down at her stomach.

"Of course."

"I have three children. Two girls and a boy," Amelia said. "And Anna has five. All boys."

Eva gawked at her. "How do you have time to do anything for yourself?"

"We have a nanny that helps."

153

"You would need one. I can't even imagine having that many children. I will probably be done after this one."

The women looked at one another. "Won't your husband have something to say about that?"

"I don't know, but it's not his decision. It's mine." They stared at her like she had just insulted their Führer. Eva didn't want to feel like a broodmare, which is how she thought the Germans looked at women in this time.

Lorelei cleared her throat. "I hear they have delicious food here. Why don't we order."

As they ate, Eva learned the ranks of their husbands, how long they had been stationed in France, their children's names, and what they enjoyed doing with their days. But they also kept the questions coming at her too.

"To be newly married and have your husband gone so much must be hard," Petra exclaimed. "I would demand that he be home more."

Eva smirked to herself. "Well, no one really demands Wilhelm to do anything."

"Yes, I've heard about your husband," Lorelei said. "I think some of the men stationed here are afraid that he will arrest them if they step out of line."

Eva wanted to say that wasn't true, but it probably was. "I wouldn't put it past him. He takes his duty and others very seriously."

"My husband said he was surprised that he got married. He told me his only love was his job," Amelie stated as she sipped her tea.

"It certainly is one of his loves."

"Let's do this again next week. I thought after we had lunch, we could meet at the Le Petit Palais Museum."

All the times Eva had been to Paris, she had never been to one of the museums. "I would like that. Do your husbands work on the weekends too?"

"Yes. I feel like I don't have a husband sometimes, but I understand it's necessary for the war effort and the victory of Germany."

Sunday was her birthday, and Eva was starting to think she would be spending it alone. She wondered if Wilhelm even remembered her birthday was coming up.

September 13th, 1942

Over the next few days, she hardly saw Wilhelm. She was beginning to hate this more and more. She didn't work and barely had things to occupy her time. She would clean the apartment that wasn't dirty, go for walks, and browse the bouquinistes, looking for a good book. All the while, in the back of her mind, she could not stop thinking about Jon, what they were doing to him, where he was, and how he was her key to their time.

After looking for a book and failing to find one at the street vendors, she watched the local men fish from one of the bridges and realized this was how she was going to be spending her birthday. Alone in the city, doing nothing of significance. Wilhelm had gone to work after they had breakfast together, but he said nothing to her about her birthday. The only thing he asked her was if she would pick up some of his shirts that were at the cleaner being steamed and starched. He told her when they would be finished and gave her the address and the slip. It upset her more than she had expected when that was all he said to her, and obviously didn't remember it was her birthday.

She rode the subway to the cleaner his shirts were at. She couldn't figure out why he had taken them to one so far away. It took over twenty minutes to get there, and it would take the same to get back. She walked into the building and stood behind two women who were there before her. After waiting over ten minutes, they were finished, and it was her turn.

Eva went to the counter and laid the slip in front of her. "I am here to pick up some shirts. The last name is Bauer."

The man picked up the slip and studied it. "Let me go get them." He laid the paper on the counter and disappeared into the back. After a few minutes, he returned without the shirts. "I'm sorry, but they aren't ready yet."

"My husband told me they would be ready."

"He was mistaken. Again, I am sorry. If you would like to wait, they should be finished soon."

"Yes, I will wait." She sat in one of the chairs in the small lobby. She observed people as they came to get their clothes and then left. She watched the man behind the counter sort through clothes, go to the back, and then return to the front, but he never brought her the shirts. After waiting for half an hour, she stood and went to the counter and rang the golden bell near the register. The man appeared from the back and stood in front of her on the other side of the counter.

"It has been half an hour. Aren't the shirts done yet?"

"I will go check." He disappeared into the back and then, a minute later, returned without the shirts. "Not yet. It should only be ten more minutes."

Eva was frustrated. What on earth was taking them so long? What a way to spend her birthday. She returned to the chair, sat down, crossed her arms over her chest, and tapped her foot on the floor. Almost twenty minutes later, the man came out of the back with four white shirts and laid them over the counter.

She stood and walked over. "What do I owe you?"

"Nothing. They were paid for when they were dropped off."

"Alright. Thank you." She took ahold of the hangers, pulled them off the counter, and draped them over her left arm. She had been there so long she was thirsty, tired, hungry, and had to pee. She would go home and eat whatever was left over from last night.

She got on the subway, laid the shirts on her lap, then leaned her head against the wall. Two soldiers got on and took the seat in front of her, and she watched them, thinking how strange it was that the sight of them was normal to her now. She finally closed her eyes as she waited for her stop. When the subway arrived at the arrondissement, she got off and climbed the long flight of stairs to the surface. She put her hand on the wall at the top to catch her breath. She got more winded now that the baby was bigger.

It was close to seven, and the sun hung low in the sky, so the street lights had already turned on. She walked the rest of the way to the apartment with the shirts, thinking she might lay down after she ate.

The guard at the door let her into the building, then she took the key from her purse and unlocked the door to the apartment. As soon as she pushed it open, she paused on the threshold as the smell of food wafted out into the foyer. She pulled her brows together in confusion, then stepped inside and closed the door. She set the shirts on the hall table along with her purse and crept to the kitchen but stopped before she got there. Looking into the dining room, she saw that the table had been set. There were candles lit in the middle and a place setting for two. She cracked a smile because she knew this had to be Wilhelm's doing. She continued to the kitchen and stopped in the entryway. Wilhelm had his sleeves rolled up and an apron tied around his waist. She crossed her arms and leaned against the doorway as she watched him pull something out of the oven. This was a sight Eva never thought she would see.

"And I thought you said you couldn't cook?" she said from the entryway.

He sat whatever he had taken from the oven on the counter and turned to her as he pulled off the hot pads. "I can't."

She smiled. "Then what are you doing?"

"Attempting to cook."

"Should I be worried?" her tone was of amusement.

"Possibly."

She unfolded her arms and went to the stove, looking down at the dish he had just taken out. It was a cake of some sort. "What kind of cake is this?"

"Oh good, you can tell it's a cake."

She laughed. "Of course."

"It's Schwarzwaelder Kirschtorte that we will have after we eat the Königsberger Klopse."

She looked at the two plates that had meatballs in gravy with piled steamed potatoes on the side. "That actually looks really good." The fact that he did remember it was her birthday and would go through all this effort to make her a meal and dessert made her feel emotional. She blinked away tears that were trying to pool in her eyes and gave him a warm smile. "Thank you."

"I called my mother, and she gave the recipe for everything and offered some advice about how to prepare it."

"No matter how it tastes, it is still better than any restaurant you could have taken me to."

"You might not say that after you've tasted it."

She shook her head. "This is still better. And it is the best gift you could have given. Being able to spend my birthday with you is exactly what I wanted."

"Who said this was your gift?"

Her face took on a perplexed expression. "I don't need anything else."

He stepped towards her and wrapped his arms around her waist, pulling her against him. "You deserve all the nice things Paris has to offer." He leaned in and kissed her on the forehead. "And you deserve all that I have to offer."

She didn't want that. She didn't want him to feel like the only way to keep her happy was to give her things. She pulled back a few inches and looked at him. "You have given me everything. My life, my freedom, a baby, your love, and even my friend Jon. As contradictory as this sounds, the only thing you can't give me is my family and my home."

He squinted his eyes at her and started to speak, but she leaned up and kissed him, placing her hand on his cheek. She pulled away and looked into his eyes. "Don't try to contradict me."

He pursed his lips and let out a long breath. "I would put you on the counter and have my way with you if the food wasn't getting cold, and if we didn't have somewhere we needed to be in," he looked at his watch, "an hour and a half."

She eyed him suspiciously. "And where do we need to be in an hour and a half?"

"Oh, that's for you to find out." He let go of her and picked up the two plates on the counter, and she followed him into the dining room. He sat them on the table, pulled the chair out for her, and then went to his own.

She watched him as she ate, and when he offered her wine, she declined and had water instead. She remembered that in the 1940s, they didn't yet know the effects alcohol had on unborn babies. "So I don't get to know anything about where we are going?"

"No." He gave her a mischievous smile, and she loved the playful manner.

After they ate dinner, he told her to wait in the dining room while he got the cake. He brought the it in along with two small plates, and sat them at the end of the dining table.

"Come here."

She stood and walked toward the end of the table, and once she was standing next to him, he took her by the shoulders and turned her so her back was facing him. He covered her eyes with his hands, and she reached up and put hers over his.

"What are you doing?"

"Relax," he whispered. "Start walking, and don't worry; I won't let you hit a wall or trip."

She let go of his hands, put hers out in front of her, and started walking. After a few seconds, he told her to stop and turn to the right, and then he had her walk a few more feet before telling her to stop again. He moved his hands, and she opened her eyes. She drew in a deep breath, bringing a hand to her open mouth.

A large American flag was hanging from the wall of the sitting room. On the coffee table were a few books in English, some American candy, and beside them, a vase filled with a mix of orchids and evening primroses. Sitting on top of the stack of books was a small wooden box. Her first reaction was shock, followed by an overwhelming sense of awe at what he had given her, and then came the guilt mixed with sadness at how he must have come to be in possession of these things. She turned around to face him, her eyes clouding with tears.

She shook her head. "Where did you get all this?"

"From American soldiers who had been fighting in Africa."

"Men who were captured or men who are dead?"

He knew why she asked. "Both, I suspect."

She didn't know if she should feel happy or let the sadness for the men who suffered so she could have these things take over. Wilhelm wanted to make her happy and give her the closest things he could to her country, and he didn't deserve her anger or frustration for trying. The only emotion she would show him was gratitude.

She slid her arms around him and kissed him softly on the lips. "Thank you. I actually was convinced you had forgotten my birthday."

He shook his head. "I forget nothing."

She let go of him, went to the flag on the wall, and rubbed her fingers along the fabric. It looked funny to her because there were only forty-eight stars on it, not fifty. And they were in neat rows, not the alternating six-star rows to the five-star rows that were on the flag in her time. But regardless, she had an American flag, and she would take it back with her if she ever went home.

"Open the box," he instructed.

She walked to the table and picked the little glossy wooden box off the books. She lifted the lid, and inside was a golden necklace. Hanging from the chain was a gold circle with writing engraved on it. She brought it closer to her face and looked at the inscription but had no idea what it said.

"What does vita mea mean?"

"It says my life in Latin."

She should have guessed that. "And why did you choose that?"

"Because you are my life, and my life belongs to you."

She pressed her lips together and rubbed her index finger over the shiny gold piece, feeling the engraved words. The sentiment was so tender, and she loved it more than any diamond he could have given her.

"Would you put it on?" She wanted him to know how much she liked it, and wearing it would be the best way to show it.

He came up to her, took the box from her hand, and removed the necklace, then laid the box on the table. She turned her back to him and pulled her hair to the side. His hands came around the front of her, then pulled the chain to the back and clasped it. She looked down at the necklace; it was cool on her skin. She turned to face him and gave a warm smile.

"I will always wear it."

He kissed the top of her head. "Let's eat our cake so we can go."

"I still think you should tell me where we are going."

"Not a chance."

After they ate their cake, they went outside to a waiting car. It hadn't been there when she came home, so he must have told his orderly what time to be at the apartment. Wilhelm opened the back door and then slid in after her. The car drove down Avenue Foch to the Arc de Triomphe, went through the roundabout, turned down Avenue d'Iéna, took it all the way to the Seine, and then turned onto Pont d'Iéna Bridge. The car pulled off on the side of the street of Quai Jacques Chirac next to the Eiffel Tower.

"Are we going up in the Eiffel Tower?" She looked from the window at him.

"You think I would tell now that I am so close to showing you?"

"I guess not."

He opened the door and stepped out, holding his hand for her. She took it, and he helped her from the car, then looped her hand through his bent elbow, and they walked together toward the Eiffel Tower. There was a lot of noise coming from the grounds around the tower, the voices of many people, and the sounds of other things. She looked up at him, and he smiled. The anticipation was building, but her question was soon answered as they stepped onto the gravel walkway leading to the tower. Under the Eiffel Tower was a very large red and white striped tent, and the area around the tower was covered with smaller tents with various rides from bumper cars to a carousel, and in the middle of it all was a Ferris wheel. It was a carnival set up on the grounds around the Eiffel Tower.

She didn't even try to hide her shock and excitement. Her mouth was open, and she slowly turned to look at Wilhelm. "I haven't been to a circus since I was a child."

"Well, now you can experience one as an adult."

She felt like it was too much, everything he had done for her birthday. But she loved it even more because it was his way of showing he cared.

She took his hand and pulled on it. "What are you waiting for? Let's go." She could see the pleasure on his face at her excitement. "Where should we go first?" There was so much she wanted to do.

"It's your birthday, you decide."

"Alright. Let's ride the Ferris wheel."

He grinned at her. "You know what Ferris wheels are for, don't you?"

She gave him a side glance. "Besides riding, should I?"

"They are for couples to make out."

She raised her brow. "Are they?"

She led him to the ticket booth and asked the man in the box for two tickets. As she was getting money from her purse, Wilhelm handed the man some cash. "I was going to pay for those," she protested.

"Eva, my money is your money now too? Besides, any money you have in your purse is most likely what you made while being a nurse, and that money belongs to you."

She found his views so strange, but he was right. She nodded and took the two tickets from the man's outstretched hand. They found a seat on the Ferris wheel, and when they sat down, it rocked back and forth. It was small, and they had to sit close; she liked it. She laid her hand on his leg, and he put his hand on top of hers. The Ferris wheel jerked, and all the chairs rocked, then it started to move.

"Have you ever been on a Ferris wheel before?" she asked.

"No."

"Then how do you know what they are for?"

"I just do." He leaned in and kissed her, and she felt his lips moving against hers. He pulled away and looked at her; in his eyes, she could see how much he cared for her. He turned his head and then pointed. "Look."

She turned to see what he was pointing at. They were at the top now, and you could see over the entire circus with all the lights blinking, some white and some multicolored, and it was amazing. Farther out, you could see the city of Paris lit up like diamonds, reflecting off the Seine. She knew it would soon close because of the lights out, and all the magic of it would be over.

When the Ferris wheel stopped, they went to the cotton candy tent, and he got them one that they shared. "Maybe we can do the bumper cars now."

He started to say something, then paused before finally speaking. "No, I don't think that is a good idea for you."

She thought about saying something to that but then reconsidered. She tried to go through the list of things pregnant women were told to avoid but couldn't remember if that was one of them. In her time, she knew that water slides were a no, as were roller coasters, so maybe he was right. Bumper cars did jerk and bump you around a lot, hence their name.

"Maybe the carousel then...?"

"Sure, we can do the carousel."

They stepped up on it, and she chose a white horse, and he picked the zebra beside it. She held onto the pole and watched him as they moved up and down. It was strange to see him like this, relaxed, playful, in civilian clothes, and not as this scary, intimidating person. She liked this side of him and wished that other people could see him as she did.

They watched the elephant show and the juggling, and then the last thing they did before it was time to leave was dart throwing. Wilhelm won her a brown teddy bear by popping eight of the ten balloons. She held onto it as they walked back to the car.

When they were home, she put the bear in the room that would be the baby's, then showered and went to bed. It was the best birthday she could have asked for, but she was tired and wanted to fall asleep in Wilhelm's arms. That would be the perfect ending to her birthday.

Chapter Eleven

September 18th, 1942

"It just isn't the same without you there," Ingrid said as she sipped her tea.

"You know I would love to go back if I could. But even if Wilhelm didn't oppose it, the hospital wouldn't hire me, not with me being pregnant."

"I realize that, but you were such a good nurse. Somedays, I turn around and expect to see you there, but at least I can visit you now that I live in Paris."

"How are you liking your apartment?"

She snorted out a laugh. "Well, it certainly isn't as nice as yours. I think it might be the size of this room."

Eva looked around. "Trust me when I say it was not my idea to live here."

"You are crazy if you don't like it. I would love to live somewhere so nice."

"But it's not real. What I mean is it won't last. The Allies will eventually take back Paris, and then I will no longer be living here."

Ingrid's demeanor was now uncomfortable. "We don't know that."

"Yes, Ingrid, I do."

"Do you share your thoughts with Wilhelm?" she asked in a tone suggesting Eva was crazy if she did.

"Of course not." She checked her watch. "I have to go. I'm meeting the Stopford wives in twenty minutes."

"The who?"

"Oh, it's just a name I call the other officer's wives that I meet on Thursdays."

"Why do you call them that?"

"It's a joke we have in America. It wouldn't make sense to you. But if you hear me say that, you know who I'm talking about."

"You are meeting with other German officers' wives? That doesn't sound like you."

"I only go because Wilhelm thinks it's good for me to socialize." She laid on the sarcasm at the last word.

"Speaking of Wilhelm, how are you finding married life?"

"Well, it's not how I imagined it would be."

"How do you mean?"

"It's just not how my life was."

She couldn't tell Ingrid that in her time, women worked and didn't stay at home to make dinner for their husbands, clean the house, and tend to his needs. Unlike this time, when men had all the control, and women had no say. In her time, that would not be tolerated in most developed countries.

"Not working, for one thing, is strange for me. Sometimes, I don't know what to do with my days."

"I can see how that would be hard. But I personally would love to be in your shoes."

"Ingrid, I'll try to come by to see you at the hospital soon. I can't work there with you, but I can at least see the hospital."

"I would love it if you did."

Eva saw her out and then took the subway to the restaurant where she was meeting the women. It was a different restaurant than the last one and farther away, but she didn't mind. Eva was happy it wasn't just lunch today; plans had been made to visit a museum afterward. She had never been to any museums in Paris and was excited to see one. There was a lot in Paris that she still hadn't experienced, and she now had time to.

She stepped off the subway at the Quartier des peupliers and took the stairs to the top. She spotted the women waiting at an outside table in front of the restaurant. This time, she didn't hesitate but took a seat without waiting for them to invite her to do so.

As they had lunch, she learned the others couldn't make it to the museum, that it would only be her and Lorelei going.

"My husband is out of town, so my calendar is pretty empty," Lorelei said.

"Mine is pretty open too."

"It's a shame when a young bride is left alone so often, especially a pregnant one."

Eva forced a smile. "I would like it if I saw him more."

"I'm sure you would."

"My husband is taking me to the opera tonight," Anna announced joyfully.

The mention of the Paris Opera House caused a stab of pain in Eva's heart. She vowed to herself she would never go there again, not even with Wilhelm. She wanted the memories she made with Wilhelm to be new and in new places.

After lunch, she said her goodbyes to the other three women and walked with Lorelei to the museum. "Have you been here before?" Eva asked.

"Oh yes, many times. You haven't?"

"No. There are actually a lot of things in Paris I haven't seen."

"Well, if your husband is too busy to take you, I would be more than happy to go with you to see the sites of Paris."

"That would be nice. I might take you up on that offer."

"Please do."

The Le Petit Palais Museum was made of white stone and a grand set of stairs that led up to a large entryway covered by a dome. The front of the building was long and flat, but the rest was curved into a circle that enclosed an atrium. Part of the roof was glass, offering a skylight over the displays to give a certain mystique to the art. It was nowhere near the size of the Louvre but was beautiful in itself and a hidden gem of Paris. It looked like a palace to her, with high arched ceilings covered in Greek-style paintings, pillars that held up the corner arches of the rooms, and the winding marble staircase with its black metal railing twisted into elaborate shapes that led to the top. Eva loved the atmosphere of the building and the warmth of the sun shining down on them from above. It was a beautiful place. Most of the art was sculptures, but there were a few galleries with paintings from 19th-century French artists to Italian Renaissance oil canvases of Madonna and Child.

"How many times have you been here?" Eva asked Lorelei.

"Oh, maybe a dozen." She gave a crooked smile as she glanced around the long hall, admiring the painting that covered the walls.

"I can see why. Have you been to the Louvre?"

"Yes. Have you?"

"Sadly, no. I haven't even gone up the Eiffel Tower. But I would like to do that with Wilhelm."

"Of course. It's romantic." Eva's cheeks flushed a light shade of pink. "But if you want, we can go to the Louvre sometime together."

"Maybe next week."

"I will plan on it." She looked at Eva sidelong. "Are you happy here?"

"Yes, I love France," Eva said with a smile as she scanned the beauty of the art around her.

"No, I mean in occupied France? And being married to a German?"

Eva's face fell, and now she was guarded. "Oh. I mean, it has its challenges."

"Sure, sure. You must love him very much to have married him and given up your home for his."

"I don't know if that is what I did."

"But you have. And you solidified Germany as your home the moment you became pregnant with his child."

Eva stared at her, surprised and confused by her words. She wasn't sure what point she was trying to make. "Maybe he would move to America someday with me."

"No, dear, he won't. If you ever go home, it will be alone."

She needed to know this woman's reasons for telling her this. "I don't understand. Why do you think he wouldn't come with me?"

"His home is here. And he has given so much for Germany, do you think he would leave it all behind?"

Eva thought about her question. "I guess it depends on why he would be leaving."

"He wouldn't leave by choice." She eyed Eva. "Do you think that your country would let him immigrate there anyway?"

An uncomfortable, breathy laugh escaped her lips. "I'm not sure because I don't know what the laws are."

"It's not about the laws of immigration; it's about who he is. They wouldn't let him come over and live a happy life with you and your child. They would arrest him and put him on trial for war crimes. That is the ending you would get, not a fairytale. Let me ask you something else. If you had the opportunity to go home right now, would you?"

"Uh...I...don't know." She felt like she was being interrogated. What was this woman hoping to learn?

"Of course, you don't. It's a hard decision for you to make now that you are married to a German and are going to have his baby. But really, it comes down to where your loyalties lie."

Eva was uncomfortable now. "Did my husband set this up? Did he send you here to ask me these questions?" The anger rose above the controlled calmness she was able to maintain a second ago.

"Heavens, no," she chuckled. "I'm just pointing out who you are because you seem to be confused about who that is. You don't have to pretend in front of me that you are loyal to Germany and its causes just because you are married to a high-ranking German officer. You might fool Anna, Petra, and Amelia, but the wool isn't pulled over my eyes so easily. Your country is where your loyalties lie."

Eva didn't know what was happening. She wasn't sure why Lorelei was asking these kinds of questions, and it made her feel afraid. The nature of the questions and the things Lorelei said sent a chill through her like a ghost had just walked over her grave. "I don't want to have this conversation anymore."

She turned to walk away, but Lorelei caught her arm. "Please, don't be so hasty to leave."

Eva looked at her hand on her arm. "Let go of me."

Lorelei didn't let go but drew closer. "Have you been to the Arènes de Lutèce?"

Eva found her question odd and out of place with what was happening. "No."

"It's on 49 rue de Monge. We will finish our visit through the museum as planned, and then we will part ways. At ten o'clock on Monday morning, you will meet me on the steps of the Arènes de Lutèce."

"And why would I do that?"

"Because you want to know what it is I have to say."

Eva pulled her arm away and eyed her with distrust. "Who are you?"

"Lorelei Vogel," she gave Eva a calm, pleasant smile.

"I know your name. I meant, who are you on the inside?"

"Come on Monday, and I'll tell you." She looped her arm through Eva's and started pulling her along. "Let's walk. People are watching us."

Eva self-consciously glanced around the room, noticing a few people at the far end staring in their direction. "How do you know you can trust me?"

"I have a way of reading people. When you go home tonight, mention none of this to your husband. Do you understand?"

"Yes."

"Good."

They walked arm in arm through the rest of the museum, then separated just outside as if nothing had transpired. Eva watched this older woman walk away in utter bewilderment. Who was she? What did she want? And why did she seem to think she was interested in whatever she had to say? But she would keep her word and not mention this to Wilhelm.

All that night, Eva couldn't stop thinking about the cryptic conversation with Lorelei. The woman had seemed eager to befriend her, and now she was starting to think she knew why. She rolled onto her left side and looked at Wilhelm, lying still as he slumbered beside her. She couldn't get the woman's words out of her head about what would happen to Wilhelm at the end of the war if Germany lost or if he emigrated to America. The words haunted her, and she fought back the worry that was rising inside. The fear of losing him was real, and it scared her more than anything. She hadn't known it before, but her love for him was more precious than her own life.

She placed her hand on his arm and rubbed it softly with her fingertips. She could feel the muscles under his skin and the arm hair moving with the motion. She moved her hand to his and laced her fingers through his, holding tightly. She knew Lorelei was wrong because she would stay for him. He was where her loyalties lay.

When she woke, Wilhelm was gone, but a piece of paper was on his side of the bed. She sat up and took it from the comforter, unfolding it.

Eva,
Stay home today. Make sure you are ready by noon.

Wilhelm

Why was everyone being so cryptic as of late? She looked at the clock on the nightstand. It was just after nine. She got out of bed, ate some breakfast, took a shower, and did her makeup and hair. Either he had something planned for her at noon, or something was happening before noon that he didn't want her to know about, but then why would he tell her to be ready? She was planning on visiting Ingrid at the hospital, but that would have to wait now.

She went to the living room and looked at the English books Wilhelm had given her for her birthday. She picked up the first one and read the title. It was *As I Lay Dying* by William Faulkner.

The second book she picked up was *Burmese Days* by George Orwell, the third book was *Brave New World* by Aldous Huxley, and the fourth was *The Grapes of Wrath* by John Steinbeck. The last one was *South Riding* by Winifred Holtby. That one she had never heard of, but the others were classics in her time. She decided to start reading The Grapes of Wrath. She had never actually read the book or watched the movie, but she remembered her parents owned the film on VHS when she was little. She sat on the couch and covered up with a blanket, then opened the book to the first page.

She was on chapter eight when a knock came from the front door. She looked at her watch, and it read eight minutes till twelve. She laid the book on the coffee table and moved the blanket, placing it on the couch, then stood and went to the door. Whoever it was had got past the guard, so Wilhelm must have sent them. She opened the door, and Wilhelm's orderly was standing just on the other side.

"Frau Bauer, I am here to pick you up."

"To take me where?"

"Your husband's office."

"Why?"

"He didn't say."

So this wasn't a date. If he was having her brought to his office, then it was something else, something formal, work-related. She wondered if it had anything to do with Lorelei.

"Let me get my purse."

She closed the door and took a second to calm her nerves, then retrieved her purse from the hall table and opened the door again. Wilhelm's orderly was still there waiting for her. She followed

176

him outside, and he opened the back door of Wilhelm's black military car. She slid in and put her purse on her lap, holding tightly onto it as she waited in the backseat. His orderly got in the front and started the engine, then pulled out onto the street. They weren't far from the Gestapo headquarters, so it only took a few minutes to get there. The car pulled in front of the building, and then the orderly got out, opening her door. He walked her to the front, and the man at the door led her inside to a chair in the hall and instructed her to wait.

German soldiers were everywhere as she eyed her surroundings, her gaze lighting on a flag with the swastika flying in the distance through the window. Her eyes bore into the black, red, and white as it danced with the breeze, but a noise pulled from her from the intense focus. A few doors down were two young soldiers leaning against the wall in their pressed uniforms and freshly polished boots, chatting about something as they each smoked a cigarette. The men stopped talking for a second and looked in her direction, then leaned in close to say something to one another. She suspected they were talking about her.

The door just to her left was open, and male voices came from inside, but neither of them was Wilhelm. She leaned farther to her left and turned her head so she could listen.

"You're lucky you have an influential father," one man said, his tone thick with ire. "If he didn't hold such a high position in the navy, his pleas would not have held as much sway. And he somehow managed to find a position for you even though you have been stripped of all your rank. But trust me, you would be better placed with a company of hardened Russians because your last commanding officer's punishment was child's play compared to your new commanding officer. He has a reputation for disciplining the disloyal most severely. Your last officer's skill, notoriety, and punishment don't compare to your new officer's. He doesn't have the same... flair for brutality."

"Who is he?" She could hear the nervousness in the young man's voice.

"SS Obersturmbannführer Bauer. He is currently attending to some other matters, so consider yourself lucky. Because if he wasn't, it would be him talking to you now and not me. Report to Lieutenant Ludwig, and he will get you settled. And I warn you, no more slips ups you don't want him punishing you."

The sound of heels clicking together and then heavy footsteps on the wooden floor echoed into the hall. The man walked out of the office, not looking her way, but headed towards the front of the building. Eva sat with her hands under her legs and tapped her feet on the floor as she waited. The anticipation was gnawing at her, eating away slowly at her resolve. Finally, the door opened to Wilhelm's office, and a soldier stepped out, holding the door open as he stood in the doorway and looked at her.

"You can come in now. He is almost finished."

She quickly stood and walked behind the man into the office. There were several other soldiers in the room talking with Wilhelm. When she entered, he looked from the men to her. He said a few words to one of them, handed him a piece of paper, and then briskly dismissed all in the room, leaving the two of them alone in the imposing office. He leveled his deep hazel gaze on her rapture hard.

"I am going to let you see Jon today. In a minute, I will have him brought into the office," Wilhelm stated, his keen eyes trained on her as if gauging her reaction.

A heavy silence hung in the air. There was a sense of relief in knowing what this was about, but it was quickly replaced with trepidation at the idea of seeing Jon again. And she didn't know if she would see him alone or if Wilhelm would be in the room with them. As uncomfortable as it was, she had to ask.

"And will this be a private visit, or will we have a guard?" Her voice was shaky as she held Wilhelm's penetrating gaze.

"That depends. What are your intentions when you speak with him?" Wilhelm was lethally calm.

"To catch up with an old friend, find out how he is, and hopefully learn something about my family."

Wilhelm rose from his chair, strode to the door, and opened it. He called to someone in the hall, and a soldier appeared in front of him. "Bring the prisoner in."

"Yes Obersturmbannführer."

The man disappeared, and Eva looked from the empty doorway to Wilhelm. Her nerves shot. His expression was unreadable, and she wished so much she knew what he was thinking. Multiple sets of footsteps echoed in the hall coming towards the office and Eva tensed. In walked Jon, his hands cuffed in front of him, and holding onto his arm was the soldier who went to retrieve him. Wilhelm nodded to the soldier, who then turned and left the office, closing the door behind him. Wilhelm pulled a key from his pocket and took a firm hold of Jon's right hand, stuck the key in the small keyhole, and unlocked it. He removed the cuffs from Jon's wrists, then walked back to his desk and casually sat on the front corner.

Jon wrapped his left hand around his right wrist, rubbing where the cuffs were. He looked at Wilhelm and then around the room, his gaze finally resting on Eva. His eyes flooded with bewilderment, and it took him off guard to see her and to see her in the condition she was in.

"Why am I here?" Jon asked.

"So you can visit with Eva," Wilhelm said, a challenge in his tone and a warning in his eyes.

Jon looked from Wilhelm to Eva, his eyes fixed on her. "It's a trick. It has to be. Some game he is playing; he wouldn't let me see you otherwise."

Eva eyed him with confusion and shook her head, trying to get him to stop talking.

He turned back to Wilhelm, astonished. "Why did you bring her here? Why did you involve her in this?" he demanded, unable to keep the surprise and obvious anger from his voice.

Wilhelm's eyes tightened with a calculating expression that indicated he could see the true Jon now. "It is not a trick or a game," he said slowly in English, a heavy German accent thick with every word. "She asked to see you, and I told her I would arrange it. And I didn't involve her in this, but I suspect you did. You are undoubtedly why she was in Europe in the first place. So, if you want to blame someone for her situation, then you should consider your own actions." He stood from the desk and walked across the room to Eva. He took her hand and leaned in, planting a soft kiss on her cheek. "You have thirty minutes." His breath was warm on her ear, and she could feel his lips brush against the

180

skin, sending shivers through her. He let go of her hand and gave her a look that confused her. His expression wasn't hard, but in his eyes, there was a caution she didn't understand.

Once he had left the room and closed the door, she rushed to Jon, and they embraced, holding on to one another as all the fear, anxiety, pain, longing for home, and suffering that she had endured coalesced into one overpowering tide of emotions that hit her like a sea wall. She gripped the back of Jon's sweater with both hands and cried, and he cried with her.

When she finally felt more in control of herself, she pulled away and looked at Jon's face. He was thin but appeared to be in relatively good health. "Come, let's sit down." She led him to the two chairs at Wilhelm's desk, sat in one, and pulled Jon down into the other. He studied her, his eyes focusing on her stomach. Finally, he looked up at her, his face full of questions.

"Yes," she answered, knowing what his first question would be.

He looked away from her and scanned the office, taking in the gravity of both of their situations. "Before I left England to come to France, I studied everything I could about this time. I read all about the German officers stationed here, what they did, and what part of the country they were in so that I could learn who I would potentially be dealing with. And I have read about SS Obersturmbannführer Bauer. He is as conniving as he is dangerous. So what cruel game does he have us playing?"

"He isn't playing a game, Jon. Just as he said."

"I can see that. When they first brought me in, and I noticed you and your condition, I wondered why you would ever sleep with him unless it was to save your life or he forced himself on

181

you? But then I saw how you were with him while ago, just before he left the room. And I realized you are here with him of your own accord because you want to be."

She didn't know what to say to this because he was correct in everything he said. "It wasn't always so," she told him, hoping he believed her. "For the longest time, we hated each other, but things kept happening that brought us together, over and over, no matter how much I fought it. And he saved me so many times. Jon, if you only knew the things he has done for me."

"When I wrote to you, telling you there was a German who could help you, I wasn't talking about him. I later learned his name. It was a man called Gerhardt von Schulz. He was the person who I wrote to you about. Whatever happened with him?"

Eva's eyes teared up at the mention of Gerhardt. "He did help me, but he is now missing on the Russian front. He has not been a part of my life for a long time, Jon." He looked away, and she watched him stare down at his hands. They were wrapped in white gauze, covering the missing fingers. "What happened, Jon?"

"Do you mean, how did I lose my fingers?"

"I mean everything. What has happened while I've been gone? What have you been doing? How is my family? Are they worried?"

"Eva, I don't even know where to begin."

She looked at the clock on the wall. "We don't have long to visit, so we need to tell each other as much as we can."

He nodded in understanding. "I have not stopped trying to find you. But the others, they aren't sure about you coming back now."

Her pulse spiked. "What do you mean?"

182

"They think it could change too much if you did or have unforeseen consequences."

"Why would they think that? What could it possibly change?"

"It's just a theory. They don't even know about the baby. I'm not sure they would let you come back if they did. Technically, it is a person from the past, and you would be bringing them to the future. You aren't supposed to bring anyone with you from this time to ours."

"Do they even know what's been happening?"

"They don't know I've been captured, and I have no way of letting them know."

"So they want to just leave me here?" Her nostrils flared in anger and disgust.

"In a word, yes. But it's more complicated than that. But don't worry, we will go back together."

"How? We are both trapped here now, and they won't know when to open the portal for us."

"I was leaving notes for Dr. Brandt. He has probably noticed they have stopped and knows something is wrong by now. But he won't give up on me, and I won't give up on you."

"And my family? What do they think has happened to me?"

He sighed. "I had to come up with a story to tell them. I didn't want them to think you were dead because I didn't believe you were, so I told them you had been kidnapped. We weren't sure by whom, but we thought it might be sex traffickers."

"What?" She looked away from Jon and to the window, trying to real in her emotions; the gray clouds were all she could see as she digested this. "They must be terrified for me, thinking I'm fighting for my life."

"What did you want me to do? I couldn't talk to you and ask what lie would be more convenient for me to tell your family. So, I came up with one on my own, one that I thought was believable. The only other thing I could have told them that would make sense was that you ran away, but I'm sure you didn't want that to contend with when you returned home. With the story I gave them, you can always fall back on the emotional trauma and tell them you don't want to talk about it. They won't push you. They will be sympathetic."

She tried to be understanding. Jon really was left with few options, and would any other lie have been better? "Thank you. I understand it must have been hard for you, telling someone that kind of news."

"It was. They have started a donation fund to find you. You have been featured on the news. The authorities have been notified, and they have even started a Facebook page. They have gone above and beyond and won't give up until you are found."

The anguish her family and friends must be going through tore her up inside. To think that she has been kidnapped. But was the lie actually worse than the truth? Her life was in constant peril, although she wasn't being kept as a slave and used for sex. She could freely walk around and was with someone she loved. The thought of returning and trying to explain things to the people she knew back home was almost as scary to her now as the thought of staying in the 1940s.

She creased her brows and focused on Jon's face. "A Facebook page? Oh, God. I don't even know how I will begin to deal with all of this if I go home." She looked at the clock again. They had less than fifteen minutes. "Do you know where they are keeping you?" This was something she could deal with in the moment.

"I do. It's here in France. It's called Saint-Denis. It's an internment camp for British and American civilians."

"I know it," she said, astonished. "It's just north of Paris."

"Yes. After they released me from prison, I was sent to a transit camp for about a week. I learned of these places while doing research. These camps serve as a collection point for POWs prior to reassignment. They are intelligence collection centers, basically. Most of the people who go to these places are soldiers they interrogate, so it is odd that they sent me there too."

She leaned in close and gently took his hands in hers. "I promise I will get you out."

He looked down at their hands and, for the first time, noticed the ring on her finger. He lifted her hand closer for inspection. "Eva, please tell me this does not mean you married him?"

She pulled her hand away and folded her arms across her chest. "You wouldn't understand."

"Oh, Eva. Are you turning a blind eye to how they are, or have you truly been deceived? The German military is ruthless and brutal. They murder their victims without mercy. I read that they killed a man just because they wanted his bike. That is the kind of people they are."

"They are not all like that. I have lived amongst them for years, and I promise you that they are people just like everyone else."

"Not just like everyone else, not all of them. Not the man you married. When I wrote you that letter telling you to seek the help of a German, did you think I was talking about him?"

"At first, I wasn't sure, but then I thought about the fact that he helped me before and how Gerhardt was already gone from my life. I assumed Wilhelm must be who you were referring to."

Jon shook his head and covered his face with his bandaged hand. "This is incredible. I had seen that a German helped you, so I told you to seek him out, but you went to the wrong person, who I believe now is the one I saw in our time who helped you. Only, I thought it was the other guy because he helped you once before. If I had not told you to seek this guy's help, you would not have gone to the wrong person. Therefore, I never would have seen it to tell you to do it in the first place."

She shook her head. "I don't understand what you are saying?"

"I'm saying I caused it to happen." Jon moved his hand in a circular motion as he thought about his words. "Sort of like a self-fulfilling prophecy. I caused you to do the thing I saw. I told you what to do, which led to your actions, and then it got recorded in history for me to see in the future to tell you to do."

"Stop. My head hurts. You are saying if you had never instructed me to seek out the help of this German officer, I never would have gone to Wilhelm?"

"Yes."

"But how do you know I would not have gone to him anyway?"

"I don't. But now, we will never know. It shows us how important even the smallest events are, or one decision can be to how things turn out. And how much people's choices really do matter."

"My life is certainly on a course I never expected it to be on. But as crazy as this sounds, I am happy. For the first time since being here. Wilhelm would never hurt me and promised that he would not let anything happen to me."

"It's a promise he may not be able to keep, even if he wanted to."

"I understand that, but he will uphold it to his best ability. He has helped me at the risk of his own well-being and reputation. I owe him my life, Jon. You have no idea what I have been through. Even just living in Berlin was dangerous. There were bombings constantly."

"Most of the time, you have been in mainland Europe and I was in London. Not in our time, but this time. Your experiences have all been on this side, but mine was on the receiving end of the Germans. The people of London have been through a lot. And like you, I have been through a lot too. In 1940, there were fifty-seven straight nights of bombings. They rained down on us like fire from the heavens, and every night, I watched the city burn and heard the sirens echo as a reminder that I could be next."

The pain she felt inside for Jon spiked. She never considered how much Jon had been through or how much he had suffered. She had always been so caught up in her own struggles. She assumed Jon was safe in their time, or at least in England and away from the worst part of the war, only now learning that he stayed for her. To find a way to get her out of Europe, risking his own life to do so. Tears freely streamed down her cheeks. "Jon, I didn't know. You should not have stayed." She looked at the clock to see that their time was almost up. "I wish we had more time because there is so much to say, but we don't. Remember what I said. I will find a way to free you."

"How? You are not even free. You aren't locked up, but you are still a prisoner, just like me."

"No, Jon, not like you. I am not trapped here physically the way you are. I am only a prisoner in my heart. I stay because I choose to."

"I feared that would happen. When you became trapped here, I worried that you would fall in love with a German or French man or become a victim of this war. But I see that you have become both."

She searched for the meaning of his words, but they didn't make sense to her. "How have I become a victim to both? I'm not dead."

"You fell in love with a German, one to whom you will be punished for attaching yourself. Eva, I don't know if any of us will live to see the sunset of this war, including him."

This was a possibility she tried not to think about. "I know. But right now, you are the one we need to worry about. Getting you out of that POW camp is my main concern. You are the only one that can get us both home."

"How will you get me out? I don't see a way you can do that." Jon looked towards the door. "He won't free me. I think if it came between freeing me or executing me, he would choose the latter."

Eva couldn't argue with that because she didn't know if he was wrong. In all likelihood, he could be right. "I know he won't, but I wasn't planning on him releasing you. I'm hoping to get you out another way, myself."

His face tensed with concern. "No, Eva. I don't want you to risk your life trying to free me. Do you know how dangerous that will be? They would have you and me both killed."

"There is no changing my mind. I'm going to get you out, even if that means at the risk of my own life."

"What about the risk to your baby's life?"

She pursed her lips into a hard line, conflicted over Jon's life and her baby's. She had to get Jon out, but preferably not at the risk of her baby. Maybe she wouldn't be caught. At the very least, she could see if it was even possible. "You will both be safe."

Just as Jon opened his mouth to protest, the door opened, and Wilhelm walked in. "Your time is up." He was calm, but there was agitation etched in his voice. He motioned for the guards to enter, and two men hastened into the room and pulled Jon from the chair, placing the cuffs back on his wrists.

He turned to look at Eva, and the fear was written on his face. They still had almost eight minutes to visit, and she didn't know why Wilhelm was taking him early. "Wait," she called, holding her hand out to stop the men. She looked at Wilhelm, trying to understand. "You said thirty minutes."

"I did, but something pressing has come up, and I need my office." He motioned for the men to take Jon away. They pulled him from the room as he craned his neck to keep Eva in view as long as he could, then he was gone, and the door closed. Wilhelm crossed his arms and leaned against his desk. "What did you talk about?"

She was struggling to come up with a plausible answer, but the words were getting tangled in the back of her throat. "We...uh, talked about my life since I've been here. He told me how he had been and about my family. They don't know what has happened to me and are worried sick."

"Why don't you write to them and I will see that they get it. Just so they know you are alright. I understand their worry. I can't imagine what I would do if you disappeared from my life and I had no idea where you were or if you were safe."

It worried her constantly the thought of what might happen to him at the end of the war, but she never really gave much thought that he worried about losing her. "I will try not to disappear."

He gave a smile that didn't reach his eyes. "Good. You know I will have to read any letter before I send it?"

"I do." This was a complication she had not foreseen. She could not have a letter sent to her parents in this time. The house they live in hasn't even been built yet. It wasn't constructed until the mid-1970s, so where would she have him send it? "I will try to write one soon." She glanced to the door and then back to Wilhelm. Jon's situation bothered her more than Wilhelm knew, and she was angry with the world at how cruel it could be. "Will I see him again?"

He coughed out a contemptuous laugh as he threw her a severe look. "No, Eva." His smile was gone, and something resembling jealousy flashed in his eyes. He looked away, his jaw clicking. "I thought letting you see him would get that out of your system. I hoped it would be enough."

She wanted to scream at him but could only do so in her mind. "Get it out of my system? Be enough? He is my friend, and friends don't abandon each other. He didn't abandon me, and I will not leave him. I don't understand why I can't see him again," she said, her voice high with outrage as the words came faster than she had expected.

He turned his head to the side and narrowed his eyes at her. "I have told you once before. I love you, but I don't trust you."

She honestly could not blame him for not trusting her. She had never given him many reasons to trust her but plenty of reasons not to. "I do understand why. But I hope you can see that I am just trying to protect my friend."

"I can see that you aren't telling me the whole story."

"I would never ask another favor of you if it wasn't life or death or of the utmost importance to me. I acknowledge that you have saved my life at least three times, possibly more, and that Jurgen would have raped me in the garden if you had not stopped him. Or that living in a camp would be my life now or ended my life if not for you." Wilhelm's mouth tensed as he stared at her, a stark realization taking hold. "I owe you my life, but I also owe so much to Jon."

Wilhelm cut her a glare. "You would not have died in the camp, Eva."

"I might as well be dead if I were sent there."

"No," he said, shaking his head. "You would have found a way to fight and survive."

"Maybe, but you were right not to tell me what you were doing. When you were deceiving me for my protection, you were being a friend to me. Just like I am being a friend to Jon."

Wilhelm let out a long breath and lost the last traces of his antagonistic demeanor. "What do you want me to say? You know I can't allow contact between you and a POW to continue." Wilhelm studied her, his expression searching. "I might," he held a finger in the air, "let you see him one last time," he finally said, his voice low. "But now you must go because I have a lot to do."

Tears burned in her eyes as she pulled in a shaky breath. She was overcome with gratitude and wanted to find some way to express it. "Thank you," she said, but her words seemed woefully inadequate for the debt she owed him. She knew this would not be enough either, but it was all she could do right now. She took four long strides in his direction and stopped in front of him, then took his face in her hands and kissed him on the lips passionately.

He put a hand on her lower back and pressed her to him, then after a few seconds, he broke the kiss. "My orderly will take you home now."

She looked into his eyes and knew she could never repay him for everything, but she would try even if it took her the rest of her life.

Chapter Twelve
ॐ

September 21st, 1942

Eva stopped at the top of the Arènes de Lutèce and looked at the circle of old Roman stone seats surrounding it, trying to find Lorelei. She spotted her sitting on the far side, reading a book. Eva carefully took one step at a time until she was at the bottom, then walked across the dirt center and up the other side. She didn't remove her hands from her pockets but stopped in front of Lorelei and looked down at her, clearing her throat.

Lorelei lifted her head from the book and gave Eva a look that indicated she wasn't surprised to see her. She laid the book on her lap and nodded to the spot next to her.

Eva sat down and turned so she could face Lorelei. "OK, why am I here?"

Lorelei looked out over the Roman arena. "Isn't it amazing, all the things the Romans built? And to think some of it still remains today."

"I know you didn't ask me here to talk about Roman architecture. So why don't you tell me why I'm really here?"

Ignoring Eva's comment, she continued. "The things they built weren't even their greatest achievement. The truly amazing thing was how they conquered most of the known world in their time."

"Why are we talking about the Romans?"

"Because. The German empire has a lot in common with the ancient Romans. They are both remarkable at science, industry, the rate of production, and their soldiers are some of the best in the world. The most dedicated and well-trained, and I am not saying that to discredit the soldiers from the Axis countries, but it is the truth. The Romans were very totalitarian, and so is the German government now. I know you do not agree with what Germany is doing or like it, but because you are trapped here, you have no choice but to keep silent and pretend to go along with it." She finally looked at Eva.

She had to think very carefully about how to respond because this could be a trap. Lorelei could be baiting her, trying to get her to say something she could use against her. "I am content being here with Wilhelm."

"I'm sure you love him, but you are not content being here."

"What is this, Lorelei? Is this a trick? I am not going to say another word to you unless you tell me why we are here and what it is that you are really trying to say."

"I think I have a proposition for you."

"No, I will not help the resistance." She could not get mixed up in that again. Especially now that she was pregnant.

194

J.L. Robison

Lorelei laughed in a high-pitched tone. "No, dear, I am not with the resistance."

"Then what do you want?"

"No, I don't work with them." She glanced around to make sure that they were alone. "I work with the British. I help them get agents in and out of Germany."

Eva could not hide her surprise at this. "Why? I don't understand why you would betray your own country and help the Allied countries."

"Because if it wasn't for my country's choices, my sons would still be alive. I was a loyal German through the First World War and have tried now through this one. But I can't any longer. I can't bring my boys back, but maybe I can help save another mother's son."

Eve understood now and couldn't say that she wouldn't do the same. "I see now, but what can I do?"

"You are married to the man in charge of all the law enforcement and most of the comings and goings of this fine country we find ourselves in."

Eva shook her head vehemently. "No... no, I will not do that again. I did once before and almost lost everything. I will not spy on my husband."

Lorelei took hold of Eva's arm. "I am not asking you to do that. I am not asking you to spy on your husband. The only thing you would have to do is know his schedule."

Eva was growing frustrated with the conversation. "Why Lorelei? Why would I need to know his schedule?"

"So he never comes home to find you gone when you are supposed to be there. You wouldn't be able to answer his

195

questions concerning your absence. There is no reason you should be out past curfew unless you are with him, doing something illegal, or—."

"I can't, Lorelei. I'm sorry."

"I was going to say or with me."

Eva raised an eyebrow. "You can't stay out past curfew either?"

"Yes. I do it all the time, and no one bats an eye at it."

"And I would be doing what?"

"You have medical training, and that is something we desperately need. You can also tell us if your husband is in the office or out in the field. All you have to do is call his office."

Eva frowned. "It would look suspicious if I started calling him all the time."

"Then perhaps you should start. Besides, isn't that what a newly married bride would do? Wouldn't it be normal for her to miss her husband, who is always gone?"

Eva chewed on the inside of her cheek, thinking. "That might work, but Wilhelm might see right through it."

"Maybe not. If you started doing it now, it wouldn't look strange in the future when you need to learn if he is in the office on a specific night."

"I will consider it."

"I understand your fear and apprehension, but none of us know the exact consequences of our actions. However, not knowing does not justify inaction. I'm afraid I need an answer now. I have to get word back to London whether or not you are in. You would not only be helping British and American agents, but you would also be helping downed soldiers get home and cargo drop-offs and pick-ups."

Eva looked at her, a little taken aback. "What did you say?"

Lorelei furrowed her brows in confusion. "Which part?"

"Did you say that you can help downed pilots get home?"

A smile broke at the corner of her mouth. "I did."

"Then I will help you under one condition."

"Which is?"

"That you help me got someone back to England."

"Who is this person?"

His name is Jon Tolly. He is an American but not a pilot. I worked with him at the Friends Service Council before France was invaded. When he learned that I was trapped here, he came to get me and fell into the hands of the Gestapo. I have asked my husband to release him, but he won't."

"Of course, he won't."

"I know. I realize that Wilhelm can't. That is where you guys come in. He is being held at the POW camp north of Paris called Saint-Denis. I need you to break him out and take him back to England. Those are my terms. The cost of my service."

"I am not sure that is going to be possible."

"That is the only way I will do it." Eva got to her feet and put the strap of her purse over her shoulder. "Once you free him, come and find me, and I will do what I can to help get him out of the country."

Lorelei stood, her eyes bore into Eva's. A pale gray-blue stared back at her. "And you? Don't you want to go with him?"

Eva hadn't even considered that. Was she really being offered a chance to go home now? Did she even want to go home? "No, I won't be going with him."

"You must love your husband a lot to turn down an opportunity like this."

"I thought I made that clear at the museum that I would not leave him. Don't get me wrong, I love my country and the family I left behind, but I also love Wilhelm. They say home is where your heart is. It's not just the place you sleep or where you keep your belongings; it's whereever the person you love is. And for me, that is Germany, or right now France."

Lorelei searched Eva's face. "I can see that. Alright, I will find out if freeing him is possible, and if it is, I will get word to you."

"Do you know when that will be?"

"No, but soon I think." Droplets of rain started to fall from the sky. "I think it's time for us to leave. I will see you next Thursday, and hopefully, I will have news by then. Oh, and Eva."

"Yes."

"Call your husband when you get home."

Eva understood her meaning. She nodded in response and then walked up the steps. She pulled her scarf over her hair and inclined her head to keep the newly falling rain droplets off her, but the cold drizzles still speckled her face. She set off at a brisk pace towards the hospital to have lunch with Ingrid. She was actually excited to be in a hospital again. She craved to work again, to help those in need. It was funny how things turned out. Wilhelm wouldn't let her work at the hospital now that she was pregnant, but he couldn't tell her no to this because he didn't know about it. For the first time since being stuck in this war, she had the opportunity to help her countryman and their allies. The thought made her afraid and giddy at the same time. And if this was how to free Jon, she would do it. She told Jon she would do anything to free him, and she meant it. She just didn't know an opportunity would present itself so soon. And she didn't have to be the one to break him out. In truth, Eva didn't know how she would do that when she promised him.

Eva walked through the large double doors into the hospital lobby. It was the same hospital she had gone to when looking for someone who did abortions. Eva wondered if the doctor she spoke with would remember her. Eva sat on the long bench in the lobby to wait for Ingrid, as she told her she would, but she didn't have to wait long when she saw Ingrid coming down the hall while removing her apron. When Ingrid looked up, Eva waved to her.

"Eva, I'm so happy you made it." Her smile was wide as she took Eva in.

"Me too. So, where do you want to eat?"

"Is there somewhere close by?"

"Yes. There is a restaurant just a few blocks away."

Ingrid looped her arm through Eva's. "Good. Let's go there then."

They stepped outside and turned the corner but didn't get far when, out of nowhere, a sharp pain twisted in Eva's stomach. She stopped suddenly and covered her belly with her hands. "Oww."

Ingrid gripped Eva's arm tightly. "What is it?"

"I don't know. There is a sharp pain in my stomach."

"We should go back to the hospital."

"No. It will pass. I just need to sit down for a minute."

Ingrid helped her to a bench across the street, then sat beside her as she rubbed her back. "Is it getting any better?"

Eva shook her head as she drew in deep breaths. "No. But it will," she tried to assure Ingrid and herself.

"Eva, I don't know. I really think we should go back to the hospital."

"If the pain doesn't go away, I will."

"Even if they do, we are going back to your apartment. We can have lunch there. I will make it while you lay down."

Eva's stomach hurt too much to argue with that. She could not understand why this was happening now. "You will not say a word about this to Wilhelm. Promise me?"

"I won't. I promise. Can you walk? We should get you to the apartment now."

"Give me a few more minutes." It was a sharp pain that was now combined with cramping. She tried her best not to worry or think the worst, but it was hard. "OK. Let's go to the apartment."

Ingrid held onto her all the way to the subway, and they rode it to the stop closest to the apartment. As the guard let them into the building, Eva tried to act as normal as she could, just in case he said something to Wilhelm. Once inside, she sat on the couch, and Ingrid went to the kitchen to make them food.

"I'm just going to call Wilhelm."

"I thought you didn't want him knowing?" Ingrid called from the kitchen.

"I don't. That is not why I'm calling him. I would hate for him to come home now and see me like this." She now had two reasons to call him. She picked up the phone and dialed the number. Soon, his adjutant came on the other end.

"Sicherheitsdienst, SS Obersturmbannführer Bauer's office."

"This is Eva Bauer. I would like to speak to my husband, please."

"I'm sorry, Frau Bauer, but your husband is out of the office. Do you want me to leave him a message saying you called?"

"Um, do you know when he will be back?"

"He should be back any minute. Do you want me to have him call you?"

"Yes, please." Right after she said that she realized she had no idea what her reason was going to be for calling.

"I will tell him. Good day, Frau Bauer."

She heard a click on the other end then the line went dead. She replaced the receiver and laid on the couch, pulling the blanket from the back and draping it over her legs. Ingrid entered the living room and set a tray with food on the coffee table.

"Eva, are you alright?"

"It's getting better." The pain was less intense now that she was lying still and not moving. She didn't even want to sit up so she could eat. All she wanted was to lay there.

"You need to eat, Eva."

"I will in a minute. You go ahead and start eating." Ingrid nibbled on one of the sandwiches as she watched Eva from across the room. Eva had just started to doze when the phone rang, making her bolt into an upright position. She picked up the receiver and put it to her ear. "Yes?" she said in a sleepy voice.

"Eva," Wilhelm's deep voice sounded on the other end. "Is everything alright?"

Her brain was still fuzzy from just coming out of sleep. "Yes, of course. I just wanted to talk to you. I hardly see you, and I miss

201

you." She could hear him breathing on the other end and knew he was contemplating what to say.

"I know I leave you alone a lot, and I'm sorry. I wish it didn't have to be this way. I can try to be home by six, and we can go out for dinner if you want to."

"I do want to." She hoped she wasn't still feeling this way when he got home because she wouldn't feel up to going out to eat if she did. "I know you can't always come home when I'm missing you, so is it alright if I call you at work?"

"It is, although I can't promise I will always be here. I'm out of the office a lot."

"I understand. And that's alright because I'll still get to talk to you more than I would if I didn't call."

"Oh my Liebchen, I am sorry I must leave you alone so much."

She smiled because that was the first time he had ever called her a pet name. Liebchen meant sweetheart in English. "I knew this would happen, but it still doesn't make it any easier."

"I will do my best to be home by six, but I have to go now. The car is waiting."

"Bye." When the line went dead, she hung up the phone and looked at Ingrid. "Do you think it is possible to be in love with two people?"

"I don't know, maybe. I mean, I guess it's possible. I think you can love more than one person in your lifetime." She looked past Eva at the wall behind her with a dreamy look in her eyes. "But there will be that one person, the one love that is like no other. The feeling for them will be strong and intense. You will know who that person is because they will have given you their

202

heart and soul in return." She looked to Eva now. "I know you are thinking of Gerhardt, but I don't believe he ever gave you his heart completely, and he never gave you his soul. You fear you will never love Wilhelm like you did him, but that is just a lie you tell yourself."

Eva felt a twinge of guilt. "I felt like Gerhardt was good all the way through. He had a pure soul."

"No, Eva, there is darkness in everybody. You are only a bad person if you act on it."

"But Gerhardt never acted on it, and Wilhelm does every day. It's like a job requirement for what he does."

"You must give all you have to Wilhelm because he will know if you don't. And he will never be satisfied with just a part of you. Some things have to matter more than others."

"I know you are right. But it's so hard to forget all the things Wilhelm has done. And you have to be careful who you give yourself to. It is dangerous to love someone too much, especially if that person is Wilhelm Bauer. My mind has always fought against and rejected him, but I knew I couldn't trust my heart, and I was right because it betrayed me in the end. But you need more than just love." She looked at her stomach and then around the elegant apartment. "I'm like that fool who will never open their eyes to the truth. It's hard to tell what's real and what's not. You can either live in a world of make-believe, or face the truth and everything that comes with it. I love him so much my heart hurts. Is that what love feels like, like pain? I don't want to live in pain or love that way. But I can't stop."

"Where is this coming from, Eva?"

"I was offered a chance to go home today, and I turned it down. But now I'm wondering for what. Please don't mistake me. I do love Wilhelm more than anyone. But he is so different than me. This is a man who had contained most of his rage to a degree and then just blew it all at once when we were in the garden. I could never do something like that to someone."

"Not even to save the person you love?"

"I don't know. I don't think I could ever be that violent, but it comes so naturally to him. I live in the same apartment with him, but I still feel like we are worlds apart. I don't think I will ever understand him or fully know who he is."

"So why did you turn down the offer to go home?"

"Because I'm dumb, I guess."

"No, because you love him, and he is your family now, and that baby."

Eva shook her head. "I'm sorry if I seem so contradictory. It's just very complicated with Wilhelm. Nothing with him is simple, nothing. But with Gerhardt, it all came so naturally; it was as easy as breathing with him. I didn't have to constantly be watching my footing, or unsure what he would do next, or find myself wondering why he did or said something."

"I do see how he could be that way. So nothing is simple with him, not even…?"

Eva eyed her, then understood. "Yes, even that."

Ingrid's mouth fell open. "Truthfully, even that?"

"I am going to tell you something, but it can never leave this room." Ingrid nodded. "I won't tell everything leading up to it, but the day after I agreed to marry him, I was at his apartment in Berlin. His mom left that morning to visit a friend for a few days, and after she was gone, he pulled me into his bedroom, pushed me over the bed, and had his way with me. It was not like any of the other times. This was painful, violent, and deliberate. He told me to never disobey him again in my ear as he pinned me there on the bed, holding a handful of my hair." This was about control and power, not lovemaking.

Ingrid gaped at her. "He raped you?"

"Well, I don't know what you would call it. I didn't tell him to stop or try to resist, so I'm unsure if he would have continued if I had."

"So… you didn't enjoy it?"

"Let's just say he wasn't gentle, and not in a good way. It hurt. But I think he feels bad about it now, even though he has never talked about it with me. He didn't know I was pregnant when he did it. And I think that in itself made him regret what he did."

"I don't even know what to say to that. But I have to be honest; he scares me a little. I don't think I could be in your shoes, Eva."

"I understand. He puts the fear of God in people. I have seen it. I never thought I could be in my shoes, either. It's this crazy ride being with him. Sometimes, when he touches me, I tremble, but he doesn't notice, and inside my stomach, it's all tied up like butterflies. It's the excitement, fear, joy, and thrill of it all mixed together. Oftentimes, it's overwhelming, and when I think about it, when I think about him, I can't breathe. And I don't know if I want it to stop or to never end. We are allies, lovers, enemies, and partners. He is a minefield of desire, rage, and pleasure. He finds release in physical pain, so he fights, which is not who I am. I believe he would never actually hurt me, but I do think he harbors a place of true darkness inside. I would never want to be in his wrath. Do you see why I tell you these conflicting things now? I don't even know if I'm explaining it very well. It is so confusing and contradictory; how can I understand it? Nothing is as I thought it would be. And you have no idea what it feels like to be in love with someone who exists at such a massive power differential to you. Why do I fall for dark, complicated, impossible men?"

"I think I know what you are saying, at least some of it. I wish I could help or give you some advice, but I have never been with someone like that." Ingrid looked at Eva's untouched food on the table. "You should really eat. Is your stomach any better?"

"A bit." She took the sandwich and a few apple slices and slowly ate them. The pain wasn't gone, and she was genuinely growing concerned. The thought of losing the baby scared the hell out of her. She chewed the food as she watched Ingrid watch her. "Sometimes it scares me to think about how much I care about him and how comfortable I am when we are together. I feel complete with him, but it doesn't make sense. It goes against logic."

Ingrid gave her a weighted look. "Maybe you should go home."

Giving her an intense stare, Eva stopped chewing. "Why would you say that?"

"Do you really want to stay here, remain faithful to him, and be confused for the rest of your life?"

"I don't know the answer to that. The simple act of loving him is easy, but liking him is a lot trickier. If I go home and give him up, I will probably always wonder if I gave up the best thing in my life or saved myself from a terrible fate that I would have to endure until I die." No matter how hard she tried, she could not fathom her feelings for him. He truly was not a nice person, so why he chose her to be with, she did not know.

"So you would stay for love?"

"I already have. Maybe you can belong to someone before we've even met them, and I have always been his. I don't know. He confuses me." Her eyes clouded with tears, and her voice quivered with the emotions she was feeling. She knew some of this had to be hormones, but everything she said was the truth. And what if she lost the baby? How would that change things? "I can't believe I love a man who is my enemy. He's the monster I allow in my bed. I understand now that just because you want something and it feels really good doesn't mean that it's good for you."

"Maybe the enemy as an individual is not your enemy. I know it will take some time to believe this, but I really don't think he is your enemy. I mean, yes, he is the enemy of your country, but he is not your enemy, Eva." She gestured around the room with her hand. "You wouldn't be here if you were."

She was experiencing so many different feelings at once she couldn't sort them out. She put the rest of the food back on the tray and lay on the couch again, covering up with the blanket. "I don't feel well."

Ingrid promptly stood and came to her side. "You need to go to the doctor."

"No. He will know if I go. It will be better if I just sleep."

"Marriages aren't built on secrets, Eva."

"This one has to be. I can only imagine what Wilhelm would do if he found out. He would have guards posted at the door to ensure I didn't leave. He has this crazy notion about women. It's archaic. I live with a man I instinctively knew was dangerous."

Why was love so frustrating?

"I have to get back to work. What will you do when he gets home?"

"Tell him I'm too tired to go out and eat."

"Do you think he will believe it?"

"Yes, I do."

She pulled the blanket further up over Eva's shoulders. "I'll come and check on you tomorrow."

"Thank you, Ingrid."

Once she was gone, Eva tried to sleep but was in and out as her emotions and thoughts ebbed and flowed without her consent. Her feelings for Wilhelm were raw and a little unsettling, and that alone was enough to keep her up. Finally, after much effort, she was able to fall asleep and stay asleep.

The closing of the front door jolted her awake. She looked around the dark room but couldn't make anything out except the shape of the furniture. She could hear heavy footsteps in the apartment, so she pushed the blanket off and swung her legs over the couch and stood. She felt unsteady on her feet, shaky as if she might pass out. A little dazed and still feeling like she was drowning in her emotions, she gripped the wall as she made her way to the hall. A light came on, and she squinted from its brightness, trying to let her eyes adjust. Wilhelm was just hanging his coat in the closet when he turned and looked at her. Seeing him after her conversation with Ingrid elicited raw emotions, and the force of her own feelings worried her. He winked at her, and Eva's eyes filled with tears. For a long, quiet moment, he did nothing but stare at her. He was unreadable, unfathomable. For the briefest second, she could see a struggle in his eyes, a feeling, but it was gone before she could analyze it. Then, he motioned with his finger for her to come to him, and she walked into his arms.

"Hey," he whispered into her hair.

She looked up at him. "Hi." He planted a soft, chase kiss on her lips and then kissed her forehead. He touched her cheek, and she leaned her face into his palm. She looked into his hazel eyes, and his gaze held no expectations. She reached up to touch his face, but he caught her hand and then kissed each of her fingers. She closed her eyes as a sharp pain settled in her lower back.

He lowered her hand to her side. "Is that better?" She nodded. "Good. Now you are going to tell me what this is about."

She opened her eyes and looked up at him again. "It's just been a long day." She needed to sit down, still feeling unsteady on her feet. She took his hand, led him to the couch, and pulled him down. "I get so bored during the day. I need something to do. I have decided to find some kind of employment."

He shook his head. "No."

She frowned. "I can't sit around the apartment all day."

"And I don't expect you to."

"Then why are you so against me getting a job?"

"I was willing to let you work after we were married, but then I learned that you were pregnant."

"Yes, I'm pregnant, not an invalid."

"This is not an argument you are going to win," he said, the tone of his voice making it final.

She let out a long breath in frustration, then blinked several times, trying to shake the lightheaded feeling. "I wanted to know if you cared if we ate at home. I'm kind of tired, actually. I had fallen asleep on the couch when I heard you come in."

He reached up and brushed a strand of hair from her face. "You know I don't care where we eat."

She forced a smile, then looked at the tray with food still on the coffee table. "I thought we could eat the rest of the food Ingrid prepared for lunch."

He glanced at it and then back to her. "That's been out a while."

"It's still good. I'm too tired to cook tonight."

He gave her a sidelong glance. "Alright."

Again, she smiled, hoping he couldn't see the strain on her face. They ate the rest of the food, and Eva took a quick shower while Wilhelm was on the phone. When she got out and walked into the bedroom, she could hear him in his office. He was cursing and swearing at whoever was on the other end.

"As soon as you find them, let me know, and first thing in the morning, bring them to my office. Yes. Yes. No, don't say anything. Alright, I have to go." He slammed the phone down and came into the bedroom. He pulled the suspender from his shoulders, sat on the bed, and started unbuttoning his shirt.

She lay facing his back. "What was that?"

"Just work."

"Did a prisoner escape?" Her thoughts went to Jon.

He turned his head to the side. "No. It's a soldier in serious trouble who decided to go missing."

"What will you do to him when he is found?"

"Nothing good," he growled.

She flinched at his harsh words. She would not want to be in that man's shoes. Wilhelm stood and went to the bathroom, then the shower turned on. She would have joined him if she felt better. When he returned to bed, he kissed her and then laid down. She knew he was tired tonight, which worked well for her.

She lay awake studying his face as he slept. His features were rough with the stubbles from his whiskers, but he looked relaxed. It was late, but she couldn't fall asleep, and the thoughts were swirling through her mind. She moved the blanket back and went to the living room to read her English book for a while and to get a snack from the kitchen. As she ate, she watched the dark city from the window, the searchlights streaming across the sky in dancing motion as they looked for planes. This was her world now, but it wasn't going to last. Although her time no longer felt like where she belonged either. She went into the bedroom and patted over to the bed, where Wilhelm was still fast asleep. She laid down facing him, her eyes drinking in his lovely face as she watched him breathe. "I love you," she mouthed before the dark of sleep claimed her.

Her eyelids fluttered open to Wilhelm's hazel eyes, intent on her. She reached up to caress his cheek, and his eyes softened. She slid closer and put her arm around him. He let out a hard exhale and then folded her in a loving embrace. Eva sighed and sank into him, his heartbeat strong against her, their bodies pressed against each other. It felt so right, like knowing where she truly belonged, that here with him was her home. She didn't believe it was in the West anymore because America was not where he was. She pressed her lips to the warm nave of his neck, a thrill surging

211

through her as Wilhelm shivered against her. She stroked his back, his side, his shoulder, and his body responded to her touch, her body warming with every caress. Eva felt better than she had earlier but was torn between whether or not she should keep going or stop before she lost the will to or rousing him to the point of frustration if she didn't follow through. She decided it was worth risking. He had been gone so much, and she missed the intimacy between them. She thought he would make more advances toward her if she wasn't pregnant.

"I want you," she breathed against his neck.

He raised up, resting his head on his hand as he looked down at her. The hint of a smile at the corner of his mouth. "I have an early start tomorrow, maybe another time."

She didn't entirely believe him. She suspected he was saying no because of her, not because he had to get up early. She sat up in bed and peered down at him. "Is that the real reason?"

"Partly."

"I knew it was not just about that."

"Come here."

She laid back down, and he pulled her to him. "Let's go to sleep."

She was disappointed, but it was probably for the best. She needed to make sure everything with the pregnancy was fine. She would call Dr. Möller in the morning.

"Eva, I know that caring for a German can't be easy."

"Caring for you isn't the hard part. It's all the other stuff that comes with it. But I know that I will always be yours. Wherever you are is where I belong."

He moved his head back and looked at her intently. "I'm not sure you know what you are saying, Eva."

"Yes, I do. I will be yours even when this war is over. So, I don't care if that is here in France, Germany, or America. But the strange thing is, I have never been closer to anyone, yet I've never felt further from someone than I do you. There are so many mysteries that seem to surround who you are."

"What do you want to know? Ask me anything, and I will tell you."

"Tell me about when you were a boy."

He sighed. "Ask me again later because that could take a while. It is too late to go into that story tonight."

"I won't forget."

He kissed the tip of her nose. "I know you won't."

The following morning, Eva called the hospital in Berlin and waited on the phone for the nurse to locate Dr. Möller. If only she was in her time and could get an ultrasound. She heard a cracking sound, and then Klaus' voice echoed on the other end.

"Eva, it is so good to hear from you. How is life in Paris? How is he treating you?" he asked in a more serious tone.

"Paris is lovely as always, and he treats me like a delicate flower." The last part, she said to complain.

"I'm glad to hear it."

"I mean, he is overbearing. He treats me like I can't do anything."

"I understand your frustration, but it is good for pregnant women to not exert themselves."

213

She rolled her eyes, knowing he couldn't see her do it. "I'm calling because I have a medical question for you. Yesterday I started having sharp pain and cramping. Is that normal?"

"You say this started yesterday?"

"Yes."

"Is it gone now?"

"When I woke up this morning, it wasn't there anymore."

"It is normal to have pains that come and go during pregnancy."

"So what causes it?"

"Well, a few things. Most of the time, it is caused by the ligaments and uterus stretching to support your growing baby. Also, it could be constipation, dehydration, or an infection in the bladder. It's good that it went away because the normal kinds of pain usually do, but when there is an actual problem, they don't. Have you had any bleeding?"

"No."

"That's good. What about diarrhea or pain in the shoulder or neck?"

"No."

"Again, that is good. Any dizziness or lightheadedness?"

"I did feel lightheaded and dizzy yesterday, but I get that a lot."

"It can be normal for some women, and where you don't have any other symptoms, I don't think there is anything to worry about."

She felt relieved. "How is Berlin, Klaus?"

"Not a lot has changed unless you count fewer buildings. The bombings have not stopped. I'm glad you are there and not here.

It is a sad state of affairs. I don't know how much more this city can take."

"Maybe you should come back to France."

"I am needed here, Eva. But I will come and visit you soon. I have surgery in ten minutes, but please call any time."

"I will."

"Try and rest, alright."

"That's all I do."

He laughed on the other end. "Bye, Eva."

"Bye."

That evening, Ingrid came by after her shift to check on Eva. "How are you feeling?"

"Much better. I called Klaus, and he said what I experienced was perfectly normal. Basically, just pain from the growing baby."

"I am so relieved. And Wilhelm, did he suspect anything?"

"Not a thing. But he acts like he will break me if he touches me. I tried to be intimate with him last night, but he wouldn't even touch me."

"He is just worried about you and hurting the baby."

"He isn't going to hurt the baby or me. Don't make excuses for him."

"I'm not making excuses for him. I'm just telling you why I think he won't sleep with you."

"I know why he does it, but it's still frustrating."

"Maybe try again tonight."

I might.

When Ingrid left, Eva read but could not keep her mind on the book. Her thoughts kept going to Jon and the proposal Lorelei made her. She wanted to see her family again and return to her time, at least for a while, but it wasn't as crucial or pressing as it used to be. But Jon had to get out of here. If he stayed in the camp, there was a chance he would not survive the war, and she would not allow that.

The front door closed, and boots on the wood floor echoed in the apartment. Eva laid the book on the coffee table and walked to the foyer. She watched him lay his cap on the table and hang his coat in the hall closet. When he closed the door, he turned to her, and without saying anything, he took four long strides and was in front of her. He took hold of her arm, his fingers gently pressing her forearm.

"I wanted to ask you something." He gave her arm a little tug, and she took a step forward. She swallowed down the rising mix of fear and lust that rose in her because she had no idea what was about to happen.

"What did you want to ask me?" Her voice was shaky as she fought against the fear of anticipation.

Instead of answering, he dipped his head and kissed her. His lips played over hers, and he put his free hand in her hair, closing his fingers, pulling at her curls, some falling out of the clip that held them in place. She gripped the lapels of his uniform, trying with all her might to never lose this moment. He pulled back, and she stood there, breaths coming fast. There was a softness in his eyes and a pang of hunger that hung in the air. She could not help but feel that he was toying with her, but it was such a sweet game, and she craved his touch. He leaned in again, and his lips traced down her neck as he brushed her bottom lip with his thumb, his other hand sliding up her thigh, pushing under her dress, arousing her with his fingers. He moved his head from her neck, and she felt his lips at the top of her cleavage, just at the opening of her dress, and the shock of his kiss passed through her while the pressure between her legs intensified. Her breaths were coming sharp and fast as her heart thumped erratically in her chest. He slid his suspenders off in one swift motion, undid his pants, then took her underwear and pulled them down, letting them drop to the floor around her ankles. She quickly stepped out of them, and he brought his hands up, cupping just under her butt, and lifted, pressing her against the wall as he held her weight. She drew in a breath when he entered her and gripped him fiercely. He put a hand on the wall beside her and moved with hard, quick thrusts, and everything in her screamed as he lit her up, her mind needing this, her body wanting this.

Chapter Thirteen

September 30th, 1942

Eva walked beside Lorelei as they headed towards the catacombs. Lorelei had told her there was something she wanted to show her but wouldn't tell her what it was. Eva glanced in her direction, but Lorelei's face was set in an expressionless pose.

They took the narrow stairwell down into the cool, damp air of the combs. She followed Lorelei as she weaved through various tunnels. They came to a small opening and stopped. Lorelei lit a candle and sat on a stone.

"What now?" Eva asked her.

"We wait."

"For what?"

"You'll see." She handed Eva a candle that she lit from hers.

Eva sat beside her and looked around the dark space surrounding them, only the soft glow of the candles giving them light. "Did you learn of a way to free Jon?" Lorelei looked over to her, then turned her head to look forward down one of the dark passages. Eva let out a long breath, a little agitated that she was being kept in the dark. The flicker of light illuminating the passage in front of them caught her attention. She squinted and focused on it. Voices echoed throughout the catacombs as the light grew brighter. The first two people entered the space they were in, and Lorelei and Eva stood, and then three more people followed behind. Eva's breath caught in her throat when she saw Jon. Without hesitation, she ran and embraced him. He grunted when she did, so she released him. A tear spilled over and ran down her cheek.

"I can't believe they were able to free you." She looked around at all the other people. "How did you get him out?"

Lorelei sat back down, crossed her legs, and cupped he hands over her knee. "You're not going to like it?"

Eva's face fell. "Why?"

"When Patrick," she pointed to a young man standing near the back with sandy-blond hair, "and Pierre," she moved her hand to an older man with dark brown hair and the beginning of a beard, "snuck into Saint-Denis tonight to free your friend they were spotted by a guard on their way out. They had to kill three of the guards to escape. The city is on high alert, and the Gestapo will be out in force, so we can't get him out right now. He is stuck in Paris until things calm down. We will hide him down here, but you must bring him food, water, candles, and some blankets."

Eva covered her mouth with her hand, bile rising. This was bad. It would now be harder to get Jon out, Wilhelm would work

219

even more than before, and when he found out it was Jon who escaped, he would instantly suspect her.

"I can bring him those things. Did anyone else escape with him?"

"No. We wanted to get more out, but it was too risky. Just going in for him was dangerous, and the odds were against us. You are lucky they got him out and all made it from that camp alive."

"I am grateful to all of you for what you have done for Jon." She looked around at the people in the room and nodded in acknowledgment. "I will bring the stuff he needs tomorrow."

"We have given him a gun just in case he is found down here or has to use it on himself."

Eva looked to Jon to gauge his reaction to what Lorelei said, but he seemed calm. "Do you know how long he might have to stay down here?"

"No, that really depends on your husband. But, we hope to have a transport plane come in maybe a week. You and Jon will know when we know, so stay available." She looked at her watch. "It's getting late, so we better get back, Eva. We have left him some water and food, but he will have a cold night."

Eva shrugged out of her coat and handed it to Jon. "No, I won't take your coat. Besides, won't your husband notice if you go home without it?" She looked at him as she continued to hold it out.

"I will give him my coat," a man said that she was not introduced to. "Keep yours."

Eva put her coat back on, and Lorelei nodded for her to follow. They walked in the cold night until they were only a few blocks from Eva's apartment. "Go as early as you can tomorrow and bring him that stuff. I will try to check on him as well."

Eva squeezed her arm. "Thank you. You have no idea what this means to me."

"I hope he's worth it. This will fall back on you more than anyone else. Do you think your husband will suspect you had something to do with it?"

"I don't know, but I wouldn't be surprised if he did. There isn't much he misses. He has a sharp eye and a keen sense for this kind of thing."

"Which is why he has the job he does." Lorelei leaned in and planted a kiss on each of Eva's cheeks. "I hope this doesn't turn bad for you."

Eva forced a smile. "Let's hope not." In truth, she was scared shitless. She knew Wilhelm would suspect her and would be pissed. She wanted to run and hide, but he would find her no matter where she went. Eva jogged up the stairs to the front of the building, and the doorman let her in. She hurried inside the apartment and went to the bathroom. She wanted to be in bed before Wilhelm got home. She stripped off her clothes, stepped into the bathtub, and turned on the water. She wrapped her arms around her bent knees as she thought. She would have to lie to Wilhelm, even though she told him she would never lie to him again. He already didn't trust her, and this was going to make him trust her even less.

Eva thought she heard a sound in the apartment and jumped, splashing water on the floor. Her heart felt like it was going to beat out of her chest. Tears burned in her eyes. She was so scared of what might be coming and petrified of Wilhelm. She pulled the plug and stood, taking the towel from the hook on the wall. She dried off, mopped up the water on the floor, then opened the bathroom door and peeked out. She did not see anyone in the apartment, and it was quiet. The only light was the one she turned on. She picked her clothes off the floor, turned out the hall light, and hurried to the bedroom. She dressed in her nightgown, flipped the light out in the bedroom, felt her way to the bed, and then sat on the edge. She watched the dancing lights of the aircraft spotlights through the window as coherent thoughts returned. She told herself that she was strong and that she could face Wilhelm and stand up to him no matter what happened. In truth, she was petrified and knew she would break under his scrutinizing gaze alone. Everything she told herself was empty words, completely untrue. She knew exactly what frightened her and made her want to flee Wilhelm as if he was going to try and kill her. He was ruthless, and she knew it. She was scared of him coming home.

She said mantras of courage to herself, all the while staring out at the night sky. Wanting to curse, weep, sleep, all the while feeling regret for betraying him again. But how could she not help Jon? She couldn't just leave him in there. Jon was their only hope.

She laid her head on the pillow and pulled the blanket up around her neck. Her heart beat at a fast, steady rhythm, and she felt sick to her stomach like she was going to vomit, swallowing against it. She knew it was from the anxiety and fear that surged through her.

The seconds passed like minutes, and the minutes passed like hours. She lay as still as the dead, waiting for him to come home, and after what felt like an eternity, she heard the front door open and then slam. Her first instinct was to bolt or, at the very least, sit up, but she didn't. She continued to lay still and feign sleep. The last time she checked, it was already past one in the morning, but she wasn't sure what time it was now.

She heard the heavy footsteps approaching, and then the bedroom light came on. She opened her eyes and blinked a few times, pretending to have just woken up from the light. She drew on all the courage she had and spoke, praying her voice didn't shake.

"What is it?"

He walked briskly to the side of the bed, and her fear rose like the tides. He roughly took hold of her arm, and she was stunned into silence as she went through the whole range of human emotions in those few seconds. She looked into his face, but his expression was military blank. There was no sign of any emotion in his eyes. He pulled her from the bed, and the gesture was not lost on her. She had never imagined that Wilhelm would ever be so forceful with her, now that they were together and she was pregnant.

He nearly drug her into the hall and stopped next to the coat closet. "Where is Jon?"

Eva swallowed against the dryness in her throat. "Are you arresting me?" She tried to hide the fear in her voice.

"Perhaps, but that depends on what you say next. Where is Jon?" he repeated.

"I can't tell you because I don't know."

"Cannot or will not?"

"Cannot."

His eyes filled with anger. "Put your coat and shoes on, now!"

For the first time since they got married, she saw him in a different light. She wanted to tell him not to look at her like that because it was as if he didn't even know her. She searched his eyes for a hint of his old self but found no trace. She stared at Wilhelm, stunned by the change in demeanor from just a few nights ago, but now he simply looked at her with an expression of unmovable resolve. She gathered up her tan wool coat and slid her feet into her brown leather shoes, hitching her purse over her shoulder. She wanted to hide all of her in the coat, but she stood tall, hoping to project a confidence she didn't feel.

He took her by the elbow, and she blanched from it, her whole body feeling numb as he led her outside. The wind blew through her clothes, and it felt like it reached her bones, or maybe it wasn't the cold night air but the situation. He opened the back door to the car, and the first time he made her get into his car in La Chapelle flashed through her mind, and she could no longer keep her dinner down. She turned and threw up all over the sidewalk, heaving as her face flushed from the heat. Her hair stuck to her damp skin, and she tried to move it as she threw up a second time. Her stomach cramped as she dry heaved. Wilhelm did not come to her, but he left her alone as she tried to gain control. She straightened and wiped her mouth with the back of her hand.

"Let's go," he said.

It sounded so uncaring, and her fear and despair hit her like a train. Overcome, she started crying in front of him. She never thought she would again be on this side of Wilhelm's feelings. He motioned with his hand for her to get into the car. She hesitated but knew there was no chance of her escaping. She walked past him and slid into the back seat, then he got in next to her. She

224

could not think of what was going to happen. There was no way he would torture her, especially now that she was pregnant. That at least she knew.

The car only drove a few blocks and stopped in front of the Gestapo headquarters on 84 Avenue Foch. Her eyes grew wide, and without giving herself time to think about what she was doing, she opened the car door and hopped out. Wilhelm opened the door and jumped from the other side, and was behind the car in an instant. He was only a few feet from her, and she backed away from him. His orderly was out of the vehicle, too, watching the two of them, waiting to see if he was needed. She felt like she was hyperventilating. Her breaths were deep, but she thought she might faint.

"Don't come any closer."

"Eva, stop this."

She turned and ran, her feet pounding the pavement. She could hear Wilhelm instructing his orderly to stand down, that he would get her. The click of his boots on the road was fast approaching behind. There was no way she was going to outrun him. She might have stood a chance before she was pregnant, but she wasn't able to now. He caught her arm, pulling her to a stop. Then he took her other arm and pulled them both behind her back.

"You should not have run."

Her knees buckled as her legs gave out, and she felt his arms go around her, catching her before she fell. Then, there was only darkness.

Her eyes flew open, and she could hear the rain hitting the outside of the wall she was lying next to. There was a sense of foreboding as she looked around, but only a faint light came through a small window at the top of the wall. She sat up and rubbed her hands over the bedding she was on. It felt like a cot with a rough wool blanket. The room smelled dank and musty, like a basement. She hopped off the bed and moved around in the limited confines of her dark enclosure the best she could with her chained ankles. Her searching hands found nothing, so she went around the room again and positioned herself by the door. She slid to the floor and leaned against it, feeling the cold cement through her thin nightgown. She drew in several shaky breaths as the pounding in her ears eased some.

"Think, just think," she told herself. It seemed almost impossible that she was in jail again at the hands of Wilhelm. She wondered if he was going to let her out or keep her in here, and how was this going to change them? How would it change her?

There was a stabbing sensation in her side, so she cupped her hands over her stomach and cried. She was tired, scared, cold, thirsty, hungry, and had to pee, but she didn't even know if there was a toilet in the cell. She stood and felt her way around the room again, this time searching for a toilet or a bucket. In the corner of the room was an inlet with a toilet but no sink that she could find. She relieved herself, then returned to the bed and sat on the edge. Her eyes wandered around, looking for anything to distract her. There was something beside the bed that she had not noticed when she got up. She put her hands out and ran them along it. It was a small wooden table set against the wall. She felt the top, and her fingers bumped something made of glass. She cupped her hands around it and realized it was a glass filled with water. She brought it to her lips and drank deeply but stopped before she finished it, in case she was thirsty later. She put the cup back on the side table and laid down, pulling the blanket tight around her to keep warm. She knew Wilhelm must have left her the water. For the next few hours, she went between anger, utter terror, and crying. She would pound on the door with her fists and scream into the void to be let out until her voice was hoarse and her hands throbbed. Jon was not going to get the things he needed in the morning. She could only hope that Lorelei would go to the catacombs like she said. Lorelei would also notice she hadn't been by and wonder what had happened to her. Eva was venomous now as she thought about Jon, cold and alone in the catacombs. She despised Wilhelm with a passion she had never felt for him. She hated him to her core. She thought back to the wedding day and remembered what Klara had said to her about Wilhelm expecting total loyalty and obedience. Maybe she was right about that, and perhaps she was also right when she said that she knew him better than her. A wave of utter exhaustion came over her, fatigue fogged her brain, and no amount of anger or fear could keep her awake any longer. She drew in a long breath. She had cried enough. She drifted into sleep, hiccupping as she did.

The loud creaking sound of metal on metal pulled her from sleep and the deafening silence of the cell. She opened her eyes to see Wilhelm closing the door behind him as the early morning sun coming through the small window made the room look like an odd yellow color. She bolted up in bed and scooted against the back wall, holding the blanket. When he turned and saw her this way, he paused, looking down at her as he held a plate with food. He

227

took a chair he must have brought in with him, set it beside the bed, and then placed the plate on the little table.

She fought viciously against the tears that were burning in her eyes. "Let me go!" Her voice was shaky, but she could not control it.

He leaned back in the chair and crossed his arms over his chest, watching her unsympathetically with none of his usual gentleness towards her. She searched for something of who he had been just a few days ago, the man she had given herself to completely and allowed to have her against the wall, but now he was hard-edged and closed off. His demeanor was almost confrontational. On some level, she did understand his sudden harshness, even though it stung. Her reaction to him made it clear that she was too emotional, too quick to panic, and too quick to cave under pressure. She pulled in a quivering breath and tried to rain in her anger and fear.

He stared at her, his expression dauntingly severe. "Poor captive bird, Who, from the narrow cage, pourest such music, that it might assuage the rugged hearts of those who prisoned thee, were they not deaf towards sweet melody. This song shall be they rose, its petals pale, are dead, indeed, my adored Nightingale," he spoke to her in English, but his words were confusing and his tone mocking.

Although he spoke in English, she had no idea what he was talking about. "What? I don't understand what that means."

He tilted his head to the side. "I'm surprised you don't know it. It's from a poem by an English author, Percy Bysshe Shelly." He leaned closer to her and rested his elbows on his legs. "It means that you have been captured and sweetly plead to the person who imprisoned you, hoping they have a heart. But the person is deaf to your words, and your plea is wasted because they can't hear you. You have put me in a difficult situation, Eva. I have let you off one too many times. If you keep misbehaving, we will both take the fall for it. Sometimes, it's futile to keep fighting. You have to accept the situation and try to make the best of it. Rules must be obeyed." He picked up the plate of food and held it out to her. "Eat."

She looked at the fresh fruit, vegetables, meat, cheese, and bread as hunger clawed at her stomach, but she wasn't going to take it. "Do you give the other prisoners food?"

"Yes. Of course, we give them food."

"And do you personally bring it to them?"

He laid the plate in her lap. "Eat, Eva."

She narrowed her eyes at him, then roughly moved it aside next to her on the bed, taking out her ire at Wilhelm's emotional distance on the plate. "I'm not hungry."

He smiled slightly, with a hint of restraint. "You are always hungry. And you are going to need your strength." He got out of his chair and came down on one knee in front of her, yanked up the hem of her nightgown, took a key from his pocket and, unlocked the ankle cuff on her right leg, then did the same to the other leg.

She watched Wilhelm and swallowed as he pulled the chains off with grim concentration, his hands on her sparking a remembrance of them caressing her the last time they were intimate. His sensuous touch up her thighs, how he murmured her name in the heat of passion. But there was no trace of this ardent affection now, and she felt his emotional withdrawal most acutely, even as she struggled to see past her own reflexive emotions. If their positions were switched and he had betrayed her in such a huge way, she would be livid with him.

Once the cuffs were off, he let the hem of her nightgown drop to cover her ankles, then stood, scrutinizing her once more like she was no one to him, and sat back in the chair.

"I don't want food from you. Next time, have someone else bring it."

His demeanor changed. "You amaze me. After all this time, you still think I'm made of stone. I have helped you survive for all these years, but there is only so much I can do."

She looked into his elevated gaze. He was intense and intimidating, but she had to stand her ground if she could. "So is that it then, you are going to keep me in here? Oh wait, are you going to send me to a camp? Or maybe you are just going to have me shot. This should be interesting to tell your child that you had to think about which punishment was more fitting for their mother."

He leaned over so quickly and with such force that she jumped, grabbed hold of both of her arms and pulled her to the edge of the bed, only inches from him, and shook her a couple of times as adrenaline fueled her, bringing all her senses to attention, her eyes wild with terror.

His stare had darkened, and the mocking smile that he had now gone. His words were low and unforgiving when they came. "Stop this, Eva," he warned through clenched teeth, his tone rough and brooking no argument. She held her breath and didn't dare look away as she stared at him, violently shaken by what she was feeling inside as Wilhelm's hands tightened around her arms, his gaze catching fire. He was so intimidating that she kept silent. She could imagine him dropping a man with a single blow, and she saw what he was capable of in the garden, so she had a good idea of what he could do to her.

His eyes seared into hers, and he squeezed his fingers tighter around her arms, his fingers digging into her skin. "Do not test me, or you will see me lose my temper. You drive me up the fucking wall with your infuriating bad behavior." She didn't want to hazard a guess as to what he meant by that. "You are the reason you are in here. Look around you. Do you think the other prisoners have a bed, an actual toilet, water, and fresh fruit and vegetables with meat and cheese to eat? No. They sleep on a hard floor, chained to a wall. They have nothing but a pot to piss in. Do you really believe I would put you in those conditions? But I have to punish you. You broke the law, Eva, again."

Her eyes blurred with the tears she had been holding back and the raw emotions that burned her throat and ran down her cheeks onto her nose. She tried to retain some of her dignity and not blubber like a child.

When she spoke, she would not meet his eye. "I had no other choice. Without Jon, I can't go home."

"Why," he growled.

"I can't tell you why. But it is the truth. Jon is the only way I will ever see my family again."

He loosened his grip on her a bit. "So, you want to go home?"

His question seemed to have a double meaning. "Of course I do."

He released her and leaned back in the chair, crossing his arms over his chest again. "One day, we will part ways, that I am certain of. I always knew you would leave me for Gerhardt or home, which always pained me. And I knew that a relationship with you would lead me down a rabbit hole from which I would never emerge. You have given me so much pain, and I knew it would have been better not to have entered a relationship with you in the first place. But love makes us do fucking ludicrous things. Things that surprise even us."

She drew in a breath, surprised that he would say that and all the things he could mean by it. "Are you saying I can go home?"

"No," he growled.

"Why?"

"Because I'm not ready to tell you bye. I have yet to come to terms with the truth that you won't always be here."

"Why?"

He gave her a look that suggested she had asked a stupid question. "You know, in the past, I tried to have you taken away, disciplined, and I tried to ignore you when you were in custody. I tried to be angry with you. And I tried so many times to do the right thing, but I failed. I failed because I'm in love with you. I have tried hard not to. You have brought me so much trouble I often ask myself if you are worth it."

"Then let me go and forget about me."

"I can't forget about you. Believe me, I've tried."

"Maybe you haven't tried hard enough."

"Do you think I like always having you in my mind messing with my thoughts? I have loved you for years and hadn't asked you for anything in return for a long time." He looked at her with soul-searching eyes. "But there it is. I love you, whether it is right or wrong to do so." He looked at the angry red spots on her arms from his fingers. "I lost control, and I'm sorry that I hurt you. Men are deplorable, and I am no different." He stood and pointed to the plate of food. "Eat. You don't want me coming back because I learned you were still refusing it."

She swiftly stood. Fear gripped her. "Wait, you are leaving me in here?"

"Of course, you are a prisoner."

He turned to walk to the door, so she ran in front of him and stood between him and the door. "No, you can't leave me in here."

For a few seconds, she stared him down, and he stood firm and glared back at her, unmoved by her protest. She wanted to cry because she felt like a shattered fragment of herself. He walked forward, closing the small gap she managed to put between them, forcing her to take steps backward until she hit the door. And like always, when he was near, her heart beat like a caged animal, wild with the desire to free itself. She hated it. She hated that he bested her again. This was all a game that he continued to win. She cursed that being close to him made her feel things she shouldn't for a man who had been so cruel to her on so many occasions. She hated even more that the look in his eyes told her that he knew exactly how she was feeling. The fact that she was reacting so strongly to him when all he seemed to feel for her was contempt. It was humiliating.

He leaned in and pitched his voice low. He was careful not to touch her. "We like to think that love and altruism are the things that define us, that human nature is inclined towards selfless concern for the well-being of others, but that's not always the case. In war, the part that dominates is our savage traits and hatred because that is easier than caring," he said in a razor-sharp whisper.

Wilhelm was predatory as he smiled unkindly, daring her to challenge him again. She couldn't move because he was standing so close to her, so she stayed frozen against the door, breathing heavily as she focused on the buttons of his jacket. Finally, he took a step back, and she darted to the bed and sat down, folding her knees up. He didn't look back at her but opened the door and stepped out into the hall, slamming it behind him. She rested her head on her knees and wept.

The days passed in a slow haze, and the only interaction with another person was when someone would bring her food and water, but never once did Wilhelm come back to see her. All this time, Wilhelm remained aloof and closed off, and her emotions became increasingly tumultuous in response to the jarring withdrawal of his ardent attention and bolstering affections, even though she understood with her rational mind why he was doing it. She was aware that she had to force her emotions aside so she could stand firm in the face of loneliness and isolation, as well as exhaustion and terror, but it was becoming more difficult with each passing day. Homesickness hit her in waves now. At work while she went about her daily life, she could suppress the sadness, but now that she was all alone in this small, confined room, it was barely possible. She had lost so many years of her life stuck in the past.

Her pain was building and building to the point she wanted to hurl everything she was feeling at Wilhelm to alleviate the hurt. Could he not give her even an hour or two of respite? Could he not take a little time out of his day to come and see her or let her have some outside time? She thought this treatment of her was cruel, even for him.

She continued to pound on the door daily, but no one ever came. She didn't know how, but being in jail tired her out more than walking the city would. She was so exhausted when night came that she was asleep as soon as her head hit the pillow, all alone in the dark cell as Wilhelm slept far removed from her. She would fall into an exhaustive, dreamless sleep, only to be woken by the shrill screams of other prisoners, bringing all her senses to attention.

After the third day, a guard brought her a pale of water, some of her clothes, and a cloth. When he left, she rushed to the bucket, pulled her clothes off, and washed herself, never remembering it feeling so good to be clean. She could hear a man screaming on the other side of the wall and tried to block it out. During the days she had been here, she had listened to the screams of people, crying, the sound of gunfire, guards yelling, and what sounded like someone being whipped. The sounds kept her awake at night, put her on edge, and stressed her out. Her nerves were shot, and she felt sick and weary.

She lay on the bed, looking up at the window. It was set high in the wall, and rays of light streamed down onto the floor by the bed. Tears had dried on her face as she lay there for over an hour, staring at the wall of the now familiar room. Most days, she would pace the small space, but today, she was too tired and didn't have the energy to get up. The breakfast that had been brought to her that morning was still sitting on the table, untouched. She was worried about Jon and the baby but was finding it harder to stay positive. And as much as she hated to admit it to herself, she was lonely and frightened. She missed Wilhelm even though she told herself she hated him, but how she felt and acted when she was with him was so clear that even when she hated him, she still loved him. She wanted him to come and see her so badly, yet she thought she might slap him if he did.

She had fallen asleep and woke to the door opening as the guard brought in her dinner and took away the plate of uneaten food from breakfast. She opened her eyes and watched him, then closed them again once he had left. A scream echoed loudly from the room next to hers, and a hard thud on the wall made plaster dust sink to the floor and settle on the table.

She scooted against the outside wall and covered her head with the blanket, pressing it tight against her ears. She squeezed her eyes shut. "Make it stop, please make it stop?"

She had not heard the door open or close and let out a shirk when someone pulled the blanket from her head. Wilhelm was sitting on the edge of her bed, staring at her, but his face was unreadable and his eyes guarded. Just the sight of him brought tears to her eyes.

"I know you don't want to see me," he said as she cried. "But you need to get up and come with me."

She sniffed and roughly wiped at the tears in her eyes. "Go with you where?"

He pulled back her blanket swiftly, almost violently. She should have protested, but she didn't. She honestly didn't have the energy to fight with him. He offered her his hand, and she took it. He pulled her up from the bed and then let go of her hand as if he was repulsed by her. He walked a few feet ahead and spoke to the guard at the door, telling him to collect her things. He looked over his shoulder at Eva, and they exchanged an uneasy glance. "Follow me."

She tried her best to keep up, but he was walking fast, she was exhausted, and her feet were swollen and hurt. He led her outside and opened the back door of the car for her. She slid in, and he got into the back with her. Once he closed the door and the car was in motion, he spoke.

"I am taking you back to the apartment for now. Early tomorrow morning, I will be leaving and will be gone for a few days, and when I return, I'm sending you to Berlin to stay with my mother."

She was shocked. This was rejection on a whole different level. Maybe it was for the best, though. "How long will I be in Berlin?"

He barely looked at her. "I will notify my mother that you are coming."

"Are you trying to rid yourself of me?" She didn't know if she actually wanted to know the answer to that.

"There is no escaping you." He glanced at her and then back to the window. "Don't worry, I will still provide for you. I meant what I said." His tone was heartfelt. "I offered you my protection and care, and you have it."

Jagged relief exploded through her as fresh tears stung her eyes. She turned from him and looked through the glass at the passing city. She knew he was sincere, but she was still fearful of the future. Not where she was going to get her next meal. He would see to that, but she didn't know what would happen to her or if he would be in her life after today.

Chapter Fourteen

☙

November 17th, 1942

E va had been in Berlin now for almost a month and a half. She
had not heard or seen Wilhelm since being here. She chose
not to tell his mother why she was there, just that he was busy with
work and didn't want her to be lonely. She had visited with Heidi
and Liesel on several occasions but spent most of her time with
Klaus and Marie. She talked on the phone almost daily with
Ingrid, informing her of all that had happened. Ingrid wanted to
come and visit her, but she told her to stay in France and that she
would eventually be back.

Her stomach had grown notably in the weeks she had been in
Germany, and for the first time a few days ago, she felt the baby
move. It was an incredible thing to experience, and she found
herself wishing Wilhelm could have been there to feel it. Having
so much time alone and being away from Wilhelm gave her plenty
of opportunities to reflect. She never wanted what she did for Jon

238

to tear her and Wilhelm apart or to put a wedge between them. But she was happy in the knowledge that Jon was now safely back in England. When Wilhelm brought her back to the apartment the day he released her from jail, Lorelei visited and told her a plane was coming to get Jon in two days. Eva informed her that she was going to Berlin and had no idea how long she would be gone. She also told Lorelei about being arrested by Wilhelm, which was why she was leaving. Lorelei said she would wait for her return, and when Eva told her she couldn't do it anymore, Lorelei reminded her that they had made a deal and that she had upheld her end of it by helping to free Jon.

Eva watched Marie knit from across the room. She was so happy to have Eva stay with her but felt terrible that Wilhelm had to leave her alone for so long. Marie looked up and saw her watching her.

"Don't despair, Eva. I'm sure he will come to get you soon."

She toyed with a piece of her hair. "I doubt that."

Marie laid her needles and yarn in her lap. "Now, why would you think that?"

Eva sighed. "Marie, I am here because Wilhelm doesn't want to see me. We got into a fight in Paris, and the fallout from it is far-reaching and most likely permanent, I'm afraid."

She moved the yarn and needles from her lap onto the armrest of the chair and stood, coming to sit beside Eva. "Couples fight. It is normal. He will be back to get you. I know my son has an overpowering desire and love for you, but he is caught between that love and his duty and devotion to his country. It is hard to juggle both, and being a soldier is part of who he is."

"Even if he does, I think it's over between us. We are not right for each other. The differences we have are irreconcilable, and he struggles daily with his inner demons, and he can't seem to find an escape from them."

"He is what his obligations and childhood have turned him into. He has had to shut down who he is to get the job done. He must do his duty while also trying not to feel as others do. But the feeling when someone you love disappears right out from under your hands is devastating. Like a piece of your soul has been torn away. So I don't think his reasons for doing things are always clear to other people who don't understand what he has been through or understand the way his mind works."

"But he doesn't talk about any of this with me. Most of what I know about him, I learned from you. He hasn't even talked to me about his childhood."

"He is private and does not like talking about his personal life or drawing unnecessary attention to himself."

"But I'm his wife. I'm the one person he should talk about these things with." Eva attributed their differences to upbringing and temperament and not depth of feelings, and she was pining for him because he was the man she loved.

"Then ask him to, and don't let him avoid it."

Eva was a little surprised that her anger and hatred for him had mostly faded with their time apart, and she wondered if he still despised her. "I will if I ever see him again."

"Oh, dear, you will see him again. He calls almost every day and asks about you."

Eva's head snapped up. She had not talked to him once since being in Berlin. She didn't even know he had called. To hear that he asked about her made her feel warm inside but also angered her. "And you didn't think it was strange that he never once asked to talk to me?"

"I just assumed that the two of you talked at other times."

"No. I have not spoken to him since I came here."

"I'm sorry, Eva. I had no idea. Next time he calls, I will give you the phone. Before you came here, he would only call me once a week, but now he calls almost every day, and it is because of you. He thinks about you a lot."

"You wouldn't know it by how he has been treating me."

"We always seem to hurt the ones we love."

That resonated with Eva. It was true. She had hurt Wilhelm so many times, and he, too, had hurt her. "I wish he were here. If even just to talk."

"I know you do. I couldn't imagine being in your shoes. I'm sure Wilhelm will call again tomorrow, and I will make certain he talks to you."

Eva was going to meet Klaus at his house, but she was patiently waiting for Wilhelm to call first. She did not want to miss it. She could not believe how empty she felt inside without him. When the phone rang, she tensed and waited for Marie to answer it. His mom picked up the phone and said a few words, and she knew it was him. Then his mom told him to hold on a second and nodded for Eva to come over. She handed the phone to her and whispered in her ear.

"I will go to my room and give you two some privacy." She patted Eva on the arm, then was gone.

Eva put the receiver to her ear, and the adrenaline spiked. "Hello, Wilhelm." For a second, she didn't know if he was even still on the other line.

After a minute, he spoke. "Hi, Eva."

She closed her eyes. Just the sound of his voice made her emotions swirl and knots twist in her stomach. She had not realized until now how much she needed to hear from him. "How are you?" She had no news of him for almost two months, but he had been getting information on her daily.

"I am well. My mother tells me you are bigger now, and your dresses barely fit."

"They fit well enough."

"You have the money I have been sending you, right?"

"I do."

"You should buy some new dresses then."

"Soon, I will have to."

"I'll have to hang up soon." His tone was guarded but not unkind.

She felt a spike of panic tight in her chest. She had only talked to him for a minute. She feared he no longer loved her, that she was just an obligation to him now. She was still grappling with her own feelings and wants. She loved him. That was impossible to deny to herself, but the thought that he would do something like arrest her even now made her blood boil. She was finding it hard to forgive him for that. But still, there was the emptiness inside that only he could fill. An intense loneliness and sadness were caused by his absence, and she would be silly to make herself suffer just to torment him. She wasn't going to cut off her nose just to spite her face. She had lost someone she loved once before, and she wasn't about to let it happen again. "Wilhelm…?"

"Yes."

She wanted to ask if he still loved her, but she didn't want to seem weak. She knew that he despised weakness. "Tell me… tell me I can go back to Paris." She heard him let out a breath.

"Eventually."

She sighed. "But you don't want me to?"

"Of course I want you to."

"Then why am I still here and you there?"

"Because right now, that is how it needs to be."

"I don't understand why." She wanted to tell him the truth, but she couldn't now. *Yes, I helped Jon escape, and I would do it again in a heartbeat. I am not sorry for what I did. I'm only sorry for what it did to us. I was offered a chance to go with him back to England, but I stayed for you. Because you aren't in England, and wherever you are is where I want to be. I know you are mad at me, and I'm not too happy with you about putting me in jail, but it didn't change my wanting to be with you. At first, I despised you for it, but that faded,* she said inside her head, wishing she could say it out loud, but instead chose to tell him she was upset he did not call her.

"Do you know how long I waited, hoping you would call or show up one day? It has been a miserable existence and cruel of you to do that to me."

"I'm sorry if I made you miserable. But I am gone so much that you would be alone most of the time, even if you were here. No, it is better if you are with my mother. That way, you have some company."

"I don't mind being alone."

"You can come back to Paris later."

"And when will that be?"

"I don't know. Eva, I have to go now."

Her eyes blurred with tears, and she angrily wiped them away. Their conversation changed nothing. "Alright."

"Take care of yourself."

"Sure." He stayed on the line for a few more seconds, then hung up, and she did the same. He said she couldn't go to Paris now, but he said nothing about her going to France. She had a non-restricted pass because she was married to him, so she would go to La Chapelle with Ingrid and then to Vichy France. She picked the phone back up and called the hospital.

"Ingrid, how would you like to visit La Chapelle with me?" Eva asked when Ingrid came on the other end.

"I would love to. When are you going?"

"When is the soonest you can get time off?"

"I can ask today for some time off next week."

"Great. Let me know the dates, and I will get a ticket and meet you in La Chapelle.

November 23rd, 1942

Eva cupped and blew on her hands in an effort to keep them warm as she waited for Ingrid's train to arrive at the station. She had called Madame Blanc last week and told her they were coming. Adele was supposed to pick them up at the train station in twenty minutes. She had not told them she was married or pregnant. That was going to be a shock.

Ingrid's train pulled into the station, and Eva scanned the people filing out, watching for Ingrid. When she saw Ingrid, she waved to her. Ingrid picked up her brown suitcase and hurried towards Eva.

She put her suitcase down, embracing her. "It is so good to see you." She pulled away and took Eva in, focusing on her stomach. "Oh my goodness, your stomach has grown so much. Can I feel?"

"Of course."

Ingrid placed her hand gently over her stomach and smiled. "It is so strange but amazing. Aunt Ingrid is going to spoil this little one rotten."

Eva felt her heart swell. She was so happy that Ingrid could be a part of her life and a part of her baby's for however long that was going to be. "Come on, I'm sure Adele is here by now."

They made their way off the small platform and crossed the tracks. Eva put her hand over her eyes, looked down the little dirt road leading to the station, and searched for Madame Blanc's black car. She saw it parked on the side of the road near the station, then picked up her suitcase and headed in that direction. She tried to pull her coat over her stomach and hold it closed with one hand so it wouldn't be the first thing Adele noticed.

Adele got out of the car when they were close and came to greet them. "Eva, I can't believe you are back in La Chapelle. Here, let me take that for you." Eva handed Adele her suitcase, but when she reached for it, she paused, both of their hands resting on the handle. Her eyes grew wide, and she slowly looked up at Eva. Her face was full of confusion and questions.

"I will explain at the house. I am tired and want to get out of the cold."

"Very well." Adele took her and Ingrid's bags and put them in the trunk.

They rode in relative silence back to the house, and Eva was dreading having to explain her pregnancy to them. Adele pulled the car to the side of the house as she usually did, and they carried their bags inside and up the stairs. Eva would stay in her old room, and Ingrid would stay in Gerhardt's old room, which had also been Wilhelm's.

"We have already had our dinner, but I will serve tea in the sitting room."

"Thank you, Adele." When Adele was gone from the room, Eva turned to Ingrid. "Well, this is going to be unpleasant."

"You weren't joking about her not liking Germans."

"It's not you she doesn't like. It's who she thinks the father is."

Understanding spread across Ingrid's face. "Oh. So she knows then?"

"She suspects. We better go down."

Ingrid followed Eva downstairs to the sitting room. There was a fire burning in the fireplace, and the lamps on each end of the couch were turned on, lighting the room in a soft yellow glow.

Madame Blanc rose when she saw them enter. "Eva, dear. How are you?" She gave Eva a hug but didn't mention her obviously swollen stomach. "And this must be your friend."

Ingrid held out her hand. "Ingrid Braun."

246

Madame Blanc took her hand and gently gave it a shake. "It is nice to meet you. Please, have a seat."

They all took a chair, and Madame Blanc poured a cup of tea each. Eva found it so odd that she never mentioned her condition. She handed them their tea, and Eva drank as she watched the fire crackle in the hearth.

"So, where is the baby's father?" Madame Blanc sipped her tea and looked at Eva.

And here it was, the question. "He is in Paris."

"And what is his name?"

"Wilhelm."

"So he is German? Is he a Nazi?"

"Yes, he is German. You know him but not by his first name." She placed her tea cup on the saucer. "And who is it?"

"SS Obersturmbannführer Bauer."

Madame Blanc cleared her throat. "I see. I take it this baby is not wanted?"

"This baby is wanted. It is his, and I want it. And when this war is over, I'll be waiting with his child."

"I must say, Eva, I am deeply disappointed in you. I knew you were with Gerhardt, and I liked him. He was one of the few good ones. But to go with that SS man... it saddens me. He will bring you down. He is an evil man, and I am sorry that you are with him."

"He didn't force me. It is strange to say it, but I love him."

"I would think so if you are choosing to keep his child. We should go to bed so we can get an early start to Vichy tomorrow."

Eva knew that Renée was not going to talk about it further. She probably felt it was pointless to try to convince her that

Wilhelm was evil and that she should leave him. "I agree. And Renée, I wanted to tell you, so it came from me, and you didn't find out some other way."

Renée stiffened. "Tell me what?"

"I am not just having his baby. I am married to him."

"Oh, dear lord. Why would you do such a thing? Can you even go home now?"

"I don't know why I couldn't."

"And what of him? He can't go with you."

"No, he cannot. But… I might stay even after the war is over."

"In Germany?"

"Yes, in Germany."

"Well, I say, you have changed. When you lived here, all you wanted was to go home to your family."

"That is true. I did, and I have changed. But you have to understand that he is also my family, so I have two families now. I'm sure I appear insane to you."

"A little bit, yes. I hope this war won't be the end for you as it was for Fabien and Sabina."

"I hope so too. But I would have been dead a long time ago if it wasn't for him. He has saved my life more than once. Renée, you have no idea what he has done for me."

"Eva, why are you going to Vichy?"

"Because I want to see the Mediterranean Sea, and I know he will never have time to take me."

"It won't be like you think it is?"

Eva furrowed her brows. "What do you mean?"

"You haven't heard?"

She shook her head. "Heard what?"

"The Germans occupied Vichy France seven days ago. It is no longer a free zone."

Eva's eyes grew wide. She knew that the Germans took the rest of France sometime during the war, but she didn't know when that happened. That would now mean Wilhelm oversaw even more territory and would be busier. He probably wasn't even in Paris. As a matter of fact, he could very well be in the south of France. This idea made her more excited to go but also apprehensive at the same time.

Eva felt tired but was too anxious to sleep. She sat next to Ingrid across from Adele and Renée. "You know, Eva, with your pass, you could go to Spain, which is a neutral country," Renée said, gauging her reaction.

Eva had not been sure that Spain was a neutral country until now. Her heart rate spiked, and all eyes were on her. This was something she had to honestly consider. "I had not thought of that."

"And you have all that money he has been sending you."

Eva felt like she had just been hit by a tidal wave and was stuck in the confusion of its undertow. Never had she had the resources or opportunity to go home at her feet like now. She felt frantic; she had to make a decision fast.

"At the next stop, you could get a ticket to Spain instead of Marseille. Think about what that means." Adele eyed her expectantly.

Eva shook her head. "I don't know. This is such a big decision."

"It should be an easy one," Renée told her.

"But it's not. And what if he caught me before I got there? All he has to do is put a bulletin out on my name, and I'm done for. Now that southern France is occupied, at least he might believe me when I tell him I just wanted to see the sea and wasn't trying to run. But there is no way I could lie about my reasons for going to Spain."

"True, but if you get there before he gets to you, then you are free."

"That's right. If, and that is a big if." The truth was Eva was conflicted. She was so enticed by this opportunity but did she want to be free of him. The answer to that was yes, but also no. Her head was in a pulsating ache, her thoughts coming in a rush. She closed her eyes and pressed her forehead against her palm.

"You don't have to decide right this second. The next stop isn't for at least half an hour," Renée said gently.

Eva moved her head from her hand and leaned back in the seat, then looked at Ingrid. "What do you think I should do?"

"I don't know."

"What would you do?"

"I think I would be conflicted. What is your heart telling you to do?"

"Stay."

"And what is your brain telling you to do?" Adele asked.

"It's just a muddle like it's caught in quicksand."

"That's because love clouds the brain. But if it were clear, it would be telling you to run."

Eva knew she was probably right. Suddenly, the breaks of the train were engaged, and it slid on the tracks, Eva and Ingrid almost falling out of their seat. Eva placed one hand on the glass and the other on the seat for support and waited for the train to come to a complete stop. As it coasted, she looked out the window. Military cars were waiting at a crossroad, and she thought her heart was going to stop. She looked to Renée and Adele, then Ingrid in confused terror. Ingrid took hold of her hand and held it tight. Eva did not need to say what she suspected. They could see it written on her face.

The train gave one last jolt, then ceased to move, the hissing of the steam from the engine filling the air as it clouded the ground outside. The sound of the outside door being opened resonated through the car, and there was a sudden awareness of Wilhelm's presence. She turned in her seat and looked at the sliding door to their compartment, then it slid open with force, and Wilhelm burst through into the little room. Their eyes met, and a fire ignited in her, the sight of his uniform triggering a rage in her that was so raw she might strike him if he was standing closer. She dropped her gaze to the floor but could feel Wilhelm staidly watching her.

He cleared his throat, and she looked up. He held out his hand. "Give me your pass, Eva."

Confusion flared, and she drew slightly back from him. "Why?"

His mouth tightened, and he looked at her in disbelief. "Why?" He said indignantly. "Because you are in France without my permission and traveling to the part that was the free zone only a week ago." He gave her a poignant look. She pulled her pass from her purse and held it out to him. He jerked it from her hand and tucked it into the breast pocket of his jacket. "Eva and I will be sitting in another compartment. You three will stay here."

She considered this, her brow lifting at his words. "Why are you riding the train to Marseille?"

"Because it might be a good idea for me not to lose track of you." He took her hand, pulled her from the compartment, down the narrow passage, into an empty compartment, and slid the door closed. He pointed to the seat across from him. "Sit," he commanded. She lowered herself onto the soft cushion, and he sat across from her, one brow raised in a strident question.

"I wasn't running. I was taking a trip to see the Mediterranean because I knew you would never take me." Wilhelm remained silent. "I didn't tell you because... well, because you are upset with me, and I am not too happy with you either."

He cocked a brow at her. "You honestly thought you could come here without me knowing?" he glanced out the window before shooting her a look of incredulity.

"No, I just hoped I could."

He watched her, considering. I suppose you can stay with me in Nice for tonight."

"Why are you in Nice?"

"Because I have to oversee the establishment of Gestapo presence in Vichy France, now that I am over this part of the country too."

"Of course."

She couldn't help but admire his sense of obligation in fulfilling his duties. Some men were made for war. Born for it, and Wilhelm was one of those men.

"To be honest, I never expected to see you again."

His expression took on a hard edge. "That's presumptuous. What gave you that idea?"

"Your actions."

"I would not miss being there when the baby is born unless I am in the field when that happens."

"You would come back only for the baby then?"

He shook his head. "No."

She got so frustrated sometimes at how brief he was when he spoke and how closed off he always seemed to be. "What is this? What are we doing here? You had me arrested. What kind of husband does that?"

"What kind of wife betrays her husband over and over?"

"So it's agreed then? Being together was a terrible idea for us." Eva couldn't understand how it was possible to love someone who was so wrong for you.

"No, I do not agree. But there needs to be a certain level of commitment on your part. I have had your body, but it's not enough. I want your heart and need total loyalty from you."

"What does that entail?"

"I don't have to tell you. You already know. It has long been overdue to have this talk with you, and what you say next will decide your future."

To her, that sounded like a threat. And honestly, she didn't know what to say. The train began to slow, and she looked out the window, noticing again that military cars were waiting at the Marseille station. Did he lie? Was he actually having her arrested when they stopped? Wilhelm looked to the window, and while he was distracted, she bolted for the door, slid it open, and pushed her legs to the limit as she ran the length of the train car. She darted into the first open door and closed it in front of her as she watched him close on her. She locked the door and fell back onto a toilet, realizing she had locked herself in a bathroom. She heard Wilhelm's footsteps on the carpeted floor but was too afraid to open the door and see if he was gone. In less than a minute, the footsteps were back, and a key was inserted into the lock on the bathroom door, then it clicked open. Wilhelm stepped into the small space and shut the door, then turned the lock back into place.

She reached down, grabbed the small metal trash can, and leveled it at him, hoping it was threatening enough to keep him away. The bathroom was small, with only a few feet between them. Her arm trembled as she tried to put more space between them by stepping back until she was against the wall, caught between him and the toilet as it pressed into the calfs of her legs. Defiance and the fear of being put back into a cell whipped through her as her body froze, her arm outstretched towards him.

"I know what you are planning, Wilhelm. And now you are going to listen to me. There is no way I am going to let you put me back in that awful place or control me."

His eyes roamed over her, and he calmly took in the trash can and nodded to himself. His gaze moved to the door, then back to her. "Eva..." he said, a sliver of annoyance running through his measured tone. "Put the trash can down. I am not arresting you."

"I don't know what to believe. I am not certain I can trust your words," she yelled at him as chaotic feelings ripped inside her. "But if a single thing you told me is a lie, I will fight you, and I don't care that I'm pregnant. Do not underestimate what I'm capable of."

Wilhelm moved his hands out in a placating gesture. "I have known you long enough to have a pretty good idea of what you are capable of." He dropped his right arm and turned his left hand over, holding it out, palm up, his tone calm but firm. "Eva, give me the trash can."

All the muscles in her body were tense, her hand still trembling, but she lowered the trash can a fraction. Wilhelm lost his placated expression, strode over to her, took the trash can, unlocked and opened the door, then threw it into the hall, the can bouncing on the floor before it rolled. He shut the door back and locked it. He turned and closed in on her, his voice a determined whisper. "We are at the station, and it's time to get off."

She looked into his eyes. "Was what you told me a lie?"

"No." His frustration was beginning to show through.

She turned this over in her mind. She had to trust him. What other choice did she have? She squeezed her fists tightly closed, trying to retain some level of calm, but he mistook it for anger. The corner of his mouth lifted. "Go ahead, hit me," he prodded, leveling his eyes on her, a smile playing at the edge of his mouth.

She gaped at him, deeply put off by his humor at her distress. She squared her shoulders and narrowed a glare at him. She forced out a snort of frustration. "I was trying to calm myself, not preparing to hit you."

Wilhelm's mocking grin widened. "It wouldn't hurt much."

"You are so infuriating," she spat out. "There, did that hurt?" She tried to pull back from him, her emotions tumultuous as she shot him a potent glare.

"No, not in the least." He gave a short laugh, but then his smile faded, and she could no longer read his mood as his eyes bore into hers.

She straightened and unsuccessfully tried to equal his penetrating gaze. "I want to be clear. If you try to arrest me, I will resist with everything I have."

His expression turned serious, his deep hazel eyes guarded. "I told you the truth. I am not arresting you. And you know I would never pit myself against you if it ever came to it. Why would you think that?"

"Because you are unpredictable and aggressive," she countered. His tone was unexpectedly caring and tugged at something raw and vulnerable inside her. She bit her lip as she tried to assess the situation.

He reached up and pushed a loose strand of hair behind her ear and stepped closer, his gaze searching, his words low but firm. "Unpredictable, yes, aggressive towards you, no."

She let out a breath of disbelief. "You are nothing but aggressive towards me."

"Not in the way you meant, I would never hit you, Eva."

She shook her head, no longer able to meet his eyes. "You don't understand what it's like to experience you, to be around you. I know it's impossible for you to imagine. But it's hard to love you." When she finally looked back up at Wilhelm, there was a storm of emotions in his eyes that was so fierce a flush spread across her cheeks. There was an intense hurt in his expression, and she was taken back and humbled by the realization that she had inadvertently given such a wounding blow. "Wilhelm, I'm sorry. Let me explain."

His hand fell to his side, and he pulled back as if collecting himself, but she could feel the turbulent emotions coming off him in waves. In his eyes, there was a struggle for control that was also visible in the rigid way he was standing. It was his attempt to bring his sudden, unbridled hurt and anger under reign.

When he spoke, his words were clipped. "We need to get off the train now. We are holding it up."

In the short amount of time they were in the bathroom, the conversation and chemistry between them had hit so many highs and lows, but now it was off its rails, and she had no idea how to get it back on course again. She figured it was better to say nothing right now and followed him out of the bathroom and off the train. The silence and tension between them hung heavy in the air.

Ingrid, Renée, and Adele were all waiting on the platform for her. They hurried over to her when they saw her get off the train. "Eva, what is happening?" Ingrid said in a rushed, concerned tone.

"I am going to Nice with Wilhelm," she whispered. "Please come there? All of you."

"Where will you be staying?"

"I don't know," she said, realizing she didn't know where Wilhelm was staying in Nice.

"I am familiar with Nice, and I know the city well. I will get a room at the Excelsior Hotel," Renée told her. "If you can, meet us there."

"I will." She hugged them and noticed that Wilhelm's orderly had gotten her bag off the train and was putting it in the car. Wilhelm waited by the open back door for her, and she walked towards him but looked over her shoulder at Ingrid, Renée, and Adele one last time before climbing into the back seat.

They had ridden in silence for over twenty minutes before she decided to speak to him. "Where are you staying in Nice?"

"In a hotel." He never looked at her but kept his head turned towards the window.

She reached over and touched his head. "What is going on in there?" What she said about him being hard to love had some deeper meaning to him than she had known. It hurt him in a way she had not understood, and there was a nagging, unwelcome guilt that gnawed at her gut over it.

He slowly turned his head to her. "Nothing I will talk about with you."

"You don't think the things you keep deep inside your mind and soul should be spoken about to your spouse?"

"Depends on the spouse."

"Why are you being like this? You said in Paris that you would answer any question I had. I asked about your childhood, and you told me you would tell me the next time I asked."

"Did I?"

"Yes, you did."

"So you really want to hear about how a boy, a little girl, and a woman were mistreated by the man who was supposed to care for them?"

She thought about why she wanted to know this, and she realized it was because she loved him. Because he was the sum of all his experiences, and this, sadly, was one of them. "Yes, I want to know you and everything about you. The good and the bad, because everything that has happened in your life made you who you are now."

He looked in the front at his orderly, then turned his gaze back on her. "Not now."

She remembered what his mom said about not letting him get out of talking about himself. "At the hotel, then."

He turned away from her and looked back out the window, and she did the same. They rode the rest of the way in silence, and she couldn't help but wonder what a mystery box he was. You finally pry one secret out of him just to realize there are hundreds more inside. He was a puzzle she could not solve, but then again, she also had her fair share of secrets. But nothing he did was by chance or done rashly. Even when he lied to her, he told the truth. The truth was in the telling of the lie.

It was dark when they arrived in Nice and pulled in front of the hotel. It was an upscale establishment, and she was not surprised he was housed there.

The orderly waited in the car, and Wilhelm got her bag for her and carried it to the room on the top floor. She followed behind, watching him, trying to gauge his mood from his body language. He took a key from his pocket and unlocked the door, setting her bag by the bed once inside. He removed his cap, gloves, coat, and jacket, then laid on the comforter with his boots still on.

"You can use the bathroom first."

She looked at her bag on the floor where he had left it. "Thank you." She lifted it onto the bed and unsnapped it, then opened the lid. She took out her nightgown and toiletry bag, gave him one quick glance, and went to the bathroom. She didn't lock the door but doubted he would come in. She decided to shower so he didn't have to wait long, but when she came out of the bathroom, he was gone. She paused, halting in her tracks. She looked around the room and noticed his jacket, coat, and hat were also gone, but his gloves were on the nightstand. She had mixed feelings about him leaving. She pulled her nightgown off and put her dress back on, but left her hair down. Then grabbed her coat and scarf off the bed where she had laid them and left the room. The door clicked behind her, and she stopped. "Shit." She turned and looked at the closed door, remembering she didn't have a key. She read the room number, 612, then hurried to the lobby.

"Excuse me," she said to the man at the desk. The man in room 612, SS Obersturmbannführer Bauer. Has he left the hotel recently?"

"Yes, Madame."

"Do you know where he went?"

"He went to the bar across the street."

"Thank you."

Eva stepped outside and sprinted across the street to the bar directly opposite the hotel. She pulled open the heavy wooden door, and the smell in the air suddenly changed. She was assaulted by the pungent stench of sweat, cigarette smoke, alcohol, and men. The room was dark and mostly empty, just a handful of German soldiers, most of whom stopped what they were doing and stared at her. She was sure it looked strange for her to be there. Piano music echoed through the building, and she searched the room. To the front of the building was a baby grand, and Wilhelm had his sleeves rolled up and his jacket and cap beside him on the bench as he played, a cigarette hanging from the corner of his mouth. She did not want to disturb him, so she took a table in the back and watched as he played. This must be an escape for him, but an escape from what? Work, the war, her, or the demons that tormented him?

It was past midnight, and he was still playing, but she continued to watch. A man from two tables away stood and came over to her table, a beer in his hand. "What is your name?" he asked in broken French.

"Eva," she answered back in German.

He smiled. "Can I sit with you, Eva?"

"If you like," she answered back in German.

He pulled out a chair and sat across from her, turned, and looked at Wilhelm. "He plays well."

"Yes, he does. He pours his feelings into the music." She was watching Wilhelm and not the man.

"I guess so." He looked at her stomach. "Are you new here in Nice."

"Yes, I only arrived today."

"And how long will you stay?"

"I don't know."

Wilhelm brought the song to a close, took his jacket and cap from the bench, and stood. He pulled the jacket over his shoulders but held the hat in his hand. He walked towards the door but suddenly stopped, taking a few steps back, so he was even with her table. His eyes narrowed.

"Eva. Why are you here?" He looked at the man sitting at her table, his gaze growing predatory. The man was frozen in his seat. "Don't you have your own table?"

"Yes, sir." He quickly stood and left.

Eva got up from her chair and picked her purse up off the table. "They said you would be here."

"You should have been in bed a long time ago."

"You aren't."

261

"Yes, but I'm also not pregnant." He held his hand out to her, and she gladly took it but found it odd that he would offer.

When they were back in the hotel, he tossed his jacket and hat in a chair and pulled his shirt out from his pants. She undid the three buttons at the top of her dress and started to pull it off, then hesitated. It was awkward for her to undress in front of him now, and the fact that it had become awkward was strange to her. She also felt fat, and he had not seen her naked with her stomach this big before. She waited, trying to decide if she should change in the bathroom or just do it now. She resolved to step out of her comfort zone and change in the room with him. She pulled the dress over her head and was left standing naked in the room. Wilhelm turned to sit on the bed so he could take off his boots but paused when he saw her. She had her gown in her hands when he turned, and she froze, all of her out for him to see. He didn't avert his gaze, and her face flushed crimson. She was embarrassed because he wasn't looking away and felt a little shameless that she was changing in front of him. She hurried and pulled her gown on over her head and turned away.

"You don't have to hide from me."

She inclined her head to the side to look at him. "I don't look like I did. Not the way you are used to seeing me."

"You are pregnant with my child. Why would I be turned off by seeing you that way?"

She thought about that and didn't know why she figured he would. Because she wasn't a man, and Wilhelm was always so cryptic, she honestly wasn't sure if it really was ugly and a turn-off to him or to men in general. No one had ever told her if men liked or disliked seeing women that way or if they were indifferent to it.

"Because I look like a whale."

He pulled his brows together, then suppressed a smile. "Believe me, you don't look like a whale."

"Alright, but a little fat."

"No, you don't look fat, Eva." To her surprise, he walked around the bed and came to stand in front of her. "When I saw you standing there naked from across the room, I thought, she is beautiful. The curve of your back, the size your stomach is now, the way your breast hang without a bra, the smoothness of your skin," he rubbed the back of his finger up and down her arm, "and the color in your cheeks when you saw me looking at you."

Her heart raced at his proximity. "I didn't know if you would want to see me this way."

He didn't answer but kissed her on the forehead, then returned to the other side of the room and sat on the bed to remove his boots. "I'm going to take a shower." He got his pajamas from the armoire, then went into the bathroom and closed the door behind him.

She wanted to still be upset with him for arresting her, but then he goes and does stuff like this, and she also hurt him on the train. She wanted to explain what she meant about him being hard to love so she would when he got out of the shower.

She patiently waited on the bed with the lamp on but felt nervous about spending the night with him. It had been so long. When he came out of the bathroom, she spoke before he had time to ask why she was still up.

"Wilhelm, I wanted to talk about what I said to you on the train."

"There is no need."

"Yes, there is."

He turned out the bathroom light and came to sit beside her on the bed. "It is late, Eva."

"I know, but if I don't get it out now, it will only get harder for me to say later." He gestured with his hand for her to go ahead. "The simple act of caring for you is easy, but us being from two countries who are at war with each other is hard, and the way you are also makes it difficult. Sometimes, I think you forget I am your wife and not one of your soldiers. But on the flip side of that, when you do remember I am your wife, you treat me like I can't do anything. I don't want to be treated in either of those ways. I don't want to be a kept woman or someone you think you can control."

"It's not that you can't do anything. It's that you shouldn't have to. And I'm sorry if you think I'm trying to control you because I'm not. But I will not apologize for the times I have saved you from others and yourself. Or when you need to be shown your errors. And I know that you and I have very different views of what is and isn't acceptable and appropriate for women to do. You are the only woman I have met who thinks as you do. I don't know if it is just your family or other Americans who believe that way, but you are no longer over there or the responsibility of your father. You live in a country controlled by Germany and are now my responsibility. That duty has been passed from your father to me."

She could protest or argue with his views, but there would be no point. He was from a different time and a different culture. "I just wanted you to know what I meant. Not that you were unworthy of love, only that you make it hard." She watched him carefully, waiting for his response. He has remained closed off to her, but she really did understand rationally and emotionally why he was being distant, and she tried to accept it. But since seeing him on the train, she would catch him staring at her, giving her an ardent look every now and then, and sensed the heat in his gaze before he carefully reeled it back.

"I am not upset with you for what you said. I would also find it difficult to be with me. I pity you because you are stuck with me."

His tone was unexpectedly warm, but a rush of sadness filled her. Did he really think he was so unworthy of love? But at least he could acknowledge how hard he made it for others to care for him. She glanced appreciatively at him, her eyes drawn to the site of his lean chest in the dim light from the lamp. The scars on his skin from the attack were visible, and a lump formed in her throat. He hadn't put his pajama shirt on when he came out of the bathroom. Heat simmered in her, hot as fire, as she took in his handsome form and considered how their nearness affected her. How was it so easy for him to seduce her without even trying? But she wouldn't make love to him tonight. And she doubted he would even if she asked him to.

"Can we talk about your upbringing?"

"No. Not tonight. It is late, and we both need sleep."

She noticed that he did not follow up with a time they would talk about it. She nodded and slid down on the bed, laying her head on the pillow and covering up with the blanket. She couldn't dismiss the feeling that plagued her when they were apart. It was more than just distance between them.

She woke to the sound of water running and opened her eyes, blinking to clear her blurry vision. The bathroom door was open, and Wilhelm stood over the sink as he shaved. She pushed off the blankets and came to stand in the bathroom doorway. She watched him, realizing she had never watched a man shave before except her father. He looked at her through the mirror, and there was something in his eyes that she could not read, but his expression was severe. She could not just stand by and let their relationship crumble and them drift apart. She didn't want to hurt him with what she said, but she had to tell him how she felt to save their marriage. She didn't know if he shared her opinion, but she thought they were good together.

"I have given myself to you, and now it's like I'm nothing. You say it's better this way, but you won't tell me why it's better and treat me like a burden, and that's it." Pain coursed through her body, and she wanted to lash out at him with all she had, but instead, she was falling apart with unfocused thoughts as her voice cracked. "I need you, Wilhelm, and I want you in my life, and I want to be in yours and not just as a responsibility to you." She felt as if she was on the brink of an emotional and physical cataclysm as unwanted tears stung her eyes. She didn't have time to think things through as reality rushed over her. The fact that she was married to a Nazi, pregnant with his baby, was still trapped in World War II Europe after all this time, and that it would all come crashing to an end soon. And that he had broken their connection now when she needed him the most, and even worst yet, she still might lose him when it's all over.

He laid the razor on the edge of the sink, then turned to face her, and for a long moment, they were locked in a silent battle. Wilhelm's gaze was so severe on her that it was almost violent in its intensity, and then he strode towards her, his expression fiery as he came at her. She tensed, preparing for him, whatever he was about to do as she focused on his face, and that is when she saw a change in his eyes, a part of the old him slipping back. He leaned in closer, his lips coming down hard on hers as their bodies made contact, pushing her back, pressing her against the doorframe behind her as he grasped hold of her and drove all of his passion onto her in an overpowering rush. Lit with his force, her desperate want for him took over, and she pushed her body harder against his, her hands grasping at him fiercely as she kissed him back just as intensely. One of his hands went to the back of her head, his fingers twining through her hair, then he bit her bottom lip as his other hand slid down to her butt. His tongue was in her mouth now as her hand rubbed up his back and under his shirt as the heated tension between them turned into an inferno. He slid his hand up from her butt and cupped her right breast, his breaths coming faster and deeper. Her whole body was on fire, and she struggled to catch her breath.

Finally, Wilhelm drew back, both of them breathing heavily as he continued to hold tight to her, his eyes savage. "I love you, Eva. Is that what you want to hear?" She looked at him, still breathing heavily, shocked and speechless. "Is it?" he demanded, his voice hoarse. "Are those the words you are aching to hear me say?"

"Yes," she said in a rough voice as he held onto her arms, staring at her with ferocity. She swallowed, her mouth feeling dry.

"I love you," he said again, lashing the words out with a vehemence that made her breath hitch in her throat. "But you have committed so many acts of treason, assisted in the murder of my countrymen, and lied to me repeatedly. So, if you are going to survive, I cannot coddle you, and I want you to survive. I did not risk my life and reputation to save you just to have you risk it again due to your own stubbornness. But it's going to be hard from now on, and I will be tough on you and force you to do things you won't like. Do you understand?" She nodded stiffly, holding her breath, shocked by his words. He stepped back and extinguished the fire in his eyes, then collected himself as his breathing was forced into a more even rhythm. When he looked at her, his face was again distant, any emotion held firmly back. He glanced at her nightgown. "Get changed; we are leaving soon," he instructed, then turned back to the sink and picked up the razor.

She sat quietly in the car beside him, wondering what would become of her now. Would he send her back to Berlin, home to Paris, or allow her to go to stay in Marseille? She hoped he would let her stay in Nice with him, but she didn't see that happening.

She looked over at him. "Where are we going?"

He didn't look at her but continued to stare out the window. "The train station."

This is what she figured. "And where am I going?"

Finally, he looked at her. "Paris."

She relaxed a little at his words. If she wasn't going to stay here with him, she wanted to go back to Paris. At least she would be in the same country and in the home they shared. She had to find a way to get word to Ingrid, Renée, and Adele that she was leaving. "And I will be going alone then?"

"Yes. I have a lot of work to do here, and I can't have you distracting me."

"Of course, I would never want that," she said with ire. "Worrying that I'm going to run would take up so much of your precious time."

He looked angry now. "That is not the manner I meant. I believe you when you say you weren't trying to flee, but when you are around, it is too distracting. It takes away my focus and motivation to do my job and remain at work instead of going back to you. I only have so much time to achieve what needs to be done here before returning to Paris, so I can't have anything else competing for my attention."

She didn't know if he was using that as an excuse or was telling her the truth. She wanted to believe him, but the way he had been treating her painted a different picture than the one he wanted her to see. "I understand." She looked out the window, but he didn't look away, and she could feel his eyes still on her.

The car pulled in front of the platform at the train station and stopped. "I'll get it," she heard him say to his orderly. Wilhelm got out of the car and came around to her side, opening her door. He held his hand out for her to take, and she stared down at the large palm outstretched in front of her. She finally placed her hand in his, and he closed his fingers around it, helping her from the car. "I don't know when I will be back in Paris, but you can call me here. I will phone you in a few days and give you the number." She nodded, and he leaned in and gave her a soft kiss on the cheek. She forced a half smile, and he handed her the ticket as his orderly retrieved her bag from the trunk and set it on the platform at her feet. "I will call you." He gave her hand a squeeze before getting into the car. The orderly shut the door and got into the front, then the car turned around and drove away.

She felt hollow and drained. She looked at the ticket, then dropped her hand to her side, picked up her bag, and walked towards the bench to wait.

Chapter Fifteen

ॐ

December 17th, 1942

Eva was keeping track of the time that had passed since Wilhelm put her on the train in Nice. It had been over four weeks. He had kept his word and called her, leaving the number to reach him, but she didn't call him as often as she wanted out of the anger and hurt she was feeling. He would call her on the days she didn't call, but they always only talked about simple things, safe things. He gave nothing away as to what he was doing there, and she didn't tell him how she was feeling. The night she arrived in Paris, she called Renée at the hotel she was staying at and informed her that she was back in Paris. The following day, Ingrid, Adele, and Renée caught the next train to Paris, and Renée and Adele stayed a few days before returning to La Chapelle.

Once they had left, and after she had rested for a few days, she contacted Lorelei, and they agreed to meet in the Louvre. Eva arrived early because this was her first time there, and she wanted to explore the museum and see the art, but she was surprised and disappointed as she walked the halls. So much of the artwork was gone, being kept safe from the Nazis somewhere, no doubt. But the building itself was magnificent and worth the trip.

She checked her watch and saw it was time to meet Lorelei in the lobby. She descended the stairs and waited near the front door. She wasn't there long when she spotted Lorelei entering the building, wearing a green dress partly covered with a fur coat, gloves, mat-black heels, and a hat pinned to her head. She looked exquisite, more elegant than Eva ever could. She waved to her, and Lorelei made her way across the foyer towards her.

She eyed Eva's stomach, and her lips curled up as she flashed a smile. "I see it is getting closer to your time."

Eva looked down, no longer able to see her feet. "Yes. I'm in the third trimester now, but I try to tell myself this baby is never coming out because I have no idea what to do when it does."

Lorelei's face was warm and kind. "You will, and there will be people to help."

Eva thought of Wilhelm's mother. "I know."

Lorelei linked arms with Eva's, and they walked the long hall. "We now need your assistance."

Eva knew this day would come and feared it. "What do you need my help with?"

"On a farm west of Paris, we are hiding a downed British pilot. He was wounded when his plane crashed, and we have treated his wounds the best we can, but he needs the help of someone skilled in medicine."

Eva was relieved that she had not asked her to help kill someone. "And you want me to go to this farm and treat him?"

272

"Yes."

"But I no longer have a pass. Wilhelm took it when I went to the south of France."

"That isn't a problem. We will sneak you out of the city."

Eva pulled her arm free and stopped walking, searching Lorelei's face. "But how? I can't think of a way that would be possible."

"Leave it to me. Plus, it will be easier while your husband is still gone."

"When do you need me to go?"

"Tonight."

That wasn't the answer she was expecting. "Tonight? I...."

"Wait in your home. We will be by to get you at five sharp."

Eva didn't know what to say, but she was confused and a little worried about this plan of Lorelei's. "Can I ask how you will get me out of the city?"

"Of course. I would be surprised if you didn't. The guards will not question my driver and me leaving the city for a party at a château."

"But I don't have a pass, so that still doesn't work."

"We will put you in the trunk. They won't check it."

Eva was not so confident they wouldn't. "Are you sure?"

"They never have before."

"But you are leaving late."

"I do it all the time."

Eva hesitated for a second before finally answering. "I will trust you."

They left the museum and went their separate ways, and Eva waited at their townhouse. She anxiously paced the hall and constantly checked the window. The phone rang, making her jump. For the first time, she didn't want it to be Wilhelm. She picked up the receiver and put it to her ear. "Hello."

"Eva," Ingrid's voice echoed on the other end.

"Hi, Ingrid."

"I was wondering if you were free tomorrow?"

"I believe so. Why?"

"Well, I have the day off and thought we could go to the Eiffel Tower."

Eva had been saving that for Wilhelm, but she didn't know why anymore. He didn't seem to be the least bit interested in spending time with her. "I would love that. Just come by tomorrow before noon, and we can have lunch together too."

"I will."

Eva heard a car engine idling out front. "I have to go, Ingrid, but I will see you tomorrow."

"See you then."

She could hear the excitement in Ingrid's voice. She hung up the phone, and a loud knock came from the front door. She grabbed her coat and purse and then hurried to the door. She pulled it open, and Lorelei was waiting on the other side.

"Are you ready?"

"Yes." She closed the door behind her and followed Lorelei to the car.

Once they were in the back of the car, Lorelei spoke again. "Shortly, we will park in an alley and hide you in the trunk. I have put some blankets in there for you to make it a bit softer. Your condition is uncomfortable enough, especially in the later months, and we don't want you to bounce around in there too much either."

"Thank you."

They drove only a few miles when the car pulled into a dark alley, turned off the headlights, and killed the engine. Lorelei and her orderly helped Eva into the trunk.

"Watch your head," Lorelei said as Eva lay down in the small space.

She watched the lid close, engulfing her in total darkness. She breathed a little heavier as panic started to rise. She tried to remain calm, but it was hard. She kept reminding herself that this was payment for them rescuing Jon.

The ride was uncomfortable and felt like it was taking hours. The car went over bumps, made sharp turns, and stopped suddenly. It made her feel sick, and the baby didn't seem to like it either. It moved a lot, kicking her in the back and pushing on her stomach. She placed her hands over her belly and felt the constant movement. "Please stop, little one." She rubbed her hands up and down her stomach, hoping it would soothe the baby, but it only made it move more. It changed position, pushing against her bladder, and she had to press her legs together so she didn't pee in her underwear. She poked her stomach with her finger anytime it moved, but it only moved to the other side. "You are definitely Wilhelm Bauer's child," she said, tapping her stomach with her palm.

Finally, the car stopped, and then she heard voices right before the trunk lid opened, and Lorelei and her driver looked down at her. "That wasn't too bad, was it?"

"I guess it could have been worse," she said as they helped her from the trunk. She felt stiff, but the baby had finally stopped moving. She looked around, noticing the outline of a forest through the darkness. She looked to the two-story farmhouse they had parked in front of.

"Follow me," Lorelei said.

"Before I help him, I need to use the bathroom."

Lorelei pointed to an outhouse about thirty feet away. "That is the only toilet. You are no longer in the city, Eva."

Eva sighed, then walked to the outhouse. She quickly used it and then followed Lorelei to the front door of the house. Lorelei pulled the string to the little brass bell beside the door and then it opened. An elderly woman stood before them. She was older than Lorelei and wore a simple, worn dress, nothing like the one Lorelei was wearing.

She looked to Lorelei, then to Eva, and back to Lorelei. "Who is this?"

"Her name is Eva. She is the one I told you about. She is a nurse and can help the pilot."

"It's good you brought her when you did because his condition has turned for the worse this afternoon." The woman moved to the side and motioned for them to enter. They followed her upstairs and down a hall to a small bedroom at the end. The woman pushed the door open, and it squeaked on its hinges. Eva peered around her into the dimly lit room. A man was lying on the bed, still wearing his British pilot uniform. He looked to be in his late twenties with dark brown hair. His skin was ashen, and sweat was beading on his forehead. His eyes were closed, and his chest moved with slow, deep breaths.

Eva looked to the woman for approval to enter, and she nodded. Eva came to his bedside and looked at him closer. His jacket was unbuttoned, and his once white shirt was soaked in blood. She pulled the chair from the desk beside the bed and sat down. She leaned over him, but he didn't upon his eyes or stir. She lifted his shirt to look at the wound and saw a piece of cloth balled over it that was held in place by a long strip of material tied around his torso. She gently pulled the rag back, exposing a bullet hole. She turned in the chair and looked at the woman.

"Has he said anything? Do you know his name or how he got shot?"

"I don't know anything about him. He spoke frantically when we found him in our barn, but I understood none of it. He only spoke in English."

Eva turned back to him. "I will learn who he is. English is my mother tongue too." She put both hands on his shoulder and arm and rolled him slightly to his right side but did not see an exit wound. "The bullet is still in him. We have to get it out, or he will die. What do you have that I can use?"

"I have some pliers, alcohol, and salve for wounds."

"I can't use the pliers; they are too big. Bring me some boiled water, the alcohol, and all the clean clothes you can spare."

"Is there anything I can do?" Lorelei asked.

"Help me get his shirt and jacket off." Lorelei came to her side of the bed, and each began removing an arm from his jacket. He opened his eyes then, and his pupils dilated. His eyes darted from Eva to Lorelei, then he tried to sit up, moaning in pain as he did.

"Slowly," Eva said to him in English.

He instantly stopped moving and really looked at her. "You are... not French?"

"No, I am not. I'm American. This is my friend Lorelei. She is German but is here to help you."

His head snapped to her. "You brought a German?"

"No. She brought me. She is the reason I am here to help you. She is working with the British." He coughed and then winced as he brought his hand to his side.

"You have a bullet in your abdomen, and I have to get it out, but first, we need to remove some of your clothing."

"Do you know how to do that?"

"I used to be a nurse."

"And you aren't anymore?" He looked at her stomach. "Because you are having a baby?"

"Something like that." She helped him out of his jacket and pulled his shirt over his head as gently as possible. "Lay back." She helped him lie down, and he closed his eyes once his head was on the pillow. He breathed heavily from the exertion of sitting. The woman brought the things Eva asked for and set them on the nightstand next to the bed. Eva cleaned her hands with alcohol, then removed the temporary bandage and poured some over his wound. She set the bottle back on the nightstand, wet one of the cloths in the pan of water, rang it out, and wiped the blood from his stomach.

"I'm going to do something now that will hurt a lot." He tensed and stared at her with large, brown eyes dilated from fear. "I have to stick a finger in the hole to find the bullet and see how deep it is. I don't have the correct tools to remove it, so I will have to improvise." In truth, she didn't know what she was going to use to remove it. She handed him a cloth to put in his mouth and bite on. Once he had it firmly clenched between his teeth, she stuck her index finger in the hole, and blood ran out onto the sheet. He grunted and closed his eyes, squeezing them tightly. She couldn't feel the bullet with her finger and knew it was deeper than she could reach. She looked at the woman. "Do you have any pliers with a long pointy nose?"

"I do, in the barn."

"Get it.

The woman left the room and returned after a few minutes with the pliers. She handed them to Eva and watched. "Are you ready?" Eva asked him. He nodded but was sweating profusely, and his skin was burning hot. She cleaned the pliers and his wound again, then poked the tip down into the hole until she felt the piece of lead. She opened the pliers to grip the bullet, and he cried out, losing the cloth in his mouth, his head slumping as he lost consciousness.

"That's for the better," Lorelei said. "The farm is out of the city, but there are still other houses close enough that someone might hear.

Eva looked at his face and how pale it was. He had lost a lot of blood and needed a transfusion, but she knew he wouldn't get one. He also needed antibiotics and pain medicine, but he probably wouldn't get those either. If he survived the night, he might just make it.

"It is."

Once again, she opened the pliers and pinched the bullet with the tip. "Bring me a threaded needle." The woman left the room again but returned only a few seconds later and laid a needle on the bed beside Eva. She pulled the pliers up with the bullet, and blood ran from him in a steady flow. She quickly laid the pliers on the table and placed a towel over the wound to soak up some of the blood. She removed it and then began sewing the hole. Once it was stitched, she cleaned the remaining blood from his skin, rubbed some ointment over the wound, and put on a clean bandage. She pulled the blankets up over him and stood.

"Check the wound daily, and if you have any pain medicine, give it to him. I will return when I can and hopefully bring some medicine with me."

"Thank you for your help. Will he live?"

"I don't know. It's too early to say."

"Would you like a cup of tea?"

"I would love one." She cleaned the blood from her hands, and the three of them went downstairs to the kitchen.

The woman put a kettle on the stove. "Please, have a seat." Eva and Lorelei sat at the little round table, and the woman joined them. "Where are you from?"

"America."

"And here you are now, in the heart of the war."

"I have been here a long time."

"And you have found yourself a man, or just what they leave behind?" She gestured with her eyes to Eva's stomach.

Eva smiled at her comment, understanding that during the war, there were a lot of unplanned pregnancies. Some were made in love, some by lust, and some by rape. "He is still in the picture. I married him."

"And is he fighting in the war?"

"He is."

"And he knows he is going to be a father?"

"He does."

"War hits families the hardest. Do you know where he is?"

"In the south of France."

The woman creased her brows. "He is a resistance fighter?"

Eva looked to Lorelei, who shrugged her shoulders. "You might as well just tell her."

Eva let out a long breath. "No, he isn't in the resistance. He's German."

"You are an American in France who married a German. You don't hear that one every day. I take it he doesn't know you are helping this downed British pilot."

"Of course not. I might be married to a German, but I am not a traitor. I can love a German and still be loyal to my country."

"Well, it is not my place to judge. Do you know when you will return to check on the pilot?"

"Hopefully soon. Maybe in a day or two."

The tea kettle whistled, and the woman stood, removing it from the burner. She transferred the water into a teapot and then sat back at the table. "I apologize, but I don't have real tea. We will have to make do with the fake stuff. I know it's bitter, but it's better than nothing."

"It's alright," Lorelei told her. "I will try to bring you some real tea the next time I come."

"I don't have sugar either. If you are feeling generous, you can bring me some of that as well." She wasn't being ungrateful or rude, just honest. There seemed to be an understanding between the two women.

Eva looked to Lorelei. "If it's possible, I will come back tomorrow."

Lorelei looked at the clock above the stove. "It is late, and we should go. We never know when we can come back. It changes from day to day. We assess the risk and then decide. If it is

281

possible to return tomorrow, I will call you. If I don't call, it means it isn't safe."

"I will wait for your call."

December 20th, 1942

Eva had been back once to check on the pilot the day before. He was still alive but wasn't out of the woods yet. She was actually considering telling Ingrid about him in hopes that she could smuggle some medicine from the hospital. He badly needed some pain meds and antibiotics. While working as a nurse in Germany, Eva learned that the Germans and the other Axis countries could only produce a small amount of penicillin, not enough to meet their military demands. Because of this, they had to rely heavily upon the far less effective medicine called sulfonamides. Even if that was all Ingrid could get her hands on, it would be better than nothing. Without a bit of help, he still might die.

Eva had sat on the couch reading another book Wilhelm gave her for her birthday for close to three hours. She laid it over her leg and looked around the room. It had grown darker in the time she was reading. The nights fell quickly in December.

The house felt empty and lonely without Wilhelm. It was strange how once you got used to someone, it was hard when they weren't around. You craved their presence, the sound of their voice, the noises they made, the interactions, and the feel of them. It was strange the things you missed. She wondered how long he was going to stay mad at her. She felt like she lost a part of herself the day he had her arrested because that was the day he withdrew from her. She doubted he would forgive her, but he could at least treat her like a friend, seeing how he wasn't treating her like a wife. He had completely pulled away from her and closed himself off. He never talked for long on the phone and was hardly ever home anymore, and when he was, he ignored her most of the time. If he wasn't even willing to communicate with her, he sure the hell wasn't going to be intimate with her. He treated her like some unpleasant thing he had to deal with. Would he even want to be a part of his child's life? This thought worried her because she didn't want it to go down the same path he had, with an uncaring father. She didn't believe he would ever mistreat the child like his father did him, but not caring could still scar you.

She laid the book on the coffee table and stood to stretch when something moving outside the window caught her attention. She turned her head to look at it, but all she could see was a foggy white. She briskly walked to the window and put her face close. Outside, a heavy blanket of snow was falling gracefully onto the street. She smiled, giddy as she watched it. The brilliant white powder dusted over everything. She had never seen snow in Paris before, making the city feel even more magical. She hoped it was still on the ground for Christmas. It was only five days away, but the snow could be gone by then. Her happy feeling about the snow faded as she realized she would likely not be spending it with Wilhelm.

She moved away from the window, no longer in the mood to watch the snow. She had to accept that, for all intents and purposes, Wilhelm had left her. By this point, she was used to spending Christmas with friends and not family. But she still couldn't keep the depressing feeling from crashing into her that the little family she had built was over, even though it was still in its infancy. She didn't want to wallow in her self-pity and sadness anymore, so she took a shower and went to bed, hoping to quickly fall asleep so she wouldn't have to think about it. She was trying so hard to keep it together, at least in front of others, but inside, she was falling apart.

She was lying on the lawn near the reddish brick wall, looking at the weathered wooden fence that surrounded the backyard of her parent's house in Provo, the flower garden nestled aesthetically in the corner. The summer sun warmed her as the hot, dry air carried pieces of her hair with it. The scent of the peonies that lined the fence and the sweet fragrance of the rose bushes that ringed the house wafted over her. Her skin was so warm, and she was happy; she was home. A deep, familiar voice filled her ears. She turned her head, drawn to a figure coming out of the house through the rear sliding door, but she was blinded by the sun. She could only see the outline of him, his dark hair moving slightly with the breeze, but she could tell he was wearing a button-up shirt with jeans. *Wilhelm.* The wind picked up, and the scent of the flowers grew even sweeter. She lifted her head, closed her eyes, and inhaled it, but when she opened them, he was gone.

Eva woke with a jolt. She wasn't sure what, but something abruptly brought her out of sleep. She blinked and scanned the darkness in front of her. The room was quiet, and she didn't see anything, but as she grew more alert, she suddenly noticed the presence of someone sitting on the bed behind her. She whipped her head around and rolled onto her back, squinting at the silhouetted figure.

"I apologize. I wasn't trying to wake you."

She couldn't believe it. Wilhelm was home and before Christmas. She didn't know what to think. Should she be happy, worried, or cautious? Was he going to be cold and closed off to her like he had been? She didn't quite know how to act right now. She wanted to hug him, kiss him, cry, slap him, scream at him, and tell him to go away, only to make him come back.

"What time is it?"

"Almost four."

She pushed herself into a sitting position and turned on the lamp beside the bed, then folded her hands in her lap. He straightened, and their eyes met. "Are you coming to bed?"

"In a minute. I'm going to shower, and then I will. I have to get up early and need to get a little sleep."

"Are you leaving again tomorrow?"

"Yes, but you will be coming with me."

Her heartbeat ticked up a notch, and her palms moistened. She cleared her throat. "And where will we be going?"

"Berlin."

"Why?"

"I have to attend a meeting that is being held there."

"And will we be spending Christmas in Berlin?"

He took her hand and turned it over in his like he was inspecting it. "No."

She was growing concerned. "Here then?"

He sighed and looked up at her. The worry on her face was visible. "I thought I would take you and mother to Spain. We could also see the south of France while we're there."

Eva drew in a breath. He was taking her to Spain, neutral Spain. "For Christmas?"

"Isn't that what you wanted, to see the Mediterranean Sea?"

"It is, but I never thought I would see it with you."

"I was allowed to take Christmas off and haven't seen Mother or you in a long time."

"What time do I need to wake up?"

He raised an eyebrow. "You don't need to get up when I do."

"But I thought we were going to leave early. Isn't that why you are getting up early."

"No, I have to work in the morning. I should be home by noon, though." He stood from the bed. "I'm going to take a shower now."

He removed his jacket, then his suspenders, unbuttoned his shirt, dropped it to the floor, and pulled his undershirt over his head. She couldn't look away. She hadn't seen him in a very long time and was drawn to him. He turned to walk to the bathroom and noticed her staring at him. Feeling embarrassed, she looked away.

"You can look."

She raised her eyes to him. *But not touch*, she thought. "I know," she finally said.

He pursed his lips, and his face became guarded. "You can go back to sleep now. I'll try not to wake you when I crawl into bed."

Without answering, she pulled the chain on the lamp and slid down into the bed. He left the room, and she heard the shower turn on and waited. She didn't want to fall asleep. She wanted to talk to him, hold onto him, and be close to him. She was frustrated with her body because sleep was winning, and she didn't want to sleep. Her eyelids grew heavier by the second and took longer to open each time until she drifted into a light sleep.

She stirred and shifted, waking from her doze. She wasn't sure how long she had been asleep, but Wilhelm was lying on his back beside her. She thought he might be sleeping and had missed her chance to have any kind of interaction with him. When they go to Spain, his mother will be with them, and they will have no time alone, and then when they get back home, he will immediately return to work. Was this his plan all along, to use his mother as a divide between them? She had to fix this before the rift between them was too great to repair. Did he no longer love her? He told her he did in the south of France, but that didn't mean he wasn't lying. Did he think she didn't love him? After all, she had never actually said those words to him, even though she felt them. She loved him more than life, but she was afraid to say it and didn't completely understand why.

"Screw it," she mouthed to herself. She put her hand under his pajama top, took one finger, and, with her nail, skimmed down his stomach and over his abdominal muscles, circling his navel. She sensed his sleepy smile as her fingers slipped under the waist of his pants and towards his pubic hair. He caught her hand and brought it to his lips.

"Haven't we done enough damage to last a lifetime?" he said, then kissed each finger in turn to lessen the sting of rejection.

She pulled her hand away and leaned up on her elbow. "What does that mean?"

"What we do to each other, what we have done to each other."

It was true that they had both hurt each other, but she couldn't help but wonder if he was using that as an excuse. And there was always more to it than what he said. She yearned for him and wanted to scream out in frustration. "Please," she whispered and planted a kiss on his neck.

He cupped her cheek and shook his head. "We shouldn't."

She was so frustrated and lonely that a tear slipped from her eye. She placed two of her fingers on his lips to silence him. "Don't say no. I need it. You have no idea how much I have missed you, or have you not even given it a thought?"

He groaned. "I think about it every day, what I have put you through these last few months, and what it must be doing to you."

"Only you have done nothing to ease my misery."

"That is what I'm trying to do by taking you to Spain."

"But that isn't enough. I want more of you. Do I need to beg? Is that what you want me to do?"

"Shit, this is hell," he groaned. "No, I don't want you to beg."

"Then what do you want? I told you what I wanted."

"I want you to be safe and happy, but I also want you to stay in your place and not lie or go behind my back."

She felt a knot form in her stomach because she was still doing that. "So what are we going to do then? Stay in this lonely, miserable limbo for the rest of the war?"

"I would like not to."

"So would I." Out of nowhere, the baby kicked her hard in the side. "Ahh." She put her hand on her stomach and pushed.

He placed a hand on her arm. "Eva, what's wrong?"

She could sense the change in his tone and body language. "Nothing, just getting kicked." She took his hand and placed it on the side of her stomach, holding it there with her hand. The baby kicked again. She heard him draw in a breath. "Pretty incredible, huh?"

"I... have never felt anything like it. And it does this a lot?"

"Yes, she does."

"She?"

"I think it's a little girl."

"Why do you think that?"

"I don't know. I just feel like it is. Would you be upset if it was?"

He moved his hand to another part of her stomach as he spoke. "No, I will be happy with either."

She so wanted to kiss him right now. She leaned close to him, and her lips found his as she laced her fingers through his hair and pulled. She got up on her knees and slid her other hand into the front of his pants, frantic now. He caught her wrist before she had time to wrap her hand around his erection.

He broke the kiss and leaned back, breathing heavily. "Eva, it is not a good idea."

"Why Wilhelm, why is it not a good idea?" She struggled to hold back her frustration and want.

"To name one, you are in the late stages of the pregnancy."

"I'm a nurse, Wilhelm, and I can promise you the act of making love isn't going to harm the baby unless maybe you lay on me." He had stopped her advances in their tracks, but it felt different to her somehow.

He didn't let go of her wrist but considered what she said. "Eva, you might not think that I have, but I anticipated your hesitation and am acting in your best interest, even though I don't think you are necessarily prepared to act in your own interest. Your active attempt to seduce me isn't lost on me. Even though I am willing to be seduced, I'm not going to let you, because I understand that you are not as ready as you let on. What I did was severe but necessary, and I know you are still angry with me somewhere inside, and I don't blame you. And I do understand that you are lonely, but I don't think you are ready to be intimate with me so soon."

There was the anticipation of what she thought was going to happen building in her, only to be squashed because he was attentive to her body language. She was surprised at how good he was at being perceptive of her in a way that wasn't necessarily overly presumptuous, which was sweet to her. When he was gone, she spent so much of her waking hours and many of her sleeping hours on thoughts and dreams of Wilhelm. And sometimes the thoughts and dreams were erotic ones of him, and in these thoughts, she used every ounce of her sexual energy on the idea of having him like he was a delectable, shy accountant and her the temptress who was going to corrupt him. How could he not see that she desired him and that she was deeply, deeply attracted to him? She thought about sex with him. She thought about ravishing him and having him ravish her. This was not something she hasn't put thought into.

"That's not true. I am ready."

"Sex is a highly emotional act. I have allowed in your feelings for me, but love is not just about being ready to receive care, affection, and attention. It is also about giving it in return. Eva, you can have respect, attraction, desire, and you can want the other person. You can have all those things simultaneously. You may be with the perfect person for you, whom you care about, but that still doesn't equate to readiness and consent in the moment. Just because you want something doesn't mean it's the right time, especially now because you are susceptible. You think you want something that you are not ready for."

He let go of her hands, and she placed them in her lap. She understood that her emotions were running hot and that her feelings and thoughts were in a dizzying cyclone inside her. Maybe he could see what she couldn't. Without saying a word, she laid on her side, facing away from him, and pulled the blanket up to her chin. He leaned in and kissed her on the cheek, then contoured his body behind hers and folded her in his arms. She wasn't going to pull away, knowing that this was the only part of him she was going to get right now. And it would have to do because she still wanted to be close and feel him, and she was. Not how she had imagined or wanted, but still, it satisfied her enough to fall asleep in his arms.

Chapter Sixteen
಄

December 25th, 1942

The south of France was everything Eva thought it would be, but Spain surprised her. It was absolutely stunning, with the crystal blue water and the ancient buildings made of stone and tan stucco, covered with red roof tiles. The city of Barcelona was like something you would see on a postcard, only it could never do it justice. You had to be here to fully experience the city's beauty and captivating charm. There was a leisurely pace to the city as people moved about in an unhurried manner as if the sun had made them lethargic and relaxed. The weather was warm and inviting; she loved it and wanted to never leave. The only downside was that she couldn't speak Spanish, but Wilhelm could. She enjoyed watching him converse with the locals and the easy manner in which he dealt with them.

They had spent a lot of time at the beach and visiting the street markets. He bought her any food that caught her eye, from bread to fruit, and Gazpacho, a tomato-based Andalusian soup that was strangely served cold. It was a shock when she took a bite because she wasn't expecting it, but the hot day made it enjoyable.

Eva bought a souvenir for Ingrid and Klaus but struggled to buy Wilhelm a Christmas gift. He insisted he didn't need anything, that being there with her and his mother was all he wanted. But she didn't listen and turned to Marie for assistance. Together, they searched the shops and found a watch he would like, one far nicer and better than the one he had. His was dying, and she knew it drove him crazy because he was very punctual. Once she had the baby, she hoped to get a portrait taken of them all together as a family and give it to him. She planned on getting one made for herself too. She had told him not to buy her something and was very persistent. She had set on him, held his arms to his sides, and told him she wouldn't let him up unless he promised not to. He didn't seem to mind the punishment and didn't cave until he needed to get up.

"Finally," he said, "I submit. I will not buy you a Christmas gift. Whatever you want, it is yours, Eva. You need only ask." He had a carnal look on his face, but in his eyes was a much deeper feeling, one that didn't reach the surface.

It was now Christmas Day, and they were gathered on the couch in the hotel room. Wilhelm and his mother wanted to open the gifts on Christmas Eve, as is traditional in Germany, but she insisted on doing it on Christmas Day like they do in America. Wilhelm and his mother didn't have a problem with it. After all, she hadn't been back in years, and they understood that she wanted something that reminded her of home.

To Eva's surprise, Wilhelm had gotten his mother a separate room, and she relished their alone time, but Marie was in their room now for the gift exchange.

Wilhelm handed a small box and something wrapped in brown paper tied with string to his mother and then an envelope to her. Eva eyed it as he held it out to her. She drew her eyes up to him.

"You said you weren't going to buy me anything."

His face stayed unreadable. "I didn't." His mother handed him his gift, then he sat beside Eva on the couch.

She looked at Marie. "You open yours first."

"Alright." She opened the box and pulled out three rolls of yarn and some new knitting needles. "I needed more yarn, and extra needles are always appreciated." She looked at Eva and Wilhelm. "Thank you."

Wilhelm smiled warmly, and Eva placed a hand on her knee. "Open the other one."

Marie tore the brown paper and pulled from it a fur shawl. She looked to Wilhelm and narrowed her eyes, and it reminded Eva so much of Wilhelm, the way he did that to her.

"You should not have spent so much money on me. I will never wear it."

"Well, now you can say you own one," Wilhelm told her.

She blew out a long breath and laid the items on her lap. "Open yours now."

He opened the small box and smiled when he saw the watch. With only his eyes, he looked at Eva and back to the watch. "Now, this is useful. I cannot be late, and mine loses time constantly." He leaned in and gave her a long, deep kiss before breaking away. He then looked at his mother. "Thank you, both of you."

Marie smiled back at him. "It was Eva's idea to get you the watch." Her eyes settled on the envelope in Eva's lap. "And what is in there?"

"Open it, Eva," he told her.

She pulled the flap that was tucked inside the envelope and removed the contents. She gasped when she saw what was on top. In her hand was a photo of Fabien, Brigitte, and Sabina. The eyes in the photo stared back at her, and she couldn't believe she was seeing their faces again. She was starting to forget what they looked like, the memories fading. She looked to Wilhelm.

"How? Where did you...?"

"It was in the file we have on them. We don't need the photo anymore because they are deceased, so I thought you would like to have it."

She threw her arm around his neck and whispered in his ear. "Thank you."

A smile broke at the corner of his mouth. "Look under the picture."

She lifted the picture to look at the paper behind it. Her pass had been in the envelope with the photo. "You gave me my pass back?"

"Yes. And I expect you to use it wisely."

She knew exactly what he meant. To not run. "I will." Her gift to him was wholly inadequate now, and she wished she had gotten him more or something better. He kept to his word and didn't buy her anything, and she was okay with that because this was so much better than anything he could have bought her.

They ate lunch in the hotel room then Eva decided to nap while Wilhelm visited with his mother. They were in a suite, and the bed was in a separate room. She left the door open a crack, then laid down, closing her eyes. She fell asleep quickly and slept for hours. When she opened her eyes, the sun was in a different position in the sky, and she knew it was getting late. She heard voices in the other room and realized Wilhelm was still talking with his mother. She rolled, with some difficulty, to her other side, then laid still and tried to listen.

"It was the best decision of my life," Wilhelm said.

"But when she told me you two were lovers and that she was pregnant with your child, I knew you were in love with her, but I also knew it would cause you pain."

"What else did you expect me to do, Mother? I wanted to give her what she deserved."

"But you took a huge risk for her and almost lost everything because of it, including her."

There was silence between them before he finally spoke. "Isn't that what you do, risk everything for the one you love?"

"I suppose it is. And her love consoles you?"

"When you love someone so completely that they are your whole world, that is what Eva is to me. It is hard for me not to give in when she asks for something, even when I know I should. Love is supposed to be wild and passionate, and that is what I have with her, but I'm not sure that is what she has with me."

"What makes you question if she does?"

"Because she has never once told me she loves me."

"She'll tell you someday, Wilhelm. One day, she will say it."
Again, there was a brief moment of silence. "I'm going to return
to my room now." Eva heard Marie walk across the floor. "Thank
you for the gifts." There was a sound of a kiss, then the door
opened and closed.

Eva closed her eyes and pretended to be asleep but listed.
Wilhelm walked into the room, and she felt the mattress dip as he
sat beside her. He gently placed his hand on her stomach, then
leaned in and kissed her on the forehead. She opened her eyes,
looked up at him, and smiled warmly.

"Hi."

He brushed his thumb on her cheek. "Do you want to go for a
walk by the sea?" She nodded her head. "Alright. I'm going to put
my shoes on."

He left the room, and she closed her eyes and thought about
what she had overheard. What else had they talked about while
she was asleep? She had been asleep for a while, so they talked
for a long time, but she didn't want to ask what they had discussed.
It would be rude and wasn't any of her business. She hadn't heard
him return to the room when she felt him kiss her eyelid.

He rubbed the tip of his nose along her jaw. He hadn't shaved
since they had been on vacation, and his whiskers tickled her skin.

"You have to get up if you want to go for a walk."

She opened her eyes and looked at him. His hair wasn't
combed neatly to the side like it usually was and looked unkept,
and his eyes were warm and inviting. She reached up and rubbed
her hand over his whiskers. "I'm going to get up now." She moved
her hand and put it on the bed to push herself into a sitting position,

and he took her by the elbow, helping her up. "I know. I'm fat and sometimes need help getting up."

He pursed his lips. "Not fat, pregnant."

She got out of bed and went to the front door and slipped her shoes on, then they left the hotel and walked at a slow pace towards the sea. Eva had her arm linked through his while he had his hands in his pockets.

"Will you return to work once we're back in Paris?"

"Yes, but we will go to Berlin again first."

She tilted her head up to look at him. "Why?"

"I want to see my mother home safely, but also, I have business in Berlin."

Of course you do. She decided to ask him about it and see if he would tell her. "What business do you have in Berlin?"

"Just a meeting with my commanding officer. I have been promoted, and he needs to make it official by pinning on my new insignias."

She pulled on his arm, stopping him. "Were you not going to tell me you got promoted?"

"I was, once we got to Berlin."

"Why then?"

"Because now I have extra responsibilities, which means I will work more."

"Oh."

"Yes, oh. I knew you wouldn't like it, so I wanted to wait to tell you until after the holidays and we were back in France."

"What rank are you now?"

"Well, I was an Obersturmbannführer, but now I will be a Standartenführer."

"What ranks are those again?"

"I just told you."

"No, I mean the English equivalent."

"An Obersturmbannführer is the same as a Lieutenant Colonel, and a Standartenführer is a Colonel."

"What did you do to warrant a promotion?"

"My job."

"Isn't that something every German does?" she said, giving him a teasing smile.

The corner of his mouth pulled into a playful grin. "You think you're funny, do you?"

He came at her, and she backed away. Eva squealed, holding both hands in front of her to fend him off. "Wilhelm, don't." He grabbed hold of her wrist and pulled her to him, then tickled her. She tried to turn away or bend over the best she could, anything to get him to stop. "Wilhelm, no, she cried. You're going to make me pee my pants." She couldn't stop laughing as she said it.

He stopped, then put his hand on her chin, lifted her head up, and placed a gentle kiss on her lips, his soft and warm against hers. She closed her eyes, enjoying the sensation of his mouth on hers, the butterflies in the pit of her stomach, and the warm, tingling sensation in her pelvis. But then he moved away and laced her arm through his again.

"The sea awaits," he said.

She pushed against her desires and thought about the walk to distract her from it. She wanted to ask him about his past again but waited a bit before broaching the subject. Once they were on the beach, she decided it was a good time.

"Can we talk about your childhood?"

He took in a deep breath and slowly let it out. "I knew you wouldn't let this go." He stopped walking and shrugged off his jacket, laying it on the sand so she wouldn't get her dress dirty. He helped her down and then sat beside her.

"Are you sure you want to hear it?"

"I'm sure. I need to know the truth."

"The truth about what exactly?"

"About you."

"I'm not convinced that you are ready to hear it."

He consistently dodged the questions about his life, and it frustrated her. "I am ready to hear. I have waited a long time to know what is going on in that Kraut head of yours."

"I know you think you want to know, but you don't trust me." He pointed to his head. "You don't want to know what it is here."

"Then how is this marriage supposed to work? You told me it needs to be built on trust, but you won't trust me with your secrets. It will never be built on trust if only one of us speaks of what's inside. So I am ready. I want to know everything there is about you."

"You only say that because you don't know what I'm about to say. It's not that I don't trust you with it; I'm afraid of what you will think once you've heard it."

She grew worried. What was Wilhelm going to tell her? "Whatever it is, I want to know."

He sighed and looked out over the sea. "Do you remember me telling you I'm not a good person?"

"Yes, but—"

"No buts. That is what I am. And you have known for a long time, but only recently did you learn what I am truly capable of."

She knew he was talking about what had happened in the garden. She had seen a darker side to him that night, and it scared her. When she still hated him, she imagined him doing unspeakable acts, but she hadn't witnessed his full rage until then.

"I'm sure this makes me sound like the monster you have always thought me to be, but I don't regret anything, except what I've done to you. I did these things because I felt they were necessary or because it was my duty." He narrowed his eyes as he looked out over the water. "Or they just deserved it."

A chill ran down her spine as the hairs on her arms stood on end. "What are these things you have done?"

She broke his concentration, and he looked away from the water back to her. There was something playing behind his eyes, a scene or a memory.

"We will only talk about my past, not my work." She nodded once. "I grew up in Cologne but moved to Essen after my stepfather was gone. We moved there so I could find work in the mines. It was a noisy, dirty place. Large holes were everywhere, and the smoke hung over the city like fog. The machinery worked late into the night, making it hard to sleep. Everything was covered in black soot, including our bodies, but it didn't matter much because our apartment was a piece of shit. The conditions were abhorrent, and the people of the city were suffering in more ways than one. On my way to work in the mornings, I would see men fighting in the streets and outside of the mines. Sometimes, it was over a job, and other times, it was food. There was so little of it, and most people could scarcely afford what little there was. You could not find butter, meat, milk, or fruit, and few vegetables, mostly root vegetables like beets and potatoes. The bread was made with sawdust, so it didn't sustain you. The cakes were made of mustard powder and water. Our bellies ached all the time from hunger, but that wasn't the worst of it. Rheumatic fever was spreading rapidly through the city, killing people, mostly children and the elderly."

She wanted to cry as she listened. Her life had been so different than his. She never once wanted for a meal, or a safe, clean place to stay, with a warm bed and soft pillow to lay her head on. Even now, she didn't want for those things because he provided them for her. She felt guilty that he did, and a need arose in her to provide for herself.

"By that point, I was in my twenties, but my childhood wasn't much better," he continued. "My mother always struggled to provide for us, but she did the best she could. I enjoyed it being just the two of us, but I understand that she was lonely for a kind of affection I couldn't give her. I was so angry when she told me she was getting married. I was only eleven and didn't understand why she would bring someone else into our little family, someone who would take her away from me. I viewed it from the eyes and understanding of a child. But I didn't know then what would come later."

"What would come later?"

"I'll get there. I needed a way to channel my emotions, especially my anger. I was constantly getting into fights with other boys, and it didn't matter if they did something to me or not. I hit them because they were mean to me, I would hit them because they cut in front of me at school, but I especially enjoyed beating the boys who taunted me about not having my real father around. At that time, I didn't know who my real father was, but I knew he

302

had left my mother when I was a baby. That in itself made me angry, and whenever I would hit another boy, I would imagine it was him I was punching in the face or kicking in the gut." He looked down at his hands. "It was obvious that my mother was disappointed in me, and she had every right to be, but she never said it. Not long after Charlotte was born, my stepfather grew more abusive. I was thirteen and had gotten pretty good at fighting, and was stronger than most thirteen-year-old boys. But I wasn't strong enough to fight him yet."

Wilhelm's eyes darkened, and a simmering violent expression settled on his face. Eva watched the change in him, and she knew he was about to tell her something truly awful.

"I never wanted him to be around Charlotte or hold her, so whenever mother was not with her, I would take her out of her crib and go outside with her if the weather was warm or hide with her in my room if it was cold. When he would slap my mother, I would stand between them, and that made him angrier, and he would take it out on me. But I would rather him hit me than her. Whenever he drank, it was in excess, and that only made him worse. I didn't want him to ever lay a hand on Charlotte. When she was five, we learned that she had diabetes. He didn't want to get her medicine, so Mother and I snuck her into the car and took her to the doctor in town. To my knowledge, he never hit Charlotte because I saw to it. But over the years, the treatment towards my mother continued, and mine grew worse. He seemed to like me less the older I got. We lived on a small farm that they had bought after they were married, but he gambled and drank away all our money and then the farm. We had seven days to vacate before the new owners moved in. This was the last straw for me. I was a man by then, already twenty-three, and Charlotte was ten. I helped on the farm and fought for money in my free time as a way to release my frustration and let go of the pent-up anger. I was now bigger than him and much stronger. It was midday, and Mother and Charlotte were in town selling what they could, and I stayed behind to pack. I waited in the barn for him, knowing he would come in to drink the liquor he had stashed there. And when I saw that drunken piece of shit that showed up in my life from fuck knows where walk through the open barn doors, I smiled at the thought of what I was about to do to him. I didn't care where the motherfucker came from, but I was about to send him to hell. I took the rusty ballpoint hammer from the hook on the wall, and before he even knew I was there, I hit him in the leg so hard the ball of the hammer went into his knee cap. I didn't want to kill him right away, you see, I wanted him to suffer the way he made us suffer, so I hit him in the leg so he couldn't run. I poked hay in his mouth to shut him up, and he looked up at me with those icy blue eyes, and I saw the fear in them. I didn't need to tell him why I was doing this; he already knew. Next, I unhung the saw from the hook on the wall and cut off his fingers, slowly, one after another, and then his hands for all the times he had hit my mother and me. He cried, and tried to say some bullshit through the hay in his mouth, but he couldn't. So, I pulled it out, just so I could listen to him plead a beg for his life. I wanted to hear the pain, the suffering, and fear in his voice, knowing I was causing it. It was music to my ears. Then, I cut off his penis, the life almost leaving him when I did, but I wasn't going to let that bastard get off that easy. I took the pale of water and poured it over his head, and then I sliced off his balls, stuffing them into his mouth. I told him he didn't need them because a real man wouldn't hit a woman or a child. I threw his penis in the dirt beside his hands and watched as he bled out in the hay, but that was too easy a death for him. I wanted him to feel the agony as he died. I continued to remove pieces of him slowly until he was dead, then I took him out in the woods and burned his body and the blood-soaked hay."

Eva stared at him, frozen. This man she loved with all her heart was capable of something so heinous and evil. She now saw how Wilhelm was created and why the mold was made. But what was the difference between a bad guy and a good guy who did bad things? Some people only have a sense of right and wrong, but lack the understanding or reasoning as to why something is right or wrong. Her thoughts briefly went to Gerhardt and what he had to do to the girl in Poland in order to save her family. She believed that he had a good understanding of what defined right and wrong. If Wilhelm had been in Gerhardt's shoes, he would have let the girl die.

"You killed him?" she breathed in disbelief, the knowledge of his actions hitting her like a rushing torrent.

"Yes, and It's a crime I would gladly commit again. I made a choice. I could be a good man, or I could be a good son and brother." There was a wicked glint in his eyes when he looked at her, but all the anger and rage faded when he noticed her face. "I said you wouldn't like what you heard. But you told me you wanted to know me better, and now you do."

"I thought he abandoned you, your sister, and your mother?" Her words came out shaky.

"That is what they thought because that is what I told them. We needed him out of our lives, and that was the only way to rid ourselves of him. He never would have left on his own. I don't usually let my rage take over, and now you know why."

He reached for her, and she unintentionally flinched, so he withdrew his hand. "I'm sorry," she whispered, her voice barely auditable. She felt a need to apologize, but truthfully, she was scared of him.

"Don't be afraid of me, Eva. I would never hurt you. Men are predatory, but they should only be predatory to other men, not women. I know what you probably think of me now. But what happened to me as a boy did not produce a soulless caricature of a man. What it did do was stall the normal growth of softness and sweetness that is usually found in children and drove other qualities I possessed, like intelligence, ruthlessness, and determination. I learned from all my past experiences that a man with nothing to lose can obtain anything he wants. And a man without feeling cannot be hurt, or so that is what I told myself. I understood that I was doing wrong even as I did it. Not that this awareness of the evil in me stopped me for a second, only that I paid for it in pain and self-torment later. And then I found you, and you gave me peace, something to focus on other than my pain, and something to care about other than my work. Only my sister and mother had ever done that for me."

She could never change him, and she knew it, so she could either love him for who he was or leave. And she tried that before, ultimately failing at it because her heart was his now. She had always questioned why he was so good at hurting others, especially the dangerous people who crossed his path. Then she began to question whether he was any different than the man he saved her from.

306

"I'm not afraid of you." That wasn't exactly the truth, but she didn't want him to think she was. She needed to process this new information and then figure out what she would do with it. "I'm sorry you have been through so much bad stuff, and that it causes you pain."

"Until I met you, it was a hellish purgatory." He stood and brushed the sand off his pants, then held a hand out to her. She stared at it for a fraction of a second, then took it, and he pulled her to her feet, picked up his jacket, and shook the sand from it.

They ate dinner at a restaurant close to the hotel, and when they were finished, his mother turned in for the night. Eva showered and then read in bed, trying to not think about their conversation.

Wilhelm came out of the bathroom and crawled on the bed. He looked at the book in her hand. "Is it good?"

"It is."

He caught her off guard when he scooted down and laid his head on her stomach, resting his hand on her thigh. She lowered the book and looked at him but could only see the back of his head. She could smell the soap coming from his freshly washed hair. He seemed to be fine with her reading, so she lifted the book up to eye level and ran the fingers of her left hand through his hair. She played with it and gently pulled on pieces as she twisted her fingers around sections, but after some time had passed with them this way, she lowered the book again and leaned over so she could see his face. He had his eyes closed, and his breathing was even and shallow, and she wondered if he was asleep. His face was set in a relaxed expression, and for some reason, he reminded her of a child, peaceful and harmless, so unlike when he was awake. He wasn't at peace when he was awake and was a dangerous person. She had seen how merciless he could be to others. She liked him this way, vulnerable and at rest, sleeping with his head on her like she was his pillow. She wanted to stay like this and not leave after the new year because she knew once they were back in Paris, everything would change. And some of these things terrified her.

Chapter Seventeen

ೲ

January 3rd, 1943

Eva had thought a lot about it, and it was decided. She was going to tell Ingrid about the British pilot when she returned to Paris. She needed access to medicine, and frankly, she could use some extra help, especially now that she was in the third trimester.

"Eva, I don't think it will come out." Marie stood in the kitchen entryway holding Eva's tan coat that was covered in tomato stains. Eva had dropped an open can of tomato sauce on the floor, and it splattered all over her dress and coat. She was getting ready to leave when she saw Marie struggling to get the top of the can off. It had fallen down into the tomato sauce, and she was trying to dig it out.

"No." She crossed the kitchen and took it out of Marie's hand. It's all over my dress too. I only brought six dresses because I didn't know we were going to Berlin before Paris, and they are all still in the washing machine. Wilhelm is supposed to be here any minute to pick me up. He is dropping me off at Dr. Möller's house before his next meeting. What am I going to do now?"

Marie held up her index finger. "I think I have an idea. My dresses won't fit you now, not with your stomach, but I still have some of Wilhelm's old clothes from when he was a boy."

Eve eyed her in confusion. "Why do you still have his old clothes?"

"For sentimental reasons, I guess. I still have some of Charlotte's too. Let me get them." Eva followed Marie to her bedroom and watched as she opened an old trunk. Marie pulled out a pair of trousers, a white button-up shirt, and a brown wool jacket. "Here, try these on."

Eva eyed the musty-smelling clothes on the bed. "How old was he when he wore these?"

"I think about fourteen."

Eve picked up the jacket and inspected it, then the other two pieces of clothing. "I guess this will have to do." She took them to the bathroom, stripped her clothes off, slipped on the shirt, and pulled on the pants. She couldn't button them, and they were tight in the butt and hip area. The sleeves of the shirt were too long for her arms and came to the end of her fingers. She put the jacket on, which was equally as big as the shirt. She wondered if Marie would have some string to hold the pants up with. She held the waist of the pants with one hand and opened the bathroom door, stepping on the pant legs as she walked. They were too big in some places and too small in others. "Marie, do you have something I can use to hold the pants up?"

Marie couldn't suppress a smile. "Oh dear, you look... well..."

"I know, it looks pretty ridiculous."

"I do have something to hold those up." She took some yarn from her knitting basket, put it through the belt loops, and tied it around Eva's bare stomach. "You might want to leave the shirt untucked."

"I think you're right."

Marie knelt and rolled up each pant leg. "There, that should help."

The front door opened, and Eva had the sudden urge to hide. Heavy footsteps echoed on the tile, then became quiet once on the carpet. "Eva?"

She turned to look at him, her face turning red. She lifted her arms to her side and then dropped them to 'say this is me.'

"Why are you in those clothes?"

"Because I got tomato sauce on my dress and coat, and the others are in the wash. "These were yours when you were fourteen. I know it looks terrible, but I'm only going to see Klaus."

A smile formed at the corner of his mouth, and something lit in his eyes. He laid his cap on the back of the couch and sauntered toward her, taking her in. He took the open part of the coat and pulled it back, then lifted the shirt and chuckled when he saw the yarn holding up the pants. "No, I like that you look like a fourteen-year-old boy," he said in a playful manner.

"Good, because I put it on just for you." Two could play this game.

He slipped his hand in the coat, resting it on the small of her back, and leaned close to her ear. "You shouldn't have worn anything for me." His breath was hot on her skin, and his voice was deep and rough.

She stiffened and drew in a breath. It was so easy for him to get under her skin, making her want him. She licked her lips. "I think we should go."

He straightened and gave her a wink. "Yes, we should." He checked his watch. "I have to be back at the Reich Security office in fifteen minutes."

When they pulled in front of Klaus' house, Wilhelm got out and helped her from the car. He kissed her forehead, then gave her a stern look, and a question hung in the air. She creased her brows, confused by the way he was acting.

"I'll see you back at the apartment."

"Alright." She held his fingers and stood on her toes, pressing her lips to his. She could feel him smiling, and it made her smile.

He pulled away. "Enjoy your visit."

"I will." He got back in the car, and it drove through the gray, slushy snow. She knocked on the door, and it didn't take Klaus long to open it. His face brightened as soon as he saw her, but then his look turned to confusion.

"Eva, why are you dressed like a man?"

"Oh," she laughed. "I didn't have any clean dresses and can't fit into Marie's right now, so I'm wearing some of the clothes Wilhelm wore as a boy."

"Here, come in out of the cold." He took her arm and led her into the living room. He helped her out of her coat and hugged her, then they sat on the couch. "I can't believe your time is almost here."

She looked down at her stomach and rubbed her hand over it. "I know. I can't believe it, either. It's starting to feel real, and that is scary."

"You'll have all the help you need. And I will be there when you have the baby. It should be the first or second week of March, so I have taken those weeks off so I can be in Paris."

She smiled at this man who was willing to use his vacation time to come to Paris and deliver her baby. "How am I ever going to make it up to you?"

"Just deliver a healthy baby, and that will be payment enough."

"I'm going to try. You know, I think it's a girl."

"Really."

She nodded. "I just feel like that is what it is. I haven't told Wilhelm yet, but I want to name her Charlotte after his sister, who passed away at fifteen."

"I didn't know he had a sister."

"He doesn't talk about her often. I think it is too painful for him. He loved her a lot, so I want to give him this."

"You are giving him a baby. Isn't that enough?

"Klaus."

"I'm sorry, Eva. It is still hard for me to accept that you are with him. I wish you would leave him and go home. Take that baby back to America, where it can be safe and away from him."

"He would never hurt this baby, and I couldn't do that to him. Leave with his child, making him lose both of us at the same time. He doesn't deserve that."

"He doesn't deserve a family, and he doesn't deserve you."

"I am not leaving him, Klaus."

"I know you're not."

She wanted to tell him about the pilot, to let him know she was still the same old Eva, even though she was with Wilhelm. In a way, she still trusted him more than Wilhelm because he wouldn't punish her for what she did. "I haven't changed, Klaus. In France, I am helping a British pilot."

His eyes grew wide. "Why would you tell me this?"

"Because I trust you and wanted you to know that I have not been corrupted by Wilhelm."

"I never thought you were, just that you were blinded by your love for him. Why would you do something so stupid and dangerous under his nose? He could have you killed for this."

"He wouldn't, and he won't find out."

"You don't know that."

"Yes, I do. A friend from America came to France to try and save me, but he was captured by the Gestapo. They tortured him and put him into a camp. I helped him escape, and Wilhelm suspected I had something to do with it, and of course, he was mad, so he had me arrested."

Klaus clenched his jaw and held his hand up to stop her. "He had you arrested, and while you are pregnant?"

"Yes, but I was only in there for a few days. I had a bed, food, and water. I had the cell to myself, and no one laid a hand on me. Then he had me released."

Klaus stood and paced with one hand on his hip and the other on his chin as he so often did when thinking. "I cannot believe he did that. I can't. That bastard thinks he can do whatever he wants. If he is capable of that, then he is capable of anything, Eva."

"I promise you that he will not hurt me. He loves me, I think, to the point of obsession."

"That is dangerous too."

"It is, but not nearly as dangerous as being his enemy or getting on his bad side. I do know, Klaus, what he is capable of. I just don't think he is capable of doing that to me."

"You don't know what's inside the minds of men like him, but I do."

She thought of how he killed his stepfather and the way he mercilessly beat the man in the garden. "Actually, I do."

"And that isn't enough to make you leave him?"

His question stumped her. Her logic and the love she had for him were constantly waging war with each other. But love always seemed the victor. Life would be cruel if it took him from her. Maybe she was being selfish and stupid, but she couldn't help it. There was a time when she told herself she was with him because she had to be, but she needed to be honest. She was with him because it felt good. She didn't want to be alone, and she loved him.

"No, I guess it isn't enough to make me leave him. Can we talk about something else, please?"

He sat back beside her. "Of course. How about we talk about where we are going to eat?"

He was still trying to take care of her. A wave of emotion hit her, and she started to cry. "I don't know what I would do without you."

He pulled her to him, holding her as he rubbed her hair. "I'm here as long as you need me. And I can't wait to meet that baby. It's the closest I will ever get to being a grandfather."

Eva pulled back and looked at him through her teary eyes. "And she will love you like I do."

"I have to ask, Eva. What if he decides he wants another child?"

She recalled his conversations with his mother the night before the wedding. He had told her that this baby was the first of many to come, he was sure. Was he just saying that for his mother's benefit, or did he really mean it? Even if he was, she couldn't tell Klaus about this. "No, I don't think he does. He didn't even want kids."

"Maybe after it is born, he will realize that he likes being a father. You can't give him another one, Eva."

She laughed, a little embarrassed. "It's not that easy."

"It is. Just make sure he always uses protection."

"And what if he doesn't want to?"

"You will just have to make him."

"That won't be an easy thing to do." She pointed to her stomach. "This happened because he only used a condom once."

"Just be persistent. And if he won't wear one, don't have sex with him."

She huffed. "You think a man will just stop having sex with his wife?"

"I never said it would be easy."

"I'm not going to think about that right now. This one isn't even out, and we are already talking about a second one."

"But it soon will be, and not long after, you can get pregnant again. Don't you miss being a nurse and being free to make your own decisions?"

"Of course, I miss being a nurse and working with you. But I was never free. I have been a prisoner since this war started."

"But now you are worse than a prisoner. You can't divorce him. It's not allowed."

"I don't want to divorce him."

"Because you are used to your chains. If you decided to go to... let's say Austria or Poland tomorrow, do you think he would let you?"

She cast her eyes down. "No."

"Exactly. He probably knows who you talk to, where you go, and everything you do. That is his mindset. It's why he is in the Gestapo. He will never let you go home. He has you trapped here, and has such a firm grip on you he is confident and secure in the idea that you will always be his and be here."

"But I don't think that is a bad thing like I once did. I like being his. The only thing that makes me sad is that I will remain here, and my family is in America."

"No one should have to give up their family for the one they love."

"He didn't ask me to."

"He didn't have to. He already knew you would."

The conversation was upsetting her, and she didn't want to think about what she was and wasn't giving up. "Let's go eat now."

"Alright, let me get my coat. Are you sure you want to go out to eat dressed like that?"

"I don't mind as long as you don't."

"Not at all."

317

She looked at Klaus from across the table as she picked at her food with the fork. "What are your plans when the war is over?"

He swallowed the food in his mouth and then took a sip of water. "Before the war, I worked at a hospital, and because of the war, I still work at a hospital, but I think when it is all over, I might open my own practice. That is always something I have wanted to do, but not in Berlin."

"Why not in Berlin?"

"It's too big for my liking. Besides, there might not be much of it left by the end of the war."

"Where is it you would like to go?"

"Probably near Ingolstadt."

"Why there?"

"Because it's in Bavaria, where I am from."

Eva only now realized that she had never asked Klaus about his home. "Where are you from, Klaus?"

"Köshing, just north of Ingolstadt. It's a small town, too small for me to have the practice I want."

"I hope you get to do that one day, Klaus."

They ate the rest of their dinner in silence, and then he took her back to Marie's apartment. "I will see you in Paris soon." He kissed her on the cheek. "Try to rest these last few months."

"I will." She obviously wasn't going to rest as much as Klaus was suggesting. She couldn't stand to just lay around the house.

Two days later, Eva and Wilhelm left for Paris, and he returned to work the following morning. She made sure to get up early, and after he left, she called Lorelei.

"I'm sorry I haven't been here to check on the pilot. How is he doing?"

"He is better. I have continued to visit him while you have been gone. I do think you should come and check on him soon."

"I might be able to tomorrow. Do you think you could sneak me out there?"

"When does your husband get home?"

"He will probably work late into the night. What time could we go?"

"I think early in the morning would be better. Call me as soon as your husband leaves."

"I will. I also wanted to talk to you about something. I think I have a way to get my hands on some medicine."

"Oh, how?" Her tone was skeptical.

"A good friend of mine is a nurse, and I can ask her if she can take some medicine from the hospital."

"You want to tell her about the pilot."

"I do."

"Can she be trusted?"

"Yes. I have known her for a long time. We worked together in Berlin."

"She is German?"

"Yes."

"That could be a problem. I'm not sure you should tell her."

"Why?"

"Because she is German."

"You are German. I don't know why that is an issue."

"Most Germans will run and tell the Gestapo because they don't have a reason to not be loyal to Germany."

"She isn't like that. She already knows that I helped the resistance in Berlin. She would never turn me over or intentionally betray me."

"And you think she would do this for you, steal medicine from the hospital?"

"I think she will try."

"You seem certain that she will put herself at risk for you."

"I believe she will if I ask, and I wouldn't ask if we didn't need the medicine."

"Alright, ask her. But only have her do it if she thinks she can without getting caught. And make sure she tells no one else."

"I will talk to her today."

After she hung up with Lorelei, Eva took the tram to the hospital. She searched each level and found Ingrid helping a patient on the second floor. When Ingrid saw her, she smiled and held up a finger, letting her know that she was almost finished, so Eva waited in the hall.

"How was your time in Nice?" Ingrid asked as she walked out of the patient ward and embraced Eva.

"Good."

"But…?"

"But nothing. It was good."

"So he is still being closed off and distant?"

Eva did not want to have this conversation in the hall of the hospital where other people could hear. "Let's talk somewhere else. When do you get off?"

Ingrid looked at her watch. "In twenty minutes."

"I'll wait downstairs."

She went to the lobby and sat on the hard, wooden bench, then leaned back against the plaster wall. Eva was worried that Ingrid would not agree to steal the medicine. She wondered if it would be better to show her the pilot first, then ask her to take the medicine, but maybe that would be too risky. She needed to decide quickly but was worried she would make the wrong decision. *Crap.* She determined it would probably be better to tell her about the pilot first and then ask her to take the medicine after.

Ingrid came down the hall towards her, untying her apron. "Where would you like to go?"

Eva stood and linked her arm through Ingrid's. "Let's go to the catacombs."

Ingrid pulled her arm free and wrinkled up her face. "No, I hate the catacombs. They are dark and musty, and the bones scare me."

"Like I told you last time, they aren't going to come alive. Don't be a child. Those things shouldn't scare you anymore." Eva felt a little bad for chastising Ingrid because she was still afraid of the dark, only Ingrid didn't know.

"Can we just walk somewhere above ground, please?"

"Fine. Let's go to the Parc Monceau. It's a beautiful place to have a stroll."

Ingrid gave her a half smile. "Thank you."

Eva linked arms with her again but waited to talk until they were outside and away from so many people. "To answer your question, yes, he is still being kind of evasive. I do understand why, and I even partly agree with it, but I don't exactly like it. It's complicated. He is complicated."

"I'm sorry he is being that way towards you. Do you think he will change after the baby is born?"

"Honestly, I don't know. But I didn't come to see you to talk about him. I came to ask you a question."

Ingrid gave her a side glance. "Alright."

"Let's sit down."

Eva lowered herself onto the grass in front of the Roman colonnade that curved around a pond. Floating on the murky water were water lilies, and following along the water's edge were rose bushes speckled with small red roses. Ingrid lowered herself beside Eva and looked at her expectantly.

Eva cleared her throat before speaking. "Before I tell you why we are here, you have to promise that what we talk about will not go beyond you and me."

"Should I be worried?"

"No, not as long as you don't speak of it to anyone, for both of our sake."

"Alright."

"I need your help with something. On the edge of town at a farmhouse is a wounded British pilot, who I have been helping." Eva watched Ingrid's eyes widen. "I have managed to keep him alive, but he is in desperate need of medicine, which I can no longer get now that I'm not working at a hospital."

"You want me to steal it?" Her voice grew louder with each word, and her tone was accusatory.

"Shhhh, keep your voice down." Eva glanced around, making sure they were still alone. "Yes, I need you to take some."

"That is a huge risk. What do I get out of this?"

"The knowledge that you are helping save someone's life."

322

She shook her head. "No, I want to come with you. If I'm going to risk my life for someone, I want to meet them."

"I don't know if that's possible."

"Why? You go out there to see him."

"Yes, but it isn't easy. They have to put me in the trunk of a car and sneak me out of the city. I don't know if we can both fit in there."

Ingrid looked horrified, her mouth agape. "They put you in the trunk of a car while you are pregnant?"

Eva didn't see why it was such a shocking concept. "Yes."

"Oh my God, Eva, no. That is so dangerous. Wilhelm would be so angry with you if he found out."

"I'm pretty sure that is not the thing he would be upset about. Sneaking out of town to help a British pilot would probably trump me riding in the trunk of a car."

"You are right. He probably would be even more upset over that. But you could still get hurt or lose the baby."

Eva chuckled at her level of concern. She knew Ingrid really wanted her to have this baby and didn't want anything to put the pregnancy at risk. "I promise you it is not that risky. It's not much different than riding in the back seat of a car. I will ask if you can come. Do you think you can get the medicine tomorrow?"

"I'll try. When do you go back to see him?"

"As soon as you get the medicine."

Ingrid nodded. "I'll come by your apartment tomorrow after work."

"Alright."

Ingrid had snuck the medicine from the hospital, and Eva told Lorelei that it was a success. Now, they were both crammed into the trunk, waiting for the car to arrive at the farm. It was much more uncomfortable now that Ingrid was in the trunk with her, but she didn't dare tell her. The ride this time made her feel nauseous, and the hard floor was causing her back to throb. When the car stopped, she couldn't wait to get out.

The lid to the trunk opened, and a bright light shone in. Eva had to squint against it. Lorelei helped her out first, then Ingrid. Eva stretched, rubbing her lower back with both of her hands.

"Ingrid looked around the vast fields and trees that surrounded the house. "This is where you have been coming?"

"Yes."

"This is beautiful. I am jealous you have been coming here without me."

"We didn't know if we should tell you at first."

Ingrid's face fell. "You know I would never say anything."

"I do, but I had to convince them, and I didn't want to get you involved if I didn't have to."

Ingrid took a step closer to Eva and spoke in a hushed voice. "Why is Lorelei helping the British and Americans? She is German and married to a high-ranking officer, so I don't quite understand."

"I am married to a high-ranking officer and am helping them, and you are German, and you are helping them."

"Yes, but she is both."

"She lost her two sons, and now she is tired of the war and wants to see it end."

"Ahhh," Ingrid said in understanding.

324

"Follow me, ladies," Lorelei called to them.

They went inside the house and up the stairs to the room at the end of the hall. When they entered, Eva's nostrils were assaulted by the pungent smell of body odor. She looked to Ingrid briefly, then to Lorelei. "Has no one given him a bath since he has been here?"

"I haven't, and I don't think Madame Aubert can do it alone. I wasn't going to ask you to do it, not in your condition."

"I can do it if you'll help," Ingrid said to Lorelei.

"Yes, I can."

While they were gone preparing water and getting towels, Eva checked under the bandage. It was as she had feared. The wound had become infected, and he was running a high fever. She wasn't sure the medicine they brought was going to be enough now. He looked pale, and his lips were dry from dehydration. She prayed he would survive, but he really should be in the hospital under the care of a doctor, with access to more medicine than they had, like a saline drip in his arm and at least a two-week supply of antibiotics.

When Ingrid and Lorelei returned with the towels and water, Eva pointed to the wound. "I don't know how much more we can do for him. He needs to be in a hospital." They all turned their gaze to the sleeping man. He reminded Eva of a dead person with his ashy, pale complexion and the purple circles under his eyes. The red veins on his eyelids protruded through the thin skin, and he was clammy with shallow, irregular breathing.

Ingrid looked at Eva. "He can't go to any of the hospitals in Paris. The Gestapo would find him and send him to a camp or have him shot."

"You mean my husband would have him shot. It's alright, Ingrid, you can say it."

Ingrid looked back to the pilot, not wanting to make eye contact with Eva. "I'm sure he would know about it."

"Of course, he would. He is the one who makes those kinds of decisions. I've come to terms with the fact that I love a bad person."

"There is another way," Lorelei said. "Not far from where you live, Eva, is an American hospital."

Eva's head shot to her. "What?"

"Yes. It's on 55B du Château, Neuilly-sur-Seine. It's a huge building with a wall around it and a gate at the front that says American Hospital at the top. You didn't know about it?"

Eva was shocked. She had never heard anything about this. She had been to Paris so many times, and now she lived here and had never walked by it or heard it spoken of by any of the Parishioners.

"No, this is the first I have heard of it. Are the doctors and nurses there American?"

Lorelei smiled. "Yes, all of them."

Eve felt like she was going to faint. She took hold of the metal footboard and sat on the edge of the bed at the pilot's feet. "Would Wilhelm know of this?"

"Oh yes. They keep a close eye on the hospital and the head doctor there, who actually lives on the same street as you."

Eva wasn't sure she heard her right. "Same as me?" she asked breathlessly.

"Yes. But you can never go to the hospital or to that doctor's house."

"Why?"

"Because you cannot be seen at the hospital or anywhere near him. He is an active member of the resistance. He secretly assists Americans and British, as well as members of the resistance. He gives them medical care and helps them sneak out of the country to Spain. His apartment serves as a rendezvous for messages and money, the kind of information meant for the Allies. Stay far away, Eva. Your husband already suspects him and his family."

Eva had an odd feeling inside, rising from her stomach. There was so much about her husband she didn't know, and so much he kept from her. Her hands were tingling, and she felt strangely numb. Then she could no longer keep the contents in her stomach down, and before she could stand the vomit rose in her mouth then went all over the wood floor, getting some on the rug. She wiped her mouth with the back of her hand.

"I'm sorry. I'll clean it up."

"No, don't worry about it, Eva. We'll clean it up," Lorelei said. "Go sit downstairs."

"I really should be the one to clean it up."

"It's alright, Eva," Ingrid told her. She took Eva's arm and helped her downstairs. "Are you alright?"

"Yeah, I just didn't expect to hear that."

"I'm going to go back up and help. We shouldn't be too long."

"Alright." Ingrid gave her hand a squeeze and then disappeared up the stairs. Eva lay on the couch and ran everything Lorelei said over in her mind. This new bit of information made her feel even more distant from Wilhelm when all she wanted was to be closer to him and longed to break through the barrier that stood between them.

When she heard Ingrid and Lorelei coming down the stairs, she sat up, feeling ill from the stress of the day. "How is he?"

"Not well. We're going to take him to the hospital as soon as we can. I will need you to write a set of instructions in English for him."

"I can do that. What will happen to him when he is better?"

"We'll find a way to get him to Spain or put him on the next transport plane when it returns to England."

"I want to go when you do that."

"No." Her answer was stern.

"You told me to stay away from the hospital and the doctor's house. You didn't tell me I couldn't see him off."

"It's going to be dangerous, and I can't guarantee your safety."

"That's alright. I don't expect you to. I want to come."

"Is it common for the pick-ups and drop-offs to go wrong," Ingrid asked.

"Not usually, but we never know if it's been compromised. It's always a risk."

"I didn't get to see Jon off, so I need even more to see this through."

"I'll let you know when it's scheduled."

Eva went to bed as soon as she was home. The ride back into Paris did her in, and she didn't care that it was only eight. She felt utterly spent and was ready for the day to be over. She also couldn't wait to get this baby out, but that thought petrified her. She couldn't even think about the labor without her heart racing, and then the thought of caring for a baby had her on the verge of a panic attack.

She snuggled under the warm blanket and closed her eyes, listening to the icy rain hit the window. She hadn't been in bed long when the front door slammed, making her jump. She pulled herself into a sitting position and threw the blankets off, not wanting Wilhelm to know that she was in bed this early. She didn't want him to worry or ask questions, but she wasn't fast enough, and just as she swung her legs over the side of the bed, he walked through the doorway into the bedroom.

He paused when he saw her, flipping on the bedroom light. "Eva, why are you in bed?"

She looked at him standing before her in wet clothes, water dripping onto the floor around him. "I was tired. Why are you wet?"

"It's raining." The sarcasm in his voice cut through the concern.

"I know it's raining. I mean, why were you outside without an umbrella?"

He shrugged out of his wet leather trench coat and carried it out into the hall, and when he returned, he had removed his boots, hat, and gloves. "I am wet because I had to be outside, and an umbrella would have gotten in the way."

"Oh." She lowered her swollen feet to the floor, the squishy soles pressing against the cold wooden floor.

He looked at her squarely. "Are you feeling alright?"

"I'm fine."

"In a few weeks is a formal dinner we are expected to be at," he said as he unbuttoned his shirt.

"What day?"

"It's on the sixteenth."

She watched him, thinking about how he was hiding the truth about the hospital, the American doctor who lived down the street from them, and so much more. She had always heard that life is what you make it, but she was a firm believer now that it was up to fate. She knew she needed to let this man go, but she couldn't escape him now. Another choice of fate that she had no control over.

He looked at her, his eyes bright as they pierced hers. "What?"

"Nothing."

He took her in, standing beside the bed in her nightgown, one arm behind her back, the other hanging at her side. "Do you want to shower with me?"

This was the first time he offered something like this since denying her advances. She fought against the smile that pulled at the corner of her mouth. "Yes."

She followed him to the bathroom, and he stripped off his clothes and then turned on the water. She hesitated, but after a few seconds, she pulled her gown over her head. She hadn't seen him naked in so long. Her eyes roamed over his muscular frame, and she wanted to reach up and touch him but didn't know if he would stop her. Why had she fallen in love with this devil in the form of a man? She must be cursed, and her punishment was to be tormented by him. Tormented by the fact that she loved him, tormented that he loved her, and haunted by the knowledge that he could be taken from her one day.

Slowly, she reached up and pressed the tip of her fingers against his left peck muscle, sliding them down his torso and over his hard stomach, feeling the line of hair that ran down to his pelvis. It didn't matter if they had sex. She just wanted to be intimate with him, touch him, and be close to him.

He watched her touching him as if he was a perfectly chiseled sculpture. "The water is going to get cold."

His smooth, deep voice brought her out of her reverie. It was soft and affectionate, without ire or his usual evasiveness. She looked up into his warm eyes, trying to read him. She couldn't make out any one feeling because there were too many coming through in the way he looked at her. She turned her gaze to the water pouring from the shower head.

"You are right. It will get cold."

He took her hand and pulled her into the shower with him, then put his hand on her stomach with his fingers sprawled out over it. "I can't believe it's almost time."

"I have to admit I'm a little scared. I always thought I would have my mom to talk to. To ask her about the birth and how to take care of a baby," she said with a nervous chuckle.

"You'll be fine. You know you can ask my mother anything about it, and she will answer to the best of her knowledge."

"I know. It's just different than how I thought it would be." A realization hit her that Wilhelm would not be in the delivery room with her. It wasn't until the late sixties that they started allowing fathers to be in the delivery room. She had read about it in a medical journal at the university library one night while studying. She put her hand over the top of his and looked up at him. "Wilhelm, you have to promise me that you will be in the delivery room with me when I give birth?"

"I don't think they will let me stay with you."

331

"I don't care what they will and will not allow. I want you in there, and Dr. Möller is delivering, so he will let you if I plead with him."

His face hardened. "Is he?"

"Yes, because I asked him to."

"And what's wrong with the French doctors here in Paris?"

"I don't know them, and I trust him."

She thought about what Klaus told her the last time she was with him, about Wilhelm possibly wanting another child and that she needed him to always wear protection or deny him sex. It made her think about whether or not she wanted another baby. In truth, she knew it was a terrible idea and that she shouldn't add to the many mistakes she had made with him.

"Do you think you will want more children after this one?"

He made a snorted laugh. "Where did that come from?"

"I was just wondering because I don't think I want anymore."

Under better circumstances, she would love to have more children with him, but he needed to think she didn't. She could instantly sense the change in his mood and body language. He pulled his hand away and tensed.

"Why don't we see how we feel after this one."

She had to be firm. "I don't need to. I already know I don't want another baby." His expression wasn't one of anger, but it wasn't far off. Maybe anger mixed with hurt, but he tried to hide it.

"I have to get up early, so we need to hurry."

She hated how he always shut down and never wanted to talk about his feelings, his wants or dislikes, or anything about himself.

"So you don't feel the same way?"

"I don't know how I feel, Eva. We don't even have this baby yet." He turned away from her, picked up the bar of soap from the dish, and started lathering it over his body.

She placed the palms of her hands on his back and leaned in, kissing softly between his shoulder blades. "I'm sorry."

"You don't have to be sorry. You say that is how you feel, and who am I to tell you that you don't have the right to. I had told you before that I didn't want children either."

He didn't say another word to her, and she watched him clean his skin and hair. Then he stepped out onto the rug and pulled the towel from the hook, leaving her alone in the shower. It felt empty, and not just the space. She hurried and cleaned herself, then got out and went to the bedroom. He was already in bed with his back turned to her side. It didn't matter if he told her or not. She knew he was upset by what she said. Did it mean that he did want more children? It was just another unanswered question she could file away with all the others.

She pulled the blanket back and crawled into bed, scooting close to him for the warmth and just to be near him. He didn't turn, so she put her arm over his waist and pressed her stomach against his back. She was going to enjoy his company even if he didn't want hers.

Chapter Eighteen

January 16th, 1943

Eva fidgeted in her chair, tapping her fingertips on the table. The pilot had been taken to the American hospital almost two weeks ago. His health had improved, and he was now well enough to travel. Lorelei had called her the day before to inform her that the plane would be there to get him tomorrow night. The whole thing made her nervous, and she was having a hard time controlling her anxiety.

Wilhelm was in the corner of the room smoking with several other officers, and she was left alone at the table with people she didn't know. That, too, was setting her nerves on edge. There was only one other woman at the table with her, but she was on the other side talking to the man seated beside her. Some of the men were in uniforms, and others in suits, and Eva wondered if all of them were Nazis.

"So you are Frau Bauer?" the man to her right asked.

"Oh, um, yes."

The man had a chubby face with red cheeks and thinning blond hair. "And I see that you are expecting. That is wonderful. Germany needs loyal Germans for future generations who will continue the thousand-year Reich. Keep up the good work."

She wanted to slap him across the face and scream that she was not German and that there was no way in hell she would raise her baby to believe the Nazi ideology, but instead, she tapped her fingers faster on the table and gave him a forced smile. "Thank you."

"Are you liking life in Paris? Avenue Foch has such beautiful homes. I dare say your husband picked the nicest one on the street, and for you, no doubt. We were all so intrigued when we found out he was getting married. He was always so outspoken against it and said he didn't have time for a wife. We were convinced he would never get married and remain a bachelor with only lovers. But then I heard that he was getting married, and I had no idea he was even dating someone." He gave a broad, genuine smile, exposing his crooked teeth. "How did you two meet?"

"Many years ago, in La Chapelle."

"Where is that?"

"It's on the Belgium border."

"Was it love at first sight?"

"Not even close. We didn't actually like each other when we first met. We didn't form a friendship until he was wounded and wound up in the hospital I worked at. I guess you could say it started then, long after we had met."

He laughed, delighted at her story. "Wow, so enemies to friends to lovers, and now soulmates."

335

"I guess you can put it like that."

"And when are you due?" He looked at her stomach. "It can't be long now. Does he move a lot?"

Without asking, he placed his hand on her stomach, and she froze. Her eyes darted quickly to Wilhelm, making sure he wasn't looking in their direction. He had his back turned towards them, and she relaxed a fraction. She didn't think this man meant anything by it. He just lacked boundaries. But if Wilhelm saw, it would anger him.

"Sleeping, I guess." He moved his hand away and laughed.

She gave a nervous laugh. "I guess so."

The man looked up, and Eva saw Wilhelm sit beside her from her peripheral, placing his hand over the top of her fidgeting one.

"Wilhelm, I was just talking with your lovely wife. She told me how she made you work for her affections." He gave another deep-chested laugh.

Wilhelm glanced at her. "She still does." Eva's face flushed. The orchestra was playing a slow song, and Wilhelm took her hand. "Shall we dance?"

She had not expected him to ask her this. "Yes."

Wilhelm looked at the other man. "I'm afraid I must steal my wife away."

"Of course."

Wilhelm led her to the dance floor and slowly glided her over the glossy wood. "He seemed to be enthralled with you," Wilhelm said once they were mingled among the rest of the people on the dance floor.

"He was just curious about me because I married you."

"I'm sure. So many of the men I work with are nosey. They are always trying to find out about my life. I think they do that because I'm Gestapo. They do that to other members of the Gestapo as well. I think there is a bet amongst them to see who can find out the most. They seem to think we are this mysterious group of men with dark secrets."

"Aren't you? I have to pry anything I want to know from you. You are the most secretive person I have met."

"Second only to you."

That was a fair and accurate statement. She was keeping the most important things about herself from him. "So we are both guilty of keeping secrets."

"True, but I have told you more than you have told me."

"You don't know that."

"I do."

"What am I keeping from you?"

"What are you not keeping from me?"

"Stop answering my questions with a question, and tell me what you think I am keeping from you."

"For starters, you won't admit that you helped your friend Jon escape."

"And what else do you think I am hiding?"

He raised his brows. "Where do I begin. From the moment I met you, I knew you were hiding something big, and I'm still trying to figure out what that is."

"I don't know what big thing you think I'm hiding."

"Did you help Jon escape, Eva?"

She tensed. Why did he want to know so badly? "And if I did, would it make any difference?"

"At this point, no. I already know you did, so you might as well admit it."

"If you already know, then why are you asking?"

"So that you are one step closer to being honest with me."

Eva focused on his face as they moved across the dance floor. "No, I won't admit to it. You don't tell me most things, and I have to find them out from someone else. You want me to lay out all my secrets on the table for you to see, but you won't do the same. Trust has to be mutual."

"Then how will we move forward from this point."

"I don't know, but I do know that it doesn't have to be that way."

"It does because I can't tell you everything."

"I accept that you have work-related things that you can't discuss with me, but you don't talk to me about things that have nothing to do with your job."

"Like?"

"Well, for example, you wouldn't tell me how you really felt in the shower when I told you I didn't want any more children."

He took a deep breath and let it out slowly through his nose. "I honestly can't say if I want more children at this point because I haven't experienced what it's like to have one yet. However, I think I will like being a father, so the natural thing would be to want more."

She so badly wanted to tell him she would do whatever made him happy, that he was special to her, and that she would gladly give him all the children he wanted. But her future and his were so uncertain it would be irresponsible to tell him the truth or to give him all that he wanted. She wondered if this impasse they were at was the final nail in their coffin.

"I guess it would be."

She let him lead her in the dance, moving with him, his hand warm on hers as his other hand was low on her waist. The music was soothing, and as they danced close, she couldn't help but feel that they were strangers, neither willing to give nor trust. There had always been a silent battle between them, and from the moment they met, they were at odds. She still struggled to comprehend how they managed to fall in love, but then opposites do attract.

When the song ended, he took her by the hand and led her back to the table. She was growing tired, and her feet now hurt from dancing and were pressing against the sides of her shoes. She felt a little sick from the food they ate, the stress of the evening, and the anxiety about tomorrow. Wilhelm was in a conversation with the man beside him, and she hated to interrupt but didn't think she could stay any longer.

She tapped him on the arm, and he turned to her. "Can we go?" she asked in a whisper.

He looked at his watch. "We have only been here an hour and a half."

"I know, but…" She had to tell him she didn't feel well, or he would insist they stay. "I need to lay down. I can find my own way home if you want to stay."

He creased his brows. "Don't be silly." He turned back to the man he was talking to. "My wife is tired, so I'm afraid we will have to continue this conversation tomorrow."

The man patted Wilhelm on the shoulder. "I understand. Get her home. I'll see you in the morning."

Wilhelm helped her into her coat and held her hand as they walked to the car. She wondered if he was worried she would fall on the ice. He opened the door for her, then shut it once she was in, and walked around the back to the other side of the car. A wave of exhaustion hit her once the car pulled away from the curb, but the motion made her feel more nauseous. Her feet, her back, and her head hurt, and a new cramping sensation radiated through her stomach. She didn't care how Wilhelm felt about her or how she felt about him. She desperately needed to lay down and simultaneously wanted to feel comforted. She lowered herself down, putting her head in his lap and curling her legs up on the seat. His legs were warm against her cheek, and she closed her eyes, taking in his heat.

He placed a hand on her hip. "Are you cold?"

"A little." Mostly, she was tired. She could feel him moving, then his leather trench coat was being draped over her. She could feel him pulling it over her bare legs and her feet. He tucked it around her neck, then rested his hand on her again, but on top of the coat.

She opened her eyes, blinking against the haze of sleep. A hand rubbed over her cheek and hair. "Eva," Wilhelm's voice was low and soft. "We are home. Let's go inside, and you can go to bed.

When she sat up, the coat slid off her shoulder, and she looked around. She picked up the coat and handed it to him. "Thank you."

He gave her a faint smile and took it from her hand. He opened the door and stepped out, holding his hand out to her. She placed hers in his, and he helped her from the car. He didn't let go of her hand and helped her up the steps to their apartment. Once inside, she pulled off her shoes, her feet throbbing from being crammed in them all evening. She rubbed each one for a few seconds, wounding how they fit into her shoes. He pulled her coat off her shoulders, and she walked to the bedroom. She unbuttoned her dress and let it fall to the floor, then went to the bathroom, brushed her teeth, and watched her face. When she was finished, she slowly walked back to the bedroom, each leg feeling like it was made of lead. She all but fell on the bed and didn't see Wilhelm anywhere. Once she was still, she could hear him in his office on the phone with someone. She couldn't understand most of what was said, but she could tell it was work-related. She didn't move, trying to keep the contents of her dinner down. She listened to him hang up the phone, then his bare feet on the hall floor.

The bed dipped from his weight, and she could see his dark shape beside her. He moved the blankets from her feet and took her left foot. His hands were invitingly warm, and she closed her eyes, enjoying the soothing feel of them. With circular strokes, he moved his thumbs over the arch of her foot, massaging the tight ligament. His strong fingers kneaded her sore foot, and it felt amazing. She released the breath she was holding, along with the tension, and felt drowsy. He worked her foot methodically, then put it under the blanket and took her other one, doing the same thing to it. She looked at him with heavy eyelids. "Why are you so nice to me?"

"I thought that was obvious."

"I know I don't deserve you."

"Go to sleep, Eva." He moved his hands from her foot to the calf of her leg.

She closed her eyes and let herself drift into sleep.

The honking of a car horn woke her, and she rolled onto her back and looked at the window. The bright sunlight lit up the room in a warm yellow color. She looked at the clock on the wall near the door, and her heart skipped a beat. It was almost one o'clock in the afternoon. How had she slept so long? She set up in bed and leaned against the headboard. She felt like she had only slept for a few hours, but she didn't know how that was possible. She threw the blankets off when she saw a note on Wilhelm's pillow. She took the piece of paper and read it.

Eva,
I don't know when I will be home, but it will be late. I won't be in the office, but I told my adjutant that you might call. A storm is predicted for this evening, so you should stay in. You need to be resting anyway.

Wilhelm

She laid the paper on the nightstand. So there was to be a storm the night the pilot was supposed to leave. She went to the bathroom and then called Lorelei.

"Hello."

"Lorelei, it's Eva. Wilhelm told me there is supposed to be a storm tonight. Is that going to be a problem?"

"Did he say what time the storm would be here?"

"He didn't. Also, he is working late, which is good for us, but he did say that he will be out of the office all day. I don't know what he is doing or where he will be."

"I haven't had any reports that the Gestapo are on to us, so I don't think there is any reason for concern. Unless I get new instructions, we will go forward as planned."

"Alright." If Lorelei wasn't concerned, she told herself she shouldn't be either. "What time will you be here to pick me up?"

"At six."

"I'll be ready."

She ate lunch, read some of her book, tidied the apartment, and then took a nap. The day passed quickly, and six o'clock arrived in record time. She already had her coat and shoes on, and when she heard the knock on the door, she grabbed her gloves, hat, and scarf off the entryway table along with her purse and opened the door. She followed Lorelei's driver to the car, and he held the door for her, then closed it once she was in. Ingrid was sitting in the middle, and Eva was a little surprised to see her. She knew that Ingrid had been secretly going to the American hospital to check on the pilot, and Eva suspected that they had formed an attachment.

"We will stop just before we are out of town as usual, and you two can get in the trunk."

The sky had blackened, making it darker than it already was, and the snow fell in little flakes. They didn't get a lot of snow in Paris, so why did tonight have to be one of the few nights they did?

The car pulled into an alley and stopped, then Eva and Ingrid crammed into the trunk, and the driver closed the lid. Lorelei had put a blanket in there for them, and Eva was grateful. She closed her eyes, trying to endure the ride, feeling suffocated in the cocoon of darkness surrounding them. She focused on her breathing.

"Are you alright?" Ingrid whispered.

"Yes. We can't talk, remember?"

"I know."

The ride seemed to take forever, but finally, they were there. The lid of the trunk opened, and a wash of cold air filled the space, and her breath came out in a cloud in front of her. The driver helped her and Ingrid from the trunk, and she saw Lorelei waiting for them. "Where is he?" Eva asked.

"He is already here. We brought him here by another means. The plane should be landing any minute.

They walked through the trees and then hunkered low in the tall weeds that surrounded the opening where the plane would land. Eva noticed the silhouette of several other people, maybe eight or nine. They were squatting in the grass near the edge, each of them with a weapon at the ready. The only one who wasn't armed was the pilot. Eva came beside him and sat in the grass because she couldn't kneel down like everyone else.

"I wanted to thank you for all you have done for me?"

"You are welcome. I'm sorry I wasn't able to come to see you at the hospital, but I can't be seen anywhere near there."

"I understand. I know this is dangerous for you." He looked to Ingrid, then back to Eva. "I had no idea I would grow fond of a German."

Eva looked at her stomach. "I didn't either."

"The father is German?"

"He is. So you like Ingrid."

"I am fond of her, yes. I gave her my address back in England and asked if she would write. I know she can't speak English, but I hoped you would transcribe the letters for her."

Eva gave him a warm smile. "Of course."

He looked her over. "Isn't it risky coming while you're pregnant?"

"It shouldn't be. We don't plan on there being any action." She looked at the men with guns. "Are they?"

He glanced at them. "I think they are just being cautious."

The approaching sound of distant plane engines echoed off the trees. She looked to the sky but couldn't see anything yet, only could hear the sound it made. "It's almost time," she told him.

Lorelei came to Eva's side and knelt. "That is the plane. Everything needs to happen quickly, and then we need to leave. When the plane lands, it will not shut off its engines. They will unload the cargo, and he will get on board, and then they will take off. The longer it is on the ground, the more dangerous it is."

"I understand."

Ingrid moved to his side, and Eva smiled at her and took her hand. Eva was actually happy for Ingrid. He was the first man Ingrid liked that she approved of, not because he was British, but because he seemed to honestly like her. His being British and her German, while their two countries were at war, meant he would have to. That thought made her consider Wilhelm and how he must truly love her. He didn't even seem to really like Americans, but he still risked so much for her. He was kind to her and often treated her like a queen. She smiled at that thought.

They could now see the plane, and one of the men who was hiding came out into the opening with a flashlight in each hand to help guide it in. It landed in the grass and taxied to the end near where they were hiding, turned so the tail was facing them and the nose was facing the direction they came from, and then it stopped. They all stood and came around to the side of the plane, and the door opened. A man was standing in the doorway.

"Which one of you is coming with us?"

"I am." The pilot took a step forward.

"Right. Get on board, and we will start unloading the cargo."

"Aye, sir." He gave Eva and Lorelei a quick hug. "I owe you my life." Then he turned to Ingrid and embraced her, holding on to her longer. He kissed her on the cheek, then released her. He hurried and climbed onto the plane while several of the men unloaded wooden crates off the aircraft.

"Who are these men?" Eva asked Lorelei.

"Members of the resistance."

"I thought you said you didn't work with the resistance."

"I don't directly, but they are crucial to the Allies and the war effort, so we all work together when it is necessary."

Just as they were unloading the last crate from the plane, a bright light came from seemingly nowhere, illuminating them and everything around them. Before Eva could process what was happening, she was being forcefully pulled away towards the weeds. She looked to see that Lorelei had her arm around her waist as they were both springing away from chaos. There was shouting in German, French, and English, and then gunfire echoed over the roar of the plane engines. Eva was jerked down roughly once they were in the weeds, and she fell to the ground with Lorelei. She had landed at an angle, partly on her side and partly on her stomach. A sharp pain radiated through her stomach and back, but she bit the inside of her cheek to cope with the pain. She got to her hands and knees and watched the events unfold. She frantically looked for Ingrid but couldn't see her anywhere. People were firing at each other, and instructions were given in German for them to surrender. She watched the plane door close and then accelerate down the short stretch of grass. The fighting continued, and she watched in horror. One German was hit in the shoulder and fell to the ground. Eva felt a hand on her back, and she almost screamed. She turned to see Ingrid behind her.

"Oh God, Ingrid. I had no idea where you were."

Ingrid's hands were shaking, and her eyes were watery. "I'm so scared, Eva."

Eva put her arm around her. "We will be alright. They don't know we are here." She looked back to the fighting, and somehow, while she was distracted, more Germans had arrived. Most of the resistance fighters were now dead, but there were still a few fighting. Her heart caught in her throat when she saw Wilhelm appear in the clearing. She clasped her hand over her mouth and watched. She felt stupid for not considering that this was where he would be tonight. Three men from the resistance were left, and they had them in the middle on their knees at gunpoint, with their hands behind their heads. One stood and ran, and a soldier lifted his machine gun, but Wilhelm pushed it down.

"No. We need him alive." He pulled his pistol from the holster and pointed it at the fleeing man, then pulled the trigger, a loud ringing echoing in the night. The man fell to the ground, clasping his hand over his leg as he cried out in pain. Wilhelm holstered his gun and walked toward the man. He was next to one of the crates when another man leaped out from behind and slashed Wilhelm across the stomach with a knife.

Eva involuntarily let out a squeak, and Ingrid clasped her hand tightly over her mouth. Desperation for Wilhelm reared through her, and she wanted to run and help him, but she had to stay back. The only thing she could do was watch as this man attacked the man she loved.

Wilhelm rounded on the man and grabbed hold of his wrist, trying to wrestle the knife from him. Wilhelm's men stood by, watching, not wanting to shoot for fear of hitting him. But the whole thing happened so quickly that they were stunned.

The knife was inching closer to Wilhelm's throat, so he reached up and gripped the blade, ripping the knife from the man's hand. He tossed it onto the ground, his blood covering the shiny metal, and then Wilhelm swung his bloodied fist at the man with such force that a cracking sound came from the man's face as Wilhelm's knuckles contacted his eye socket. The man staggered backward, and before he could regain his balance, Wilhelm put a hand on each side of his head and twisted it with such force that it turned to the side at an unnatural angle as it popped and cracked. The man's lifeless body fell to the ground, and Wilhelm cursed under his breath, breathing heavily as he glared at the dead man lying at his feet. He gritted his teeth as he looked at his hand, then inspected the cut on his abdomen. Blood had now soaked through his shirt and military jacket.

He turned to his men. "What the fuck!" he yelled menacingly. "Were you somehow rendered useless?"

The man closest to Wilhelm stood at attention. "No, sir, we didn't want to hit you."

Wilhelm strode toward the man and ripped the rifle from his hand, then leaned in close. "Next time you shoot. If you can't do that, then use your damn hands," he said through his teeth, the muscles in his jaw tight. He shoved the gun into another one of the men's hands. "Spread out. There might be more of them."

Lorelei grabbed Eva's hand. "We have to get out of here now." Eva took Ingrid's hand, and the three of them ran as fast as they could in a stooped position. When they got to the car, Eva and Ingrid hurried and climbed into the truck, and Lorelei got into the back. The driver started the engine but didn't turn on the headlight until they were on the main road.

Eva was shaking from the cold and from the adrenaline. The pain was severe now, and she worried about Wilhelm. She didn't know how badly he was hurt and wondered if he would go to the hospital or come straight home. And the poor men who lost their lives and those who were captured. She wondered if they would give her, Ingrid, and Lorelei up, or would they be able to keep it to themselves. At least the pilot was able to escape with the plane. She silently cried in the dark of the trunk.

The car stopped in the alley, and they both climbed out and got into the backseat. "Make sure you don't have any dirt or grass on you, Eva."

She looked at herself but couldn't tell in the dark if she did or not. "I will shower when I get home."

"Now we know where your husband was tonight. How the hell did he find out?"

"It wasn't from me, if that is what you are thinking."

"I don't think it was you, but there is a leak somewhere. Somebody talked." The car pulled in front of Eva's apartment. "Let me know if you learn anything?" Lorelei told her.

"I will." She gave Ingrid a quick hug and then got out of the car. She tried to act normal as she passed the guard just outside the front door. She gave him a smile and hurried to the apartment. As soon as she was inside, she went to the bathroom, peeled off her clothes, and got in the shower. She made sure it was fast, then picked up her clothes and poked them under the pile of dirty laundry. She got in bed and covered up, only now fully noticing the pain from falling. She moaned and put her hand over her stomach, curling into a ball.

She couldn't sleep, so she watched the hand of the clock as it moved annoyingly slow. She wanted to know how Wilhelm was or if he was going to come home at all. Finally, the front door opened and she resisted bolting from the bed to go to him. She had to act like she didn't know anything had happened. Wilhelm didn't come into the bedroom but went to the kitchen instead and turned on the light. She watched it shining into the bedroom and couldn't stand it any longer. She had to see how he was. She got out of bed and walked the long hall to the kitchen. Wilhelm was standing by the sink with a towel in his hand, his jacket off, his shirt unbuttoned, and his undershirt pulled up with his other hand. He had a piece of material wrapped around his left hand that was stained with dry blood as he pressed the towel to his stomach. Wilhelm moved it back a fraction, and she could see that it had fresh blood on it. Then he pressed it against his stomach again and clinched his jaw like he was in pain.

"Oh my God," she cried, then rushed to his side and tried to pull the towel from his stomach, but he held it tight."

"Eva, it's nothing."

"Wilhelm, let me see."

She was not going to back down. He kept the towel pressed firmly against the cut, so she slapped his hand. "Move it!" He relaxed his fingers, and she pulled the towel away. Her gut tightened as she took in the gash about four inches long and roughly half an inch deep on his stomach, which was slick and sticky with blood.

"Oh, Wilhelm, you need stitches. How many towels have you used?"

"This is the first towel."

"But how many pieces of material have you used to soak up the blood?"

"Uhh, three or four."

She pressed the towel back against the cut and took him by the arm, leading him to one of the chairs at the kitchen table, and he staggered, making her wonder just how much blood he had lost. "Sit down." He did, and she took his left hand and unwrapped the cloth. It, too, was bad and needed stitches. The cut was so deep it had to be to the bone. She went to the phone in the kitchen and turned the dial.

"Who are you calling?"

"Your orderly. We are taking you to the hospital." She was glad that Wilhelm came home so she could go to the hospital with him, but at the same time, she was upset that he did. He didn't try to stop her from calling, and she turned the dial to the last number. As she listened to the ringing on the other end, she could hear that his breathing was labored, and his face was frighteningly pale. His usually olive skin had now turned to an ashy white color. When his orderly picked up, she told him that Wilhelm was hurt badly and that he needed to hurry to their apartment. The orderly told her he would be there in ten minutes, and then the line went dead. She hung up the phone, got a clean towel, then returned to Wilhelm and sat in the chair beside him. She laid his hand on her leg and gently wrapped it.

"Are you going to tell me how you got these?"

He sighed. "A bad day at work."

"I figured that. But how exactly did you get them?"

"A surprise attack."

"And did you catch them?"

"No, I killed him." There was not an ouch of regret in his voice.

She stopped wrapping and looked up at him. She was surprised he had told her the truth. She knew he had killed the man because she watched him do it, but she hadn't expected him to tell her. "Oh." His eyes met hers, and she could see he was waiting for her reaction. She licked her lips and went back to wrapping his hand. When she tied it, he winced under his breath, so she placed a soft kiss just above the bandage. "Sorry.

"It's alright."

She searched his face and saw the agony etched all over it. She looked at the clock, willing his orderly to hurry up and get there. When she heard the knock on the door, she quickly stood and went to answer it. She pulled the door open and motioned for him to enter.

"Help me get him to the car."

He followed her to the kitchen, and Wilhelm was slumped slightly in his chair as his breathing came in fast, panting breaths. She went to his side and put an arm around his back to help him stand.

"No, Frau Bauer, let me do it. He is too heavy for you, and I don't want you to strain yourself."

She moved away and let the orderly help him up but took Wilhelm's uninjured hand, her heart thudding with intense concern as they took him out to the car. She was shocked and worried that his condition had deteriorated so quickly. She knew now that he had lost a significant amount of blood, more than he had obviously realized or her. They got him into the backseat of the car, and the orderly drove faster than usual through the empty streets of Paris. She didn't care that she was still in her nightgown. All she was concerned about now was Wilhelm and getting him to the hospital. She couldn't even focus on her own pain because of her worry for him.

His eyes flashed towards her. "I'm not going to die. You are worrying too much."

"Of course I'm worried," she said, tears pulling in her eyes as she listened to his ragged voice.

He gave her a forced smile through his obvious pain. "It's nice to know you care, Misses Bauer," he said to her in English with a strong German accent, too tired to try and force an English one.

She liked to hear him say it in English. They seldom spoke in English, but primarily German and sometimes French. "I thought that was obvious?" she said with a friendly challenge, repeating what he had told her the night before.

They arrived at the hospital, and the orderly waited in the lobby while Eva followed Wilhelm to the room. They stitched up his hand and stomach and gave him a blood transfusion. He was prescribed antibiotics and pain medication. They administered the medicine at the hospital and told him he could go home if he was monitored. Eva informed them she had been a nurse and said she would be the one giving him the medicine.

"He will be groggy and not completely lucid while he is on the pain medication," the doctor said as he held out the two brown glass bottles to her.

"I know. I've seen its effects before when I worked at the hospital."

"If he shows any signs of an infection, you need to bring him back as soon as you notice."

"I will."

"He can have another pain pill when you get home, but I wouldn't give him any sooner than four hours after that."

"Thank you, doctor."

When they were back at the apartment, the orderly helped him to the bedroom and laid him on the bed. "If you need anything, call me."

"I will. Thank you. I don't know what I would have done if you weren't just a phone call away."

"That is why I'm here."

Once he was gone, she went to help Wilhelm change out of his bloodied clothes. She sat on the bed beside him, and he gave her a tight smile. "Can I get you something?"

"A glass of brandy would be nice right now."

"You can't have alcohol, not with the medicine you are taking."

He shifted his position on the bed and slightly gave a sharp wince. A small amount of blood was beginning to show through the bandage, and she could see the pain he was in from the expression on his face. She went to the kitchen, got a glass of water, and brought it back to the bedroom. She took one of the pain pills from the bottle and handed it to him along with the glass of water. He gave her an appreciative look, took the pill from the palm of her hand and the cup, then put the pill in his mouth and drank the entire cup of water. He let out a long sigh, and she took the cup from him and sat it on the side table. She helped him out of his button-up shirt, then he lifted his arms slowly, and she pulled the bloodied undershirt over his head. She inspected his wound, and then her eyes roamed over his muscular chest, lingering as she took in his handsome form. Her cheeks prickled from the heat, and she felt embarrassed that she was noticing him in this way at the moment and in his condition. Her own pain had slowly subsided, and she was glad. She didn't want to worry about herself or the baby while she was concerned for him. She looked up, and their eyes met. He was smiling at her wickedly, and she feared he had noticed her eyes lingering on his naked chest. She broke their eye contact and started to get up to get a pair of pajamas for him when he reached up and placed his hand over her breast despite his obvious pain. She didn't move his hand but didn't look at his face.

"I don't think that is a good idea," she said, almost in a whisper. "You are not in a condition for that."

She finally looked up, and he gave her a wanting look. There was humor in the smile playing at the corner of his lips. She knew his emotions were not well constrained under the powerful pain medicine he was taking. He leaned over and reached for her with an unexpected, untethered boldness. Her heart raced, and she struggled to keep her breathing even as he rubbed his knuckles up and down her arm.

"You are under the influence of the medicine, Wilhelm."

"Probably, but the pain is less now."

"I can tell by the provocative way you keep touching me."

His lip turned up. "And why do you think that is because of the medicine?"

"Because you have utterly refused any of my advances in the last few months, and you are in pain and only can't feel it because of the medicine. But yes, I can see that you are feeling better." She looked at his hand which was still on her arm.

He breathed out a laugh and shot her a suggestive look before his expression grew more serious. "Does me touching you bother you? It's always hard for me to hold back when you are so close."

She considered his question and also his unchecked honesty. She was not used to being around Wilhelm when he was not tightly controlled. "I'm happy you are not in pain." What she really wanted to tell him was that she wished he would make advances toward her when he wasn't under the influence of drugs.

She helped him change into pajamas and then crawled into bed beside him. Suddenly, she was aware of the emotional and physical exhaustion from the events of the day. She laid her head on his shoulder, and he pulled her closer, his cheek brushing her hair as he angled his head down to nuzzle against her. To her surprise, he kissed her temple, soft and lingering. Wilhelm certainly wasn't shy in private. When they were alone, he wasn't the reserved and formal Wilhelm she was used to. Although, lately, he has treated her almost the same in private as he did in public, so she was frustrated by his open display of affection now. Part of her wished that she could take some of the pills to deaden her grief, the future that lay before her, and the memory of the horrific events that happened today. She didn't want to remember that the world was at war, a war that threatened everyone she loved in this time. She wanted to forget that Wilhelm could have died tonight. Just the memory of it shook her to the core. But at last, she was pregnant and couldn't take memory-altering drugs. Plus, with Wilhelm wounded and under the influence of the medication, she needed to keep a clear head.

"How is the pain?"

"It is better now," he said while staring at the wall, but then he looked at her, and his mouth curved into a lazy grin. "I am feeling much better." His eyes glided over her as he brushed his fingertips along her thigh. "You are so beautiful," he mused. "Your love is more powerful than these drugs. Before I met you, I had never encountered something that would or could ever come before my duty. But you have thoroughly quenched that fire, and now the only one that remains alight is for you; only it burns."

She raised her brows at this demonstrative explanation of his feelings. She knew exactly what he meant by her fire burning him. He perceived Germany as constant and loyal but her as ever-changing and deceitful. His hand slid up her leg and under her nightgown, and she was amused at the knowing look he was giving her. He had been sedated for a while in the hospital after

357

the attack in Berlin, and when he woke, the medicine they gave him was not this strong.

"You have never been under the influence of so much medicine before."

"No, I have not. But I've also never been at home in this much pain before or wanted something so much."

She suspected she knew what he meant, but she wasn't going to admit that she did. "You've never wanted medicine this much?"

Wilhelm's smile faded. "No. I've never wanted anything as much as I want you." There was frustration in his words and a yearning in his voice. The silence in the room was heavy, and she was acutely aware of the tension between them and an unsettling thrill that was pulling her through an ocean of mixed emotions. She glanced up, and Wilhelm was steadily watching her, his expression unreadable, but there was still the subtle look in his eyes from before. So he did want her and was just denying himself as well as her, and she only knew this now because he was not the least bit in control. She was growing even more flustered by how intensely Wilhelm stared at her. She moved away from him to her side of the bed.

He smirked at her. "Keeping a safe distance?"

She swallowed hard, unsettled by him and her attraction to his masculine physique. It was hard to resist her draw to him. His gaze was steady on her, and he beckoned with his finger for her to return to his side, the longing still in his eyes as he patiently waited for her. They were both quiet, only the sound of their breathing and her beating heart thudding in her ears. She finally gave him a seductive look, knowing she was being reckless. Wilhelm smiled as he caught her gaze, then reached over and rubbed his thumb over her bottom lip, his eyes boring into hers wantonly. Her breathing increased, but she remained still, trying to control her body as it pulsed with heat, the pleasure of his desire for her hard to ignore. His breathing had also increased, and he shot her an intensely carnal look. The look in his eyes was a desire so fierce that she knew it would override any concern for his own well-being.

He took her hand and tugged on her with firm insistence, wanting her to move to his side of the bed. "Come here." There was nothing gentle in his request, only a demand fueled by overwhelming want that was wild and enticing but also intimidating at the same time.

She glanced at the bandage on his hand. Wilhelm, no. You are not well enough."

He didn't let go of her hand but smiled wider, desire hot in his gaze. "Then you be on top." There was a command in it like before, a rough edge to his passion.

"You are hurt," she reminded him again, all the while fighting her own desire.

"My hand is wounded, and my stomach, not the rest of me, it works just fine." His eyes were alight with a wicked gleam.

She wanted to do this with him, to give in to his passion and his desire. Some days she wanted him so much it was almost painful, and now he was offering it to her and she wanted to be reckless, to let herself be pulled into his overwhelming, all-consuming passion. She wanted to let him take her any way he wanted, as many times as he wanted.

He sensed her hesitation and pulled on her more insistently, losing any remnant of amusement. He was intense, highly affected by the medicine, and consumed by a domineering want. She pulled her hand from his and kept it firmly at her side.

His expression tensed, and his frustration was palpable. He withdrew his hand, and his breaths were deep and slow. Eva looked at his face, and when her eyes met his, there was a hunger in them that was so intense it shocked her.

When Wilhelm spoke, his voice was quiet but impassioned. "I have never wanted something more in my whole life than I want you."

She understood the deeper meaning that he conveyed in his tone and intense expression. He was not just talking about this moment or wanting to take her now, but something far greater and much more significant. His honest display of these feelings for her, as well as his desire, moved her.

She looked at the ring on her right hand. "We are married. You already have me."

To her surprise, his eyes gave a harsh flare, and he looked away. "No, Eva," he said. There was a different kind of pain in his voice. "I don't." He rolled onto his back and looked up at the ceiling, his feelings firmly pulled away from her. She only now noticed the chill in the air that seemed fitting for the grief she was feeling. The pain seared through her because she knew it was true. She had grown to love him in so many ways, and she had given herself to him with no reservations, freely surrendering to the fierce attraction they had for each other and her strange longing for the intense love he showed her. Craving to be able to let go of the grief that was lodged in her heart. She believed it was possible for her to love him fully in return, and even though she hadn't professed her love for him, she hoped he could read it in her eyes.

But she felt her love, her passion for him was never as his was for her. His was unwavering in its strength, blazing and ardent, completely unfractured. She was painfully aware that a small piece of her heart still belonged to Gerhardt and might always be his, and she knew that Wilhelm could sense the truth as well.

She pulled the blankets over her and lay there for a long time, unable to sleep. Wilhelm was quiet and still beside her, and she didn't know if he was awake. Her guilt and the conflicts that waged inside kept her awake for hours until, finally, her eyelids grew heavy, and she welcomed the sleep that eventually took her, but it was not peaceful or restful. The memory of Wilhelm's passion, his unchecked words, and her inability to return his feelings completely played out in her dreams.

Chapter Nineteen

January 21st, 1943

Wilhelm returned to work after only five days, against her protests. He told her he felt fine and would continue taking the antibiotics and the pain medicine if he needed it. She didn't believe he was actually fine, but he always pushed the limits when it came to himself.

To her dismay, the pain and cramping she felt after falling returned but had intensified. She tried to downplay it to convince herself that everything was fine. She was scared. Scared of the pain, fearful of what it meant, and afraid to tell anyone about it, but deep down, she knew something was wrong, seriously wrong.

The sun was shining outside, but it was a cold January day. She had protected herself from the weather and went for a walk, hoping it would ease the pain, but it didn't, so she returned to the apartment and decided to read. The pain was severe, and she couldn't focus on the book, so she laid it down and scooted to the edge of the couch, her legs apart to accommodate her stomach.

She rubbed at her lower back, then froze when she felt something discharge into her underwear, something wet. She stood, lifted her dress, and pulled down her underwear. Inside was blood mixed with other fluids. She held her breath, panicked, as she looked at the bright red color. She pulled up her underwear and went to the phone. When she got the operator, she asked to speak with the hospital in Berlin and gave them the name. A nurse answered, and Eva asked to talk to Dr. Möller, then gave her name. She put the palm of her hand against the wall and leaned over while she waited, taking controlled breaths. She heard Klaus' voice on the other end, and relief washed over her.

"Eva."

"Klaus," she said through her labored breathing. "I think I'm in labor."

There was silence on the other end, but finally, he spoke. "Why do you think you are in labor?"

"Five days ago, I fell, and immediately I started having pain, but it went away that night. Yesterday it came back, and the pain is so much more intense now. And just a few minutes ago, I started bleeding."

"Eva, I'm going to try to get there as soon as I can. But you need to go to the hospital. Why didn't you go when you fell?"

"Wilhelm was seriously injured that same day and had to go to the hospital, or he might have died. Besides, I didn't think it was that serious because the pain subsided."

"He didn't make you go after the fall?"

"He doesn't know."

"So he doesn't know about any of this?"

"No. I didn't want to worry him."

"I understand that, but he is going to find out now anyway."

"Not if I go to the hospital and nothing is wrong, then I will have no reason to tell him."

"But something is wrong, Eva. Nothing about what you described is normal at your stage of pregnancy.

A sharp burst of pain radiated through her whole body, and she cried out. "Owww, God."

"I'm going to hang up and catch the next train. Call him!"

"I will."

"I mean it, Eva. Call him."

"I will, I promise." When she hung up the phone with Klaus, she redialed the operator and asked to speak to Standartenführer Bauer at 84 Avenue Foch. The operator put her through, but his adjutant answered the phone.

"SS Standartenführer Bauer's office."

"Yes, can I please speak to my husband?" She fought the pain and tried to keep her voice level.

"I'm sorry, Frau Bauer, but he is out of the office."

Of course, he was. "Dammit," she said in English. "When will he be back?"

"I don't expect him back for a while."

Right now, she really missed cell phones. "Would you please tell him I called and will be at the hospital?"

"I will, Frau Bauer. "Are you unwe—"

She cut him off by hanging up the phone. She would have to find her own way to the hospital. She called Lorelei Vogel and asked if she would take her.

364

"Of course I will. We are leaving now."

Eva put on her coat and shoes, got her purse, and waited on the front steps. The pain was excruciating, and tears trickled down her face, cooling her cheeks from the cold January air. When the car arrived, she slowly made her way down each step. Lorelei and her driver both came to help her. They put her in the backseat, and she turned to her side because it hurt too bad to sit on her butt. Her breaths were shallow and fast. She squeezed her eyes shut and gripped the door.

Lorelei rubbed her arm. "Control your breathing. It helps."

"How do women do this?" Eva kept her eyes shut. "I don't think it can. It hurts so bad."

"You don't have a choice. That baby is coming."

Eva shook her head. "It's too early."

"Sometimes they don't wait. Does your husband know?"

Eva shook her head. "I called his office, but he wasn't there." She drew in a breath and held it.

"Did you leave a message?"

She nodded and let out a long exhale. "They will tell him." She looked to Lorelei. "I don't want twilight sleep. I don't."

"They will do what is best."

She vehemently shook her head. "No, I don't want it. And I want Wilhelm there, in the room."

"That is not how things are done."

"I don't care how things are done." She was in too much pain to care about 1940s customs.

The car pulled in front of the hospital and stopped. They helped her out and into the lobby. Lorelei got two nurses to come and assist. They put Eva in a wheelchair and rolled it into the elevator, taking her to the third floor. She was scared out of her mind. She didn't have anyone there, not her mom, not Wilhelm, or even Ingrid. She realized she was going to deliver her baby alone in 1940s France.

She looked up at the nurses. "I don't want twilight sleep. I want to have it natural."

"That is not recommended."

"I don't care. I am refusing it. If you try to force me to take it, I will tell my husband exactly who it was that forced me. I will give him each nurse and doctor's name. He is head of the Gestapo in France, and I will make sure he knows who did it to me." She hated using Wilhelm and his position as a threat, but right now, she was terrified and alone, and that was all she could think of.

The nurses exchanged a glance. "I will tell the doctor," one of them assured Eva. They pushed her into a room and got a gown. "Let's get this on you." They helped her out of her clothes and into the gown, then went to find the doctor.

Eva looked around the cold, sterile white room. "Where are you, Wilhelm? I need you." Her eyes nervously darted to each side of the room, lighting on all the things around her, and she wanted to cry, and not just from the pain.

A doctor and three nurses came into the room. "Can you please call my husband?" she asked, panicked.

"Yes, we will have someone call him," he said as he slipped on a pair of gloves and prepared the instruments.

"He is SS Standartenführer Bauer of the Gestapo."

The doctor paused and focused on her, his brows pulled together. "That is your husband?"

She groaned through the next wave of pain. "Yes."

He nodded to one of the nurses, and she left the room. "They tell me you don't want twilight sleep."

"No, I don't."

"I wouldn't recommend doing it without it."

"I don't care. And when my husband gets here, I want him in the room with me, not waiting in the hall."

"I'm not sure he will make it in time. Lie back, and we will see how close you are." She laid on her back the best she could, and the doctor put two fingers inside her. "Lay still," he instructed. He pushed his fingers hard into her, then pulled them out. "You are eight centimeters, but your water hasn't broken yet." He took a long piece of metal that was hooked at the end. "I'm going to break your water with this. Don't worry, it won't hurt." He stuck it in her, and she barely felt anything. Then, there was a warm sensation as fluid poured out of her.

"I am only around thirty-four weeks. Why did I go into labor now?"

"Sometimes that happens. It's not always understood why."

"I fell five days ago. Could that be why?"

"It could be, yes."

Her eyes blurred with tears. "Will it survive?"

"There is no way of telling, but there is a change. You are far enough along, so I wouldn't lose hope yet."

The nurse returned to the room. "He is on his way," she informed Eva.

Eva cried out in joy. "Thank you." The cramping intensified now that he had broken her water. "Why does it hurt so bad?"

"The contractions will increase in severity the closer you get."
He put his fingers in her again and checked. He pulled them out
and looked at her. "It is time for you to push now."

"No," she shook her head. "He isn't here yet."

"We can't wait. You have to push." He put each of her feet
into a stirrup and positioned himself on a chair between her legs,
the nurses coming to stand at his side. "OK, push now." She
sucked in a deep breath and held it, then pushed down towards her
butt as hard as she could. She let the breath out and panted,
dropping her head back onto the pillow. "You need to push again."
She lifted her head and pushed again, then let the breath out in a
long groan. Her face felt hot and flushed from the pressure. She
pushed several more times and was utterly exhausted, and every
time it felt like her insides were being torn out.

She looked up to see Wilhelm enter the room and held her
hand out to him. He came to her side and took her outstretched
hand, kissing it. His face was strained, and worry was etched on
it. He brushed some hair from her sweaty forehead and kissed her
there too.

"I'm sorry, Eva. I left as soon as I heard." He kissed her on
the forehead again, his lips lingering. "I'm so sorry."

"You're here now."

"Push," the doctor yelled. She did as he said and squeezed
Wilhelm's hand as she screwed her eyes shut, fighting against the
pain, trying to focus on the feel of the baby descending. Wilhelm
rubbed his thumb on the palm of her hand in circular motions, the
only thing he could think to do. "The head is crowning," the doctor
told her. "Just a few more." She pushed, but her energy was
waning fast.

"Good girl, you're doing great," the nurse told her, patting Eva on the leg. When the next contraction climbed to its peak, and she had the urge to push, she did, and the top of the baby's head and forehead were finally out. The doctor took hold of the head with both hands and pulled, then both shoulders popped out, and the rest of its body slid out with ease.

Wilhelm tightened his grip on her hand as he watched, his face set in an intense concentration. She leaned up to see a tiny body with pink skin on the table between her legs. The doctor tapped the baby on the back several times, and she cried a loud, piercing wale. He cut the umbilical cord and tied it off, then a nurse cleaned her off with a damp cloth, wrapped her in a blanket, and handed her to Eva. Eva looked at her squished, tiny red face. Fuzzy white hair covered her body, and on her head were sparse strips of light brown hair. Her eyes were blue, and she had her hands curled into tight fists. She was so small and thin, and Eva was uncertain about her baby's next few hours. She had not originally wanted this child, but at that moment, all the regret and anger washed away, and was replaced by love.

Eva took her thumb and index finger and pried up the baby's little fingers, and she gripped Eva's index finger. She blinked up at Eva and squalled, then started crying, kicking her feet, uncovering her legs in the process.

"She is too small to hold her body heat, so we will put her under a light. But she needs to eat first," the doctor told her.

Eva realized what he was suggesting. "You mean now?"

"Yes. The nurse will help you." The doctor pulled on the umbilical cord gently, removing the amniotic sac from inside Eva, then placed a towel underneath her butt because she was still bleeding. The nurse came to her side, took hold of Eva's gown, and pulled one side down, exposing her left breast. Eva was embarrassed and felt a little violated by what was happening to her. Her body had not felt or seemed like hers since she learned of her pregnancy, and now it felt even less like hers.

"Move the baby to this side," the nurse instructed.

Eva very carefully turned the baby around so its head was facing her left side. The baby screamed so hard that her face turned a purplish red color, and the sound stopped coming from her open mouth. Eva's heartbeat spiked, and she looked at the nurse.

"Why isn't she breathing?"

"She will."

Finally, the baby drew in a breath, and a sound came from her. It was so loud Eva thought she might go deaf. The nurse took the back of the baby's head and held it straight, then moved her head forward, guiding her until her open mouth was over Eva's nipple. Immediately the baby stopped crying and closed her mouth, sucking as she made quiet whimpering sounds.

"Good, she latched," the nurse said. "Babies this young sometimes struggle with the sucking, swallowing, and then breathing motion."

The sensation was odd as Eva watched this tiny person feeding from her. Finally, she looked to Wilhelm. He, too, was watching the baby, amazement on his face. But Eva could also see the delight and utter joy in his expression.

"You can touch her," she told him.

He looked at her and blinked several times as if she had pulled him from a trance. He took ahold of one of her feet that was sticking out from the blanket. They were tiny, red, and pudgy. He rubbed the top with his thumb, and it was larger than her foot.

"What do you think?"

He let out a breathy laugh. "I think she is the most amazing thing I have ever seen." He stared at the baby, who was greedily sucking at Eva's breast. "You were brave and endured it so well."

"I was not brave. I was terrified out of my mind. But you being here gave me courage. I don't know what I would have done if you hadn't gotten my message in time or if they wouldn't let you in."

He caressed her arm and hair in a comforting gesture. "You would have been fine. I only watched. You did all the work. You didn't need me here to do what you did."

"I did. Believe me, I did." She was so tired now she could hardly keep her eyes open.

"Let's turn her to her other side." The nurse took the baby, who was falling asleep, and Eva pulled the other side of her gown down, and then the nurse handed her back. She was awake now and starting to cry, "It's good to change sides. You try getting her to latch on."

Eva put her hand on the back of the baby's head and brought it towards her. The baby moved her head from side to side, rooting, before eventually finding her target and latching on.

"Soon, we will move the two of you into a room," the nurse told her.

"Alright." She looked to Wilhelm. "Would wanting you to stay with me tonight be asking too much?"

"You know it wouldn't."

She smiled at his response and watched as he lovingly observed his daughter. "I want to name her Charlotte," Eva told him. He moved his focus from the baby to Eva and looked at her with intense eyes. "I'm sorry. I should have talked to you about it first."

"No, I like that idea. I just didn't expect you to choose that name."

"Very early on, I felt like it was a girl, and from that moment, I knew her name would be Charlotte." She watched as he fought back against an unwanted emotion. "I wanted to give you that, a piece of her." He leaned over, cupping her chin with his hand. He pressed his lips to hers, planting a soft kiss. The baby started to cry from the disruption, and he moved back. She found Eva's breast again and quieted, falling asleep after she latched on.

The nurse came back to the bedside. "We have to burp her now, then we will move you and her to a room."

Eva looked at the sleeping baby. "How do I do that?"

"Let me show you, then once you see it done, you will know how. I have three children, and the first one is always the most difficult. They are the one you learn from." The nurse took Charlotte from Eva's arms and pressed her to her own chest, Charlotte's head resting against her shoulder. The nurse gently tapped her back, and Charlotte let out several small burps. The nurse then laid her on a table, folded a white cloth into a triangle, and pinned it around Charlotte for a diaper.

The reality of what the nurse just did hit Eva like a sucker punch. They didn't have disposable diapers in the 1940s; they only cloth diapers that would need to be washed with every use. Then her mind went to the thought that Charlotte might die and she wouldn't have to wash diapers, and instantly felt guilty.

Wilhelm kissed her on the temple. "I will be right back." He stood and walked over to the doctor, taking him by the arm and leading him away from the bed.

She watched as they spoke, wondering what they were talking about. She knew it was on purpose that he led the doctor away from her and out of earshot. She looked around the room, then her eyes settled on her still partly spread legs, and for the first time after giving birth, she assessed her body and how every inch of her seemed to hurt. She pulled her hospital gown back up, covering her breast, noticing how sore her nipples felt. The nurse brought Charlotte back to her and placed her in Eva's arms, bundled in a blanket, sleeping, her one hand sticking out as her fingers curled around the edge of the blanket. Eva kissed her tiny hand and forehead, then rubbed her finger over Charlotte's round cheek. Eva leaned in and smelled the top of her head. She was surprised that it smelled good, kind of a pleasant, sweet smell. Eva didn't know how, but she already loved her so much. She couldn't believe she once considered aborting her, something Wilhelm still knew nothing about, and she never planned to tell him.

"She weighs just over two kilograms," the nurse said. "And she is a good length, fifty centimeters."

Eva wasn't sure how big that was. "And that is good?"

"For a baby born early in the third trimester, that is good. She will need to eat around eight to twelve times a day for the first few months, then it will go down to between seven or nine."

Eva looked up at her, shocked. "Eight to twelve times a day?"

"Yes, that's right."

"How will I get anything done?"

The nurse smiled. "You will find a way, but babies are like an appendage, especially at first."

Eva looked back at her baby. Simply her being born turned her world upside down. At least while she was pregnant, she could easily go places and didn't have to soothe a crying baby, feed it, or change its diaper just to repeat it all over again. She also remembered that they didn't have a stroller or much of anything for the baby yet.

The doctor followed Wilhelm back to the bed. He perched on the side and took her hand. "They are going to move you now." The nurse pulled the bloody towel from underneath her, and Wilhelm and a nurse helped her into a wheelchair. They took her to a small room, and in the corner was a baby bed with a light attached to the top. The nurse took Charlotte and placed her in the bed, put another blanket over her, and turned on the light. Eva noticed that there was another bed next to hers and wondered if they had put it in there for Wilhelm.

The nurse looked to Wilhelm. "We are going to take your wife to the bathroom where she can bathe and change into a clean gown."

"Alright."

They left her alone to bathe, and it felt heavenly, being able to clean off the blood and other fluids from the birth and the sweat from the labor. When she was finished, they gave her a pair of underwear with a thick pad, then helped her into a gown. They pushed her back to the room in the wheelchair, and Wilhelm helped her into the bed.

"I need to go home and get a few things. I will also call my mother so she can come. I also need to go back to work for a bit. But I will return as soon as I am finished."

She looked at him with heavy eyes, hardly able to keep them open. They had given her a pain pill before she bathed, and it was now in her system. She took his hand and placed his large palm on her cheek. "I will sleep."

A smile cracked at the corner of his mouth. "Yes, my sweet Eva, you sleep." He pulled his hand away so he could leave, but she caught it. "Lorelei Vogel is in the lobby. She is the one who brought me here when I couldn't get ahold of you. Would you tell her to come back tomorrow, so she can see the baby then? I also would like to thank her for coming to get me and bringing me here."

"I will tell her. And make sure she knows how grateful I am for what she did."

"And would you let Ingrid know? But also tell her not to come until tomorrow. I don't feel like having any visitors today. I don't have the energy for it."

He kissed the top of her head. "No one will bother you. I'll be back in a few hours." He turned out the light and closed the door. The only illumination in the room was from the light over Charlotte's bed. She closed her eyes, and soon, the exhaustion consumed her.

Chapter Twenty

§

April 22nd, 1943

The last three months had passed in a blur. Eva was so consumed with taking care of the baby and learning how to be a mother, along with trying to catch some sleep whenever she could, that she hardly noticed the passing of time. Klaus had made it to Paris that following day and came to see her, as did Ingrid and Lorelei. Eva called Adele and Renée and told them the news when she got home from the hospital. They, of course, were thrilled and enquired when she would bring the baby to La Chapelle. Eva told them she didn't know, but hopefully soon.

The air had warmed, and the trees now had buds on them, so Eva took Charlotte on a walk anytime the weather was nice. Ingrid was at the apartment almost daily, and Eva knew if Wilhelm was home more, it would drive him crazy. He had taken two days off to be home with her and Charlotte, but no more. His job seemed even more demanding as of late, if that was even possible, now that he had been promoted.

Wilhelm's mother had stayed with them for the first two months to help with Charlotte. Eva could tell she was in her element and on cloud nine anytime she was with Charlotte. She held her, rocked her, and would sing to her German lullabies that she used to sing to Wilhelm and his sister when they were babies. Eva didn't mind and enjoyed watching her interaction with Charlotte, but it also made her a little sad because her mom and dad couldn't be there to see their granddaughter. Marie had returned to Berlin but was planning another trip to Paris soon. Eva knew it would be hard to keep her away.

She pushed the baby stroller along the brick platform of the train station, watching the people emerge from the cars, searching for Klaus. He had to return to his work and the hospital in Berlin a few days after he came to Paris but finally got some time off to visit her again.

He stepped off the train wearing his field gray uniform. His shiny bald head was not covered with a cap, and his round glasses were pushed up high on his nose as usual. He carried his small leather bag in his right hand and searched the platform. Eva waved to him, and he spotted her over the crowd of people, an advantage he had by being tall.

He smiled at Eva and made his way along the platform. When he reached her, he leaned in and gave her a side hug, then looked into the stroller at the sleeping baby. "How is she?"

"She is doing great, better than me, I think. She is the only one who really gets any sleep." She laughed at the thought of her suffering at the hands of her baby.

"It should get better soon. I would say babies usually start sleeping longer at around this age."

"Hopefully. Charlotte is happy when she is awake but is a terrible sleeper. Although she doesn't have her days and nights mixed up, so that is a blessing."

"Oh, but she is so worth it."

Eva focused on his face, the gentle smile he had as he looked at Charlotte, and she realized the significance her baby had in other people's lives besides just hers. To Klaus, she was the closest thing to a grandchild he would ever have. To Marie, she was her only grandchild and possibly would remain that way, but it was still something Marie never really believed would happen. To Ingrid, it helped her cope with the loss of her own baby. Renée and Lorelei, who had lost all their children, took comfort in welcoming a new life into theirs. As for Wilhelm, Charlotte had the biggest impact on him. She was something he never knew he wanted. All the pain and hurt from his past, his hatred for his father's people, and the bitterness he harbored seemed less important now. He wasn't home often, but he made up for it when he was, to her and to Charlotte. He just enjoyed simply being with them. Eva taught him how to change a diaper, but he had done only one. That was the one thing with Charlotte he didn't enjoy. But he was more than happy to hold her, carry her, and push the stroller, but he particularly liked reading to her. She would look up at him with big eyes like she understood every word he said. Eva made it a point to only speak to Charlotte in English because Wilhelm, Marie, Ingrid, and Klaus only talked to her in German, and she was constantly surrounded by French. She was Charlotte's only source to English right now.

"Does she bother her father when she cries at night?"

"He has never said anything about it and has never been to work late because of it. But then he wouldn't. It's not like him to."

"I suppose it's not."

Eva and Klaus left the train station and walked the streets of Paris, finally stopping at a park. They found a bench to sit on, and Eva parked the stroller beside it, then turned to Klaus and crossed her legs.

"How are things in Berlin?"

"Worse. The bombing continues, and the war in the east is not going well." He looked out over the grass with a look of contemplation. "I don't think Germany is going to win this war."

She had never heard him say anything his country would view as defeatist talk. In their eyes, it was criminal to speak or think that way. "No, I don't think they will," she agreed.

He looked at her. "Does that worry you or make you happy?"

She considered this. "Both. I feel sorry for what will happen to the German people and what that means for Wilhelm. But this war is awful and needs to end. I guess it's like an infected leg that you know needs to be cut off, but you simply can't imagine parting with it."

He eyed her, understanding on his face. "I know the conflict you are struggling with. Germany is my country, and it saddens me to see what is happening to it, but this can't go on. Germany has to lose."

"Will you stay if they lose the war?"

"Yes. Someone has to remain behind to pick up the pieces. We will have to try and rebuild what was lost to us and pray it is enough."

She looked at Charlotte, sleeping in her stroller. To Eva, she looked more and more like Wilhelm every day. "I can't lose him, Klaus. I don't think I could survive that. I didn't think I would love him, but I do. I grew to care for him in a short amount of time, and that eventually turned to love. I already lost someone once. I can't do it again." It was still strange admitting the momentous shift that had happened in her relationship with Wilhelm.

He lowered his voice. "I heard about what happened to Gerhardt von Schulz, and I know what he must have meant to you. I'm sorry for your loss," he said, compassion in his tone.

"Thank you." Tears pulled in her eyes at the thought of him. The full force of the grief she had been suppressing unwillingly came to the surface. She choked on her tears as she stared at the distant trees. She couldn't speak and hated that she was crying in front of Klaus, but better him than Wilhelm. "I loved him," she forced out finally. "I loved him with everything I had. I think he will always be my one real love." The tears ran onto her lips, the salty taste of them on her tongue. She felt like what she told Klaus could only partly convey what she felt in her heart. "I lost something important to me, and this war is threatening to now take something else that is important to me." Her words trailed off as her voice choked with more tears.

He gently took her hand in his. "Eva," he said, his voice serious but also kind. "Look at me." She lifted her head and met his gaze, no longer trying to hide her agony. "We will all lose something by the end of this war. People that we love, and things that are important to us." His words were emphatic but hard, stripping Eva's emotions raw because they were terrible in their finality. He let go of Eva's hand and gripped her chin, forcing her to not look away. "Eva, I want you to really listen to what I'm telling you. You will lose, again and again, one precious thing to you after another. Do you understand what I'm saying? That is what this war does, what it means to be in Germany and love a German." Eva nodded, the tears continuing to flow as he held tight to her face. "There is the real possibility that you will lose every last thing that you hold dear, and so will I, and so will Wilhelm, and so will Ingrid, and so will everyone else in Germany, and this country, and England, and even yours. But it has to be done so our children won't lose those things." Her face was rigid, and the misery of the awful truth of his words sank in. "Make sure that you don't forget this."

She nodded. "I won't."

"You need to let go of everything that is precious to you except for her." He pointed to Charlotte. "Do you understand what I'm telling you to do?"

Eva held his gaze, his fierce blue eyes boring into her. The fear of reality was trying to claw to the surface. "What you are asking me to do is hard. It is so hard. I don't know that I can."

"Then you have to learn how to. The two things that should matter to you most are your life and hers." He let go of her chin and moved away a fraction.

She wiped the tears from her face. She knew there was no way she could do what he said. "It's funny because I almost had her aborted. I even went to the person who did it, stripped off my clothes, and laid on the table, ready to be rid of it. But when I saw the thing they were going to put inside me to take her out, I couldn't do it. I could not bring myself to make her suffer and pay the ultimate price for my mistake. She was innocent, the only innocent in that situation. Wilhelm and I, we were the guilty ones."

"Correct. Just don't bring another innocent into the world who will suffer at the hands of others' bad choices." He stood. "Let's walk to the apartment. It looks like it might rain soon. She peered to the dark clouds that hung low in the east, then stood and followed him as he took hold of the stroller.

She kept the conversations lighter on the walk to the apartment. Her chest felt tight, and her stomach was uneasy from the severity of their last conversation. "You should stay with us. There is no need to spend money on a hotel."

"Thank you for the invite. I would take you up on it, but I don't want to upset your husband. I'm sure he would rather me not."

Eva loved how astute he was. "You are probably right. Wilhelm prefers the company of only certain people. But please, come for dinner."

"Now that I won't say no to. Will your husband be home for dinner?"

"I believe so. Wilhelm called me earlier today to tell me he wouldn't stay late today. I think it's because he knows you are here and doesn't want to be rude."

Klaus let out a laugh that rumbled deep in his chest. "I don't think he cares about being rude. I think he cares that I am here."

Eva wrinkled her face. "That is not why."

"I am pretty sure that he hates it when I visit you. I do not like him and have never tried to hide that fact. He probably thinks I'm trying to turn you against him or take you away, which isn't too far from the truth. But the feelings are mutual. He also dislikes me. He only tolerates me because of you, which I guess says something about his character."

"Klaus, you know that he does love me?"

"I believe he does love you, but there is something in him, a core that no one and nothing touches."

She wanted to disagree with him, but she couldn't. There was always a place deep inside Wilhelm that seemed forever out of reach.

Once at the apartment, Klaus carried his bag and the stroller up the steps, and Eva held Charlotte. To her surprise, the door was unlocked, meaning Wilhelm was already home. He had obviously left work early, which was highly unusual. Klaus placed the stroller and his bag in the hall and followed Eva into the living room. Wilhelm was sitting on the couch, his legs crossed, still wearing his shiny boots and uniform. He was flipping through one of the English books he gave Eva for her birthday. When he saw them enter, he laid it on the coffee table and lifted his head to them.

"How was the train ride, Hauptmann Möller?"

"It was well. Thank you."

Eva thought she could hear the irritation in Wilhelm's voice. She went to the couch and sat beside him. "Would you take her, and I will go start dinner?"

His whole demeanor changed when he looked at her. "Come here, my Bärchen," he said as she leaned in and placed Charlotte in his arms. He always called her Little Bear because whenever she was hungry, she would make grunts that sounded more like growls, which would turn into a cry if she wasn't fed soon. He moved her fisted hand up and down, and she grasped onto his finger, holding on tight.

Eva went to the kitchen, but before she started dinner, she stood in the entryway and listened, making sure they were getting along. They talked a bit about Paris, the bombings in Berlin, and then Charlotte. When she was satisfied that they would play nice, she began preparing the food. She made a traditional German meal with meat and potatoes covered with a creamy sauce and apple turnovers for dessert. She could hear Charlotte fussing from the other room and hoped she would go back to sleep, but it had been a while since she fed her. She left the kitchen and peeked in the living room. Wilhelm was standing now, rocking, trying to quiet her. Eva went back to the kitchen and put the apple turnovers in the oven, then stirred the food in the pan. Charlotte was crying now, and after a few minutes, the sound grew louder.

Wilhelm appeared in the kitchen doorway, holding a red-faced screaming Charlotte, her lip quivering with each cry. "I can't get her to stop. I think this little girl needs a nip."

Eva smiled at his choice of words. "She probably does. I haven't fed her for a few hours because she had been sleeping."

She laid the wooden spoon on the stove and came to him. He leaned in, sliding his arm around her and pulling her into an impassioned kiss, sending a hard rush through her. He then gave her a softer kiss before handing her Charlotte.

"Watch the food, and I'll go feed her." She could feel the flush hot on her cheeks. His nature was all-encompassing, and it never failed to make her gasp and her body come alive when it was against him.

"Sure," he said, monotone.

Even though she understood the word, his answer seemed cryptic to her. His voice, the look on his face, and his body language told her he wanted to say more but didn't. She took Charlotte to the nursery so she could feed her in the rocking chair. She fed Charlotte in the living room a lot of the time because it was just her and Wilhelm, but now that Klaus was here, she figured it was better to do it in a more private place. She didn't know if it would be strange for Klaus, and she didn't want to make him uncomfortable. He was a doctor, not a father.

She unbuttoned her dress and pulled the pieces of material out of her bra that she kept there for leaks. She slipped the strap over her arm as Charlotte rooted her head, crying. "Come on, it's right here." Charlotte latched on, then Eva leaned back in the chair and rocked it with one foot. Charlotte curled her fingers around a piece of Eva's hair and pulled. Eva smiled down at her. "Why do you always do that when you eat?" She pulled her hair out of Charlotte's fist and brushed it over her shoulder so she couldn't get ahold of it again. She hummed the Wizard of Oz tune, then started to sing it to her.

There was a knock on the partially closed door. "Eva, is there anything I can do?"

"I think Wilhelm has it under control in the kitchen." She pulled the baby blanket from the back of the rocking chair and draped it over her and Charlotte. She thought she would try inviting him in. She felt a little bad that he was sitting alone when he was their guest. "Do you want to come in?"

"Won't that be strange?"

"No, I'm covered up with a blanket."

He pushed the door open and stepped into the room. He looked around at all the things they had in there. The crib, baby books, toys, and all the stuff that made it a little girl's room. "I heard you singing to her; it was beautiful. What was it?"

"It's a song from an American movie called The Wizard of Oz. I have the book too."

"You must really like it."

She smiled to herself. "I do."

"What's it about?"

"It's about a little girl named Dorothy who lives in the state of Kansas, and one day, a tornado comes through her farm and carries her house away with her and her dog Toto in it. It drops them and the farmhouse into Munchkin County in the magical land of Oz. When the house falls, it kills the Wicked Witch of the East, the evil ruler of the Munchkins. The Good Witch from the North arrives and gives her a magical pair of shoes that belonged to the dead witch. The Good Witch tells Dorothy that the only way she can return home to Kansas is to follow the yellow brick road to the Emerald City and ask the Wizard of Oz to help her, who is great and powerful. Dorothy then embarks on her journey. On her way down the yellow brick road, Dorothy frees a Scarecrow from a pole, puts oil on the joints of a rusted Tin Man, and meets a Cowardly Lion. The Scarecrow wants a brain, the Tin Man wants a heart, and the Lion wants to be brave, so Dorothy convinces them to go with her to the Emerald City so they can ask the Wizard for these things. They have many adventures on their way to the Emerald City. Once there, they all meet the Wizard, and he agrees to help them if they kill the Wicked Witch of the West. They are told that no one has ever defeated her. The witch sees them coming and sends many different kinds of creatures to stop them, but the Tin Man, the Scarecrow, and the Lion fend them off. Finally, she sends her Winged Monkeys to capture them. She takes them and makes Dorothy her slave while she tries to figure out how to steal her magical shoes. She finally tricks Dorothy into giving her one of her shoes, which makes Dorothy mad, so she dumps a bucket of water on the witch, and she melts. When Dorothy and her friends meet the Wizard again, they discover he is just an ordinary old man who came to the land of Oz a long time ago from Omaha, Nebraska. Another state in America. But he keeps his word. He gives the Scarecrow a brain, the Tin Man a heart made of silk, and the Lion a potion for courage. He agrees to take Dorothy and Toto home in his hot air balloon and then return to Omaha. Toto chases a cat, and Dorothy goes after him, but the rope to the balloons breaks, then it floats away, and she never gets on it. Dorothy summons the Winged Monkeys and asks them to take her home, but they explain they can't cross the desert surrounding Oz. They tell her about the Good Witch of the South named Glinda, who might be able to help her. The monkeys fly her there, and Glinda tells Dorothy that her magical shoes can take her home. Dorothy says bye to her friends, all of whom will return to their new kingdoms. The Scarecrow to the Emerald City, the Tin Man to Winnie County, and the Lion to the Forest. Dorothy takes Toto in her arms and taps her heels together three times, repeating the words, 'There is no place like home.' Instantly, she begins whirling through the air and rolling on the grass of the Kansas prairie, up to the farmhouse, though the magical shoes fall off her feet enroute and are lost in the Deadly Desert. The book and movie differ a little from each other. In the movie, in the end, she wakes up in her bed with a cloth on her injured head and is being attended by her aunt, uncle, and farm hands. There is also a professor there, and they all look like the people from her dream, so she thinks that they are. They don't believe Dorothy, but she doesn't care and gratefully exclaims, 'There is no place like home.' There is obviously more to the story, but you get the gist."

"It seems she really wanted to go home. I see why you like the story."

"I like it for many reasons. Dorothy is bored in the beginning, but after her adventures, she realizes how much she loves her home, even if it is the prairies of Kansas."

"Will you read it to her?"

"Someday." She moved Charlotte to the other breast. "When will you return to Berlin?"

"In a few days."

"Wilhelm opened the door and walked in. "The food is done." He looked to Klaus, not attempting to hide the disapproval on his face.

"I will wait in the dining room." Klaus disappeared through the doorway and closed it behind him.

Wilhelm crossed his arms and leaned against the wall. "So that is what the story is about? A girl who learns that there is no place like her home."

"I don't share her opinion. It's just a story."

"An American story about a girl who is in a strange land and wants to go home that was given to you by Gerhardt von Schulz."

He didn't need to tell her that he was upset. "I like the story, and I am not trying to relate to the character. I know you would prefer if I got rid of the book, but it is the only thing I have from

Gerhardt. He is dead, and I would like to keep it. It's not there as a reminder that he is competition because he isn't, and it's not. He wouldn't be even if he were alive. It's all I have of him, but you gave me her." She looked at Charlotte, who was asleep now, occasionally still suckling. "And you have me, something he never will."

Wilhelm's face was set in a rigid scowl. "That's only because he is dead."

"That's not fair. I was with you before he died."

"Because he didn't want you," he spat, venom in every word. "But if he were alive and greeted you with open arms, you would run into them without hesitation."

She wasn't going to have this discussion. She was furious with him now. "Get out, Wilhelm, get the hell out." Her words were low but full of fury. What he said hurt her for so many different reasons.

He pulled the door open and walked out of the room, then she heard the front door slam. She fixed her dress and then laid Charlotte in her crib. She went to the dining room and looked at Klaus.

"I take it you heard?"

"Some of it. I heard him talking about Gerhardt von Schulz, and I heard you tell him to get out, but that was really it. Did you intend for him to leave the apartment when you told him to get out?"

"No, only for him to leave Charlotte's room." She looked to the door. "Where do you think he went?"

"Somewhere to cool off. Don't worry, Eva, he will be back. He is upset with you, but I think he only left because I am here."

"I'm not worried about that. I'm worried about what he will be like when he returns. He has never hit me, and he wouldn't. He rarely yells at me. What he does is shut me out, and I think that is almost worse."

"He is a complicated man, but his reasons are simple. He doesn't think you love him."

She turned towards him. "But I do. I love him so much it hurts."

"But in his mind, he will always be second to Gerhardt."

"Do you think it's possible to be in love with two people?" She had asked Ingrid that same question, but she wanted to get his opinion.

"It's hard to say because I've never been in love with one person, but I suppose it's possible. The question you need to ask yourself is who do you love more."

She put her hands on the back of the wooden dining room chair and leaned over. "I don't know. But Gerhardt is dead, and I am with Wilhelm now. I've had his child, so I guess it doesn't really matter."

"It does to him."

"I don't know who I love more, but I do love him. And I don't know how to make him see that. I have given him everything I have. My love, my body, my freedom. I have taken his home as my own. What more does he want?"

"He will never be happy with the way things are. He wants all of your heart, and you cannot give him that. I don't like him, but I do understand. I wouldn't want to always feel like I was second fiddle to someone else."

"But he isn't. I chose to be with him when Gerhardt was alive. And it's not because he picked someone else. I mean, it is and isn't. If Gerhardt hadn't left my life, I would never have seen Wilhelm as anything other than a monster. But Gerhardt leaving made me really see Wilhelm and forced me to change my mind about him. That led me down this path of love I have for him now. And now I know that I don't love Gerhardt more. But no matter how hard I try, I can't convince Wilhelm of this."

"And you probably never will. Maybe it's for the best. If he thinks you don't love him, he won't be as hurt if you go home."

"But I'm not going home."

Klaus looked to the kitchen. "The food is growing cold. Let's eat. I'm hungry."

He used the food as a diversion, and she knew it, but she was also hungry and decided to let it slide. They ate dinner in silence, and then Klaus left for his hotel and told her he would be back in the morning. She was planning on taking Charlotte to the park with him and Ingrid.

She cleaned up after dinner, showered, read some of her book, fed Charlotte again, then went to bed. Wilhelm still wasn't home, and the rain had finally reached Paris. The curtains were open, and she lay facing the window, looking at the darkened sky, studying it. The rain beat against the window and roof, and in the distance was the muted roll of thunder from the storm that had been gathering since that morning. When she saw the dark clouds in the distance at the park with Klaus, she suspected it would be quite violent when it came. The wind whipped the rain around as the storm intensified. She rolled over, staring at the empty side of the bed, then turned back to the window, giving it an uneasy look as the worry tightened in her chest. She jumped, startled when thunder cracked nearby and lightning scattered across the sky.

As the night went on, the storm continued to build like an angry beast. She didn't know where Wilhelm was, and her worry for him made her anxious. Now that her anger towards him had subsided, her consciousness was heavy with guilt about telling him to leave. She had no idea he would leave the apartment. If it wasn't for Charlotte, she would brave the storm and look for him. How different the evening had ended compared to how it began. Wilhelm had been warm and affectionate when they were in the kitchen. Pulling her to him and kissing her the way he did. If she was being honest with herself, she hungered for the next time Wilhelm would pull her into his fiery kiss as the terrible world around them momentarily blurred away. But she didn't know if he would ever again.

Eva was having difficulty shaking the chill that seeped into her no matter how tightly she pulled the blanket around her. She continued to watch as the winds rose to a howling sound and the rain hit the window with a punishing force. She was sure she wasn't going to get any sleep this night. She went in and out of light sleep throughout the night, but nothing restful. Several times, she had to get up, feed Charlotte and change her diaper.

The storm had calmed, but it was still a hazy gray outside as dawn broke. Rain dripped from the roof of the building, hitting the sidewalk below. Wilhelm never came home, and she was now sick with worry. She threw the blankets off and went to the phone by the bed, dialing his office. His adjutant answered, and she wasn't surprised.

"Hi, I was wondering if you knew what time my husband would be at work this morning?"

There was a pause before he answered. "He is already here, Frau Bauer. Did you need to speak with him?"

She sighed with relief that he was alright and she knew where he was. "Yes, please."

"I will tell him."

After waiting for over ten minutes, he finally picked up the phone. "What, Eva?"

Her first instinct was to be angry with him at his curtness, but that would not help her accomplish what she was trying to do, which was mend things. "You didn't come home last night. You had me so worried." She couldn't keep her voice from shaking. "You could have at least told me you were going to sleep somewhere else."

"You were well tended by Hauptmann Möller."

"Where did you go, Wilhelm?"

"The office."

"You slept at your office?"

"Yes. I came in and did some work, then slept on the leather couch. It made it easier for me this morning, anyway. I was already here to start the day early."

"You didn't have to do that. I intention wasn't for you to leave the apartment, just Charlotte's room. I wanted you home last night, with me, sleeping in our bed. And you didn't eat dinner, and what will you do for breakfast?"

"I will eat at a café."

"And what about tonight?" She could hear him breathing on the other end.

"If that is what you want, then I will come home."

She closed her eyes. "Oh, my love," she said aloud on the phone. "There is no longer anyone but you. It is you that I want. I crave your love and your touch, not anyone else's. I am yours, but I question if you are really mine."

"I have never been anyone else's."

She smiled. "I will be here when you get home. I will wait all night again if I have to."

"I won't make you wait."

"I will hold you to that."

"I have to get back to work now. Give Charlotte a kiss for me."

"I will."

She hung up the phone and chewed on the inside of her cheek. She went to the bedroom and pulled a box from her wardrobe closet that had been hidden discretely under some clothes. She set it on the bed and pulled off the lid. She lifted Sabina's bear and laid it beside the box, then the dried flowers, and finally The Wizard of Oz book. She rubbed her hand over the worn cover, then placed her lips to it, gently planting a kiss. She put the other things back in the box and returned it to her closet. She got ready for the day, fed and changed Charlotte, then left the apartment and headed to the park.

The air smelled fresh from the rain as she took in deep breaths. She always loved being outside after a rainstorm. She walked along the Alexandre III bridge, taking in the landmarks along the Seine River. It was like an open-air museum with all its history, and to her, it was also the prettiest bridge in Paris.

She had brought some blankets and food so they could eat at the park. She found a dryer spot under a tree, laid out the blankets, and then set the basket on it. Charlotte was asleep, so she left her in the stroller. She sat on the blanket, bending her knees, and waited for Ingrid and Klaus. She was nervous about seeing Wilhelm again tonight. She was going to do her best to make the bond between them stronger. This distance that was growing between them was killing her. She loved Wilhelm, and he was the man she chose, so she had to put him above everyone else, including Gerhardt. She didn't want Wilhelm to feel like he was competing with his memory. There was nothing she wouldn't do to show him that she loved him.

Ingrid and Klaus stopped beside the blanket. "We waved at you, but you didn't even notice," Ingrid said.

"I'm sorry. That storm kept me up last night, and I didn't get much sleep. And then Charlotte woke up several times wanting to eat."

Klaus sat across her, and Ingrid sat on the blanket beside her. "I know, it was crazy."

Klaus gave her a knowing look. "Did he ever come back?"

She shook her head. "No."

Ingrid looked between the two of them. "Who are you guys talking about?"

"Wilhelm. He had a lot of work to do, so he stayed at the office all night." She looked at Klaus, asking him with her eyes to not say what really happened.

"I can imagine he stays very busy with his job."

"He does, but he told me that he will be home tonight." She watched Klaus, waiting for understanding to register on his face.

He lifted a brow. "That is good."

Eva stood and reached into the stroller, taking from it The Wizard of Oz book. "Ingrid, would you keep this for me?"

She looked at the book in Ingrid's hand. "Um, sure," she said, her confusion evident.

"It reminds me of Gerhardt, and it is too painful. I don't want to have it near me right now." She would tell Wilhelm that she got rid of it, which was partly true. She couldn't bring herself to fully part with it, so this would have to be enough.

"Also, don't tell Wilhelm that you have it. He knows it came from Gerhardt and thinks I'm getting rid of it."

"Oh. I promise I won't say a thing." She took it from Eva's hand and laid it on the blanket beside her.

Eva passed out the sandwiches she made and poured them each a glass of water. The sun was finally peeking through the clouds, and she loved how it warmed her skin. Charlotte moved in the stroller, making little grunting sounds as she kicked off the blanket and swung her arms.

"She is hungry." Eva stood to get her, and Ingrid got to her feet.

She went to the stroller with Eva and looked in. "Oh, she is so pretty. I can't believe you get to look at her every day and hold her."

"You can hold her after she is fed."

"Oh, that would be lovely."

Eva covered her and Charlotte with the blanket and undid her dress. As Charlotte ate, her legs and feet stuck out of the blanket, and Ingrid leaned over, touching her them.

"I want a baby so bad."

Eva chuckled. "You need a man first."

"I have one. He just isn't in the position to give me one."

Eva's brows pulled together. "Who?"

"That British pilot. We write to each other almost every day."

"I knew he asked you to write him and if I would transcribe them for you, but you never told me you wrote him even one letter. Why didn't you say something?"

"Because you were far too busy to worry about that. Wilhelm got hurt, and then you had Charlotte. It seemed selfish to ask that of you."

"Ingrid, I wouldn't have minded."

She shrugged. "I know."

Eva turned Charlotte to the other breast and watched Ingrid flip through The Wizard of Oz.

"Would you teach me English?"

Eva smiled. "I would love to."

"I want to write him a letter in English, and maybe someday I can teach him German."

"I think he would be willing to learn, and I will help you write the letter."

Ingrid put her hand on Eva's arm. "Isn't that the woman who was at your wedding? The one who came to see you while you were getting ready?"

She looked up to see who Ingrid was talking about. Eva didn't think it was her because she couldn't imagine Klara would show her face around her. But it was Klara, making her way across the grass towards them, her blond hair reflecting in the sun.

"Oh my God, it is her."

Klaus turned around and looked behind him. "Who are you talking about?"

"That woman coming towards us. It's a long story that I will tell you some other time."

Klara stopped just a few feet from the blanket. "Hello, Eva?" She looked at Charlotte under the blanket in Eva's arms as she fed. "And this is your daughter, Charlotte."

Eva drew in a long breath through her nose. "How do you know her name?"

Klara's lips lifted into a leer. "I know a lot of things." She looked to Ingrid and Klaus. "Can we take a walk?"

She normally would tell Klara no but was curious about why she was there. "Alright." She gently pulled her breast out of Charlotte's mouth, and she started fussing. She handed her to Ingrid. "Will you burp her?"

"Of course."

Eva buttoned her dress under the blanket and then handed it to Ingrid. "I won't be gone long." Klaus gave her a questioning look as she stood. She gave him a little nod, letting him know everything was alright. She came to stand beside Klara, who was now watching Charlotte. She looked mesmerized at the infant, and Eva thought she could see affection, envy, jealousy, and a certain level of pain in her eyes. "You wanted to talk, so let's talk."

She lifted her eyes from Charlotte to Eva. "She looks so like him."

Eva looked at Charlotte. Her newborn blue eyes had changed over time to a greenish hazel like Wilhelm's, not brownish hazel like her own. "Yes, she does." She turned and started walking, and Klara followed.

"I always knew he would make beautiful children."

Eva's lips drew up into an appreciative smile at what Wilhelm had given her. Eva didn't think she could be more perfect. "Yes, he does."

"But I was always under the impression that he didn't want children."

"He didn't, at first, but when he found out I was pregnant, he had a change of heart. He thinks the world of her."

"He is different. I can see it. More gentle somehow and peaceful. When we spent time together, he was wild and passionate, a storm of uncontrolled fury. He is strong and smart, but he used to have no direction. There was his duty and loyalty to Germany. He had always been single-minded and driven when it came to his country, but that isn't what I'm talking about. In every other aspect of his life, he was adrift but craved the more refined tiers of human needs, like love, belonging, and mutual respect. It is hard for me to say this, but I can see that you make him happy in a way I never did."

Eva was floored that she would admit this, but Klara had her worried. How did she know that she made Wilhelm happy unless she had been in contact with him? And what did she mean when she said he was passionate?

"I do make him happy, but I think it is also hard for him to love me sometimes. You are right about what you told me in Berlin. You are better suited for him. Your personality matches his better than mine ever could."

Klara stopped walking, her eyes meeting Eva's. "I'm glad we can admit these difficult truths to each other. But one thing you should know about Wilhelm. No matter who he loves or how much he loves them, with all he's seen and been through, he can only be his own man. No one will ever tell him how to live his life because they will die trying."

Eva understood her meaning. "You said he was passionate. What did you mean by that?"

Klara smirked. "I'm sure you don't need me to explain that to you."

Wilhelm told her he had never slept with a German woman before, but maybe he wasn't being honest. "So you and he...?"

"No."

Eva was still as she looked at Klara. "No?"

"I wanted to, but he never would. He only slept with women who wouldn't expect more from him, like a commitment. Lots of women vied for his attention and affection, but you are the only one who succeeded."

Eva remembered him telling her something about that. "I didn't vie for his attention. It just happened over time. Were the women who wanted him to notice them the girls in Poland?"

Her lip curled up. "You are well informed. Yes, and girls in Germany too."

"He told me about the girls in Poland when we were in Dieppe."

"I met Wilhelm when he was attending the university, studying to be a lawyer. That is also where he met Jurgen Pflüger."

Eva's face hardened at the mention of the man who tried to rape her. "Wilhelm told me."

"Jurgen was outmatched when he went up against Wilhelm, but why do you think that is?"

Eva shrugged. "He is a better fighter?"

"Not just that, but to do what he did to Jurgen, even if it was to stop him from doing something bad, Wilhelm had to be okay with the violence, and not everyone could do that. And what made Jurgen outmatched was that Wilhelm was willing to be violent on another level, one that was worse than even Jurgen's, because you can't defeat the bad guy unless you are worse than the bad guy, even if just for a time. You have to be willing to do a truly awful thing in order to stop the bad thing from continuing."

Eva thought about the bombs America would soon drop on Japan and how that was the only way to get them to end the war. She understood what Klara meant. "I am aware of that. And if you are hoping I will think less of Wilhelm because of it, I don't. I was there and saw the whole thing, remember? And I married him even after that and had his child. So if you hope that you are going to have the last laugh because you got the best of me by trying to make me believe there is no good left in him, you couldn't be more wrong."

"I am not trying to do that. I was just seeing if you truly understood, and I think you do. It's hard not to get swept up in Wilhelm's energy. Trust me, I know."

"Yes, I do know."

Klara peered over the grass at some children playing a few yards away. "Did you know that Jurgen is out of the hospital now?"

Eva's heart spiked, but she remained calm on the surface. "No, I hadn't heard."

"Yes, he has been out a few weeks now. They have him working at a desk job in Berlin."

"I hope what happened in the garden is a lesson he won't forget."

"Oh, he will never forget what Wilhelm did to him." The nuance in her voice left Eva wondering what she really meant. "Can I hold Charlotte?" Klara asked, changing the direction of the conversation.

Eva's jaw tensed. Did she want this woman, who she knew was in love with Wilhelm and who had tried to break them apart to hold their baby? But what harm would it do? What was she going to do, try to run away with Charlotte?

"For a minute." Klara gave a brief nod and followed Eva back to the blanket. "Klara is going to hold Charlotte while we pick up." She looked at Ingrid, who was still holding Charlotte. Ingrid frowned, uncertainty in her eyes. "It's alright, Ingrid. Give Charlotte to her."

Ingrid stood and placed Charlotte in Klara's arms. Charlotte made a cooing sound and swung her little hands that were balled into fists. Eva watched Klara, how her face lit at the sight of Charlotte. But envy was also written on it, the longing for what she didn't have. Eva knew what she felt like because Gerhardt's fiancée had what she once wanted and still did to a point.

Eva helped pick up the blankets and food, all the while keeping her eye on Klara, making sure she stayed close. Klara rocked Charlotte back and forth, moving from one foot to the other, smiling and talking to her. Eva thought that if Klara had the chance to take Charlotte, she would.

Once everything was packed and put away, Eva went to Klara. "It's time for me to leave now."

Klara looked at her, eyes glistening as her face fell. "She is precious, such a dear child."

Eva smiled. "She is." Eva reached for Charlotte, but Klara shrank back, and Eva's panic rose. "Let me have her now, Klara."

Klara looked at Charlotte, then back to Eva. "I would have given him beautiful children too."

"I'm sure you would have." Eva didn't want to say anything that might upset her. In Eva's peripheral vision, she saw that Klaus had come to stand beside her, and it made her feel more comfortable. Klara looked between the two of them, and then, after a few seconds, she kissed Charlotte on the forehead before holding her out to Eva. She took her from Klara, relief swelling in her now that Charlotte was safely in her arms.

Something waged in Klara as she took a few steps back, then finally turned and walked away. "She looked like she was going to do something foolish," Klaus said, still standing beside Eva.

"I suspected that too. She is hurting because she loves him."

"I understand, but she can't make him love her, and she has to see that."

Eva placed Charlotte in the stroller, and they made their way to the street. She turned and looked behind her across the park, but Klara was no longer there. Strangely, she found herself feeling guilty that she had everything Klara wanted and that maybe she was less deserving of it.

Chapter Twenty-One

ॐ

January 11th, 1944

Eva rolled the ball across the room, and Charlotte crawled after it. It hit Renée's foot and stopped, and Charlotte sat down and picked it up, turning it over in her hand before trying to put it in her mouth. At a year old, she was a handful. Charlotte had been crawling for some time and could pull herself up with the help of furniture, and she was already trying to walk along the couch. Her first word was in English, but her favorite word was mama in German, like mommy in English, but sometimes she would pronounce it more like it was in French. She could also say papa and a few other words that Eva couldn't quite understand.

"Such a little cutie," Renée mused, looking down at her on the floor just at her feet. "She looks so much like you."

"Really?" Eva concentrated on Charlotte's face. "Everyone always tells me that she looks just like Wilhelm." Eva suspected Renée could see that too but didn't want to say it.

"Well, maybe she is a good mix. Shall we go on that walk?"

"Yes, let's go." Eva, Renée, and Adele were planning to walk
into town with Charlotte if Renée could make it that far. Eva and
Charlotte had been in La Chapelle for a couple of days. Wilhelm
had been working long hours every day, coming home sometimes
at dawn just to get up a few hours later to return. She wondered if
all the extra work he was doing had something to do with the
Allies' invasion on June 6th, also known as D-Day. It was only
five months away, but Eva kept that knowledge pushed far in the
back of her mind. Things were going good with Wilhelm, well,
better than they had been, and she wasn't ready to return to reality.
She had thought about her life and situation over the last twelve
months since Charlotte was born, and she knew what she wanted
and what she would do. She was going to stay in this time with
Wilhelm. It was where she belonged now. She needed to ask
herself the hard questions looming that she had dismissed for so
long. Did she really want to be with Wilhelm? Could she accept
who he was and what he had done? And could she really live in
this time? Those were hard questions she needed to ask and even
harder to answer, but she couldn't put them off forever. As
difficult as it was, she finally forced herself to think about them
and now knew the answer to each one. She wanted to be with
Wilhelm and Charlotte as a family, so the other question was easy
for her to answer, which was yes, she could and would be alright
staying in this time. As to the second question, she understood that
she had to be OK with what Wilhelm had done, which meant all
of it. Was she being naive and selfish to forgive and forget all of
his indiscretions? Yes, she was, but that was the only way she

could be with him, and she wanted to be with him more than anything.

"Adele," Renée called from the sitting room. "We are ready to go. Would you bring the stroller to the foyer?"

"Of course. Are you sure you are—"

"Yes, yes, Adele. I may be old, but I can still go for walks."

"We'll go slow," Eva said for Adele's benefit. She picked up Charlotte, carried her to the front door, and put her in the stroller that Adele had retrieved. With the help of Adele, they rolled it down the stairs. Eva pushed the stroller on the dirt road, kicking up dust from the dry soil. They hadn't had precipitation in La Chapelle for weeks, and it showed. Even though it was cold, the sky was blue, and the sun illuminated the landscape in its lazy winter haze. Eva was bundled in her thickest coat, had her hat, scarf, and gloves on, and doubled Charlotte's blankets.

"We are going to pick up a few things while you are at the cemetery."

Eva met Adele's guarded eyes. "Why don't you wait, and I'll go with you?" Eva found it odd that they were going to go shopping without her.

"I don't want to keep Madame Blanc out in the cold for too long."

Eva turned to look at Renée, who was lagging a few feet behind. "I guess you're right. I'm surprised she wanted to come on a walk into town with us."

"She is afraid of growing older. She watched how her mother's health declined rapidly in her last few years, and she worries it will happen to her."

"I can understand that fear. I am still young now, but I won't always be. These last few years have given me a new appreciation for time."

Adele looked at Charlotte, asleep in her stroller. Her cheeks and the tip of her nose were pink from the cold midday air. "I'm sure it has. You know, this baby has put new life into Madame Blanc."

"How do you mean?"

"She thinks the world of you and has always wanted grandchildren, but that never happened for her. She struggled to get pregnant with her son, and after, she never could conceive again. He was very young when he died and left Madame Blanch with no grandchildren and no heirs."

"What will she do with the château when she's gone?"

"I'm not sure. I'm trying to get her to write a will, but she keeps making excuses."

"Maybe I can talk to her about it when we get back."

"I would be grateful to you."

Eva left Adele and Renée at the only general store in town and made her way down Main Street towards the cemetery. She pushed the stroller through the wrought-iron gate in the stone wall surrounding the little cemetery. She followed along the wall to the back where Sabina and Fabien's graves were, then sat in the grass in front of them and looked at the aging gray stones. They were dulled and weathered, with dirt stuck in some of the carved letters. She took her finger and cleaned it out the best she could, then rubbed her palm along the cold stone.

"I wanted you guys to meet Charlotte. She is my daughter, and I know you would both like her, especially you, Sabina. She is still little, but she likes to play with balls, and I think she will love flowers when she is older. I'll have to play pirates with her, just as we did." She gave a little laugh. "And teach her the pirate lingo." She looked to Fabien's tombstone. "And I will teach her to grow potatoes and corn. She would have loved you both so much, just as I do. But there is something I have to tell you. Her dad he is a German, but you can't hold that against her, even though he does bad things. She is just an innocent bystander in all of this. Really, it is my fault." She pulled a weed from the dead grass and fidgeted with it. "I allowed all of this to happen because I am weak. I know I am stupid for loving him, and that it is reckless but I don't regret it or would ever undo having her. I know that is bad, but I can't help it. I love her father and her. I often wonder if you guys are looking down on me and proud of who I have become or if you are disappointed. I hope it's the former. I'm sorry for everything that happened. I should have done more. If you blame me, I do understand. I wish I could see your faces looking back at me, smiling, happy."

"Eva."

She turned to see Adele waving at her from the other side of the wall. She waved back to let her know that she was coming. "I have to go now, but I'll visit you again when I can. You both are always with me." She got to her feet and looked down at the stones one last time, then pushed the stroller towards the exit.

When they were back at the house, Eva fed Charlotte, put her to bed, and helped Adele with the groceries. "Why do you need all of this food with just the two of you here?"

"The Madame likes to keep the kitchen stocked."

"She never kept this much food in the house when I would stay here." Adele wouldn't meet her gaze but kept her head down as she took food from the bags. "Adele? Why does she have all of this food?"

Adele stopped and lifted her head. "You are not the girl you used to be, the one I remember coming to stay."

Eva creased her brows. "What are you talking about?"

"I'm talking about how you have changed."

"I haven't. I mean, not like I think you mean, but what does that have to do with the question I asked?"

"It means I no longer feel that I can trust you."

Eva set the jar of jam on the counter she had been holding and stared at Adele. Trust me, trust me with what? "Adele, I don't know what you are talking about. It saddens me that you don't think you can trust me anymore. Is it because I married a German?"

"Not just that, it's who you married. You married the worst kind of German."

"He didn't change me. I still do the same things in Paris that I did here and in Berlin if you understand my meaning."

"I do, but I have a hard time believing it."

"You shouldn't because it's the truth. Last year I assisted with the escape of someone from a POW camp and helped get them to England. That is the truth."

"You have a way of getting people out of mainland Europe?"

"I do."

"How?"

"I met a German woman who no longer agrees with this war. She lost both of her sons and is tired of the fighting. She was already working with the British when we met. She approached me and asked if I wanted to help, and I agreed. We were able to send a downed British pilot home right before Charlotte was born."

"How do you manage this?"

"Planes. They come at night and land in fields. I don't contact them. She does."

"What is her name?"

"I'll tell you if you tell me why you have all of this food."

Adele motioned with her index finger for Eva to follow. She climbed the stairs behind Adele to the linen closet at the end of the hall. Adele stopped in front of the door and looked at Eva. She stared at Adele, confused, but waited for her to do something, and she did. Adele opened the door, then pulled on the middle shelf, and the whole thing moved, the wall that the shelves were attached to, and behind it was a little room. Eva squinted into the darkness but couldn't see anything except the dust floating in the air. Adele bent down and picked up a flashlight that had been on the floor just inside the room to the right of the door. She turned it on and shone it into the room. Three people were sitting on the floor in the back, leaning against the far wall. A woman in a worn dress huddled with two children, holding her arm over her eyes to shield the light as the two kids clung to her.

Eva allowed her eyes to adjust, studying the people hiding in the tiny room. She made a small gasp when she realized who they were. Staring back at her were Rachel, Esther, and Uri. She couldn't believe that they were alive. She looked at Adele. "How... um..." She was speechless.

"We found them after you left. They were hiding in the corn fields. They had been there for three days when I brought Madame Blanc to the Dubois farm. They didn't know anyone was coming, and we caught them in the house looking for food. Madame Blanc told them she would hide them at the château for protection. They would have hot meals, blankets, pillows, and clothes, but the living space would not be ideal. They come out when no one is over, but we follow a routine they had to learn. If there is the sound of a car outside, or if someone rings the doorbell, they are to make their way upstairs as quickly and as quietly as they can and go into the room. They cannot move or make any sound until they are told it is safe to do so."

Eva looked back to them again, still huddled in the back of the room. She hardly recognized the children now that they were years older. "Rachel, how are you?"

Rachel's eyes darted to Adele, who nodded at her. "I am as well as I can be."

"I had no idea you were alive. I had to leave because the Germans were after me too."

"I heard. But you are no longer in hiding?"

Eva didn't want to tell her too much because she didn't want Rachel to despise her. "No. I was able to clear my name. I'm sorry your situation isn't better, but I'm glad that you are alive. After what happened to Ezra, I feared something terrible happened to you and the children."

"They looked for us, but the kids were good and didn't make a sound. It was the worse three days of my life. Worst than even being in here."

"The war will end soon, Rachel, and you will no longer have to hide."

"That is my hope, but I'm not as certain as you seem to be."

"It will, I promise you that."

"You guys can come out now. It's only Eva and her daughter here," Adele told her.

Rachel looked at Eva. "It is your baby that we have been hearing?"

"Yes. Her name is Charlotte."

"How old is she?"

"A year old now."

Rachel pushed herself from the floor, and Ester and Uri did the same. She walked to the opening and stood in front of Eva. She looked at Eva for a long time, taking her in, then she put her arms around her, pulling her into an embrace. "It is nice to see a familiar face again."

Eva returned the hug. "I feel the same."

They went downstairs to the kitchen to make dinner, and Eva assisted as Rachel recounted the last few years, but Eva wasn't going to do the same. She told Rachel bits of her life, the things that didn't involve Wilhelm, but she would eventually ask who Charlotte's father was. Eva wasn't sure how she was going to answer if she did. Eva was relieved that Wilhelm had not come with her to La Chapelle, but she missed him terribly. She felt like a single mother over the last twelve months. He was gone so much.

Though she understood, she was a little hurt that Adele and Renée hadn't trusted her enough in the past to tell her that Rachel and her children were alive and hiding behind the linen closet. Eva handed Adele the plate she had just washed so she could dry it when she heard Charlotte crying upstairs. She dried her hands on her apron, and Rachel stood from the kitchen table.

"I can get her."

"Are you sure?"

"I would be happy to."

"Alright." Eva watched her leave the room, feeling strangely anxious. Coming from up the stairs was more crying than Rachel's voice accompanied by whimpering words from Charlotte. The sound grew louder, and Rachel walked into the kitchen carrying Charlotte on her hip. Charlotte's face was red and blotchy, and she sniffled, looking around rapidly. When she saw Eva, she reached out her arms.

"Mama," she said in a whine.

Eva came, taking her from Rachel. Charlotte laid her head on Eva's shoulder, nestling it against her neck. Eva kissed her hair and rocked her. "I'm going to go feed her."

"She is a pretty little girl. Where is her father?"

Eva didn't think Charlotte looked particularly German, so she hoped she could deceive Rachel. "In Paris."

"Go feed her, Eva. I'll finish cleaning up."

It was obvious to Eva that Adele was saving her from having to tell Rachel the truth. "Thank you." She left the kitchen, took Charlotte to the lounge, and sat on the long sofa. She unbuttoned her dress, pulled the right side down, and started feeding Charlotte. Renée came into the room and sat across from her.

"What does Rachel think of Charlotte?"

"She likes her."

"Does she know?"

"No, and I don't want her to."

"You are wise not to. It's probably good you are leaving tomorrow."

"I agree." It gave her butterflies at the thought of seeing Wilhelm again.

Adele entered the room and sat beside Madame Blanc. "Well, what is her name?"

For a brief second, Eva was confused, but then she remembered she had agreed to tell Adele who she was working with if she would tell her about the food. "Her name is Lorelei Vogel."

"And she lives in Paris too?"

"Yes. Her husband is not in the Gestapo, but he often works with Wilhelm."

Adele's lips curled up at the corner. "And you do all of this right under his nose. You live in his home and play the dutiful wife while you are deceiving him."

"I have to."

"I'm not judging. I think it is brave but also foolish."

"But isn't what you are doing dangerous too?"

"It is, but I'm not married to a German. You literally live with the Gestapo."

Renée held up her hands. "What are you two talking about?"

"That Eva is working with a high-ranking officer's wife who decided to betray her country."

Renée's face was etched into the severe expression she always had when she felt like she was being left out of juicy information. "What? Who?"

Eva looked from Adele to Renée. "The woman we spoke of, Lorelei Vogel. She lost her sons in the war and is fed up with all of it."

"Yes, and she has access to planes that can take people to England."

Renée's face lit up, and her eyebrows rose. "Oh."

"Just wait a minute. It's not that easy. She can't summon the planes anytime she wants. She is told when they will come, and that is not often. You are not to tell anyone else this information. She would be angry with me if she knew that I had told you. The only person she is aware of that I told is Ingrid, and the only reason she was OK with me telling her is that we needed her help."

"You are just full of surprises, Eva. Whether you realize it or not, you have been subversive to the Third Reich through this whole war."

Eva switched Charlotte to her other breast, wishing she had not told them. "We will not talk about this anymore, and you will never tell anyone. And I am not being subversive."

Renée looked to Adele. "Oh, but you are." She turned back to Eva. "Think about it. You can go home now. That is what you always wanted."

"It is what I did want, but not anymore."

"You can't seriously want to stay here because of him?"

"I do."

"I don't believe you are thinking straight, Eva. You can't remain here because of him. We don't know how the war will go or what might happen in the next few months. Leaving is the safest option for you and Charlotte."

415

"Yes, but not the best thing. Charlotte needs her father, and I need my husband. I don't expect you to understand."

"No, I don't understand it."

Rachel walked into the room, and they all grew quiet. "What are you guys talking about?"

"Just hoping the war will end soon," Adele said.

Charlotte had fallen asleep in Eva's arms. "I'm going to put her to bed." She laid Charlotte in her lap and buttoned up her dress. She then rested Charlotte against her shoulder and patted her back. She stood and carried her up the stairs to the room they shared. She was glad to be out of that room and away from Renée and Adele. They never did understand her, not even when she was with Gerhardt.

The following morning, she ate a quick breakfast with everyone, and then Adele drove her to the train station. She had said her goodbyes to Rachel and the children, elated that they were alive and grateful to Renée and Adele for caring for them all this time, but now she was ready to go back to Paris, back home to Wilhelm.

She held Charlotte on her lap as she watched the landscape pass through the window. The trees were bare of leaves, and the countryside looked dead, but it was still pretty in its own way.

She looked down at Charlotte, who was biting the ear of her stuffed rabbit. The ear was soaked, and saliva ran down her chin. Eva took a towel from the diaper bag and wiped it away. She was fussy and chewed on everything because she was teething. She looked up at Eva and gave her a gummy smile, and her heart melted. She loved this little person so much that she couldn't imagine her life without her now. She knew that Wilhelm felt the same as her. She could see it every time he looked at Charlotte. She would have to be enough for both of them, and Eva knew it. Since that night at the end of her pregnancy, they never again discussed having another child. They hadn't been intimate since Charlotte was born, so she was always able to reassure Klaus. She often thought she wanted another one and used to believe Wilhelm did, but she was no longer sure. She told herself they had both changed since Charlotte's birth, but really, they had both changed long before that. It was Jon's escape that had changed everything, and she never felt like they had reached that same level of intimacy or trust since. Not that Eva didn't want to be intimate with him, but she didn't know if he wanted to with her. In the first few months after Charlotte was born, she had to heal, but he still kept his distance even after she had. He was so good at keeping his feeling in check that she didn't know if he lost interest in her or if he was doing it for what he thought was her sake. She wanted things to be like they used to be, not this new norm that was a shadow of how it used to be. She ached to have Wilhelm like she once did, to have all of him unguarded and hers. He was fully submerged in his work, and she took the back burner. He did things with her and Charlotte when he was home or just Charlotte, but never just her. She was beginning to think she had lost a part of him she would never get back.

"Do you think Daddy will be home when we get there?" Charlotte let out a long grunt and swung her rabbit up and down. "No, I didn't think so either."

The train pulled into the station and rolled towards a stop, then made a final jerk before it was still. Eva stood, holding Charlotte

417

with one arm as she pulled her bag from the overhead rack. The stroller was stored near the door, and she would get it on her way out. She carried her bag and Charlotte to the door and noticed that a crew member had already put the stroller on the platform. She stepped off the train and set her bag down next to the stroller, then laid Charlotte in it.

"Frau Bauer?"

She jumped and looked at the man who spoke. Wilhelm's orderly was standing next to the stroller. She hadn't seen him when she got off the train and wondered where he had been waiting. "Sergeant Wollenberg, how are you?"

"Very well, Frau Bauer. I was sent here to retrieve you."

"I can see that. Thank you." She didn't need to ask if Wilhelm was with him because he would be on the platform waiting for her if he was.

He picked up her bag. "Follow me."

She pushed the stroller behind him through the crowd of people getting off the train. Parked on the street in front of the main station entrance was the car, shiny and black with the swastika flags on each side of the hood. She still couldn't believe that this was her life.

He put the bag in the trunk and waited for her to lift Charlotte from the stroller so he could put it in with the bag. She actually liked Sergeant Ludwig Wollenberg. He had always been kind to her and was extremely loyal to Wilhelm. He knew almost as much about her as Wilhelm did, but she never once worried that he would inform the Gestapo on her or Wilhelm. He opened the back door for her, and she gave him a warm smile as she slid onto the brown leather seat with Charlotte in her arms.

418

The car pulled out onto the road, and he looked at her in the rearview mirror. "How was your trip?"

"It was good, but it's nice to be home."

"I imagine so. A week can feel like a long time."

"It can, especially with a baby."

He cracked a smile. "I can believe that."

The car pulled in front of the apartment, and he carried her bag and the stroller inside and set them on the floor in the entryway hall. "Have a good night, Frau Bauer."

"You too, Sergeant Ludwig." As soon as the door closed, she turned on her heels, scanning the apartment. The air smelled strongly of food, food that was cooking. Still holding Charlotte, she made a beeline down the hall to the kitchen. Wilhelm was just taking something out of the oven when she entered through the doorway. Her mouth opened slightly in surprise. She hadn't expected him to be home, much less cooking dinner. He had only cooked her dinner once before, and that was because it was her birthday. "Are we celebrating something?"

"Well, hello, Frau Bauer."

She gave a little laugh. "Hello."

"No, we are not. Go have a seat in the living room."

"Alright." She carried Charlotte to the living room and sat her on the floor beside her chair, then pulled it out and sat down.

"This was my mother's favorite dish, and she used to make it all the time when I was a child. She had taught my sister and me how to make it, the only dish she taught me how to make," he said as he carried a white porcelain dish to the table, steam rising from it. He sat it on the table near her. He smiled as he looked at her, the hot pad still on his hand.

419

She leaned over and peered at the food in the dish, smelling its aroma. "I'm sure it tastes delicious." She looked up at him standing over her and thought he looked proud of himself. She was impressed, actually, because not many men in this time could cook anything, nor did they try, and he had several times. His breakfast was not very good, but his last dinner was pretty tasty, so she had high hopes for this one. But she couldn't help but wonder why he went out of his way to make her dinner and why he wasn't at work.

He sat down in the chair beside hers. "Dig in."

She dipped out a spoonful of the mystery food, and then he did the same. She took a bite and recognized it. "Oh, I have had this before. It's a potato casserole. We eat this in America too."

"Really?"

"Yes." She took another bite and watched him. They didn't talk much at the table, but he kept glancing in her direction, and she could feel his eyes on her. Charlotte started to cry, so Eva laid her fork on the plate and reached down to pick her up.

"No, I've got her. You eat." He lifted her off the floor and sat her on his lap, straddling one of his legs. He bounced her up and down, and she smiled. It always brought her so much joy to watch him with Charlotte. He was so good with her, and she seemed to love being with him. He ate the rest of his food with one hand and held Charlotte with the other.

When they finished eating, she stood and took their plates to the kitchen, putting them in the sink. He followed her with Charlotte and held her out to Eva. "You feed her, and I'll clean up."

"I can do it after I feed her. You made dinner. I should be the one to clean up."

"I don't mind."

She bit the inside of her cheek but relinquished and took Charlotte from him. He rolled up the sleeves of his white shirt to his elbows, revealing the dark hair on them. She watched but turned before he caught her staring. She got some fruit, bread, and a little piece of cheese from the fridge and fed it to Charlotte, then went to the nursery and sat in the rocking chair, and undid her dress. She nursed Charlotte as she listened to dishes clinking in the kitchen. It felt so strange that he was home this early in the day because he never was these days.

After a while, his footsteps came down the hall towards the nursery, and she felt a little strange that he was going to see her nursing. She wasn't sure why but guessed that it was because it had been so long since he had seen any part of her naked, or her him.

He stood in the doorway and watched her for a bit before finally speaking. "Once you put her in bed, we can have a drink in the living room."

She hadn't had a drink since Charlotte was born because you usually didn't while breastfeeding. But Charlotte was eating solids now and would be done eating for the night when she had the drink, and it would be out of the system by morning. "That sounds nice. I will meet you in there." He nodded and disappeared. She changed Charlotte into her nightgown, put on a clean diaper, then laid her in her crib and covered her up with a blanket. She went to the door but hesitated for a minute before finally entering the living room.

"What would you like?" he asked.

"Wine."

He poured her a glass of red wine and opened a beer for himself. He held the cup out to her, and she stepped closer to him and angled her head to look up at him. She took it from his outstretched hand but was careful not to touch him. Like any hot-blooded woman, she couldn't help but be attracted to him or want his affection. But he had been uninviting, and she knew that meant to keep her distance, so she did.

They sat as they drank, making small talk, and in that time, he had three more beers and her two glasses of wine. She poured the last of the red liquid into her mouth and looked at him. "Do you want another one?"

He gave her an intent look and set the beer can on the coffee table, then scooted down on the couch next to her. She stared at him, trying to figure out what he was doing. He took the empty wine glass from her and set it on the table next to the beer can, then leaned in and kissed her on the neck. Her whole body tensed, and she swallowed, wildly uncomfortable as she looked towards the curtained window, at the floor, the empty fireplace, anywhere but him, as she was faced with the uneasy realization that Wilhelm wanted to have sex with her. She remembered when she rejected him the night he was injured and high on medication, but he wasn't any of those things now. He knew exactly what he was doing, and it wasn't from the effects of medicine, although she wasn't entirely sure it was even then. Klaus' words came unbidden and unwanted into her mind that she could not have unprotected sex with him again. Her periods had resumed months ago, so this was risky.

Wilhelm's feral look took a turn for the darkly amused, and he reached up and slid a finger along the side of her breast. "I'm not thirsty, Eva," he said, his voice pitched low.

She gave an uncomfortable laugh. "What are you doing?"

"I thought that would be obvious."

"I think it's better if we wait and do this some other night."

That couldn't be further from what she wanted. Her body seemed extra responsive to him, and her stomach twisted with the feeling of butterflies as a tingling sensation settled lower.

He leaned back and observed her, and then he watched her gaze move to his mouth, smiling because he took it as an invitation. She lifted her eyes and paused, trying to read him. He leaned in again and kissed her, the briefest touch, lips on lips, and then he pulled back.

"You know what I want, and I don't want to wait for some other night." He looked at her quizzically, his brow furrowed. The side of his lip pulled up a fraction as his silken voice lowered to a more intimate register, and he leaned in closer. "You don't need to worry. Charlotte is sleeping, so we have all night," he said in a low murmur, then leaned back, and their eyes met.

A tide of emotions rushed through her like a storm breaking. The need in his voice was arousing, but she had to fight it. "We shouldn't," she said in a strained whisper as she watched the lightning flash in his eyes as they burned into hers.

He leaned into her and softly nuzzled her neck, his voice low. "Oh, we should," he said, his voice deep and velvet smooth.

She couldn't control her breathing as it came slow and hard, her chest rising and falling with each breath. "You don't fight fair."

"No, I don't, so this will be good practice for you then. You can start by learning how to dominate me. I'll be completely at your mercy."

She felt his mouth tilt into a smile against her neck. The heat from his desire sent a tingle down her spine, igniting her own desire. She grew increasingly flustered by his power over her as she slid her hand up his muscular arm. "I have the feeling you are harder to dominate than most people."

He laughed. "I am, which is why you should start learning how to tonight."

She remembered what he had said to her the last time he came onto her, that he had wanted her more than anything in his entire life. He leaned back and lifted his hand, rubbing his thumb over her bottom lip, the slow burn of desire in the air. She shivered at his touch, and she looked at him, his gaze unrestrained as he took her arm, his fingers curling around her wrist. His touch sparked a tingling warmth that rippled through her slowly, and she struggled to keep her focus. He was so close, his rigidly contained body only inches away from hers, making it harder to resist being completely consumed by his draw. She knew he could feel it too, his skin feverishly hot on hers. Her draw to him intensified, overtaking all caution because she missed him desperately at this moment. She missed touching him, being close to him, the only place she felt truly free from the horrors that surrounded her, and she missed the way he sent fiery desire through his kisses, through his touch. He was driving her wild.

Her own desire pulsed towards Wilhelm as she reached up and traced a finger down his chest. Then she slid her hand up and over the hard muscles of his taught shoulder, quickly growing lightheaded from heat and want. She met his eyes, and Wilhelm's hazel gaze had gone dark with feral desire. The intensity of it rippled through her, and she wanted him beyond all reason or caution. She wanted him as reckless desire swept through her. She swallowed and parted her lips, and a provocative smile reached her eyes.

He pursed his lips, then pulled her hard against him, one hand on her waist as the other traveled down her curves. He grabbed the back of her head and pressed his lips hard against hers. Klaus' words echoing in her mind told her to pull away, but she didn't resist and let him kiss her. Emboldened, she slid her hand up his neck and threaded her fingers through his thick brown hair, bunching it in her fist as she pulled him into a deeper kiss as a passion ran through her whole body. She pressed her breast enticingly against him. She could feel the curve of his mouth as his lips briefly pulled up in amusement, which quickly faded away, and all that was left was the force of his desire as she deepened the kiss, exploring his eager mouth. She kissed him passionately without letting up, wave after wave of lust emanating from her, wanting it to consume them both as she felt his own passion mounting. Then Wilhelm's hands were around her wrists, pushing her firmly away, his eyes glazed with desire.

"We have all night, remember?" Hunger heavy in his words.

Her desire pulsed through her body in a rush toward him. She wanted him so badly that she was ready to be completely reckless. To hell with what Klaus said. She didn't care anymore.

"I know."

He stood and took her hand, leading her to the bedroom. As soon as they were in the room, he began unbuttoning her dress, and she reached up and pulled his suspenders off his shoulders, rubbing her hands over his shirt, feeling his strong back muscles. At that point, he didn't even wait until they were on the bed. He lifted her up, sat her on the dresser, and then stepped in between her legs. She undid his pants as he pulled her dress out from under her. He began hungrily kissing her lips and then her neck. He had said they had all night, but it was obvious to her that he wanted her as badly as she did him and was impatient, unable to wait. He was going to take her now on the dresser and probably again before morning came. She would gladly give herself to him as many times as he wanted to have her.

While kissing her, he reached down with one hand, and she could feel the pressure of his hard penis against her and then inside of her. She gasped, and he pressed his cheek to hers, his mouth open as he let out a deep breath. She could see what he was feeling on his face, the intense pleasure of it. His cheek felt clammy against hers, as did his hands. He began to move, and it stung a little. It had been a long time since they were intimate. He bit her neck as he moved rhythmically, then kissed her, never stopping his motion. Everything he did seemed desperate, like he wanted to climb inside of her. He squeezed her shoulder as he climaxed, breathing heavily as he rested his head on her chest. He looked at her, and there was a hunger in his eyes that she had only seen once, but this time more intense, and it sent shivers through her.

He pulled her off the dresser and carried her to the bed. This was not over. He was going to have her as many times as he could that night. She wasn't entirely sure where this drive was coming from, but it seemed like he feared this would never happen again. She knew that in any sort of way, he would not give her up easily.

He was a force to be reckoned with, but she had allowed herself to be in this situation, and she wasn't altogether sure she didn't like his intensity.

He dropped her on the bed, pulled her dress over her arms, and threw it to the floor, then her slip. He unbuttoned his shirt and took it off, then his undershirt, his pants, and finally his underwear. She looked at his hard chest, the complexion of his skin, and the contours of his body. She let her eyes drop to his scrotum and his bulging penis that was hard and erect, the organ rising thickly from a nest of dark, curly hair between his legs. She couldn't stop herself from looking, she reveled it. The sight of him elicited excitement in her, a deep want. For so long, there was an endless, aching need for him. She loved this man more than life itself. Besides Charlotte, he was the most important thing to her.

His eyes burned into hers, then he crawled on top of her and began kissing her all over her body. She pulled his head up to her and kissed him. He looked into her eyes before pulling one of her legs up and placing it around him.

"You don't know how badly I have wanted to do this. I have missed the feel of your soft body. For a while, I knew you didn't want me to, then you gave birth, and I knew I shouldn't, but it's been the longest twelve months. It's strange to think that beneath me is the beauty I saw sitting across from me at Madame Blanc's all those years ago. You were a vision, an angel, and I didn't even like you, but it was hard to deny even then. I know it is different for you, but when I look at you, I see a glimpse of what heaven must be like. We despised each other then, so to think that tonight, and other nights, you have let me have this, have you in such an intimate way. But tonight, I want to lose myself in you. I've never wanted anyone like I want you."

It was such a strange feeling for her to have captured the love of a man she once viewed as being so evil and to listen to him now. He spoke the sweetest words to her like he was a completely different person than the one she met in 1939. And he was going to enjoy her now to the fullest, and she was going to let him.

He thrust inside of her hard, and she moaned as he pushed her into the mattress. He let his hands and mouth wander, but then, unexpectedly, he stopped and pulled out. In one swift motion with his strong arms, he flipped her onto her stomach. "I want to do it this way," he whispered in a breathy voice in her ear. He took both of her hands and pulled them behind her while she lay with her head on the bed. As he held her hands with one of his, he entered her from behind. Her lips parted in a silent gasp. He could always enter her so much deeper this way. He began to move, slow at first, then he picked up speed and thrust harder and deeper.

The sensation was intense, more so than ever before, but she couldn't quite put her finger on why. She clenched her teeth together as the waves of it crashed into her, and she couldn't handle it anymore.

"Stop!" She was breathless, and he was panting.

"What?" His voice was husky, and something resembling annoyance and disbelief skimmed the edge of his tone.

"I can't. It's too much and too deep right now."

He didn't try to convince her to let him finish that way, but instead, he let go of her hands and pulled out. He took her by the shoulder, pulled her up to her knees, and grazed her earlobe as the muscles tightened deep in her belly. He leaned in and glided a trail of butterfly kisses down her neck, and she could feel his hardened penis pressing against her lower back. He moved to her side and put an arm around her waist, lowering her onto her back. She watched him, thinking that he was going to move on top of her again, but he didn't. Instead, he slid his hand between her thighs and inserted three fingers inside her. With deft movement, he had her body tensing, and smiled at the reaction he was eliciting from her. He pulled his fingers out and moved down on the bed, positioning himself between her legs. He sucked her clitoris into his mouth as she writhed beneath him, his teeth biting hard into the sensitive skin. She reached down with her hand and gripped his hair, but he didn't stop. He held firmly onto her and continued, moving his mouth from her clit to the inside of her thigh and biting there too, clamping the soft flesh between his teeth, leaving a mark. She drew in a sharp breath from the surprise of it and the sting of pain that surprised her. He moved his head to her other leg and bit her inner thigh there too, close to her opening. Finally, he moved his mouth back to her opening and bit there like before, only this time a little harder. She held her breath, her eyes tearing from the sharp throbbing. He reinserted his fingers, four this time, but never relinquished her clitoris with his teeth. He worked with his mouth and fingers. Eva moaned as the climax built, sending waves through her whole body, her fingers clenched around the sheets, her head tossed back, and her mouth open. He pulled his teeth off her clit and moved up, kissing her navel, belly, and sternum, then muffling her cries as he placed his mouth over hers. He removed his fingers, and then he entered her. One, hard thrust, doing deep.

He placed kisses on her body as he moved greedily, wanting all of her. He breathed heavily, and all the muscles in his body tensed when he came, spilling inside of her. He stayed on her, his weight pinning her to the bed as he breathed heavily, his clammy skin sticking to hers as he came down from his orgasm. After a few minutes, he rolled off and pulled her on top of him, wrapping his arms tightly around her holding her to him. She reached up her right hand and caressed his hair. He leaned up and kissed her feverishly.

Finally, he moved her off him and pulled down the blankets. "Get under." She moved to the head of the bed and slid under the blankets, then he laid down and covered them both up. She guessed that they were going to both sleep naked. His arm slid around her waist and pulled her to him, then folded himself against her back and held her tightly. For some reason, he reminded her of a kid at a pet store. They see a puppy and hold onto it for dear life, knowing that they can't keep it but will get as much love as they can in that short amount of time.

He kissed her bare back. "Thank you."

"You don't need to thank me."

"It's out there now, and I meant it."

He fell asleep rather quickly, but Eva lay awake, looking at the wall, thinking about what they had done. When she was sure he was in a deep sleep, she climbed out of bed and went to the bathroom. She cleaned herself off, then hurried back to bed. It was cold in the apartment, and she was now shivering. The air was so chilly, but the bed felt warm as she crawled back in, seeing Wilhelm lying in the same spot she had left him. She liked sleeping with him. She laid down, facing him, watching him as he slept, drinking him in. He had a handsome face, a chiseled jaw, full lips, broad shoulders, and a muscular body. He looked innocent now, but she knew what terrible things he did in his waking hours. She finally drifted off to sleep, not knowing what tomorrow would bring.

Chapter Twenty-Two

February 29th, 1944

E va looked across the table at Ingrid. "Not like too, it's t-h-r-o-u-g-h. Put the tip of your tongue on your front teeth."

"I did that."

"No, you put it on the roof of your mouth, which is why it comes out sounding like too."

Ingrid dropped the piece of paper in front of her. "I can't say that word or any of the English words with th. It is stupid."

"It's not stupid. It's just hard for non-English speakers. Don't feel bad. A lot of children in English-speaking countries struggle with the th too."

"But they are children."

"Yes, who have spent their whole lives hearing English. You will get it. You are already good at pronouncing a lot of the words, and your vocabulary is growing quickly."

"My head hurts, and I'm tired. Can we take a break?" She sighed and leaned back in the chair.

"Sure. We have been going at it for two hours, so why don't we resume tomorrow?"

"Yes, gladly. So, his mother has Charlotte?"

"She does."

"How long has she been in France?"

"A few days. Wilhelm had more time to spend with me in January, but now he is back to working all the time."

"Is his mom worried about the increased bombings in Berlin?"

"She doesn't seem to be, but Wilhelm definitely is. She is tough. I think that woman is made of steel. Wilhelm is talking about selling the apartment in Berlin and moving his mother to the country. I think he should move her to the west of Germany."

"Because of the Russians?"

"Yes. He, of course, asked me why I suggested that, and I told him how bad it would be for his mother if the Russians ever took Berlin."

"And?"

"And, he agreed. I think for once he will listen to me."

"So what part would he move her to?"

"Probably around Cologne. That is where he is from."

"Oh, I didn't know that. It used to be a beautiful city, but it's dirty now, with all the factories. Have you been there?"

"No, I have not."

"The area around Cologne is still nice, though. Just out of the city is the Schloss Drachenburg Castle, and the countryside and villages are stunning."

Eva smiled at the thought, wondering why he never talked more about the area with her. "So you and this pilot are getting serious?"

Ingrid gave a bright smile. "We are. Danny is so kind and says the sweetest things to me. He is such a gentleman."

"I am glad to hear it." Eva looked around the restaurant. "Klaus is late. I wonder where he could be?"

"Maybe he got lost."

"No, he is familiar enough with Paris. I doubt that is the reason." Ingrid eyed her from across the table, her expression vague. "What?"

"I don't know. You just seem different."

Eva pulled her brows together. "Different, how?"

Ingrid tilted her head to the side. "You look healthy, or maybe it's happiness, I'm not sure."

"Healthy?"

"Yes, your cheeks have more color, and your skin is glowing. It looks dewier than usual."

Eva bit the inside of her cheek and lifted her eyes to Ingrid. "Maybe it's both."

"Alright, what has changed?" Ingrid insisted.

"I'm not entirely sure why, but Wilhelm has been more intense towards me lately."

"Intense, how?"

"Well, like he used to be. Loving and affectionate, but more so. He changed when I returned from La Chapelle."

"More so... what does that mean?"

Eva was aware of the heat on her cheeks that spread to her neck and chest. "Let me put it like this, he had the evenings off for two weeks in January, and we made love every single night for those two weeks."

Ingrid covered her mouth to stifle her surprise. After a few seconds, she moved her hand, dropping it to the table. "What was that like? I bet you were sore?"

"Ingrid?" Eva glowered at her.

"It's the truth."

"You asked what it was like? Well, we definitely hungered for one another, but sometimes his love is a little hard for me to handle."

"And?"

"And that is how it feels."

"You can't just say something like that and leave it there."

"I can... but I won't. What I mean is the things he does are intense. He is intense. So I can't figure out why I want him to do those things to me or why I let him, again and again."

Ingrid leaned over the table and put her chin in her hands. "How is he intense?"

Eva lost her smile. "That's private, Ingrid."

"Not from me. I would tell you."

"I know you would, and sometimes you divulge too much."

"I don't. And you don't divulge enough."

Eva let out an exasperated breath. "Fine. One example is, a few weeks ago, we were going to one of his work functions. We took the elevator to the top floor of the building where it was being held, but when we got out of the elevator, he pulled me down a side hall and pushed me up against the wall. His hands were all over me as he kissed me passionately. Then he pulled at my dress, and undid the buttons so he could get to my breasts."

Ingrid drew in a breath. "He didn't... not in the hall?"

"Yes, he did. He took my right breast, and pulled it out of my dress, and started to kiss and suck it, then he bit it rather savagely. He didn't know it at the time, but he left a purplish bruise on my nipple and on the skin underneath it. I yelped, I think from the shock of it, and I told him we shouldn't do it in the hall because someone might see us."

"What did he say to that?"

"Nothing, he just carried on. He was quite forceful, doing things he had never done before. Tearing at my clothes with a desperation and hunger that was new to me. It was animalistic, really, and to be honest, I was a little terrified. He gave off his emotions in waves, and I could feel them, so it wasn't just the physical part of it all. It was everything. Physically, mentally, and emotionally draining, but also exhilarating. I had never experienced such fear but also ecstasy at the same time before. I'm not even sure if I'm making sense."

"You are. So... he just did you right there in the hall?"

"Yes. He pulled up my dress and ripped my hose in the process, then tore off my underwear. They fell to the floor because there was no way they would stay up after what he did. He then used his index and middle fingers and pushed them inside me. When he had me completely and utterly under his control and to the point of screaming, he took me even higher, and I wanted it to last all night. My legs were shaking, and when I thought they were on the verge of giving out, he lifted me, holding me against the wall, and he took me that way. He had me more than once in that hall. I knew we could be seen and that I would feel it in the morning, but the rush was worth it. I was willing to suffer through the pain the next day." Eva looked to Ingrid for a reaction, but she only stared back at her with a stunned expression.

"Wow. So this is how he has been since you returned from La Chapel?"

"More or less."

"Is that the only time he was that intense?"

Eva bit the inside of her cheek. "No."

Ingrid's mouth opened into a little O. "You have to tell me."

"I don't know, Ingrid."

"Please? I don't have a man in my life, so I have to live vicariously through you."

Eva let out a breath. "Oh, Ingrid."

Ingrid tapped her foot on the floor from impatience. "Come on, Eva?"

"Fine." She hesitated for a second before speaking. "It's how he always makes me feel. I didn't think an orgasm could be that intense, but whatever it is that he does, especially recently... boy." She folded and unfolded the cloth napkin on the table in front of her. "He makes me come so hard," she breathed. "Like a little over a week ago. His hands claimed my body, squeezing my breasts as he bent me over the couch in his office. He had to put his hand over my mouth as I came, because it was so good I couldn't stop from screaming. If I ever had sex with anyone else, I'm sure he would leave me wanting more, wanting everything only Wilhelm could give me. It's him I think of whenever I feel that throbbing pull between my legs."

"And he still does this kind of thing to you?"

"Not as much the last few weeks, though, because he has been working a lot. I am already in bed most nights before he even gets home. I must admit that I miss all the attention, and I miss him. I feel this strange sensation when I'm with him like I'm on a drug. When he leaves I feel the crash, just like if I were actually high from a substance. I crave his affection, and I know people would say that is bad, but I don't care. I suspect it will only get worse."

"Why do you say that?"

"Because he wants me to leave Paris. He plans to move Charlotte and me to Cologne with his mother."

Ingrid pulled in a breath, concern on her face now. "Why?"

"Come on, Ingrid. We all know the war is going badly for Germany. They could lose France any day, and he knows it, I know it, and you know it."

Her face fell. "I do. But I don't want you to leave. How will I see you if you are in Germany?"

"You could always come with me?"

"Go back to Germany? No, I don't think so."

"But you can't stay here if the Allies take it back. And think how the French will treat you if that happens because you are German."

"I know, but I don't want to return to Germany. Do you really want to go there?"

"I've never been to Cologne, but it sounds nice. And like you, I can't stay here if the Allies make it into France, not being married to a German, especially the one I'm married to. I also have a child who is half German... and... well, soon I will have two."

Ingrid's eyes widened as they bore into her. "What?" she squealed, far louder than she should. Other people in the restaurant turned in their chairs to look at them.

"Keep it down." Eva looked around, feeling embarrassed as people in the room watched them.

"You are pregnant?"

"Yes."

Ingrid was struggling to find her words. "I didn't think you would have any more kids?"

"Well, with how often we were having sex, it was going to happen."

"Did you want it to happen?"

"Um, yes and no."

"What about him? Does he want more children?"

"Yes, he does. But I haven't told him yet. I only realized I was pregnant a few weeks ago."

"So that is why you are glowing. Does he suspect?"

"I don't think so."

"How did you find out?"

"It's a lot easier once you've had a child. Some of the symptoms are different, but many of them are the same. I'm tired all the time, and I'm sick all day long. With Charlotte, I was only sick in the mornings, but with this one, it doesn't seem to ever go away. And my breasts are a lot sorer than before."

"Are you sure that's not because of your husband?"

"Yes, Ingrid. It's not that kind of pain."

"Have you told Klaus?"

"No. He will freak, though, when he finds out."

"When will you tell Wilhelm?"

"I don't know yet. I would like to soon, but he is so preoccupied with work right now."

"He will almost certainly want you to move to Germany when he learns of it."

"Yes, probably, which is another reason I haven't told him yet. I want to have him a little longer before he makes me leave France."

"Oh, Klaus is here."

Eva turned and looked behind her, then straightened in her chair and peered at Ingrid. "Not a word about this."

"Won't it be better to tell him now and get it over with because he will find out eventually?"

"I'll tell him I'm pregnant when I feel ready, but that isn't now. I don't know who I'm more nervous about telling, him or Wilhelm."

"That is a tough one. But I still think you should tell him now."

The look Ingrid was giving confused her. It came across as worry and perhaps a little disapproving. Eva didn't have time to ask her what she was thinking or to reaffirm that she didn't want her to tell Klaus because he pulled out a chair and sat at the table just then.

"What have you girls been talking about?"

"Just how Ingrid thinks English is hard."

"He smiled. It is. I took it in school, and I don't remember a thing."

"That's because it was a long time ago." Eva tried to sound reassuring.

He laughed. "Did you just call me an old man?"

She realized how it sounded. "No, what I meant was that it's been a while since you have been in school, and that is why you no longer remember."

He squeezed her arm. "No need to apologize. I know that I'm old. But that isn't why I can't remember. It's because I struggled with it in school, so I didn't retain it when I got out."

Ingrid's eyes darted back and forth from Klaus to Eva. Finally, she spoke, interrupting Klaus and Eva's easy banter. "So Eva has some news."

Eva's breath halted, and her eyes narrowed as she glared at Ingrid. She could not believe Ingrid had said that. She didn't get upset with Ingrid often, but this was one of the few times. She was furious with her.

"Oh," he looked from Ingrid to Eva, "what news?"

Eva cleared her throat and tilted her head to him. "Just that Wilhelm is planning on moving his mother to Cologne, and I will probably go with her. He wants me out of Paris soon."

Klaus considered this. "That's not a bad idea for his mother. Berlin is the hot spot in Germany right now, and if the war comes to our doorstep, it will most likely be fought there. But for you, maybe you should stay so if there is an invasion, you can go home."

"Think about how the French will treat me because I married a German and have a half-German child."

"True, you would have to get to the Americans soon for your own protection, but he would have to be gone by then."

"Yes, and he will not leave me behind."

"Especially now," Ingrid blurted out.

"What the hell is wrong with you, Ingrid." Eva was livid now.

Klaus glanced between the two women. "Why?"

Eva looked at the table instead of Klaus. "Because I'm pregnant."

Klaus' grayish blond eyebrows rose, forcing creases in his forehead. He looked at her through the lens of his small round glasses, and she could clearly see the sadness and disappointment in his eyes. He turned his face away from her and stared out the window by their table.

"Oh, Eva. You haven't really thought this through, have you." He reached up and rubbed the top of his bald head. "I can't believe you would have another child with him. I warned you of the dangers of doing that. No, Ingrid is right. He will not let you stay in France. Does he know?"

"No." Eva could hardly look at him.

"How far along?"

"I think about seven weeks."

"When are you going to tell him?"

"Like I told Ingrid, I don't know. Wilhelm is really busy right now, so he is always gone."

"Maybe don't do anything right now. When is he planning on moving his mother to Cologne?"

"He didn't say, but I think soon. We are going on a trip to Berlin in the next few months, so he will probably inform his mother then. He knows a meeting is planned soon with the high command, and all of the SS who oversee an occupied country have to be there. He just doesn't know when yet."

"Maybe you can tell him when you get back," Ingrid said.

"Maybe. Can we eat our food and talk about something else?"

442

"We can do that. There is no reason to worry about it right now." Klaus said with his usual reassuring tone.

(

Chapter Twenty-Three
ॐ

May 22nd, 1944

Eva's yellow summer dress gently flapped in the breeze as she pushed Charlotte in the stroller. The weather was warm, and she enjoyed spending time outside. The city of Berlin, however, smelled of smoke, and some streets were entirely in ruins now. Piles of rubble that were once buildings lined the roads. The constant bombings by the Allies devastated the city. Eva truly felt sorry for the people of Berlin and London. She could have never imagined how terrible it really was in her time. You had to see it in person to truly understand the extent of how destructive the bombings were and the toll they took on the people of these cities. Germany had started the war, but many of the people who died and suffered from the bombings were children and old people.

She had seen so little of Wilhelm over the last few months, and she knew why. Even on the train to Berlin, he reviewed documents and hardly spoke to her. In the pit of her stomach had settled an uneasy feeling. The Allies would be in France soon, and she knew it, but she didn't quite know what that meant for her. Wilhelm had purchased a house on a few acres of land just outside Cologne and sold the apartment in Berlin weeks ago. His mother was staying in a hotel while they waited for the house to be ready for her to move in. Wilhelm's plan was for her to move in with his mother. He still didn't know that she was pregnant because she always wore loose-fitting dresses, and they had not been intimate for a while. They had almost been like strangers the last few months. All he did was work, and she hated it. She missed him desperately and craved his affection and attention. He told her that when they returned to Paris, he would have a little free time that weekend, but on Monday, it will be work as usual, which meant he would have little time to spend with her, and they would go back to hardly seeing one another.

Eva was taking Charlotte to stay with Marie for a few hours while she visited Heidi and Liesel. The sun was going down fast, and she didn't want to be out too late. She knew the chance of a bombing raid would increase as soon as the sun went down.

She pulled the stroller into the hotel elevator, took it to the third floor, then pushed it down the long hall lined with doors until she reached Marie's room. She lightly tapped on the door and waited.

It opened, and Marie smiled when she saw Eva and Charlotte. "Hello, Eva." She leaned in and gave Eva a kiss on both cheeks. "How are you?"

"I am doing well."

"You look tired and a little pale. Are you sure you are feeling alright? Maybe you are getting sick."

"No," she gave a forced smile. "I feel fine."

Marie eyed her, not quite believing her. "Alright then, you go have fun." Eva kissed Charlotte on the head, then Marie took the stroller and pushed it into the room.

"I'll try not to be too late."

"Take your time. I don't see this little one enough."

Eva knew that Marie loved having Charlotte, and it made her happy that she was able to spend time with her grandmother.

Eva had dinner with Heidi and Liesel, like when she lived in Berlin, then she went to a club with them, but she didn't drink any of the champagne that was served, and she didn't feel like dancing. After much insistence, she finally gave in and danced with them. It reminded her of old times, and it felt good, but she knew this, too, would be over soon. Nothing would be as it was, and before long, all that would be left were her memories. She tried not to think too much about it because it depressed her.

When she left the club, it was just after seven, and she wondered if Father Becker would be at the church. It had been so long since she had seen him. She hoped that the church was still there and had not been destroyed by the bombings. She was relieved when the steeple came into view just over the top of the buildings. She pulled open the heavy wooden door, then went through the second smaller door into the chapel. It smelled just as she remembered. Candles were burning throughout, illuminating the room and giving it a peaceful, warm glow. She followed the hall to Father Becker's office. Light shone from under the door, so she tapped three times with her index finger.

He opened the door but paused when he saw her. "Eva." There was a hint surprise in his voice.

"Hi, father."

"Why are you in Berlin? I'm happy to see you, but I don't know why you are here. Berlin is not a safe place anymore. It never was for you, but now not for anyone."

"I return to France tomorrow."

"Well, come in." He moved aside for her to enter, and she sat in the same chair she always did. He walked around the desk and took his chair. "I still can't believe you're sitting across from me."

"I know. So much has changed since I saw you last."

"What happened to the man you were worried about? The one you said was after you?"

"Not what I expected." She held up her right hand. "I married him. We have a daughter who is one and a half, and I'm pregnant."

He stared at her from across the desk. He blinked a few times, then spoke. "Well, that is not what I thought you were going to say."

"I didn't think it would happen."

"So you found a way to love this man?"

"I have. Somehow, I found a place for him in my heart, and now I can't imagine what my life would be without him. He gave me a beautiful daughter who means the world to me, and now he has given me a second child." She placed her right hand over her stomach so he would understand her meaning.

"Well, this is a turn of events I had not seen. But what will you do when the war is over?"

She knew that he was implying that Germany would lose the war. "Stay here, I suppose. This is where he is from, so this is my home now."

"But you understand that he will likely go to prison for what he has done, or worse?"

"I do. But I'm hoping that doesn't happen. Am I being naive to hope for that?"

"No, as long as you realize that hope may be a different thing than reality."

"I do. I wish that I knew how to help him."

"But then you would be cheating justice."

She focused on him. What was he trying to say? "You think I should let them take him?"

"I do because that is the right thing to do."

"But you have been preaching to me this whole time about forgiveness, and now you tell me that I should stand by and watch as my husband is dragged off to prison and do nothing?"

"Yes, because forgiving someone does not mean that it exempts them from receiving justice. It is more about you and their eternal soul than their mortal body. He has to pay for what he has done here, and if he won't repent, then he has to pay for it in the next life too."

This hit her like a gut punch, and she felt sick. She wanted to weep for Wilhelm because she loved him, and she worried that he would suffer in this life and possibly the next. She stood from the chair. "Thank you for your advice, Father."

She stepped around the chair and turned to the door, but he spoke. "Please, don't be upset. It doesn't mean he will die in prison, and you don't know that he won't ask for forgiveness. Perhaps he can be redeemed in this life and saved in the next."

She peered at him from the doorway. "Let's hope." She turned from him and walked into the hall, then hurried to the door. Once outside, she took a deep breath, her eyes burning with hot tears. She had never thought about it like that, that he could be facing so much pain, so much suffering, and she couldn't help him. It had shaken her to the core.

She walked briskly back to the hotel as the night air began to cool. She wanted to pick up Charlotte and take her back to the hotel she was staying at with Wilhelm, and she wanted to walk into his arms and not let him go. She started across the Molteke Bridge over the Spree River, watching as the lights reflected off the water, trying to contain the whirling thoughts. She turned her head forward again as a figure approached her quickly from the other end of the bridge. It was a woman, and at first, she thought nothing about it until they walked past one another and made eye contact. Eva halted in her tracks, as did the other woman.

"Eva Abrams," was all she said.

"Lina Schubert." Eva didn't expect to ever see Lina again, the one who gave up the resistance in Berlin and the reason they were all dead.

"You are supposed to be dead."

Eva gritted her teeth. "No, and none of the others should be dead now either. You traitorous bitch."

"Traitor. Oh, I'm the traitor? You are betraying your own country. And for what, because you are being fucked by a German?"

Eva slapped her hard across the face, the sound echoing off the bridge. "It is not my fault you were used by the man you thought loved you. Is that why you are so upset with me? It is because the man I'm with truly loves me?"

"No, he doesn't. He chose someone else."

449

Eva hadn't considered that Lina might not know she was with Wilhelm. "I'm not talking about him."

Lina looked genuinely confused. "Whom then?"

"My husband, Wilhelm."

Lina's nostrils flared from anger. "You are married?"

"Yes, For over a year and a half. We have a daughter."

Lina was fuming now. "I don't understand. Why did you get to be happy and not me?"

"Happy, you think I'm happy?"

"Aren't you? You are married with a child."

"Yes, and I am happy about that, but plenty of things make me unhappy."

"You don't deserve a family. You don't deserve anything. You were supposed to be dead, eliminated with the others. How are you still alive?"

"What made you this way, Lina?"

"The world," she snapped.

"Because you let it."

"You didn't answer my question. How were you the only one who made it out alive?"

"I guess you could say I have an angel looking after me."

"And is this angel named Wilhelm?"

"It doesn't matter."

"It does because he is the reason you are alive. I am going to find out who he is and report him, and then you will both be hung from the square like the traitors you are."

"You will never succeed. I will tell him who you are, and maybe it will be you hanging from the square," Eva spat, anger fueling her words.

Lina made a growling sound and lunged at her. Eva fell back, hitting the side of the bridge, and Lina pressed her back hard against the stone. Lina had her hand around her throat, so Eva brought her hand up and pushed on Lina's face, trying to get her off. When that didn't work, Eva pressed her thumbs into Lina's eyes. Lina screamed and instantly pulled back. Eva put her hands on the top of the bridge, supporting herself. The adrenaline was pumping through her, and her body was shaking. She worried about the baby if Lina tried to hit her in the stomach.

Lina regained her bearings, and like a wild animal, she came after Eva again. Eva took a step to the side and grabbed Lina's arm. Lina took hold of Eva's arm and tried to wrestle hers free. When it wasn't working, she let go and punched Eva in the face. She staggered back, and Lina came at her again. Eva swung at Lina, hitting her in the side of the neck, but Lina didn't stop. She grabbed Eva and pulled her to the side of the bridge. Lina was pushing her further and further over the edge. Eva's heart pounded so hard she could hear it thumping in her ears and pulsing in her temples, her ribs hurting from the continuous strained beats. She had to do something, so she let go of Lina with one hand and hit her in the nose with the palm of her hand, angling upward. She heard the crack, and when Lina let go, Eva hit her again in the jaw.

Blood ran down Lina's face, and she licked it from her lips. "Is that all you've got?"

This had to end. Eva ran at her, putting a hand on each of her shoulders and pushing. Lina took a few staggering steps backward, placing one foot wrong and twisting her ankle to the side. She fell into the railing, and the upper half of her body went over the bridge. Eva watched as Lina hung on, trying to balance

451

so she could push herself back up, but stood frozen in place, watching Lina struggle. Lina looked at Eva, panic in her eyes, and for a second, she considered helping her up, but what would that accomplish? Lina would only come after her again or follow through on her threat and turn her and Wilhelm in, and she couldn't let that happen.

"Eva, please!" Eva took a step towards her, but before she could take another, Lina's hands faltered, and she fell head-first into the river. Eva ran to the side and looked down just as Lina splashed into the water. Lina had her arms out but still hit her head on impact, knocking her unconscious. Eva leaned over, watching Lina's body float for a few seconds before being pulled under by the current. She drew in a breath and pulled back. No one had ever died at her hands before now. She had been in the car during the attack on the German high command, but she wasn't driving, and she never shot anyone with the gun they gave her.

Feeling the bile rising, she leaned over the bridge and vomited in the water. She wiped her mouth with the back of her hand and backed away from the edge. The urge to not be on this bridge anymore was overwhelming, so she ran towards the end. She kept going straight toward the Reichstag, which was only a few yards away. She and Wilhelm's hotel was a block from the Reichstag, and she couldn't get there fast enough.

As her legs carried her closer to the hotel, she thought about what happened over and over in her mind, replaying it like a bad horror film. She took the hotel steps two at a time and pushed the revolving door, then hurried to the front desk and asked for her key. When the man handed it to her, she pulled it from his hand and took the stairs to the room. She unlocked the door, went inside, and quickly closed the door behind her. She turned, facing the room, but halted, seeing that a lamp was on. She scanned the room but didn't see anyone. Slowly, she walked towards the bed and heard the shower running, steam coming through the partially open door. She wanted to take off her dress and get into the shower with him, to let the hot water clean the blood from her as he comforted her, but she couldn't. He would be able to see her growing stomach.

She looked down at the blood that was splatted on her dress. She ran to her suitcase, took out her nightgown, pulled her dress off, and slipped the gown over her head. She poked the dress in the bottom of the suitcase so he wouldn't see it, then quietly stepped into the bathroom. She barely turned the cold nob on the sink and cleaned the blood from her hands and face. Then she checked the rest of her body to make sure she hadn't missed any.

She tiptoed out of the bathroom, then went to the bed and crawled under the blankets. She wanted to lie down and hide that anything had happened, but she was too shaken up to do that. She needed him to make her feel alright, to hold her until she felt better.

The water shut off, and after a few minutes, he came out of the bathroom, drying his hair with a towel, the clean scent of his soap filling the air. He stopped when he saw her in bed, his hand paused, still holding the towel to his hair.

He looked around the room, then set his eyes on her again. "Eva, where is Charlotte?"

She sucked in a breath. She had forgotten that she needed to pick her up. "With your mother."

He didn't take his eyes off her, registering what she said. "Why is she still with my mother?"

How could she possibly hide what happened from him? "I forgot to get her. Would you call your mother and ask her if she will keep her for the night? We can get her in the morning before we leave."

He slowly lowered his arm, the look on his face growing suspicious. "Eva, why did you forget to pick her up?"

Eva viciously fought back the tears that pulled in her eyes. She looked down at her hands, focusing on her bruised knuckles, feeling the throb in her cheek. "I don't know how to do this, Wilhelm." Her voice was shaky, betraying her feelings.

He came and sat on the edge of the bed beside her. He, too, looked at her hands before finally taking one in his. "How did you get this?"

She had had all she could take. It was like everything she endured during all these years came at her today, every emotion, every hurt, every betrayal. Everything she had lost and will lose, and now Lina, who is dead because of her. But if she had saved Lina, it might be her at the bottom of the river or, like Lina said, hanging from a pole in the square. She let her tears fall, no longer trying to hold them back. "I can't. I don't have the strength for this. I want to go home." She cried harder. "I want to go home." He scooted closer and pulled her into his arms. She looked up at him with red-rimmed eyes, and he stopped breathing when he saw her bruised cheek. Wilhelm studied his gaze on her, his face full of unspoken emotions, but he reigned them in and remained calm for her, hugging her harder, willing her not to cry.

She didn't know how long he had held her like that before he spoke. "I will call my mother. She will be happy to keep Charlotte overnight." He let go of her and went to the phone.

She watched him pick up the receiver and turn the rotary dial. He wasn't on the phone long before he replaced the receiver. He returned to the bed and pulled her next to him, then covered them both up. He didn't ask her any more questions, but she knew he would later. At least she didn't have to talk about it right now. She fell asleep quickly, and he continued to hold her as he watched her sleep.

That morning, Eva woke, still slumbered beside him, her legs entwined with his, her head on his chest. She focused on her hand, which was curled into a ball on his stomach. His breathing was shallow and even, and she felt the rise and fall of his chest. Slowly, she lifted her head and looked at his face to see if he was still sleeping. His eyes were closed, and his face was relaxed. Gently, she moved her leg off his and sat up, then slipped out of bed. She got some clean clothes and went to the bathroom, locking the door. She did not want him to see that she was pregnant. She didn't want him to know until she was ready to tell him and until she had a better idea of what their future would be.

As she let the water cascade over her, she looked over her body, noticing bruises that she had not seen last night. She showered quickly, then stepped out of the tub onto the mat. She dried off and picked up her underwear when the doorknob turned. She froze, staring at it as if the lock would fail, fear pulsing through her.

"Eva, why do you have the door locked?"

She hurried, slipped her underwear on, put on her bra, and grabbed her dress from the bathroom counter.

He tapped on the door. "Eva?" The concern was evident in his voice.

She had to answer him, or he might break the door down, thinking something was wrong. "Habit, I guess," she told him as she pulled her dress over her head.

Now that her stomach was covered, she unlocked the door. Wilhelm was standing just on the other side, his face severe and his eyes narrowed.

"Our train leaves soon." He checked his watch. "So you have fifteen minutes to explain to me what happened last night."

She took in a deep breath, preparing herself. "I can tell you while I do my hair." She walked past him out of the bathroom and put her gown in her suitcase. She sat at the small desk by the window and started brushing through her wet hair. When she spoke, she didn't look at him standing behind her in the mirror.

"I was walking back across the Molteke Bridge last night when I ran into someone from my past. She and I weren't exactly friends. She had always hated me and thought that I had been eliminated. Those were her words. You see, she was in the resistance with me, except she was the traitor who gave us up to the Gestapo. I'm sure you know her name. Lina Schubert." She finally looked at Wilhelm in the mirror. She could tell that the name registered in his memory.

"I had seen her name in the file for the Berlin resistance."

His mood was very guarded, but Eva thought she could see regret in his eyes. "She attacked me on the bridge, and in the struggle, she lost her balance and fell over the side into the river.

The fall knocked her unconscious, and I watched her sink under the water." She left out the part where she had an opportunity to help her but made the decision not to.

He looked at her crestfallen face. "I am sorry, Eva. I never thought this would come back to you. I wasn't aware that there was animosity between the two of you. After we captured the names on the list, I never thought about the person who gave them up again. I didn't know I needed to be concerned with her, but I should have looked into her a little bit closer."

"I feel like I'm moving closer to my demise every day. I'm going to suffer a death made by a thousand cuts."

"Is that what you meant last night when you said you can't do this anymore?"

"That and everything else. It's all too much. Pebbles keep getting added to the bucket, and now it is too heavy for me to carry. I can't lift it anymore."

He came to her side and squatted down next to her. "That is why I am here, to carry the bucket for you."

The tears blurred her vision. She didn't want him to have to carry her burdens for her. It was taxing, and she couldn't ask that of him any longer. He was the most stoic person she had ever met, but it wasn't fair to him that she constantly pulled from his strength and leaned on him for support.

"It is time for me to fight my own battles. I will just have to get stronger so I can lift the bucket."

"Just because someone is strong doesn't mean they don't get tired and need someone to help them once in a while."

"I know that, but you have carried it for me for too long. And the guilt I feel at letting you has weighed on me for a while. I was just too weak and afraid to do it myself. It's just... that we are drowning in death. It's all around us, and it will only get worse. I'm not strong like you. I don't want to see any more starving people or destroyed cities. There is none of that back home. I just want it to end, all of it."

"I always suspected the bombs sounded like music to your ears because they will end the war sooner."

"No, they do not. I never want to hear another bomb. I'm tired of being stuck in this storm of violence, surrounding us from every side like a never-ending darkness we cannot find our way out of."

He rested his hand on her thigh and leaned in, kissing her bare knee. "I cannot send you home to America, but I hope that moving you from Paris to the country will allow you some solace."

She rubbed her hand through his hair, and he closed his eyes. "It would bring me solace if you were coming with me."

"You know I can't. If I have to leave Paris, I will work in Berlin until I am reassigned."

"So we will be separated a second time then?"

"Yes, and it might be a long time before we see each other."

Her chest was tight, and her eyes burned. "So my choices are to separate from you or live with the destruction?"

"No, because you don't have a choice. You can't stay in Paris."

"But I could go with you to Berlin."

"To live back in this city? No. There is a reason I'm moving my mother out of Berlin and why I would never move you and Charlotte here."

His reasoning was sound, and how could she argue with it. The war was lost, and he knew it. They stayed like that until a clock on the wall chimed. He looked at it and then his watch.

"We have to go, or we will miss our train." He stood, and she got up from the chair and turned so she could retrieve her suitcase when he caught her by the wrist and pulled her into his arms. He held her to him tight and kissed the top of her head before laying his cheek on it.

She loved the feel of him, his warm, solid frame, and how his strong arms made her feel safe. She took a deep breath, his scent filling her nostrils, and she closed her eyes, content to stay this way forever.

Finally, he pulled away. "Let's go."

She nodded, picked up her luggage and purse, and followed him downstairs.

On the train ride back to Paris, they settled into an uncomfortable silence. Charlotte was on her lap playing with a toy as Eva looked out the window, and he sat beside them, going over papers and occasionally jotting something on one of them.

When the train pulled into the station, he stood without saying a word and pulled their bags down from the overhead rack. Eva placed Charlotte on her hip, and they stepped off the train and went to the waiting car. It took them to the apartment but kept the engine running out front, waiting to take Wilhelm to the Gestapo headquarters.

He kissed Charlotte on the forehead, then gave her a quick kiss on the lips. "I will see you tonight, and when I'm back, we will talk more about the move."

"Alright." After he left, she fed Charlotte and put her down for a nap. She closed the door and looked around at the apartment she shared with Wilhelm, hardly believing she was going to leave it and him. They hadn't decided on a date yet, but she knew it would be soon. His mother was leaving to go there tomorrow, and she would probably follow shortly after.

The phone rang, pulling her from her thoughts. She went to the table and picked up the receiver. "Hello."

"Hello, dear, how are you?"

She was surprised to hear Madame Blanc's voice on the other end. "I am fine, Renée. How are you?"

"I am well. Adele and I are going to Paris to collect the rent from my tenants, and we would love to see you while we are there."

"I would like that. When are you coming?"

"Tomorrow. We should be there around dinner time. You don't think your husband will mind if we steal you for one night, do you?"

"No, I'm sure he won't." Eva hated losing any time with him because it was so limited, but it had been a while since she saw Renée and Adele, and she didn't know when she would be in La Chapelle again. "Where would you like me to meet you?"

"We will just pick you up at your apartment."

"Alright, that would be fine. I will see you tomorrow."

She did anything she could to keep herself busy while waiting for Wilhelm to return home. She wanted to see him, but she was also anxious about the topic of her leaving.

Charlotte woke up, so Eva got her out of her crib and let her play in the living room while she vacuumed. Charlotte started crying, so Eva had to stop. She came and sat on the floor, and Charlotte walked to her and sat in her lap. Eva put her hands under Charlotte's arms and lifted her above her head. Charlotte laughed and squealed.

"Why isn't he home, huh?" She lowered Charlotte, then lifted her again to make her laugh, drool running down her chin. "Where is Daddy? Why is he late?" She put Charlotte back on the floor, then pulled the basket of toys from under the side table and dumped it out so she could play with them. Eva scanned the apartment. An empty awareness hung heavy in the air, and there was a lonely sinking feeling settling over her.

Charlotte threw one of her toys and started to cry again, distracting Eva from the feeling of dread that she could not ignore. She took Charlotte into the kitchen and fed her again, then put her in her crib.

She had cleaned most of the apartment, but suddenly she felt tired. It had seemingly come out of nowhere. She lay on the couch and covered up with the blanket, quickly falling asleep.

The softest pressure was on her lips, and she opened her eyes to see Wilhelm's hazel ones looking into hers. He moved back an inch but continued to keep their eyes locked for an intense few seconds.

"Hi."

She smiled up at him. "Hi."

He placed his hand on her side to lean in again and kiss her, but she was worried he would feel the bump, so she promptly moved his hand and kissed it. He blinked, seeming a little surprised by the action. He straightened but never took his eyes off her. "I got you a train ticket to Cologne for the 26th."

She ran the dates through her head. "That is in three days. Why am I leaving so soon?"

"Because the sooner you leave, the better. I fear that it will not be safe for you here or in France for much longer."

She knew precisely why he said that. "Renee called. She will be in Paris tomorrow and wanted to take me out for dinner. Is that alright, or do you want me to not go?"

"You can go, but you need to start packing your things tomorrow."

"I will. When will you come to Cologne?"

"I don't know. I wish I had an answer for you. Probably not for a long time. We will just have to make our last night count." His tone was light, and she could hear the seduction and want in it, but his smile was fleeting.

She placed her hand on his cheek and returned his smile. "We will." She knew he didn't want to worry her, but he had to be honest with her.

She made them dinner, but as they ate, it was quieter than usual. They both were feeling the pain of their inevitable separation. He helped her do the dishes and offered to put Charlotte down for the night. Eva took that opportunity to get ready for bed. When she came out of the bathroom, he was already lying on the bed. She crawled in beside him, and he pulled her into his arms. She laid her head on his chest, and he kissed her hair. She draped her leg over the top of his and fell into a gentle sleep.

She stirred in his arms and opened her eyes, squinting against the faint morning light coming in through the bedroom window. She lifted her head and looked at Wilhelm. He smiled at her, his eyes tired, and the shadow of his whiskers was dark on his face.

"I'll go make breakfast."

"I have a better idea. I know of this place that sells the best crêpes in Paris. We will eat breakfast there and watch the sun come up."

She gave a warm smile. "I think that sounds like a fine idea."

They quickly changed, and Eva took Charlotte out of her crib as gently as she could, hoping to let her sleep a little longer. Wilhelm carried the stroller down the stairs to the sidewalk, and Eva followed, then laid Charlotte in and placed a blanket over her. She had only woken up for a few seconds but then went back to sleep in Eva's arms.

They bought the crêpes at the little French bakery, then walked to Trocadéro Square, which was a large open area across from the Eiffel Tower. It was on a slight elevation which offered an exquisite and unobstructed view of the tower and the sun that would rise behind it.

They sat on a blanket and watched the orange glow crest just above the city. It was a magnificent sunrise, and she couldn't think of a better way to spend her morning than with him and Charlotte, watching the light illuminate such a beautiful city.

He was already in his uniform. That way, he could go to work straight from the park. "You know about my father and my stepfather, but I don't think you have ever really told me about yours."

She looked over at him. "Oh." She never really thought about it. She had talked with Gerhardt about him but not Wilhelm. "Well, me and my dad are very similar in many ways. I guess you could say we are kindred spirits. We have a lot in common."

"That must be nice," an edge of bitterness in his voice, not at her but at the memory of his own father and stepfather.

"It is."

"I can see why you want to return to your family."

She felt a painful jab in her chest. Wilhelm never had a kind, supportive father figure like she did. He had his mother, but that was all. His life was so different than hers. She thought back to when she had gone to the bathroom and overheard the conversation he was having with another officer. Wilhelm had told the other man that he had very little in common with her, and that was the truth. Yet they loved each other with an intensity that was rarely seen.

"I do want to go home, but… not like I once did." He looked up from his crêpe with only his eyes. He didn't say anything, but the way he looked at her spoke volumes. "Do you know what time you will be home?"

"No."

She took another bite of her crêpe and watched him. It wasn't just her who was struggling with the impending separation. She could tell he was too. Sometimes she still couldn't believe she had fallen in love with him. Until the day she died, she would cherish every moment they had together, and she would love this man forever. The way he made her feel and the way he loved her. But more than just that, he helped her get through this war. He had the ability to calm her soul and help her not feel so afraid, making her

464

more at ease with what was happening in the world. The crushing darkness she always felt was gone because he chased it away. He was her lover, her protector, and her best friend. She didn't mind being in his world now. She once compared it to him dragging her down to his hell, but this didn't feel like hell. It felt like heaven. She couldn't be this happy if she were in hell. She would fall to her knees and beg if that's what it took for this to never end. One lifetime with Wilhelm wasn't enough. It never would be. She wanted more time; she wanted a thousand lifetimes with him. She loved him completely, and she was addicted to the way he showed his love for him. The fire in his embrace, the passion in his kisses, the intense high she felt when he took her, the pleasure from him being inside her. The things he did for her that he wouldn't do for anyone else. For so long, she fought her feelings for him because her mind couldn't comprehend what her heart already understood. Her heart was already telling her what to do, but her mind resisted. She was glad that her heart won and not her mind. She gave up everything to be with him, which was still strange to her sometimes. The way in which she was brought up and the era she lived in taught women to be independent, that they didn't need a man, and to never be at the mercy of one. But that was precisely what she had done. She had fallen right into it. Only she didn't care; wherever he is at, that is the only place she wanted to be. That isn't how she imagined she would feel when she first saw his face in Madame Blanc's parlor. But look at her now, married to him, caring for one of his children while she was pregnant with another.

In spite of all the terrible things he had done, she still loved him and cared about what would happen to him. She couldn't help it. She had tried. By this point, she had accepted that a part of her would always love a part of him.

He wadded up the wax paper his crêpe was in. "I have to go to work now." He stood, and Charlotte cried from her stroller. He walked over to it and reached in, picking her up and holding her to his chest. He kissed her on the cheek as he bounced her. Her crying turned to sniffles as she looked at him. He pretended to eat her hand as he made munching sounds, and she squealed, laughing through hiccups.

Eva watched them from the grass. It brought her such joy to see them together. She hated that he would miss so much of her younger life. She stood and came to stand beside them.

"Papa has to go. Give me a kiss," he said to Charlotte in German. She leaned in and gave a slobbery kiss on the lips. "Oh, thank you." He handed her to Eva and wiped his mouth. He placed his hand on Eva's lower back and leaned in, giving her a soft kiss. Then he moved his mouth close to her ear. "I'll see you tonight." He pulled back and gave a wink before turning and walking in the opposite direction.

She felt butterflies in her stomach. She supposed this would be the night he found out she was pregnant and learned he was to be a father for a second time. She gave Charlotte some of the food she brought for her, then looked in the direction Wilhelm had walked, but he was already gone, disappeared into the distance. She was excited to see Renée but was more excited for tonight.

She pushed the stroller back to the apartment but was surprised to see Ingrid on the steps. "Ingrid, how long have you been waiting here?"

"A while."

"It's early. Why did you come at this hour?"

"Are you going to turn me away?"

Eva was surprised by her comment. "Of course not. Why would you say that?"

"I'm sorry I didn't let you know I was coming. I just needed to be with someone."

Eva sat beside her on the step, holding onto the handle of the stroller. "Why, what has happened?"

"I would rather not think about it right now. Can we talk about something else?"

"Sure. Let's go inside."

Ingrid helped Eva bring the stroller into the apartment, then sat on the couch as Eva put Charlotte to bed. "So what were you doing when I got here?" she asked when Eva returned to the living room.

Eva smiled. "Wilhelm took me to get crêpes, and then we ate them as we watched the sunrise."

Ingrid's face fell, and she pulled her brows together like she was internally struggling with something painful. "That sounds like fun. What are you going to do with the rest of your day?"

"I will be spending the evening with Renée and Adele. They are coming to pick me up later."

"Oh, can I come? I need something to keep me busy today."

"Of course, you can."

They talked for hours, and then Ingrid helped Eva make lunch. After they ate, they took Charlotte to the nearby park and then window-shopped. Eva was going to miss this city and the life she had built here with Wilhelm. But she would make a new one with him in Cologne.

"My legs are tired. Can we go back?"

"My feet are hurting too." Eva pointed to her shoes. "And these aren't helping. My feet are swollen and pushing on the inside of the shoes."

"That sounds painful. Yes, I think it's better if we go back."

Ingrid had asked if she could take a nap on the couch, and Eva told her she could. Ingrid said she would meet them at The Arch de Triumph at around seven. She was too tired to go with her when Madame Blanc arrived.

"How was your day, my dear?" Renée asked when Eva slid into the back seat beside her.

"It was good. Also, Ingrid asked if she could come. I didn't think you would mind, so I told her yes."

"I don't mind."

"She wanted us to pick her up at The Arch de Triumph at around seven. Will we be done in time?"

"Oh, I believe so. We will collect the rent from as many of my tenants as we can between now and seven. Then we can go eat, and I will collect the rest when we are finished."

"Don't forget your new property out of town," Adele reminded Renée.

"Oh yes, we can't forget that one."

Eva positioned Charlotte on the seat between them, then turned sideways to look at Renée. "You didn't tell me you bought property outside of Paris."

"Yes... well, I did... a while ago."

Renée seemed a little nervous. Eva wondered if there was something about this property Renée didn't want to tell her.

"Alright. We can go to that one too."

They collected the rent from four different properties, then picked Ingrid up across from The Arch de Triumph. They ate at an upscale restaurant because Renée insisted upon it, and Eva would have told her no, but it was just how Renée was.

They left the restaurant just after eight-thirty and headed out of town. Renée watched Charlotte play with a toy horse. "I am happy I got to see this little one again."

Eva smiled down at Charlotte. "She is a joy. How long will you stay in Paris?"

"Not long. I plan on returning home tomorrow."

"I leave for Cologne the day after."

"Are you happy about that?"

"I'm happy because it means I will eventually get to be with Wilhelm again."

"You don't know that. No one can know what the end of this war will bring."

"True, but that is what I think will happen."

"No, that is what you hope will happen."

Eva would let her win this one. Renée was a stubborn old woman, and there was no changing her mind.

Eva looked through the window as they drove. "How far out is this place?"

"Not much farther, I think. How far are we from the place, Adele?"

"Maybe ten minutes or so."

Eva noticed a strange glance that was exchanged between Adele and Ingrid in the front seat, and it made her uncomfortable. They sat in silence as the car bumped along the dirt road. Eva pulled Charlotte in her lap and held onto her tight, a strange feeling coming over her. She watched out her window as they drove into nothingness. Not a single light could be seen outside, only an inky black.

The car finally pulled off the road into what looked like a field, but Eva could barely make anything out. They drove for another minute, then stopped, and Adele put the car into gear and shut the engine off. Eva pressed her face to the window but saw nothing except the silhouette of trees in the distance. She leaned back in the seat.

"There isn't a house out here. Where are we?"

There is something we want to show you," Adele said from the driver's seat.

Adele and Ingrid stepped out of the car, and Ingrid came to Eva's door and opened it for her. "Get out. Let's see what they want to show you."

Ingrid was acting strange, and Eva didn't know why. Cautiously, she stepped into the grass, and Ingrid closed the door. They walked a few yards in front of the car where Adele and Renée were standing.

"What did you want to show me?" No one answered, so she asked again. "Renée, why are we here?" She said a little louder, the panic rising in her.

"Hello, Eva."

She peered past Renée into the darkness. "Klaus?"

470

Chapter Twenty-Four
ॐ

May 24, 1944

"What are you doing here?" She glanced nervously at everyone, then at Klaus again. "What is going on?"

"A plane is coming tonight," Lorelei Vogel's voice cut through the quiet night air. "And you are getting on it."

Panic shot through her like a thousand knives. "I am not," she said in outrage before turning back to the car, but Ingrid stepped in front of her. "It's alright, Eva. I'm getting on the plane too."

Someone turned on a flashlight, and Eva turned her head, focusing on Klaus, Lorelei, Adele, and Renée, who were all staring at her. "Have you all lost your mind? I am not getting on that plane." Tears pulled in her eyes. "I can't believe you are a part of this, Klaus."

He took a few steps and stopped in front of her. "I love you like my own daughter, which is why I am here. Sometimes it's necessary to save someone from themselves."

Hot tears flowed freely now. "But I can't leave Wilhelm. I love him. Please don't do this, Klaus! Please!"

"Even love has its limits. The war is lost, and you can't stay here for him. We knew he would never let you go and that you would never leave of your own accord. That is why we had to do it this way. I will force you into the plane if necessary, but I hope I won't need to."

She turned to Ingrid. "You are a part of this too, aren't you."

Ingrid's eyes glistened. "I'm sorry, Eva. I'm sorry we had to deceive you like this, but you must go. You, Charlotte, and your unborn child will all be safer in England. You will be better off there. Please understand. We are all doing this because we care."

"Do not tell me how I will be better and that you care," Eva yelled. She couldn't fight the sinking feeling that was consuming her, pulling her down, deeper and deeper into the depths of despair. She shook her head and took a step back, away from everyone, the weeds scratching at her ankles. "No, I won't go. You all believe he is a bad person, but people can change. He has changed. And children need both of their parents."

Plane engines echoed in the distance, and they all turned their heads to look in the direction the sound was coming from. Her breathing increased as she became more desperate. Without warning, Lorelei came towards Eva and, put her hands under Charlotte's arms, and tugged.

"No! Stop it!" Eva screamed at her. Lorelei pulled harder, removing Charlotte from Eva's tight grip, then handed her to Ingrid. Eva fought wildly, trying to get past Lorelei to Charlotte. "Give me my baby, give me my baby!"

"No one is going to hurt Charlotte," Klaus told her in a gentle, low voice as he came to help Lorelei calm her. "But she is getting on the plane, and if you want to be with her or see her again, then you will get on too."

Eva choked on her tears, everything around her spinning. "How could you do this to me? You, the person I trusted the most, whom I love as much as my own father. You all deceived me and lied to me. Every one of you is so much worse than the man you profess to be, the devil, the man you think you are saving me from."

"Everybody does what they have to in order to survive and to protect those they love." Klaus stared at her, his intense eyes boring into her's.

"You don't love me. None of you do. Wilhelm is the only one who loves me. I can see that now."

"I hate to be the bearer of unpleasant news, but he will not survive this war." Klaus's voice was solemn.

Eva shook her head. "You don't know that."

"Yes, I do, and so do you."

"He will fight to save his life, if for no other reason than for Charlotte and me."

"Though that might be true, it won't be enough. Even if it was enough, he won't. His ideals are what is important to him. Do you really think that bloodthirsty brute of a man is tortured by a conscience? He has combat charisma, is a skilled fighter and a fierce leader, and is unwaveringly loyal to Germany. Those are the only qualities he has and the only positive things I can say about him."

"No, I won't listen to any more of this."

"You shouldn't stay here, Eva. We are German, and you are American. We belong here, and we will be judged by our actions as individuals as well as our actions as a country, but you don't have to be a part of that. No one ever needs to know what you did here."

The plane touched down in the field and headed straight towards them. All eyes turned to watch as it grew closer, and Eva used the distraction to pull free of Lorelei. But she didn't get far before Klaus grabbed her, holding her arms tight. Unlike Lorelei's grip, she knew she could not break free of his.

The plane turned just before it reached them, facing the other direction, then came to a stop, and the door opened. A man hopped down into the grass and assessed the people standing around. "Which one of you is Lorelei Vogel?"

Lorelei stepped forward. "I am."

"We have two crates."

"Yes, we were expecting them. You said you could take three passengers?"

"We can. Who is going?"

Lorelei pointed to Ingrid. "Her and the child she is holding." She then pointed to Eva, who was still being held by Klaus. "And her."

"Very well. Get them on the plane."

Eva pulled against Klaus' firm grip to no avail. Adele went to the trunk of the second car that had been there when they arrived and retrieved two suitcases and two small bags. She put a strap over each shoulder and picked up the suitcases, carrying them to the plane. She handed them to a man on board, then Ingrid started for the open door.

"No, Ingrid. Give her to me, please, I beg you!"

Ingrid turned and looked at Eva, her face full of sorrow. "I'm sorry, Eva. I'm so sorry. But this is what is best." As they helped her onto the plane, Charlotte started to cry, holding her arms out for Eva. Eva screamed, cried, and fought even harder, but it was useless.

Once both crates were off the plane, Klaus let go of her, and she whirled around to face all of them. "I will never forgive any of you." She looked to Klaus. "You broke my heart."

His eyes were watery as he stared back at her, his lips pursed tight against the emotions. "It doesn't matter. You will finally be safe and away from that awful man. I can take comfort in that knowledge."

She looked to Renée. "I should have expected nothing less of you. I underestimated your hatred for the Germans." She then turned her gaze to Adele. "Bravo, you have finally won. The war is all but lost, and in the end, you got me away from the Germans you despise so much. Wilhelm is a high-ranking officer who wields a lot of power. The war isn't over yet. As a matter of fact, it will go on for at least another year. You know that he will come after you and Renée for this?"

"I do."

He will want me back."

"Of course, he will," she replied in a tone someone would use when speaking with a child. "You have his daughter."

"And his unborn one," she spat back.

Adele's eyes grew wide. "I didn't know. But now I am even more convinced that it is a good idea for you to go to England."

"You are taking away his opportunity to see his unborn child. You are a cruel woman. You and the Germans, you deserve each other."

"We have to leave now," the man shouted over the engine noise.

"Go, Eva," Klaus insisted.

She looked between the plane and him, torn. Fresh tears filled her eyes, then she finally ran to the plane, and the man inside helped pull her into the cabin. She turned and looked through the still open door, knowing this was the last time she would see any of them ever again. That thought made her cry more. She was angry at Klaus, but she still loved him. He lifted his hand in a wave, gave a single nod, then dropped his arm to his side but never took his eyes off her. She stared at him until they closed the door, her legs giving out from underneath her as it clicked shut. She collapsed to the floor, and the man standing beside her helped her to her feet. He guided her to where Ingrid and Charlotte were sitting and gently sat her down. She looked over at Ingrid, who was still cradling Charlotte in her arms. Eva put her head between her legs and covered her face with her hands. She screamed and cried, hoping she would wake up from this horrible nightmare.

The plane had been in the air for more than twenty minutes now, and they were over the Channel. Eva had her head leaning against the side of the plane, staring at the wall across from her. She went through cycles of feeling numb, utterly consumed by her sadness, confusion, and then a wave of boiling anger from their betrayal. She wondered if Wilhelm was home now, wondering where she was. Worried, sick out of his mind, searching for her.

Did he think she left him? Oh God, did he think that? She didn't believe she could live with herself if he thought she had abandoned him, taking his child with her.

The plane shook and rattled from the turbulence, and Charlotte whimpered. Eva looked over at her little round face, her eyes red from crying. She reached for her, and Ingrid loosened her grip. She pulled Charlotte onto her lap and hugged her tight against her chest then buried her face in Charlotte's hair and cried. It was the only way she could bare the pain. She was leaving so much behind. Europe had been her home for the last five and a half years, and she would miss it. But even more than the land, she would miss all the people who touched her life in so many ways.

One of the men came to her side and knelt, speaking loudly over the roar of the engines. "We are almost there. We should be landing in about ten minutes, so prepare yourselves." Eva nodded, then he stood up and went back to his seat.

Eva looked over to Ingrid. "Where are we going to stay when we get there? What will we eat? Do you know any of this, or are we going to be left standing on a landing field, cold and alone in the middle of the night?"

"No. Jon is expecting us. He should be waiting at the field when we arrive."

This jolted Eva. She had not thought about Jon. Was he part of this too? "How did Jon know we were coming?"

"Lorelei Vogel informed him."

So he wasn't part of the great deception. At least she had him now. Eva was so tired she felt sick, and all she wanted to do was fall over and sleep. She would rest tonight and figure things out tomorrow.

The plane descended, and the tiny sudden drops made her tense, and she held Charlotte even tighter. It touched down, and everything inside the cabin shook and swayed. The plane taxied for a few minutes, then the engines were turned off, and the aircraft stopped. The door opened, and a man looked inside.

"Are these the passengers?"

"Yes, sir."

"Good. The German will come with me, and the American and her daughter can go home with Jon Tolly. Tomorrow, we will start their briefing."

Eva's gaze darted to Ingrid, wondering what was going to happen to her? She quickly stood. "Where are you taking her?"

"To a barrack on base, and tomorrow she will be briefed."

"What do you mean, briefed?"

"She is a German, and you have been living in Europe for years. We have to know what you did there. But we will discuss all of that tomorrow. The man that is here to pick you up is waiting."

Ingrid stood and looked nervously between the man and Eva. "What is happening?"

"There is nothing to worry about. They are putting you in a barracks tonight so you can get some rest, then tomorrow they will have a talk with you, like an interview."

"You mean an interrogation."

"Yes, in a way. Not like the Gestapo would, though, don't worry. They won't be mean to you. Trust me, you will see me again. Just go with this man, and don't try to resist. They are going to interrogate me tomorrow as well."

"But where are they taking you?"

"Jon is here to get me. The reason you have to stay here and I get to go with him is because I'm American and you are German. You have to understand."

"I do understand." There was a look of annoyance but also concern on her face.

The man helped Eva and Charlotte off the plane first, and then Ingrid. Another man passed down their luggage once they were off. A British officer who had been waiting approached Ingrid. "Come with me."

"She doesn't speak English," Eva told him. "He wants you to go with him." Ingrid nodded. "Oh, and Ingrid. Is that what you were doing at my apartment when I left you there?" She tilted her head towards the suitcase.

"Yes. And I want you to know that I packed all the important things."

Eva creased her brows. "What do you mean?"

"I mean, I packed the teddy bear he gave you, the dried flowers, The Wizard of Oz, Sabina's bear, and all the other things Wilhelm gave you."

The mention of his name and the things he gave her brought on a new wave of emotions. Her eyes and nose burned with the tears she tried to hold back. "Thank you."

Ingrid's eyes glistened. "You are welcome."

The man took her by the arm and led her away, and Eva watched as yet another person she loved was taken from her, even if only for now. Charlotte had her head lying on Eva's shoulder and was fast asleep, her little arms dangling beside her.

Eva followed the British soldier across the brightly lit airfield towards a chain link fence that surrounded it. Just on the other side of the fence, she could see Jon leaning against the hood of a car, his arms crossed over his chest. He was wearing a brown suit, brown shoes, and a grey felt fedora hat. When he saw Eva, he straightened, unfolding his arms. Once the soldier opened a gate in the fence and led her through, she rushed to Jon, and he sprinted towards her. They embraced, and she allowed herself to fall apart in his arms.

The man set her bags at her feet and promptly left. Jon moved away and put his hands on her cheeks. "Are you OK? How was the flight?" His eyes bore into hers. "Eva, I'm so sorry?" He felt like he had to ask and tell her everything at once.

"No, I am not OK," her voice quivered. She looked around at the British fighter planes lined in neat rows in the distance and the distinctive British landscape that surrounded the field. "I don't want to be here. I didn't want to leave. Jon, I didn't want to leave him. He has to know I'm missing by now, and he thinks I left him." She couldn't hold the tears back. "He thinks I betrayed him again, but this time in the worst possible way. He probably believes that I took everything from him. His whole world is gone in a single moment."

"It will be alright, Eva. We'll figure things out."

She shook her head. She was so sleepy that her mind was foggy, and she could hardly think. "Can we go?"

"Yes. Yes, of course." He picked up her bags and put them in the trunk, then hurried and opened her door for her and patiently waited as she got in while still holding Charlotte in her arms. He closed the door and came around to the driver's side. He started up the engine and pulled out of the parking lot.

Like a zombie, she stared out the windshield at the English town of Dover. She had never been here and never thought she would. She looked to her left at the Channel, and the tears built in her eyes. Wilhelm was just over that narrow body of water, but he felt a world away. She would swim across it if she could, just to get back to him, to the man she loved. She wiped her nose with the back of her hand and the tears away with her fingers. Her head throbbed from all the crying and the stress of the last few hours. Her eyes hurt and were puffy, and the tears blurred them.

Jon pulled in front of a tiny, narrow brick house and shut off the engine. He looked at her in the passenger seat." This is where I live. It's not much, but I have a spare room for you and your daughter. I don't have a crib for her, though."

"That's alright. She can sleep with me."

He retrieved her bags from the truck and unlocked the front door. They went inside, and she followed him up a narrow flight of stairs covered with worn brown carpet. The house smelled old and musty and of stale smoke and ash from the fireplace.

When they reached the top of the stairs, Jon turned to the right and entered a small bedroom. It looked like it had once belonged to a little girl. The walls were covered in lavender wallpaper, and the duvet was a light blush pink.

"Is this alright?"

"It's fine, Jon." Eva's voice was tired and strained.

"I will see you in the morning then."

"Goodnight."

Once he was gone and had closed the door, she broke down and cried. She cried until she had no more tears. She laid Charlotte on the bed, then went to her suitcase and opened it. Inside, there were clothes, baby toys, and on top were the dried flowers, Sabina's ragged teddy bear, The Wizard of Oz book, all the books Wilhelm gave her along with the America flag, the wooden box her necklace came in, the photo of her, Wilhelm and Charlotte, and the picture of Sabina, Sophia, and Fabien. There was also the stuffed animal Wilhelm won for her at the circus. *Thank you, Ingrid.* She took out the stuffed animal and a gown, then changed. When she was finished, she removed Charlotte's shoes and tights, put her in a clean diaper, and then got in bed, placing Charlotte against the wall and covering them up, clinging to Charlotte and the bear. She sniffed the bear's head, then pulled her gown up and sniffed it. Everything reminded her of him because it smelled like him, their apartment, and Paris. All the things that made her happy.

She cried on and off most of the night and sometimes even cried in her sleep, waking up with her face and pillow wet, as memories and dreams haunted her until morning.

Charlotte moved, and Eva jolted awake. For the briefest second, she thought Wilhelm was beside her but realized he wasn't before she even opened her eyes. Slowly, Eva lifted her lids and looked to the window at the foot of the bed. The sky was gray and dim in the early hour as a morning mist hung over the town, and she wondered what time it was. She sat up, trying not to wake Charlotte, and picked up the clock on the nightstand. It read 6:47, and she stared at the second hand as it moved, trying to register everything that had happened to her in the last twelve hours.

She heard a noise downstairs and knew Jon was up. She pushed the blanket back and put her feet on the faded rug beside the bed. Eva turned and looked behind her at Charlotte. She was still fast asleep, and Eva knew she wouldn't wake up for hours. She took the house coat from the suitcase Ingrid packed and slipped it on, wrapping it around herself and tying the belt. She quietly left the room and made her way down the squeaky stairs. She found Jon in the kitchen making eggs, and there was a plate of toast and cheese already on the table.

He turned to look at her. "Good morning. How did you sleep?"

"I'm not sure you could really call it sleep."

He placed the eggs on two plates and carried them to the table. "I'm sorry. I know you are tired, but you have your debriefing today, so we need to prepare you."

She sat down in the chair where he put the plate. "Prepare how?"

"Well, you will need to lie about who Charlotte's father is. Did you look at the documents yet?"

She furrowed her brows. "What documents?"

"The ones Ingrid put in the bottom of your suitcase. She put your marriage license, Charlotte's birth certificate, and your old ID with your maiden name on it, as well as a fake birth certificate for Charlotte. It has your maiden name as her last name and doesn't list a father. You need to hide the real birth certificate and the ID you have in your purse with your married name. As far as they know, you never got married, and Charlotte's father is French."

"How am I going to convince them of that?"

"Because you were once Eva Abrams, and you lived in France for most of the war, so it is believable that her father would be a French man. There is no way they can test and see that you are lying. And take off that ring." He gestured with his chin as he spread jam on a piece of toast.

"I will hide it with the other stuff. What have you been doing this whole time while you've been here, Jon?"

"I work now for British intelligence."

"So that is how you know so much?"

"It is. We need to invent a French name for Charlotte's father because they will ask. All they need to know is that you were a nurse and that you worked with the resistance, nothing more. It will look good if they know that, but knowing you married one of the enemies and had his children, no one will look kindly on that. You were never in love with a German, and you were madly in love with your French lover who was in the resistance with you and died at the hands of the Gestapo. You hate the Germans with every fiber of your being, and you wouldn't be caught dead with one."

"I don't know if I can pretend something that is so far from the truth."

"You have to, Eva, you need to lie. You need to believe that you are this person, the Eva Abrams I just described so much that you dream it. You don't have a lot of time to practice and remember this information. But it should be fairly easy because a lot of it is the truth." He stood from the table, got a notepad and pen from the counter, and then sat back down. "What name do you want to use for your French lover?"

She considered this. She could use the name of someone she already knew, but that might be too easy for them to learn that she was lying. "Gaston is a common French name. It's about as generic as Bob."

"Good." Jon wrote the name on the notepad. "And what about the last name?"

"Let me think a little more on that name."

"Alright."

"Jon, there is also one other thing." She held her fork and stared down at her plate, not wanting to tell Jon about the pregnancy. She knew she had to but was dreading it.

"Yes...?"

"I am pregnant."

He stopped chewing and looked at her. "What?"

She still didn't look at him. "I'm around four months along, but Wilhelm doesn't know. I never had the chance to tell him."

He laid his fork on the plate and wiped his mouth with the cloth napkin that was in his lap. "When you talk to them today, don't tell them. It's not obvious to other people that you are pregnant yet, so I wouldn't say anything unless they ask. After today you will most likely never see them again."

"Jon, you know I can't stay here. I have to go back and find him."

"You can't go back to Germany."

"I can and I will. He was there, Jon, when my world was falling apart. He watched out for me, and made me feel safe and loved. He is my best friend, and I cannot turn my back on him now when he needs me the most."

485

"You think they will let a pregnant American woman go to mainland Europe while there is still a war?"

"I didn't necessarily mean while I'm pregnant, but in time I will go back. We both know when Germany surrenders and the war ends, so with that knowledge, I know when I can return."

"Eva, you can't be serious. You want to stay here in this time?"

"I didn't use to, but I do now."

He huffed. "I don't believe it. All this time, I stayed in the past for you, so I could find you, and now you don't even want to go back."

"I did, for years. That was all I thought about and tried to do, but now... things are different. I have a reason to stay. I am married, Jon. I have a daughter, and I'm pregnant with his baby. What would I tell my parents, huh? How would I explain any of this to them? You told everybody back home that I was taken and sold into human trafficking, so I guess you expect me to say that my children are a product of rape, which couldn't be further from the truth. Both of them were conceived from the act of love."

He scooted to the edge of his chair and put his elbows on the table. "I know that, and you know that, but lying to them would be necessary."

"I would not have to lie to them about my children if I didn't go back."

"No, I would have to lie to them and tell them you couldn't be found or died. Do you truly want to do that to your parents and brother?"

"Of course not, but what do you think it would do to Wilhelm if I left? I believe that for him, it would be the worst thing that could happen. He loves that little girl more than anything, and there is no doubt in my mind that Charlotte and I are his whole world. I love my parents and my brother, and I would give almost anything to see them again. Sometimes, I wish I could pick up the phone and call them just to hear their voices, but I had to choose between this life or my old one because I can't have both. People leave home and make families of their own. That is only natural, and that is what I have done. It doesn't matter that starting a family here wasn't my intention. It doesn't change that reality because my husband and children are who I belong with. And if that means staying here in 1940s Germany, then I will. It's not how I imagined my life would be, but this is my life now, and I can't change it. Since I came to Europe, my life has been chaotic, dramatic, and complicated. I used to know what I wanted, or at least I thought I did, but in all of this craziness, death, and suffering, I found what I truly wanted."

Jon leveled his gaze on her. "You want this?"

"Yes, I do now. I have suspected for a long time that he loved me, and I wanted him to, but how could I possibly have prepared for love's tenderness or its brutality? I feel like I have had every human emotion possible thrown at me, and at times I wasn't sure I could make it through another day, but it's made me stronger, and I have grown a lot from it. I wouldn't want to go back and do it all again, but I don't regret that it's all led me to him. There are these specific moments in our lives that are more significant and important than others, that seem to define who we are, moments we keep going back to in our minds, replaying them because we want to keep reliving them. My life before Wilhelm was so simple but boring and uneventful, and now, after I've met him," she paused, "there's just after. And now I don't want to live in a world without him. I feel like I've taken love heroin, and now I can never have it again. I am going through withdrawals."

Jon licked his dry lips. "Well, we know that love has the same effect on the brain as drugs, like heroin and cocaine. But, there are things you haven't considered. What if you can't find him, or let's say you do, but he is dead or in prison?"

"I don't know. I will have to cross that bridge if it comes up, but I can't stay here in England and not even look for him. When the war is over, I can more freely move through Europe."

Jon leaned back in his chair and sighed. "You know I can't just leave you here on your own."

"I will not let someone force me to leave a place or person ever again."

Jon met her fervent gaze. "I don't mean that I will try to make you leave. I mean I will stay here with you. You are the strongest person I know, but there is no need for you to do this alone. I'm here for you."

"You don't have to do that. You have done more than enough for me. Go home, Jon."

"Unlike you, I don't have a loving family waiting for me."

"But… what will you do if you stay?"

"I don't know. Maybe continue to do what I'm doing now."

"Live in England and work for the British government?" she asked, surprised at what he was suggesting.

"Maybe, who knows. But right now, neither of us has any certainty of what the last year of this war will bring for us." He gave a slight laugh. "It's funny, really. You and I know more about what the next year will be like for the people from this time and the years to come following the end of the war then we do our own lives."

Her lip pulled up into a smile at the irony of this. "You are right. We don't."

He looked at his watch. "You should wake Charlotte. We have to go soon. I told them I would have you there by eight for your interview."

She looked at Jon from across the table. Their future stretched before them, full of uncertainty.

Chapter Twenty-Five

June 18th, 1945

The last year had been one of the toughest Eva had endured in the six and a half years she had been here. The agony of waiting out the rest of the war, worrying about Wilhelm, not knowing what happened to him or where he was, and the overwhelming sadness of suspecting that for over a year, he has thought she left him and took Charlotte with her. The thought of this constantly ran through her head, some days causing her physical pain from it. And he didn't even know that he had a son. A little boy who was now seven months old whom she named Michael. He had never been to Germany and had never seen his father or his German grandmother. She had a picture of him taken right after he was born. She also had one taken of her, him, and Charlotte, and then another one a few weeks ago. She hoped to give them to Wilhelm when she found him. If she found him. She wanted to show Wilhelm how big Charlotte was getting and to see the son he had never met. Charlotte was almost two and a half now and was running all over the house. She enjoyed sitting with Michael, babbling to him. She had long hair that Eva kept in pigtails. She seemed to think that Jon was her father, which made Eva sad but relieved at the same time. Having Jon around gave Charlotte and Michael stability and the feeling of having a family. She and the children lived with Jon but in separate rooms. After she gave birth to Michael, they moved into a larger, three-bedroom house in Dover.

She looked at Michael as she pushed the stroller and smiled at him. She loved his little cherub cheeks with the dimples on each side. Jon walked beside her, holding Charlotte's hand as they made their way to Ingrid and Danny's house. Five months after they arrived in England, Ingrid married the British pilot she had come to England for. Eva continued to teach her English, and sometimes Danny helped, and now that more than a year had passed since she started learning English, Ingrid had become reasonably good at it. Danny, in return, was trying to learn German for Ingrid.

They stopped in front of the small cottage door. "Are you sure you are ready to do this?"

Eva drew in a deep breath and let it out slowly. "Yes." She nodded her head more to reassure herself than Jon. "I have been waiting a year for this, so I am ready. The only part I hate is leaving them. That is my only regret." She looked at Charlotte, who was still hanging onto Jon's hand as she clutched her stuffed bear in her other hand. "But I couldn't ask for better people to care for them while we are gone than Ingrid and Danny."

"Isn't it too soon for you to wean Michael?"

"No. The only thing babies can have for the first six months is milk, but after that, you give them milk and solids. I won't be here to breastfeed him, but Ingrid can give him goat's milk with his solid foods."

"He won't like that."

"I know, but he will get used to it." She felt like she was being torn in two. She wanted to find Wilhelm. No, she needed to find him, but she had never been away from her children. She hated leaving them, but she had to do this, and she couldn't take them with her.

"Alright then." Jon lifted the brass doorknocker and tapped it twice.

Danny opened the door and smiled when he saw them, but there was something else on his face beneath the smile. "Come on in. Ingrid is in the kitchen making tea and sandwiches."

Eva took Michael from the stroller and left it outside next to the door. She followed Jon into the house, and Danny led them into the parlor. Jon put the bag with the stuff for Charlotte and Michael on the floor, then sat beside Eva on the floral sofa and lifted Charlotte into his lap. She was quiet and still but looked around the room with her big hazel eyes. After a couple of minutes, Danny and Ingrid came into the parlor from the kitchen. Danny carried a plate with cubed sandwiches, and Ingrid held a silver tray with a teapot and four matching tea cups. They placed them on the coffee table, and then sat across from Eva and Jon.

"I can't believe you are really going to do this, Eva." Ingrid's face was a storm of emotions.

"I have to, Ingrid. You know why."

"I do. "

"He never leaves my thoughts. I loved him before, but somehow, I seem to love him even more with every passing day. I didn't even know that was possible." She spoke to Ingrid in German, knowing that Jon wouldn't understand anything she said and Danny would only catch a few words. "Please take care of my babies while I'm gone, and write me every few days."

"I will, I promise."

"Our flight leaves in an hour," Jon reminded her.

"I know."

They each quickly ate a sandwich and drank a cup of tea, then prepared to leave. Eva hugged Charlotte tightly, kissing her repeatedly. Eva told her that she was going to stay with Uncle Danny and Aunt Ingrid for a while and that she would be back soon to get her. She made sure to tell her that Ingrid and Danny would take her to see the horses, goats, and sheep in the field nearby. Charlotte loved animals; they made her happy.

Eva looked at Ingrid. "Michael is eating solids now, but he is picky. You must be persistent, and he will eventually eat it. He has never been fed from a bottle, so I don't know how he will take to one."

"I'll figure it out." Ingrid tried to give her a comforting smile.

Eva picked Michael up off the blanket he was sitting on and kissed him. She hugged him to her, telling herself she couldn't cry in front of Ingrid and Danny, that she at least had to wait until they were out the door. Finally, she handed Michael to Ingrid. "I'll call if I can."

"Don't worry, they will be fine. Do you have everything you need?"

Eva looked at Jon. "We do. It's already in the car."

"You better get going, or you will miss your plane," Danny said.

"I know." Eva gave Charlotte and Michael one more kiss, and then embraced Ingrid.

"You will find him, Eva. And he will believe you when you tell him you didn't abandon him," Ingrid whispered in her ear.

"I know."

She pulled away, and then gave Danny a quick hug. Jon shook Danny's hand and gave Ingrid a peck on the cheek. He opened the front door, and Eva gave Charlotte and Michael one more glance before the door closed. Eva barely made it a block when she could no longer hold back the tears. Jon handed her the handkerchief from his jacket pocket.

"Thank you."

"You and I have seen pictures and videos of what Europe, especially Germany, looked like at the end of the war, but it will still be shocking when we get there to see it in person."

"I know."

"The letter Sergei sent said that he was in a company heading into Berlin, correct?"

"Yes."

"Eva, I hope that you don't get your hopes up. He might not be able to find out what happened to Wilhelm."

"I know, but he is the best chance I have. I doubt the Americans or British are going to give me that information. They are not going to share that kind of knowledge with a civilian. And they would ask why I wanted to know the whereabouts of a high-ranking Nazi. But Sergei knows why, and he can find out for me without it looking suspicious. He has some wiggle room and carries a weight in this war that I do not. He doesn't have to be upfront with why he wants to know. It would be much easier for him to lie about it."

"But you don't know that he will. He agreed to meet with you, not find someone for you."

"I think he will. I need to believe that he will. I have to find Wilhelm, Jon, I have to." Fresh tears pooled in her eyes. "I know he is in trouble, and I have to do something. He saved me so many times, and now it's my turn to save him. I owe him my life. I pray every day that he isn't in Berlin and went home to Cologne, where the Americans are. I know there will be the Nuremberg trials, and even if the Americans get him, he will face that trial, but he just might survive it. If the Russians capture him, it is almost certainly a death sentence. If they don't kill him outright, he will be sent to the Gulag where he will suffer for the rest of his life or die of starvation, sickness, or from being worked to death." She was struggling to keep it together. "I have to save him, Jon. I have to."

He squeezed her hand. "We will do what we can."

Eva stared out the car window on the way to the airfield. Her mind was racing, and her heart thumped a slow and hard beat against her chest. She folded her hands in her lap to try and stop them from shaking. It had been a year since she had been in Germany or France, and she didn't know what to expect. She often found herself wondering how Klaus was, what he was doing, and if he still thought she was mad at him. If she dwelled too much on that night, it still upset her, and the anger she felt towards him, Renée and Adele resurfaced. But in truth, she was not still angry with him. What bothered her more now was that she never got to give him a hug or properly tell him bye. They parted on bad terms, and there wasn't a day that went by that she didn't wish that night hadn't ended the way it did. She had long forgiven Ingrid for the part she played. She had to, Ingrid and Jon were all she had now, and she couldn't let the anger she felt fester and destroy the friendship they had built over all those years. The thing she worried about the most was Wilhelm. The thought of possibly seeing him again was strange and made her anxious. She didn't know how he would act towards her or what situation he would be in. Would he be angry with her, or had he forgiven her a long time ago? Maybe the pain he endured would be etched on his face, and seeing him that way would tear her up inside. The one place she didn't let her mind go was the thought of him dead. She wouldn't even entertain it or give it power.

Jon pulled the car into the grass and turned off the engine. Eva opened her door and, stepped out onto the damp soil, and shielded her eyes with her hand as she looked at the plane. The bright morning sun reflected off the gray metal hall. Jon took their luggage from the trunk and walked towards the plane but stopped and turned when she didn't follow.

"Are you alright?"

"Yeah, it's just strange going back."

"I would be surprised if it wasn't a little weird for you."

She closed the car door and walked behind Jon towards the plane. He passed the luggage up and then gave her a boost. She was glad that she wore slacks and boots and not a dress. She didn't even bring any dresses with her, only pants and button-up shirts. Jon hopped up once she was in, and they sat on the side bench.

The flight was smooth and relatively quick. Unlike when she left France and the plane had to leave a grass field outside of Paris. This time they were flying into Calais, which was just over the Channel from Dover. She gripped the seat as the plane touched down and held her breath. Not because of the flight, but because in just a matter of minutes, she was going to be standing on French soil again, but for the first time since 1939, a France that was free of German control and German occupation. She wouldn't walk the streets of Paris and see German soldiers everywhere or the German flag lining the streets, or flying from a building or a light pole.

The plane turned off the engines, and Jon stood and opened the door. He came back to where they were sitting and got the two bags. "Are you ready?"

"Yes, I think so." She stood and went to the door with Jon. He dropped the bags onto the ground and then hopped down. He turned and held his arms up for Eva, and she leaned into him, and he placed his hands under her arms and helped her down.

"The driver should be waiting to take us to Paris. Our tickets are for the five o'clock train, so we will have a few hours before we leave for Germany."

"That's good. I wanted to look at the city before we left."

The car parked in front of 84 Avenue Foch like she instructed him to. "Why are we here," Jon asked.

"Because I need to see it again."

The driver retrieved their bags from the trunk, and she thanked him as Jon handed him some cash. Once the driver was in the car, Jon spoke. "I won't go back in there."

She turned away from the building to face Jon. "It's OK. I wanted to go in alone. Would you wait here with the luggage?"

"Sure."

"And when I come out, we will walk a few blocks up the street to the apartment I used to live in with him."

"You lived on this street?"

She looked around at the elegant buildings and expertly manicured lawns, and it was like she had never left, but it seemed like a foreign place to her at the same time. "I did. He tried to give me the best he could."

"He did well then," Jon mused as he looked up and down the street.

Eva made her way down the brick walkway to the front door and paused when she reached it. The feeling she was having was intense and deeply disturbing. She pulled open the door and stepped into the lobby. She could hear people in the building but didn't see anyone. She didn't want to be noticed by them, so she crept along the corridor. The building looked so different than it had a year ago when she was here. She knew the Germans cleared out before the Americans came, but the lobby looked like they had never even been there. She made her way up to the fourth floor where Wilhelm's office used to be. She peeked around the corner when she reached the top, but the hall was empty. She walked at a brisk pace to his office at the end. The door was open, and she stood in the doorway, peering into the empty room. Dust had collected on the floor, and it looked like people hadn't been in it for a long time. She looked to the spot his desk had once stood and remembered how he used to look sitting behind it. He had been intimidating when she first saw him there, like a calculated predator who might attack if provoked. He was the man in Paris everyone feared and that everyone hated.

She stepped onto the dusty wooden floor and went to the window, the same window that he always looked out of. She missed him so much, and the pain of being away from him for so long made her chest tight, clenching at her heart. She struggled to breathe normally, and her eyes burned with angry tears.

The sound of voices in the hall made her jump, bringing her back to the moment and pulling her from her thoughts. She hurried to the door and peered around the corner. Two men were coming in her direction, and she hoped they weren't going to his office. She leaned flat against the wall and waited, listening to them as the voices grew closer. They were talking about cleaning the building when one of the men said they should eat lunch before they started. They spoke in the hall for a few minutes before finally going back the other way and down the stairs. She let out the breath she had been holding and pushed away from the wall. She scanned the room one more time before leaving and heading to the sixth floor, where the people being interrogated were held.

She rubbed her finger along the white plaster wall of the hall. It was lined with narrow wooden doors that were all opened. She looked into every room she came to, some of the small spaces only having a bucket in the corner. A few rooms had writing on the walls, so she stepped inside one and read what it said. It was graffiti written by one of the prisoners about his time there. The hair stood up on her arms as she read it. She straightened and looked around the tiny room, wondering who the people were that Wilhelm kept here. These were the cells and interrogation rooms, and Wilhelm never would have let her come up here.

She went into several more of the rooms, seeing the evidence of the horrors that occurred here. She suddenly felt like the walls were closing in on her, and she had to get out, so she turned and ran from the room, down the hall and each flight of stairs until she reached the ground floor. She stopped once she was outside, taking in a deep breath. It was a lot to take in and to know that the person who was her whole world was responsible for the things that happened here, the acts of torture that were committed. She slowly made her way back down the brick walkway to Jon.

"Well...?"

"It was not what I expected. Did they keep you up there on the top floor?" She looked up at the windows at the top of the building that lined the sixth floor. "Is that why you didn't want to go in with me?"

He looked at his hands, each missing a few fingers. "Yes, he kept me up there."

"I'm sorry, Jon. I should have known." Her voice broke with the pain and sadness she felt for him.

"It doesn't matter now. I'll never get my fingers back or the emotional things they took from me."

Guilt gnawed at her. Here Jon was, in Paris, to help her find the man who had this done to him. He was a good person, better than either of them deserved. He was even helping raise the children of the man who tortured him.

"Let's go down the street to the apartment."

They walked the few blocks and stopped in front of the building that Eva used to call home. She stared up at the front door, remembering how there was a guard stationed in front of it when she lived there. All because she and Wilhelm lived in the building and could have been targets of the opposition.

"I wonder if anyone lives there now?" she mused.

"I don't know. You could always knock on the door."

She thought about whether or not she should and finally decided it was worth it. She ran up the steps, opened the front door that led into the foyer, and stepped inside. She turned to the left and looked at her old door. She lifted her hand and knocked a few times. She didn't hear anyone inside, so she knocked again. She tried the doorknob, but it was locked. She turned to the door of the apartment that faced it and knocked. Footsteps shuffled on the other side, and then a short, elderly woman opened the door a crack and looked up at her.

"Yes?"

"I'm sorry to bother you, but I was wondering if the apartment across from you is occupied. Do you know if anyone lives there?"

The woman narrowed her eyes at Eva, focusing on her face. "No, it is empty. There used to be a German who lived there, but he left a long time ago."

"Do you know when exactly it became vacant?"

The woman scrunched up her face in concentration. "I think his wife left him, taking their daughter with her. He moved out in June of forty-four, I believe."

Of course, he did. Eva wanted to ask the woman more but didn't think it was a good idea for her to. "Thank you."

She turned to walk away, but the woman spoke again. "Why did you leave?"

Slowly, Eva turned to her. "What did you say?"

"You are his wife. I had seen you here with him, and you have a little girl."

A strange feeling settled over her. "It wasn't my choice to leave him. I was tricked into it. My daughter and I have been living in England for the past year. Now that the war is over, I came back to find him."

"He isn't here. The Germans left Paris almost a year ago."

"I know. I leave for Berlin this evening. Do you know by any chance where he moved to when he left here?"

"I don't. Sorry."

"It's alright. He wouldn't be there now anyway."

The lady gave her a nod, then backed up into her apartment and closed the door. Well, this was not what Eva had expected. She went back outside to where Jon was.

"You were in there for a while. Did you get to see the apartment?"

"No. It's empty, but the woman who lived across the hall from us knew that I was his wife."

"Seriously? That could be dangerous, Eva."

"No, I don't think so. She told me he had moved out of the apartment not long after I left. Like I said, he only lived here because of Charlotte and me. He told me that he wanted to give me the best that Paris had to offer. I never wanted for anything while I was with him. He took such good care of Charlotte and me, and I never conveyed how appreciative I was."

"I think he knew."

"Really? He thinks I was so grateful that I left him and took his daughter away."

"Well, I guess maybe not now."

Eva stood on her tiptoes and peered through the window into the room that used to be their bedroom. She could only see the ceiling and the far end of the room but could tell there was no furniture in it. Being here was depressing because it reminded her of what she used to have and the life she shared with him. "Let's go to the train station. I'm tired and want to sit down."

Jon didn't say anything, only nodded his head. They picked up their suitcases and made their way to the tram that would take them to the train station.

Eva slept on the bench as they waited for their train to arrive, and Jon read a newspaper. She felt pressure on her arm as Jon gently shook her. "Eva, the train is here."

She sat up, blinking away the sleep, and looked around the platform. "How long has it been here?"

"It just arrived. We should get on."

"I agree." She got her things, and they walked to their car and stepped on board. Jon put the suitcases on the metal overhead rack and sat down, allowing Eva to sit by the window. The passengers already on the train unloaded, and the ones waiting were all on in a matter of minutes. After sitting at the station for another ten minutes, it jolted forward, leaving the Paris station.

Eva watched the French landscape pass by and kept to herself. She was afraid of what lay at the end of this journey but didn't want to tell Jon of her concerns. Her emotions were so turbulent she thought if Jon talked to her now that, she would start crying or hyperventilating. The anxiety attack she had managed to keep at bay all day was now an overpowering force, and she was struggling as it tried to completely take her over.

When they pulled into the Berlin station, the voice in her head repeated, please, please find him. She had decided on the train ride to Germany that she would try to find Klaus too if she could.

They stepped off the train, and she looked around her at all the destruction. The entire glass ceiling of the station was gone, and the platform was packed with people. Hundreds of soldiers who were waiting to go home and children without adults sat on the edge, hanging their legs over the side of the platform. It was chaos, and she hadn't even left the station.

Jon leaned in and spoke above the noise. "We'll have to walk. There will be no transportation."

Instead of yelling above the noise, she just nodded. They picked up their bags and made their way out of the station, but Eva wasn't prepared for what she saw, the complete and utter destruction of the city. Piles of rubble is what made up the city now, and scorched cars littered the streets. The air smelled of dirt and smoke that was still rising from some of the charred buildings, but that wasn't the most offensive scent in the air. The smoke was mixed with an aroma that turned the stomach. Rotting flesh permeated the city of Berlin, adding to the ambiance.

She and Jon walked along the road, stepping over bricks and distorted rebar still encased in concrete. There was distraction all around them. People covered in dirt sat on the streets, staring out over the vest decay of the city, their eyes vacant. Some people were trying to clean up the debris, and a few people were gathered in the street playing instruments. The music playing but a lack of normal city noise like trains and cars gave the atmosphere an eerie feeling. Berlin wasn't Paris and didn't hold the same place in her heart as that city did, but still, it saddened her in a profound way to see it like this. The beautiful city she remembered from when she lived here had been reduced to nothing more than a vast pile of rubble.

She did a three-sixty and saw that the whole city was the same. The only building standing that would be saved was the Reichstag building, where Gerhardt and sometimes Wilhelm used to work. It still stood erect like a majestic symbol of the German people, though aerial bombs had blown gaping holes in the roof and bullet holes dotted the entire building, including the stone pillars that lined the front, but amazingly enough, the walls were still intact. Berlin was now only a skeleton of the city it once was.

The wind kicked up, blowing smoke and ash through the air, carrying the smell of the still-burning flames with it. It had been over a year since she had seen Berlin, and the way it looked now just showed her that time could change things so much that they were no longer recognizable.

Her heart dropped to the pit of her stomach, and her eyes blurred with tears. She felt for the German people, especially the people of Berlin. She wondered what all the other German cities looked like, especially Cologne, where Wilhelm was from.

"Are all the cities like this?"

Jon looked around them. "I believe so."

"Do you know if Cologne got it as bad as Berlin?"

"I think it is as bad, yes."

Wilhelm's mother had been living outside of Cologne, and Eva hoped with everything in her that Marie was alive and well.

"There are no street signs anywhere, and even if there where you can't tell what is what anymore. How are we supposed to find Sergei?"

505

"If I remember correctly, the Russians set up a base headquarters in the Reichstag. Let's try there first."

Entering the building this time would feel so different to her now, but she wasn't sure she would like this new feeling any more than the old one. As they made their way along the last few blocks to the Reichstag, the sight of something made Eva halt in her tracks. On the side of the road was a dead horse, and two men were standing over it, slicing meat from its body. She stared on in horror, unable to believe what she was seeing. Confused, chaotic anger mixed with sadness overtook her. Could it really be so bad here that the people of Berlin had to eat dead horses?

She looked at Jon, the shocked expression still on her face.

"It is bad, I know. But remember, it gets better."

"Not for a very long time. Jon, this is terrible. I know that they started the war, but these poor people. This is what they mean when they say it's always the innocent who suffer the most."

"Sadly, it is. Let's try and hurry. Crime was a real problem after the war, and we don't want someone to take what we have even though it isn't much."

They hurried along the street to the Reichstag and ascended the steps. When she looked down, she noticed that her once brown boots were now white from the rubble dust. All of this was so much worse than she had thought, and it was taking a more considerable toll on her emotionally than she had initially expected. When they reached the top of the steps, two Russian soldiers came toward them and said something in Russian. She looked to Jon, who held up his right hand and said he didn't speak Russian.

"Why are you here?" one of the Russian soldiers asked with a thick accent.

"We are looking for someone," Jon told him. "A Russian soldier name Sergei Ostrovsky. He is expecting us. Do you know where he is?"

"What do you want with him?" The expression on the soldier's face was severe.

"I'm a friend of his," Eva finally said. "We knew each other during the war. He sent me this letter informing me where I could find him." She held out the letter Sergei sent her in England. The soldier took it from her and slowly read it.

Finally, he looked up from the paper. "He is with the unit in the building across the street." He pointed behind them, then handed the letter back to her.

She took it from his outstretched hand. "Thank you." She and Jon made their way back down the stairs and crossed the street. Russian soldiers were milling all around them, and she watched them, all in their brown uniforms with the hammer and sickle symbol on their shoulders. It was so weird to her because she was used to seeing the field gray German uniforms, but the fact that the war had finally come to an end seemed so final to her now.

Two soldiers were standing at a makeshift desk talking and smoking when she and Jon approached. "Excuse me." Both men took the cigarettes from their mouths and looked in their direction. "I am looking for Sergei Ostrovsky. Do you know where he is?"

One man brought the cigarette back to his mouth, took a long draw on it, removed it from his mouth, and blew out the smoke. "He is over there." The man gestured with a tilt of his head to the right at a group of men sitting at a table doing paperwork.

"Thank you." She picked up her suitcase and walked toward the table. Several of the men looked up when Eva and Jon were close, and one of them was Sergei. She picked him out from the others almost instantly.

When he looked up, he didn't seem to realize who she was at first, but then recognition lit on his face. He laid down his pencil and stood. "Eva!"

She gave him a warm smile. "Sergei."

Chapter Twenty-Six

June 20th, 1945

Eva paced the floor of the dusty, cramped room, unable to sit. "It has been two days, and I still don't know where Wilhelm is."

"Don't worry. Sergei said he would find out, and he will. We knew it could take a while when we came here, so be patient."

"I have been patient. I have waited for more than a year to find him."

"I understand, but we will know soon. Sergei said he would inform us as soon as he found something out."

She sighed and went back to the bed, plopping down and staring at the peeling wallpaper. "I feel like with every passing hour, my chances of saving him diminishes. I can't stand this feeling, Jon. The feeling of being helpless. The only thing that keeps me going is the idea that there is still hope that I will find him and that maybe I can do something to help him."

"I know, Eva. I do understand. I don't like it anymore than you do."

A knock sounded on the door, and Eva bolted to her feet, almost running to the door. She pulled it open and let out a relieved breath when she saw Sergei. "Did you find him?" He hesitated, and she held her breath. "What, what is it?"

"Can I come in?"

"Yes, sorry." She moved aside, and he stepped into the room. She closed the door and looked at him, feeling like she would burst if he didn't say something in the next second.

Sergei's eyes darted to Jon, then back to Eva. He cleared his throat and then spoke. "Yes, I did find him." Eva drew in a sharp breath, and her eyes watered. She was both relieved and afraid, afraid for the next thing he would say. "But...," she tensed, "he is imprisoned in the Sachsenhausen Concentration Camp."

She felt like her legs might buckle beneath her. "What?" Her voice was shaky and barely above a whisper. Jon came to sit by her side in case he needed to catch her.

"Can we see him?" Jon asked.

"I don't know. The prisoners there are not permitted any contact with the outside world. It's what we call a special camp or silence camp."

"Could they maybe make an exception for her?"

Eva listened to the men talk, but she couldn't speak. She could barely breathe; her chest was so tight, like someone was sitting on it, and the room felt like it was spinning around her. She honestly thought she might pass out.

"It is still the early days of the camps, and I have seen them let a few prisoners have visitors from time to time. They aren't supposed to, but a few guards do if the price is right."

"So if we bribe a guard, she might have a chance of getting to see him?"

"It's possible. I can find out which guards break the rules and see what they would want in exchange. I'll try and find out as soon as I can."

Sergei turned to the door. "We will be waiting here," Jon told him.

Eva walked to the bed and sat on the edge. "I don't know what to do," she choked out. "Do you know what they do to prisoners in those camps?" She looked at Jon through the tears that were blurring her vision.

"I do. Sadly, the Germans there weren't treated any better than the people they imprisoned in those camps. Thousands of Germans will die in those kinds of camps from starvation and disease, but many died from torture or execution. Their health was completely neglected."

She broke down and sobbed, unable to hold it back any longer. "I have to fix this, Jon. I have to get him out."

"How are you going to do that? You can't have him broken out like you did me."

She looked up at him with her red, bloodshot eyes. "Tell me what you think is going to happen to him?"

He shook his head. "You won't like it."

Her lip quivered. "Don't say that." She shook her head, glaring at him.

He came and sat beside her on the bed. "We have to prepare ourselves for the worst. Why don't you lay down and try to get some sleep."

"I don't think I can sleep."

"You should try. Lay down." She did, and he went to the little kitchen to make them something for dinner.

She almost rolled off the bed when there was a knock on the door. Jon went and answered it, letting Sergei in.

"What did you find out?"

"There is a guard there tonight who is willing to let her in for the price of ten packs of cigarettes."

"Ten packs? Right now, you can barely get ahold of one."

"I know, but that is his price."

Jon let out a breath. "I will try to make it happen. If I can manage to get ten packs of cigarettes, where should I bring them?"

"I will be in the building you found me in two days ago. Hide the cigarettes in something so no one can see what they are. They are like food, and if anyone sees you with them, they will not hesitate to take them from you."

"I understand. I will meet you there." Sergei shook Jon's hand and then left. Jon turned to Eva. "I'm going to go see if I can buy ten packs of cigarettes. Wait here, and I will try to be back soon."

She slid off the bed. "I'll come with you."

"No, Eva. Stay here. Let me do this alone. The streets aren't safe, and I don't need your help to do this."

They stared at each other for a long moment. Finally, Eva nodded, not having the energy to argue with him. Jon took a wad of the money they brought and left the little studio apartment they were sharing.

She finished making the potato soup Jon had started, sat at the little table, and ate alone. She couldn't hold back the sinking feeling in her gut, the little voice in the back of her head telling her something awful was going to happen. She wanted to shout and tell it to stop, but the more she suppressed it, the louder it seemed to get.

She paced the apartment and kept checking the window to see if Jon was outside. When the front door opened finally opened, she jumped. Jon came in quickly and shut it behind him. She looked at him expectantly, praying that he got what they needed.

He pulled up his shirt to reveal cigarette packs around the waist of his pants. "I got them. Let's go." She grabbed her purse and followed him through the door. They went to the building where Sergei was, and Jon showed him the cigarette packs.

"My God, I can't believe you actually got ten packs."

"It wasn't easy. Some people asked for exorbitant prices, but I paid it."

Sergei checked his watch. "Let's go then." He said something to the other soldiers in the room, then he grabbed his jacket, and Eva and Jon followed him to a car with a red star and the hammer and sickle painted on the door.

Eva climbed into the back seat, and Jon got in the front with Sergei. They headed north, weaving around the rubble, and made their way out of the city. The sky was quickly growing dark, so Sergei turned on the headlights as he drove. Eva looked down at her hands as the car sped forward, drawing her ever nearer to her reunion with Wilhelm.

Are you OK? Are you safe, Wilhelm? she wondered as both determination and dread mounted inside.

Eva was trying to remain calm in the backseat, but when she saw the wall of the Sachsenhausen Concentration Camp come into view with its curved poles strung with barbed wire fence, she almost lost it. The reality of the situation and what she and Wilhelm both faced hit her like a Mac truck. It looked so imposing, dark, and depressing and was the only building in sight.

The car pulled up to the wrought iron gate that read 'Arbeit Mache Frei.' A man came to the side of the car, and Sergei rolled down the window. They spoke in Russian for a few seconds, then the man looked in the backseat and then at Jon.

Sergei turned to Jon. "This is the man who is going to let us in. He wants the cigarettes first, though."

"Of course," Jon said in understanding. He lifted his shirt and pulled out all the packs, handing them to Sergei, who then gave them to the man. The man smiled, his yellow cricked teeth glinting in the bright lights of the camp. He went to the gate and opened it, then waved the car through. Sergei put it in gear and drove into the courtyard of the camp. He turned off the engine and got out, as did Jon, who then pulled the seat forward for Eva. She stepped out and looked around at the brightly lit courtyard with the multiple rows of barracks.

The man said something to Sergei. "He says to follow him," he told Jon and Eva.

She walked behind them, her shoes crunching in the gravel, and continued to survey her surroundings. She couldn't believe that Wilhelm had saved her from going to a camp only to find himself in one later. She felt like her body was frozen cold with fear. How come she couldn't have saved him from the same fate? Why was she so useless?

The man told Sergei and Jon to wait outside, then motioned for Eva to follow. He led her into a small wooden building near the large, white main building.

He pointed to a chair across a table from another chair. "Wait," he said with terrible pronunciation.

He left the room, and she sat in the hard, wooden chair, looking around the dimly lit room, her nerves all but shot. She hoped to portray a serious but determined resolve outwardly, wanting to reassure Wilhelm somehow when he saw her.

She could feel something wet on her shirt. She looked down and saw that milk had leaked through. She had been using her hands to manually pump to relieve the pressure while she was here, but it wasn't enough. *Dammit, not now.* She closed her jacket over her shirt so Wilhelm or anyone else wouldn't see it. It felt like she had waited an eternity when the door to the room swung open, and the soldier walked in, holding onto Wilhelm's arm.

Eva slowly rose from the chair, all the hair on her body standing to attention. She looked at him, and her whole world crumbled. She wanted to rush to him and hold him tightly in her arms, but she stood still, not moving an inch. His head was lowered when he entered the room, but as they approached the table, he lifted it. His facial hair was long, maybe an inch, and the hair on his head was a mess. His cheeks were sunken, and his lids were heavy over his tired, bloodshot eyes, exasperating the dark circles under them. His hands were cuffed in front of him, and his clothes were dirty and ragged. He looked thin, and she noticed the bruises on his face. She felt an overwhelming urge to cry but held it back. It was apparent that they treated the prisoners poorly.

weren't here when Germany fell, and I wish you weren't here now."

It took a minute for her to register that Renée and Adele were dead. She was angry at them for what they did, but she never wished them harm or that fate. She had warned them what would happen if they forced her to leave, and they admitted they understood the risk but were still willing to go through with it. She would have to process what he had done to them later because she didn't have much time to be with him.

"There was something I was going to tell you but never got the chance. When I got on that plane, I was four months pregnant."

His head snapped to her, and he narrowed his eyes, almost daring her to say it wasn't true.

"Yes, we have another child?" She smiled and reached into her purse, retrieving the photos she had brought for him. She laid them on his leg, and he picked them up. He looked at the one of Michael right after he was born, then the one of all three of them, and lastly, the one she had taken a few weeks ago. "His name is Michael, and he is seven months old."

For a few seconds, he didn't say anything. He just looked at the pictures. "Michael, that is a good name. And Charlotte, she has gotten so big."

"She can run now, and she talks all the time. However, her two favorite things are animals and spending time with Michael. I know that all this time, you thought I left you and took Charlotte, but I would have never done that to you," her voice cracked. "There wasn't a day that went by that I didn't think of you and miss you. But I understand if your love for me is gone, I won't blame you."

"I love you, Eva. I will always love you until I breathe my last breath."

She laid her head on his leg. "And that won't be for a long time. I'm going to get you out."

"No, Eva. You will not." His voice was stern, and he seemed more like she remembered him.

"But you could die if you stay in here."

"I know."

She lifted her head and met his gaze. "Does the fact that I don't want you to die and that you will be leaving me and your young daughter and infant son fatherless mean nothing to you? Does that not bother you?"

"It does." He put a hand on her cheek. "I was willing to fight for Germany, and I would gladly die in the service of a cause I believe in wholeheartedly." With his hand still on her cheek, he looked into her watery eyes. "You will give Charlotte and Michael a beautiful life. You are a wonderful mother."

"But you will never get to meet Michael or see Charlotte grow up."

"Eva, there is no point in denying that you don't agree with the things I've done or believe in it. You think these beliefs and ideals make me a bad person. Do you honestly think that Michael or Charlotte would be better off with me in their lives? We both know you don't."

He spoke as if his own death was inconsequential to him. She moved closer and placed her lips to his, then pulled back and met his gaze, brushing some hair from his face. "No, that isn't true. I am tired of lying to myself, and I cannot act as if I don't care for you. Because I do, all of you, even the parts you believe are too dark. Every scar, inside and out, every flaw, every imperfection. You might think you are too damaged and broken to allow yourself to be happy, happy with me and the children, but you can. But you have to let me help you because I will not lose you again. I will not. I almost died when they took me away. I couldn't bare it a second time. Please, Wilhelm, you need to escape from here. Jon and I can help. We can find a way. During the first few weeks in England, there were days I didn't think I would survive the sadness, but it got better. Do you know why it got better? Because I lived on the idea that I would see you again, that I would come back to Europe and find you, and we would be together. I would save you from the Russians, the Americans, the French, the British, or whoever came after you. And that is what I intend to do."

He shook his head. "Eva, you know I would do almost anything for you but don't ask me to be a coward. I will not run away out of fear. You don't have to save me. That isn't your job."

She cried harder. "I'm not. I'm asking you to choose life, to save yourself for the children and me." She felt a desperation so intense it was consuming her. "Please do this for me?"

He placed his large hand on her shoulder and leaned in, kissing her forehead. "I love you, Eva, but I don't want you to ever come back here."

She leaned back and looked at him. "I don't understand. Why would you not want me to come back?

"This isn't a place you should be, and I don't want you to see me this way."

"No, you don't get to tell me I can't see you, and you can't stop me from coming. I have to see you. Seeing you this way doesn't bother me." She kissed him on the cheek, the forehead, the neck, then nuzzled her face against him. "Please let me help you?"

He took her hand and pressed the palm to his lips, planting a tender kiss on it. "You have helped me. There is happiness in my life because of you."

"I love you," she whispered against his hair.

He moved his head away to look at her, and for the first time, his eyes were brimming with strong emotions. Through all the pain, he smiled. "That is the first time you have ever told me that. I'm glad you finally said it, even though I'm not sure you actually mean it. To live without being loved is torture, but now, if I die, I'll know what we had was real and that you will miss me when I'm gone."

"You are not going to die!"

"We have been through so much together, but it's over now. You and I both know how this will end."

"No, I don't. I'm going to get you out, and I'm not going to give up trying. You will not die, and our time together is not over." Even as she said it, the words felt ashen in her mouth. "Wilhelm, is your mother still in Cologne?"

"She is, the last I heard."

"I promise I will try and get word to her."

Footsteps echoed down the hall, growing louder with every second. She grabbed onto Wilhelm and hugged him tightly. He closed his eyes as he took in the sweet scent of her hair, then placed his lips on the side of her neck near her ear and planted a soft kiss. "Go back to Charlotte and Michael. They need their mother," he whispered. She could feel his lips moving against her skin.

"Please, Wilhelm. It doesn't have to be this way."

The door opened, and the man burst through. "Time is up." He came to Wilhelm's side and pulled him from the chair.

The panic flowed from her. She jumped to her feet. "No! Please, not yet. Don't take him away."

"No more time," the man shouted.

"No," she shrieked. "No. Don't do this, please don't. Wilhelm, please, I beg you." She grabbed ahold of his hand and kissed it. "I love you! I love you! I love you!" she cried as he was escorted away.

"Meine Liebe," he said before being pulled from the room.

She fell back into the chair and wept, wave after wave of suffocating tears. This couldn't be happening. She would come back tomorrow, and the day after, and the day after that, until she found a way to free him. When she finally found the strength to stand, she left the room and met Jon and Sergei outside. She knew her eyes were puffy and swollen from crying, but she didn't care.

When Jon saw her coming out of the building, he walked towards her. "Eva, what happened?" His voice was weighted with concern.

"I saw him. Oh, Jon, he looked so bad. They are abusing him and starving him." She looked at Jon with a determined expression. "I am going to get him out. I told him I would come back tomorrow. He told me not to, but I didn't care. I'm coming." She turned to Sergei. "Would you ask the guard what he wants tomorrow in exchange for letting me see Wilhelm again?"

"I will."

Sergei walked towards the building, and she looked back at Jon. "It's strange. He seemed defeated and yet in complete acceptance of the idea that he might die. I was falling apart, and he sat there with perfect equanimity."

"In his situation, you have to. But I think he has known this day might come for a long time. I don't know how he couldn't."

"I told him I loved him. It was the first time I had ever said those words."

Jon raised a brow. "You married him and had two children with him, and you only now told him you loved him?"

"Yes. I had for a long time, but for some reason, I couldn't say it even though I felt it. I wanted to tell him the truth about how I felt, but I was always afraid to."

"What were you afraid of?"

"Fully being his, completely consumed by him and his love. Letting him know that he owned my heart gave him a power I didn't want him to have at the time. But the knowledge of how I felt pressed on my mind every day, and I struggled to keep it silent. At the time, I thought the best thing was to keep it to myself." She squeezed her eyes shut. "Jon, I'm afraid I'm too late, and I don't know what to do," she relented, knowing she was in over her head.

"Starting tomorrow, we can work on how we will get him out."

Sergei came to stand next to Jon. "He said that he would take three bags of potatoes."

I think we can manage that," Jon told him.

Eva got little sleep that night, but finally, it was morning, and she was ready to see Wilhelm again. Jon had left to see about getting three bags of potatoes, and she paced the apartment. She thought about yesterday and her meeting with Wilhelm. It was all too much, the matter-of-fact way they were discussing his possible death. She glanced around blankly, the whole situation sorrel and baring down on her. She should have come back to Europe sooner and tricked Wilhelm into coming with her like Renée and Adele did to her. *Oh, Renée. You and Adele were so foolish. I told you it would cost you your life, but I don't think you took me seriously.*

Jon opened the door and came in with three bags of potatoes, and she hurried over to him. "Well, they cost less than the cigarettes did."

"That's good."

They met Sergei at the same building they had the day before, put the bag of potatoes in the trunk, and then drove north again to Sachsenhausen Concentration Camp. The man let them through the gate after they gave him the sacks of potatoes and led Eva back into the building where she met Wilhelm the day before. She waited in the same chair, tapping her foot on the floor, anxiously watching the door. When it opened, she stood, but quickly, her excitement at seeing him was dampened when the guard returned without Wilhelm, followed by Sergei. She creased her brows and looked between the two men, confused.

Sergei said something to the other man, then came to her side. "He said that he doesn't want to see you and to not come back again. He wants you to stay away."

She put her hand on her hip and looked toward the window. "He is only saying that because he thinks he is protecting me."

Sergei looked around the room. "This is an awful place where bad things happen to the people here. I see why he tells you to stay away."

"Bad things? Yes, to him, and that is why I'm here. I am trying to protect him from those awful things, and he is too stubborn to see that."

"I don't think it is because he is stubborn. I think it is because he cares about you. He is the one in here, not you. So he doesn't want you being here in any way."

"Him being in here is making me suffer. Would you try asking him again, please?"

Sergei chewed on the inside of his cheek. "I don't think he will see you, even if I ask."

"But will you try?"

He looked uncertain. "Give me a minute." He went to the man still standing at the door. She watched as they spoke, and then Sergei followed him out of the room. A few minutes passed before Sergei returned alone. He stood a few feet from her but wouldn't meet her eyes, a strange expression on his face. Something had changed in him.

"Sergei, what is it?"

"He still refuses to see you. He said he won't see you no matter how many times you come and to stop wasting your time. He has asked the guards to turn you away if you come back again. But he wanted me to tell you to be happy and that he was sorry. And that he hoped you could one day forgive him for all of his mistakes."

Her dread ignited and sparked hot with frustration in a boiling rush. It was hard to quail the fury that rose like a forest fire. Her

When he saw her, his brows creased, but his eyes remained empty.

The man pushed him down into the chair roughly and looked at her. "Fifteen minutes, you have." With a scowl, he turned and left the room, shutting the door loudly behind him.

As soon as the door was closed, she ran to the other side of the table and knelt beside him. Tenderly, she placed a hand on his knee and reached up with her other to touch his face, but he moved his head away, finally turning to look at her.

"What are you doing here, Eva? Did you come so you could feel superior, finally getting to see me in prison?"

The tears escaped her eyes, running down her cheeks. "No," she whispered.

His sad, empty eyes bore into hers. "Then why are you here?"

"I didn't leave you. I was tricked by Renée and Adele." She didn't want to tell him that Klaus was involved too. "They took Charlotte and put her on a plane and said if I ever wanted to see her again, I would get on too."

A low growl came from deep in his chest, and he looked away. "I know they were involved, and they have paid the ultimate price for it."

She reached up and placed her hand on his cheek. "Are you saying they are dead?" She focused on his face.

"Yes. And I am not going to apologize for it. They had no idea what they had done when they took you and Charlotte from me. Whether you went willing or not, they were ultimately the reason you were gone." He wrinkled his forehead. "Although now I'm relieved that they did. I couldn't let you go, but I'm glad you worry and anxiety notching higher. She pulled in a deep, bracing breath and glanced out the window, trying to sort her emotions and whirling thoughts.

Finally, she turned from the window back to Sergei. He still seemed nervous, scrunching his hat in his hand. She watched his fingers tighten around it and then loosen. She lifted her gaze to his strained face.

"I know there is more you are not telling me." Dire concern was breaking through. "Tell me what's going on."

"Eva, I…" he trailed off.

"Sergei, tell me. What has happened?" She was frantic now.

He hesitated and then spoke. "He is scheduled for execution today."

She felt like someone had hit her hard in the stomach. She grabbed onto the back of the chair for support. "How… how do you know this?"

"The guard told me. I'm sorry, there is nothing I can do. I don't have that kind of authority."

Her hands were shaking, and she was lightheaded. "Are you sure?" Sergei nodded as he held her impassioned gaze. She felt skewered by sorrow and the lingering wound from so much pain.

"We should go." He reached for her arm, but she backed away from his hand and toward the table behind her. Sergei's hand reached for her arm again with a sense of urgency. "Eva, we can't linger here. We can't be here when they perform the executions."

"What time are they doing it?"

"I don't know. Soon, I think. We can't stay, and you won't want to watch that. Trust me, you will never be able to get it out of your mind."

Her throat felt like it was closing. "I need to see Wilhelm...
and I want to talk to whoever is in charge of the camp." She was
barely keeping it together now.

"You are not going to stop this. Even if you talk to the
commandant, he won't change his mind. Now let's go."

"No, I won't leave until I see him again."

Just then, Jon burst through the door, a panicked, horrified
expression plastered on his face. Then, the sound of multiple guns
firing simultaneously echoed outside. He watched her eyes widen
and brim with tears, then she screamed.

"Nooooo!" Eva ran for the door, but Jon caught her. "Let me
go! Let me go!" she cried hysterically, thrashing in his arms.

"No, Eva, don't go outside."

"I have to see him. Wilhelm!" Her voice was hoarse as she
yelled his name. "Wilhelm...!" She genuinely felt a kind of
emptiness she had never felt before as the torrent of sadness
washed over her. Jon finally let go of her, and she slid to the floor.
She lifted her head and saw the look in Jon's eyes and the
expression of contrite. Eva glimpsed the pity, sorrow, and sadness
he felt for her. She let her gaze fall and focused on the wall as the
pain drowned her, and she sank into it. She screamed until the
sound no longer came out. Jon knelt beside her and folded her into
his arms, and she heaved soundless sobs, her body shaking with
grief until an agonizing wale escaped her lips, piercing the air.

"Let's get her to the car," Sergei said. They both took one of
her arms and lifted her up, helping her outside.

She looked to the courtyard; a row of bodies still lay by the
wall, blood seeping into the gravel all around them. She knew one
of them was Wilhelm, and she wanted to free herself and run to

them. She wanted to find his body, but she didn't understand why she felt the need to. Maybe it was the only way she would know for sure that he was gone. Several soldiers came to retrieve the bodies. They each took one by the legs and dragged them through the gravel, the heads bouncing as they were pulled.

"Look away, Eva. You don't want to see this."

"I do. I need to see if he was one of them," her voice cracked.

"No, I'm not going to let you go over there."

"What if he wasn't one of them? Maybe he is still alive." Tears dripped from her chin.

"He isn't Eva," he sighed deeply, miserably. "But I will check if you stay here." She quickly nodded.

"I need to go with him," Sergei said. "They won't let him see the bodies if he goes alone."

"Alright," Jon told him.

She watched Sergei and Jon walk to where the bodies were lying. Sergei spoke to the men, then he and Jon started checking the bodies. Sergei knelt by one, then called to Jon, who came to Sergei's side and also knelt. They stayed there looking at the body for a few seconds, and Jon moved some hair from the face and looked at Sergei, and then both peered over at her.

Tears stung her eyes as she clung to the car. It was him, oh God, it was him. The full realization of this washed over her, and she lunged forward, rushing toward them. Jon ran in her direction and caught her around the waist, stopping her from coming any closer.

"Is it him? Tell me, is it him?" Her voice was thick as the words were strangled in her throat.

"Yes. He's gone, Eva."

Her face contorted, and she shook her head. "Noooo! Let me touch him," she cried. "Let me touch him." A sob rose in her throat.

"He is dead. You don't want to touch him."

"Yes, I do." She could see the blood spats still on his ragged clothes, but Sergei was blocking Wilhelm's head from her. Jon pulled her back to the car, and Sergei followed. "What are they going to do with his body?"

"Bury him with the others," Sergei told her in a gentle voice.

"But I am his family. I want to take his body."

"No one knows that," Jon reminded her. "They won't release his body to you."

She looked over Jon's shoulder and watched as a man took Wilhelm by both legs and pulled, an arm going up as his head bounced on the gravel like the others, a trail of blood left behind on the ground. She had the sensation of falling as a loud sound rang in her ears, and everything around her went black.

Chapter Twenty-Seven
℘

August 15th, 1945

I t had been two months since Wilhelm's death, but it felt like an eternity. Every night she cried herself to sleep as she suffocated in the irremediable sorrow of her melancholy and the aching in her heart that pined for him. Lying in bed, trying not to wake the others in the house as, she cried in low moans, the bitter tears stinging her face as she tried to navigate the confusion of what happened and find her way to the road of acceptance. During the day, she went through the motions but felt numb inside, but sometimes she didn't have the motivation to keep going when the weariness she tried to suppress swept over her, sucking her energy with it. Everyone around her noticed the lingering sadness in her eyes, and her face set in resigned, mournful lines. She constantly had that murky dull feeling where she wanted to cry as the ache pushed against her heart like a slow death. Now that he was dead, she would never get to clean up the mess she made, which haunted her every time she closed her eyes at night.

Jon sat the last suitcase by the door. "It's all packed up. Are you ready to go?"

She turned from the kitchen window and looked at him. "I guess so."

He watched her for a protracted moment, trying to gauge if this was one of her bad days. "Ingrid and Danny are waiting, and our train leaves soon."

Without saying a word, she went to the table by the door and retrieved her purse, draping it over her shoulder, then smoothed the sleeve of her summer dress. "I know, I'm ready."

He looked at her for a few more seconds. "Alright then." He picked up the suitcases, and she went to the living room, where Charlotte and Michael sat on the couch. Charlotte slid off and Eva picked up Michael, took Charlotte's hand and then followed Jon outside. They drove the distance to Ingrid and Danny's house to tell them bye before they took the train to Cambridge.

Jon knocked on the door, and Ingrid answered it, her hand resting on her growing belly. Ingrid had told Eva and Jon that she was pregnant a month ago. Eva couldn't be happier for her, finally getting the baby she always wanted with a man who loved her and would stay with her, supporting her and the child.

Ingrid smiled at them, trying to mask the sadness underneath. "Come on in. I have some tea steeping."

"Thank you, Ingrid, but we don't have time to stay for tea."

"Oh. Does your train leaves so soon?"

"No, but we wanted an early start."

"Well, sit down for a minute then."

Eva sat with Michael on her lap, and Charlotte sat between her and Jon. Eva was having an emotional overload, but she had to keep it together for Ingrid and Jon.

"I am so happy for you, Ingrid."

Ingrid rubbed her hand over her stomach. "This is what I always wanted."

Eva smiled. "I know it is."

Danny came into the room and sat in the other chair by Ingrid's. "Hi, guys. So you are all ready to leave then?"

Jon looked at Eva. "We are."

"I still can't believe you guys are going back to America. That is so far away," Ingrid anguished.

"But it is our home," Eva told her. She looked down at the wedding ring she had put back on. "I never thought it would be my home again, but now it is the only one I have."

Ingrid's eyes saddened. "You always have a home here."

"No, it's time for me to go back to my country, to my home and see my family." She held Ingrid's gaze. "I want you to know that if for some reason I ever stop writing you it doesn't mean I don't still love you. You will always be in my heart and thoughts," she said to her in German.

Ingrid pulled her brows together. "Why would you stop writing? You can't leave me, Eva. You and I are kindred spirts. You are the better half of me. I have never had a friend like you."

"I will always be here." Eva placed her hand over her heart. "I'm just saying if it happens, know I still love you and care about you very much."

"Oh, Eva, I wish I could pick your happiness off the ground and piece your shattered heart back together. I know I can't, but I hope there is a man who can do that for you. I love you, Eva, and I want you to be happy."

Eva shook her head. "No, my heart will always only beat for him."

"Let's tell them bye. We have to go."

They all stood, and Eva embraced Ingrid, wrapping her arms tightly around her. There would never be another friend like her or anyone who truly knew what she had been through. Ingrid understood her on a level only she could, and Eva would miss her. Even Jenny could never truly know her now, the person she had become in the years spent in this time. When you have been through that kind of trauma for so long, no one comes out the other end the same.

She pulled back a fraction and gazed at Ingrid. "You will be happy here."

"I know. Take care of those little ones."

"I will."

"And Eva, I wanted to tell you that I am happy you have forgiven me and that I'm sorry. If I knew that he would die, I never would have helped in taking you away from him. I regret that now, and I wish I could undo it." Her eyes brimmed with tears.

"It's not because I left that he is dead. I think this would have happened anyway. He wasn't willing to try and escape the camp, so he never would have left Germany, even though he knew they were losing. I think the outcome would have been the same."

A gloom overcame her, and she embraced Eva one last time. "I am still sorry." Tears spilled over onto Eva's shoulder.

"You know, I thought nothing in this world could ever take him from me. I want to feel his touch again, and I would do anything to have him again, but I'm not so naive that I don't know that I am free now and probably better off in the long run. I am basically starting from scratch and building up my life again. And the pain that I feel can only begin to fade if I go on and live my life. There is a saying that only love and regret last forever, and I don't plan on wasting the rest of my time on this earth regretting an unlived life. I cry all the time, and I can't seem to stop, but I don't want it to be that way forever. But I wouldn't undo a second I had with him. I learned so much from our time together. Being with Wilhelm taught me what it means to be best friends with your lover and to have a person who you are so complete with that when you are together, you blend like water. I will never have a love like that again, and I have accepted that because I think it is selfish to ask for that kind of love twice in one lifetime."

Tears streamed down Ingrid's face. "I love you, Eva."

"I love you too, Ingrid." Eva choked on her words.

Danny came to stand beside Ingrid. "Eva, thank you for all you have done. I will always be grateful to you for saving my life and introducing me to this wonderful person." He looked at Ingrid, and they smiled at each other.

"You don't need to thank me." She gave him a hug, and then Ingrid and Danny said bye to the children and Jon.

"Send me pictures of them as they grow, will you?"

"I will try. Would you try and locate Klaus for me, and if you find him, tell him I'm not angry at him anymore, that I have a little boy, that Wilhelm is dead, and I went home? And Ingrid, tell him that I love him."

"I will find him, and if he is alive, I will tell him."

"Thank you." They had to leave now, or Eva was going to start crying again, and she wouldn't be able to stop.

Eva looked at Jon, sitting on the seat across from her in their private cabin. The ride to Cambridge would be hours, and they wanted to be alone and away from the other passengers.

"I was surprised when you told me you were ready to go home."

"It was time," she said, peering out the window at the passing fields. "There is nothing left for me here now. And I want to see my family again."

"Are you ready to face them?"

"No, but will I ever be? After losing Wilhelm, everything else seems trivial by comparison. I survived that, and I can survive my family's constant barrage of questions. I will only be accosted by them in the beginning, and eventually, they will learn to stop asking. I didn't know if I would ever be right again. Every day, I find it hard to breathe. The anxiety that has remained feels like a weight pressing on my chest. I'm choking on the misery, and every second I'm praying that my feelings drown, but they never do. The pain inside is indescribable." She looked from the window at Jon's intent gaze on her. "He was my life, and I knew it was stupid and reckless to love him. But God must hate me for it because he took away my reason for living."

"Your children are a reason to live."

"I know, and it is because of them that I am still here."

"What will you tell your family?"

"Only what you have already told them."

"But what about Charlotte and Michael? How will you explain them?"

"I don't need to explain them. They are here, and they are mine, and that is all anyone ever needs to know."

"I respect that. Will you stay in Utah?"

"Did you ever read The Lord of The Rings or see the movies?"

Jon lifted a brow. "As a boy, I read the books, and yes, I have seen the movies."

"You might remember then at the end of The Return of The King when Frodo says, 'How do you pick up the threads of an old life? How do you go on when in your heart you begin to understand... there is no going back? There are some things that time cannot mend. Some hurts that go too deep that have taken hold.' I couldn't have said it better. Utah won't seem the same to me. My friends won't seem the same, and my family won't seem the same. And not because they have changed, but because I have changed. That was my old life. I now have to learn to navigate this new one."

The rest of the way was silent, except for Eva's gentle humming to Charlotte and Michael. It was just past midday when the train pulled into the Cambridge station. It was a clear day, and the sun was bright and hot. The air smelled of flowers, and the aroma brought Eva back to the memory of La Chapelle. She had lost so much in this war, so many people. But it was over now, and she needed to move on with this new chapter of her life.

They put their things in the car and drove out of town to the spot where this all began. "So they are going to open the portal at one thirty?"

"Yes."

"And they don't know about Charlotte and Michael?"

"No. That was something I thought was better to leave out."

Jon parked the car in the empty field and got out, taking the suitcases from the trunk. They rested on them as they waited, and Eva looked around, not really believing that she was finally going home. When she got here, all she wanted to do was go home. Now, all she wanted was to stay. Not the way it is now, but how it used to be. It is strange to think of how happy she was in the middle of a war and now how miserable she is when the world is at peace.

Jon continually checked his watch. As he was pacing, a strange sucking sound echoed off the trees surrounding the valley, then the portal opened in front of them, the black mass that would take them back to their time. Jon looked at her. "We will throw the bags through first, then all go through together."

She nodded and got off the suitcase she was sitting on. Jon took it and threw it into the portal, then the other three. He picked up Charlotte. "Let's do this quickly," he said, holding his hand out to Eva. She took it as she held on tightly to Michael, then turned and gave one last look at 1940s England. She turned back to the portal, and Jon scanned the valley, too, and then met her gaze. She gave him a nod, and he walked forward into the blackness. There was a pulling sensation, and she clung even tighter to Jon's hand and to Michael. Then, it was suddenly gone, and they all fell hard on the floor. Michael started to cry, his face turning red, and she scooped him up, cradling him in her arms. She tried to get him to stop by shushing as she bounced him. Jon helped Charlotte up, and they turned to the little window in the room. They could see Dr. Yug, Dr. Petterson, Dr. Foster, Dr. Brandt, and Dr. Jensen staring at them. They were all frozen in place, shocked expressions written on their faces. Eva knew it was more because of the children than she and Jon.

"Let's get out of this room," Jon said. He went to the door, turned the long metal handle, and pushed it open. They stepped out into the main room, and Dr. Brandt was the first to approach them.

"Whose children are these?" he asked in a low voice.

Jon turned to Eva. "They are hers."

Dr. Yug came to stand beside Dr. Brandt. "You brought children born in that time back to ours?"

Eva looked squarely at him. "Yes, because they are my children, and they belong wherever I am."

He rubbed his slick black hair. "Well, first things first. Let's start the process of going over everything that happened to you while you were there. We will work on it a little each day, then we will discuss the children and what is to be done with them."

Anger spiked in her. "Fuck this and your debriefing. I am going home. You don't get to tell me what to do with my children." She walked over to the suitcases that had already been removed from the room and picked hers up. Jon went to retrieve his suitcase, and Dr. Petterson came to stand beside him.

"This is irregular. You know it isn't how things are done. She just spent the last six and a half years back in time, and you think she should just go back to her old life like nothing happened?"

Jon stood up straight, still holding Charlotte in one arm as he lifted his suitcase with the other. "No, that is the point. It's not that nothing happened. It's that so much has happened. And she can never go back to her old life because she has been changed forever. But she has been through enough, more than you will ever understand. Hell, more than I will ever understand, and she deserves to see her family again. They are already going to ask a lot of questions. She doesn't need you asking them too. Maybe she can write it all out for you one day, but right now, we are both going home."

Eva lifted a brow, surprised at Jon's declaration. She followed him to the front door of the building, and Dr. Brandt tagged along with the other two suitcases. "I can take you into town so you can get a hotel?"

Jon stopped walking and looked at him. "How are we all going to fit into your mini coop?"

"Oh, I don't have that anymore. I drive a Land Rover now."

"Huh, well, that is an improvement."

"A lot has changed in six and a half years, Jon."

"I know. And it will take time for Eva and me to catch up. But right now, we just want to go back to America. Eva hasn't seen it in over half a decade."

"Well, the Land Rover is over here." He led them to a shiny black Land Rover and unlocked it. They stacked the suitcases in the back, and then Eva got into the backseat with Charlotte and Michael. They didn't have car seats for them, so they would have to be careful.

As they drove into Cambridge, she listened as Jon and Dr. Brandt talked in the front seat. Charlotte had her head on Eva's lap and was asleep, and Michael sucked on his hand. Eva held onto the necklace that Wilhelm gave her, feeling the warm silver in her hand, and she looked at the gray clouds that threatened to rain on them. It was going to be so strange for her to be back in Utah, under its blue, continuous sky.

Dr. Brandt took them to the Marriott hotel near the airport and pulled in front. He helped them with the luggage, and for the first time, Eva realized that she, Jon, and the children were all still wearing old clothing, and the suitcases were ones from the 1940s. It was going to look strange for people to see them this way. They would have to buy some modern clothes today, and some new suitcases.

"Would you maybe tell me someday what happened to the two of you while you were there?" He looked at Jon's hands, the missing fingers noticeable through his gloves.

"In time." He squeezed Dr. Brandt's shoulder.

Dr. Brandt got a luggage cart, put their suitcases on it, and pushed it into the lobby behind them. Jon booked them two rooms then they followed Dr. Brandt back outside to his car. He gave Eva a hug and looked at the children.

"What are their names?"

"Charlotte and Michael Bauer."

He creased his brows and looked at Jon. "Their father is German." Dr. Brandt's eyes grew wide with understanding. "And Eva is no longer Eva Abrams but Eva Bauer. She was married to their father."

He let out a long breath. "No shit."

"There, now you have part of the story," Jon told him.

Lightning forked overhead, followed by a low roll of thunder, and raindrops started falling, hitting the windshield of his Land Rover. "A storm is moving in, so I better get going. I have a challenge ahead of me. It will take a lot to calm the others, but I will try."

"Thank you," Jon told him.

"I will talk to you soon." Not his words, but his voice indicated that he was certain of this.

They went back inside, and Jon used the computer in the lobby to buy them plane tickets to Salt Lake City in two days. They had to give Dr. Brandt time to make fake birth certificates and passports for Charlotte and Michael. Then they took an Uber to Boots, a British store similar to Walmart, and bought suitcases and new clothes for them and the children. Eva bought a new purse, a diaper bag, a box of diapers, and a pack of wipes. She also got two car seats so that when they arrived in Salt Lake City, they could rent a car and drive to Provo. They would leave the 1940s suitcases and clothing in the hotel for Dr. Brandt. The plan was to leave the keys in an envelope for him and the front desk.

When they got back to the hotel, Eva got a pack-and-play from the front desk and put Michel down for the night, and Charlotte would sleep with her in the queen bed.

Eva tossed and turned throughout the night, unable to escape the nightmares. She rolled onto her back and heard the screaming again, a screaming she had heard before. In her dreams, she could hear the gunfire and watched his body be drug away like he was nothing, no more than a dead deer, and she would always scream. But this time, the screams were not in her head but were her own screams, crying out, trying to push away the flood of memories that always rushed in when she went to sleep. She never felt safe when she closed her eyes because her dreams tormented her.

She bolted up and looked at Charlotte, surprised her screaming hadn't woken her. Eva's face was covered in sweat, and her whole body felt clammy. She panted as she looked around the strange room and felt like she was losing her sanity, her grip on reality. She threw the blankets off and went to the bathroom, splashing her face with cold water. She checked on Michael, who was still sleeping on his side, sucking his thumb, then went back to bed and curled up behind Charlotte. She quietly cried into her hair, wanting Wilhelm so much that it was excruciating. There was a dull, aching pain in her chest, and she wanted to scream and fall apart, but she had Charlotte and Michael to think about now. She dreamed he was with her every night, which was a lie and felt like a sin for some reason, but she had her freedom now. She would never be chased by the Gestapo again, tortured by them, or lose a loved one to their brutality. She would never again have to hear the sound of bombs or see the destruction of war, but she didn't have him. She had suffered so much, and she cried for all of it, but she had to break out of the shell of a person she had become and live. Maybe she would see him again after she died. Perhaps he was waiting there for her. She drifted into sleep as the tears dried on her face.

The flight was long and miserable, but they finally arrived in Salt Lake City. She was happy to be off the plane and stretch her cramped legs. The airport had completely been redone and looked nothing like it did back in 2014 when she left. So much was different, and she wondered what else had changed.

They went to Avis and rented a car, put their suitcases in the trunk and strapped the car seats in the back. Eva had kept some of her old clothes just to remind her of the time she spent there, and she also kept one of the old suitcases.

They made their way south to Provo, and she grew more anxious with every passing mile. She wanted to see her family again, but she wasn't ready. They didn't even know she was coming, and she knew it would be a shock to them. Jon would occasionally glance in her direction, and she knew he wanted to make sure she was alright.

When they entered Provo, she gave him directions to her parent's house. It struck her as odd that she could remember how to get there. Provo looked exactly as it did when she left. It seemed like nothing had changed, unlike Salt Lake City. Her neighborhood seemed frozen, immune from the effects of time.

Jon turned down her street, and she could see her parent's brick house.

"Stop here, Jon." He pulled off on the side of the street, one block opposite the house. "I don't want them to see us just yet. Let's get Charlotte and Michael out of the car, and then we can walk over."

"That's a good idea. Do you know what you are going to tell them when they first see you?"

She let out a breath nervously. "I don't."

She got Michel out of the car, and Jon helped Charlotte out. They crossed the street and walked the one block to the house. Jon gave her a glance as they reached the steps. After a long pause, she slowly took one at a time. Her heart was racing, hurting with every beat. Her body was tingling, and she could even feel it in her fingers. She pushed the doorbell and held her breath. Footsteps thudded on the other side, then the door opened, and her mom stood before her just over the threshold. For a fraction of a second, she just looked at Eva like she didn't recognize her, and then she let out a scream and collapsed on the floor. Her dad came rushing over but didn't even make it to her mom when he saw her and halted in his tracks. His face went white, and his eyes teared. He dropped to his knees and cried, something she had never seen him do. It broke her heart to see her parents this way.

Her eyes burned with her own tears. "Oh, Dad, I'm so sorry."

He got to his feet and rushed towards her, stepping over her mother to take her in his arms. He squeezed her so tight she struggled to breathe, and Michael began to cry from the pressure. For the first time, seeming to notice Michael, her dad pulled back and wiped his face with his hands. "Who are these children?" He pointed to Jon. "And who is this?"

"I will tell you, Dad, but first, let's get Mom off the floor and come inside."

"Yes, yes." He shook her until she came to, then helped her off the floor and to the couch. Eva and Jon followed him into the living room. Jon tried to put Charlotte down, but she clung to him, hiding her face in his shoulder. Her dad noticed and looked to Eva for answers as Jon sat on the couch beside her.

Her mom finally spoke. "Where have you been all these years, Eva?" she cried out.

"It is not something I want to talk about, but I will tell you enough, so you won't be completely in the dark. I was taken around five years ago, but I escaped and found my way back. I don't know who took me. All I know is there was one person who was nice to me while I was there."

"Is this him?" her mom asked.

"No, but Jon never gave up on me and helped get me home."

"Is he their… father?"

"No."

Her dad came and sat beside her mom. "But they are your children?"

"Yes."

"Then who is the father if not him?"

"It doesn't matter because he is dead. Please, don't ask me any more questions?"

"No," her mom said. "You don't get to disappear for over five years and then show up and tell us we don't get to know what happened to you all that time."

"I don't even understand it myself, Mom. But it is traumatizing, and I don't want to discuss it. But these are your grandchildren, Charlotte and Michael. Charlotte is two and a half, and Michael is nine months old."

"I don't mean to push you, but can you at least tell us something about the father, if you know?"

Eva looked to Jon, and he gave her a nod. "His name was Wilhelm Bauer, and he was my husband."

Her mom brought her hand to her mouth, shocked. "You married this man, your captor?" Her dad seemed almost as worried as her mom.

"No, he was not my captor. He was the man I said was nice to me. He was German, but Charlotte was born in France, and Michael was born in England. That is all I'm going to tell you."

Over the next few weeks, Eva had talked to the police and was featured on the news as the missing girl who miraculously returned. She had been scolded by Jenny, who cried every time she saw her, and her brother seemed forever changed by her disappearance. He was married now to his long-time girlfriend, but they didn't have any children yet. Reporters were outside of her parent's house every day, and it was driving her crazy. She couldn't leave the house without her parents worrying and asking where she was going, but she understood why. She watched a lot of YouTube videos to try to catch up on all she had missed while she was gone, but she mostly spent time with her family. Her dad had already developed a special relationship with Charlotte and Michael, but she knew that would happen.

Eventually, she would have to figure out what she was going to do with her life, but for right now, it was hard enough just trying to adjust to this new reality.

Chapter Twenty-Eight

May 22rd, 2025
New York City

A t the count of three, Eva tossed her black mortarboard cap with the other hundred or so graduates. It was hard to believe this day had finally come, but she had worked so hard to get here, and she earned it. Eva was now the proud owner of an MD degree from NYU in Pediatric Endocrinology. Wilhelm's sister dying from diabetes is what first made her take an interest in the illness, but after Michael was diagnosed with diabetes, she decided to work with children who were afflicted with the disorder. Now, all that was left to do was pass the board exam, and then she would go on to do her residency at NYU Medical Center. She was going to take a short break for the summer and start in mid-August.

She made her way to the main floor of the auditorium, where the families were. She found her parents, Charlotte, Michael, Thomas, his wife Amanda, their two-and-a-half-year-old son, and

Jenny all waiting for her near the doors. Jon was also waiting with her family.

"Oh my God, you did it," Jenny rushed to her with her arms open wide. She embraced her in a tight hug and rocked them both back and forth. She took a step back and inspected Eva's graduation gown. "You are one amazing woman."

"Thank you, Jenny." Jenny had graduated with her bachelor's degree in General Education and still lived in Utah, teaching eighth grade in West Jordan, a suburb of Salt Lake City.

"Here, mommy." Charlotte ran to her, holding a bouquet of orchids.

Eva took the bouquet and hugged her. "That was so thoughtful of you. Thank you."

"It's from both of us," she said and waved Michael over. He held a single orchid and handed it up to her.

"My sweet boy." She picked him up and put him on her hip.

"Charlotte got the pink ones, but I wanted this one." He pointed to the white orchid in her hand.

"You picked this one. And why did you choose white?" He shrugged his little shoulders, and Eva laughed. "Silly monkey."

"I always knew you were the smart one." Thomas had his typical mischievous broad smile, but a proud look was in his eyes.

"Pssst. No, you are smarter than me." She put Michael down and gave Thomas a hug.

"I'm proud of you, sister."

"Don't make me cry," she laughed.

"No, you have done enough of that, and you shouldn't have to cry anymore."

"They would be happy tears this time."

"Eva, honey, I always knew you would do great things." Her dad kissed her on the cheek and handed her an envelope. "We didn't get you flowers."

She looked at the envelope he had pushed in her hand and knew it was a check. "This is better, Dad. Thank you."

"For the next chapter of your life," her mom added.

"Thanks," she mouthed to her mom and dad.

"Congratulations, Eva." Thomas' wife said, leaning in and giving her a quick half hug.

Then Jon leaned in and kissed her on the cheek. "I didn't get you flowers either. I have something better to give you."

"What?"

"So, I'm starving. Where should we go eat," Thomas said, rubbing his hands together.

"I'll give it to you later," Jon said in a quiet voice.

She didn't break their stare, wondering what it could be. Finally, she turned away from Jon and looked at her family. "There is an excellent Mexican restaurant not far from here. We can walk."

"Sounds great." Her dad waved for everyone to follow. "Let's go."

As they made their way out of the building, someone called Eva's name. "Misses Bauer."

Eva stopped and looked into the crowd to find who had said her name. Professor Sutherland was coming towards her. "Dr. Sutherland, hi."

"Congratulations, Eva. Or I should now say, Dr. Bauer." An approving half-smile cracked at the corner of her mouth.

Dr. Sutherland was her favorite professor. "Thank you. It is so strange to hear you say that, but it feels good and sounds good rolling off your tongue."

She laughed. "I imagine it does. Well, go have fun with your family. And I'll see you at the hospital."

"I start in August."

"You are going to be great. Bye." She waved at Eva as she disappeared back into the crowd.

Eva waved and then ran to catch up with her family. When they were being seated at the restaurant, Eva made sure to sit by Jon. She wanted to find out what he was planning to give her.

"So what is this you have for me?" she asked, leaning closer to him so he could hear her above the noise in the restaurant.

"You want me to tell you now?" He looked around the table at her family and Jenny.

She wrinkled her forehead, wondering what it could be. "Should we... go outside?"

"I think that would be wise."

She leaned close to her mom, who was sitting on the other side of her. "Jon and I will be right back."

"Where are you going?"

"Just outside for a second." She got up and followed Jon out to the street, where they sat on a wooden bench in front of the restaurant. "Why did we have to come outside, Jon?"

"Because it involves the past, your past." She tensed. "I had been checking for a while, and I finally found what I was looking for." She lifted her hand, gesturing for him to continue. "I found Wilhelm."

She sucked in an audible breath. "What?"

"I mean, I found where he is buried. We always thought that he had been put into a mass grave like the others, but Sergei located his mother and convinced the commandant of the camp to allow her to retrieve his body. He is buried in a cemetery in Cologne."

A pang gripped her heart, and tears pulled in the corners of her eyes. "So, he wasn't lost and forgotten in a mass unmarked grave?"

Jon shook his head. "No."

She threw her arm around his neck and pulled him to her. "Thank you, Jon, thank you. I didn't know you were even looking for him."

"I didn't want to tell you unless I found something out. It has taken me years to finally locate him."

"But you tried, and all I know is I will forever be grateful to you."

"So, what do you say, should we take a trip to Germany?"

She laughed with happy tears and nodded. "Yes." She looked through the restaurant window at her family, whom she loved with all her heart. "I want them to come too."

Jon followed her line of sight. "Are you sure?"

"I am. Even if they don't know it, I want them to see the place where their grandchildren's father was from."

"Well, let's go in and tell them."

Eva visited with Jon, her family, and Jenny, all of the places she lived during the war. While in France, they went to La Chapelle, and Eva snuck away to visit the graves of Sabina and Fabian. The rest of their time is France they spent in Paris and then

Dieppe. When they got to Germany, they spent some time in Berlin and visited the Sachsenhausen Concentration Camp at Eva's request.

She walked into the same room that she had visited Wilhelm in. There was still a table and two chairs just like it had been, so she sat in one, remembering that day so vividly like it was only yesterday. Even the walls were still the same off-white colored plaster, but with cracks and pieces peeling and chipped away that hadn't been there in 1945. She stood and went outside, walking across the gravel courtyard, the horrors of that day rushing back. She went to the spot where they shot Wilhelm and looked down at the gravel, remembering the blood seeping from the bodies onto the ground. She squatted and started brushing the gravel aside with her fingers. She didn't know what she was looking for, but she felt compelled to look.

"What are you doing," Jenny asked.

"I just thought I saw something." She had moved all of the gravel from that spot, leaving only dirt, but there was no blood there as she remembered. Eighty years of rain and wind had washed it away. She placed the palm of her hand on the spot and closed her eyes. "I'm sorry I couldn't save you," she said in German.

"What did you say, Eva?" Jenny stared down at her. "You are acting weird."

"It wasn't important." She stood, needing to leave this spot. She could only stare at it for so long before it started getting to her. "Let's find the others and go inside the museum."

"Alright." Jenny looked at her like she still thought she was acting strange.

While in the museum, Eva read every single poster and description they had. She hoped it would say something about Wilhelm but knew there wouldn't be anything.

Just after mid-day, they took the bus back to Berlin, then caught the train to Cologne. Jon had the address to the house Wilhelm's mother had lived in and the name of the cemetery where Wilhelm was buried. It was called Melaten Cemetery and was located north of the municipal district of Lindenthal. Eva was excited to see Cologne even though she knew it would look nothing like it did when Wilhelm lived there. Like Berlin, most of the city had been destroyed in the bombings, especially near the end of the war.

It was late when they arrived in Cologne, so they went straight to the hotel.

"Mom, Dad, tomorrow before we all go out, Jon and I are going to visit a few places together, just the two of us."

"Why just the two of you? What are you going to see?"

"She is a grown woman, and she doesn't have to tell us why just her and Jon are going or where it is they are going." Her dad scolded her mom.

"I know. I just thought that maybe it was something we all wanted to see."

"It's not, Mom. It's an old, run-down house and a cemetery."

She drew her brows together in confusion. "Why would you go there?"

"Because it has to do with my past. But it only holds meaning to me."

Her mom's mouth opened slightly. "Does this have something to do with when you lived in Germany?"

"It does."

Her mom nodded and said no more about it. Eva left her parents' room and went back to her own. Charlotte and Michael wanted to sleep in Thomas and Amanda's room so they could play with their little boy. She told them it was fine and was actually glad to have the room to herself.

Eva took the old photos of the kids and the one of her, Charlotte, and Wilhelm from her purse and sat on the bed, leaning back against the wall. She looked at them for a long time, rubbing her fingers over Wilhelm's face. She had gotten better over the years at suppressing her feelings. The sadness and the overwhelming longing for him, but it was just that, suppression. She couldn't get rid of those feelings. By this point, she knew she would never stop wanting him, loving him, and missing him.

She kissed the picture of him, tears rolling down her face. "I miss you. And I do forgive you for your mistakes. I did a long time ago. I just hope that you forgive me of mine." She scooted down on the bed still on top of the comforter, and fell asleep with the pictures in her hand.

She met Jon on the main floor early for breakfast, and after eating, they took a bus to the outskirts of town. They finally arrived, and Eva was a little shocked at what she saw. The farmhouse was run down from years of decay and neglect, and the land around it was covered in tall, overgrown grass and an upkept apple orchard.

Eva walked inside on the sun-bleached, rickety wooden floor of the house that had been severely damaged from water that came in through the holes in the ceiling and the broken-out windows. It smelled old and musty. Everything was covered in a thick layer of dust, and there was mold on the walls. Dirty, ragged curtains hung from the windows, torn and thin from years of being in the sun and moths eating on them. She walked through what used to be the living room and then into the kitchen. Many of the cabinets were missing, but the ones left were in bad shape, some hanging partway from where they had been attached. The walls were covered in peeling wallpaper, and an old 1940s fridge sat in the corner, the door ajar. She pulled it open, and the hinges groaned, rusted from age. Inside, it was also covered in dust and cobwebs.

"I'm not sure the stairs are safe," Jon called from the doorway.

"I want to try them."

Jon sighed. "I'll go up first. I'm heavier, so if they can support me, then they will support you." He put his hand on the banister and slowly one step at a time, made his way up. When he reached the top, he looked down at her. "I guess you should come up too, but be careful. There are rusty nails sticking through some of the boards."

"I'll be careful." Like Jon, she put her hand on the banister and climbed the stairs. They went through each room, all of them in worse condition than the rooms on the main floor. The room she lingered in the longest was the master bedroom. There was still an old metal bedframe near the window and a decayed mattress on top of it. This would have been her and Wilhelm's room. They would have slept in a bed, possibly in the same spot as this bed. They would have made love in this room, and then he would have held her while she slept. She would have woken to the sun shining through the window, and the kids would be just down the hall. It was crazy how time changed so many things.

554

"To think I almost lived here."

Jon scanned the room. "It was probably really nice in the time you would have been here."

"I wonder how long his mother lived here and why it fell into decay."

"Who knows. Maybe after the war, no one could afford to live here or its upkeep."

"Probably not. Is it crazy that the days I spent back in time were the best days of my life?"

Jon watched her as she rubbed her fingers along the metal bed frame. "No, it's not crazy."

"When I first arrived, I never thought I would say that. In the early days of France's occupation, I hated it, but by the end, I loved it. We don't always wind up wanting what we think we do." She looked out the window over the yellow grass and the city in the distance. "I wonder what happened to Gerhardt's body? I never heard anything more about him after the telegram. I don't really know what happened to him at all. I don't know if it's possible to explain how painful this all is to someone in a way that they would understand."

"I think they would have had to experience what you did to understand." She peeled some of the wallpaper back, little pieces flaking, falling to the floor.

"It's possible that Gerhardt is one of the thousands who are still missing."

She sighed. "I suppose I'll never know."

"Should we go to the cemetery?"

She nodded. "Yeah, I'm ready to see his grave now."

They walked to the cemetery from the bus stop because Eva wanted to see the city where Wilhelm grew up. On their way, she stopped at a flower shop and bought some blue cornflowers, Wilhelm's favorite flower. They entered the cemetery under an entryway made of a tan stone with a black iron gate that was left open. In front of them stretched a long walkway with rows of skeleton trees guarding over it. The cemetery was shaded because of the trees, giving it a peaceful feel.

"How will we find his grave?"

Jon pulled out a piece of paper from his picket and unfolded it. "It says he is in row three hundred, a grave on the path's edge, plot fourteen-forty."

"OK."

They followed the main road in the cemetery, reading the numbers. She walked up and down the rows of tombstones, her boots crunching on the earth, until she found it, the row she had been searching for. In the middle of the cemetery was row three hundred, and she quickly started scanning the plots.

"Jon, over here." Facing the walkway was plot fourteen-forty. The stone had overgrown vegetation covering part of it, but she could still read the name. She peered down at the words engraved into the headstone, gripping the small bouquet of flowers tighter in her hand. 'Wilhelm Bauer, born August 9th, 1903. Died, June 21st, 1945. Beloved son, husband, and father. She hadn't even noticed that Jon was standing at her side.

A small heap of leaves had settled at the base of the headstone, and dirt was stuck to the front of it. Eva knelt, brushing the dirt from the weathered rock. "Hi Wilhelm, I miss you. When you died, I knew that nothing would ever be the same again," she said in German. "I hoped that this day would never come when I had to bid you farewell for the last time. You were always my strength and my guide. You taught me how to go on, no matter what, and how to not be afraid. But now I see that I had to let you go, that God called you home. I know that your sister eagerly awaited you, and your mother is with you not too." Eva started to cry, the hot tears stinging her cheeks. "I wish I could have seen it, your reunion with them in the white halls of heaven. You were a true soldier, a hero to your people, but to me, you will always be my husband and true friend. The man who saved me, who cared for me and protected me. I swear to you that I will never forget what you did. In my heart, there will always be a place for you, and a part of you is always with me. I have loved you more than I have loved any other. Farewell, Wilhelm. Farewell, my love. I will miss you every day of my life. We will meet again one day, but I have to live in this world without you. I owe you so much, and wherever I go, you will go with me and give me courage. I will love you for as long as I live, and I will love you in the next life too." She laid the blue cornflowers in front of the tombstone and placed her hand on the smooth, hard surface. "I love you," she whispered one last time as tears blurred her vision. "I'm sorry I didn't say it sooner."

Jon tapped her on the shoulder. "Eva, look."

She turned her head to the right and noticed the name on the grave next to Wilhelm's. 'Marie Bauer, born March 3rd, 1885, died September 1st, 1967.' "She was 82 years old when she died," Jon said.

"I think she lived the rest of her life very sad and lonely."

"She had no one left. She lost both of her children, and she thought that you took her only granddaughter away. Poor woman." Jon looked at the headstones side by side.

Eva brushed the leaves and dirt away from Marie's grave too. "I want you to know that I love you, Marie. I didn't take your grandchildren from you. And I loved your son more than anything. I would have given my life for him. There isn't a single moment that I don't miss him. He never leaves me, even if I wanted him to. The memory of him will haunt me for the rest of my days, and I can't stop this pain. I have tried. I hope you are happier wherever you are now and that you are with Wilhelm and Charlotte." She took a single cornflower from Wilhelm's grave and placed it on Marie's.

When they left the cemetery, Eva told Jon she needed some time alone. He went back to the hotel, but she returned to the farm. She walked through the rooms of the house again and sat on the dusty mattress in the master bedroom, watching the rainbow colors dance on the wall. She sat still with her hands folded in her lap, and the room was quiet, only the sound of the singing crickets coming from the broken window, and it was strangely peaceful.

She made her way down the old staircase and went outside, slowly walking the land surrounding the house, rubbing her hand along the top of the tall grass, the apple orchard beside her. The sun hung low in the sky, and the fields looked like gold in the fading light. She walked towards the horizon, the house at her back. She now lived in two worlds, the past and the present. It is strange how two people can join as one and create such an incredible life together. To have someone know your private, most personal pain and then replace it with joy.

The feeling of shame was swallowing her up because she was weak and allowed someone to become so significant to her that if she didn't constantly have them in her life, it was empty, a vacant nothingness. Inside, she was dying, but only she knew. Her silent cries were deafening, the screaming so loud but only God could hear them. Somedays, the despair consumed her, and she felt so far gone that nothing could pull her back from the darkness. None of the people in her life could ever understand her pain and the constant struggle to fight through the intense hurt. It's strange how the past haunts us even though it has ended, no longer a part of our lives, and we are left only with a memory. But sometimes, you wish it was more than that. In those quiet moments alone, you almost find yourself longing to be there again, even if that means taking back all the horrible, sad things that happened because you would do anything to have the happy things again.

Epilogue

☙

August 1st, 1945

He walked through the meadow, the sun high in the sky, bright over the green field, reflecting off the water. He paused, closing his eyes, seeing the red through his lids, feeling the heat on his skin as the breeze carried the fresh scent of the grass and wildflowers with it. He opened his eyes and continued on, his boots crushing down the thick, tall grass. When he reached the tree, he stopped underneath its shady canopy. It brought back a happier time, a memory he thought of often. He started for the pond when something caught his eye. He reached into the hole in the tree and retrieved a folded piece of paper, crispy from being damp. He unfurled it, the corners sticking, tearing slightly as he pulled it apart.

When I close my eyes, I am here, in this place we shared. The leaves dance like whispering angels as they sway with the gentle breeze. High above in their branches, the finches serenade us with their songs. And when I think on that time, I see your face and how lucky I was at that moment. Someday, I will sit under the shade of the lone tree again and look out across the pond, watching its viridescent water glitter in the sun as I slip gently into eternity. The warm summer air is enduring because, to me, it will forever be that summer that we were here. And it is in this place where we experienced something intimate that I will find you again. But for now, your memory is safe with me. I will keep it in my heart. And while I wait for the cloak of this life to be removed and the mortal coil to end, knowing I am still vailed from your adoring eyes, it is here I will return. And I will take comfort in the fact that for a time, you were mine.

He let his hand drop to his side, the breeze catching the paper, carrying it across the meadow. It landed in the pond and floated, the waves moving it back and forth until it sank beneath the water.

About the author

J.L. Robison is an American author who currently lives in western Pennsylvania with her husband and two daughters. She has recently finished the fourth and final book in the Edelweiss series and is now working on a new story in the world of dark fantasy. Before becoming a writer, J.L. Robison taught English as a second language. She has had the opportunity to live in many states and has been to over fourteen different countries, experiencing their unique cultures. She writes in multiple genres, spanning historical fiction, literary fiction, romance, and fantasy. When she is not sitting on the couch with her laptop, she is outside working in her garden, playing tennis, bowling, ice skating, traveling, or doing things with her kids. She also enjoys going on walks with her husband or drinking a glass of wine to relax in front of the TV. Most of her inspiration comes at night when she can't sleep, is listening to music, or when on a walk alone in nature.

www.ingramcontent.com/pod-product-compliance
Ingram Content Group UK Ltd.
Pitfield, Milton Keynes, MK11 3LW, UK
UKHW021317120325

4964UKWH00038BA/295

* 9 7 9 8 9 9 0 7 4 5 1 0 0 *